I0843170

HOLLYWOOD PRIDE

HOLLYWOOD PRIDE

AMY KAUFMAN BURK

Copyright © 2025 Amy Kaufman Burk

All rights reserved. No part of this book may be reproduced or used in any manner without the prior written permission of the copyright owner, except for the use of brief quotations in a book review.

ISBN (paperback): 9798218371678
ISBN (ebook): 9798218371685

Cover design by Karen Quigley
Book design and production by Constellation Book Services

Printed in the United States of America

To Bernie — who stood with me, side by side, as we built our life together, on our own terms.

To Anschel, Jared, Ariela — our three grown children — for being your wonderful selves. Your core decency has helped guide our world through troubled times. You were my inspirations as I wrote this novel.

To the students I met at Hollywood High School — thank you for opening my world.

To three outstanding educators I knew during my years at Hollywood High: Mary Ellen Gormican (Latin teacher), Ella Hogan (guidance counselor), and Keith Kuhn (AP English teacher).

PRINCIPAL CHARACTERS

Caroline Black, *sophomore at Hollywood High School, transferred from Laurel Academy for Girls*

Leah Black, M.D., *Caroline's mother, a psychiatrist*

Geoff Black, *Caroline's father, a cinematographer*

J.D., *student at Hollywood High, gay, living on the streets*

Kayla, Irene, Gary, Vincent, *Caroline's group of close friends at Hollywood High*

The Duke, *assigned to Caroline for peer tutoring, leader of a gang, repeating his senior year at Hollywood High*

Doraine, *The Duke's girlfriend, junior at Hollywood High*

Valerie, *debutante, friend of Caroline's from Laurel Academy for Girls*

Carlos, *gay, student at Hollywood High*

Toni, *trans girl, student at Hollywood High*

Blake, *nonbinary, Toni's girlfriend, student at Hollywood High*

Mrs. Richardson, *Caroline's guidance counselor*

Mr. Cohen, *Caroline's English teacher*

Miss Orville, *Caroline's Latin teacher*

CHAPTER 1

Caroline Black found her way to her first period class. Her hair hung loose, streaks of lighter and darker blonde in a sheath to the middle of her back. She was slim, green eyes, no makeup. Some called her pretty, others beautiful, but when they did, she gave them a wall-eyed glare and walked away. She wore a ratty t-shirt, faded jeans, tennis shoes.

She chose the front row center seat and clasped her hands on the battered wood desktop. Trying to contain her nerves, she studied the scarred surface. *Daisy and Nick Forever. Jack Daniels for President. Daisy and Todd Forever. Algebra Sucks. Daisy and Larry Forever.* Several hearts with initials. A large hand, fisted, exceptional detail, middle finger extended. Caroline swallowed dryly, appalled that so many kids had carved up school property, but more appalled by her own admiration. *The fuck-you artist is talented with a knife.*

"Is this desk taken?"

Caroline looked up and shook her head. The girl smiled shyly and slid into the next seat. She was five-foot-two, petite, with hazel eyes, curly black hair, and milk chocolate skin.

"I'm Kayla Davidson. I'm new."

"I'm Caroline Black. I'm new, too."

They shook hands.

"I'm from Massachusetts," Kayla offered.

"I'm from Laurel Academy."

Kayla raised an eyebrow. "Is that a sovereign nation?"

Caroline's eyes widened as students swarmed in, grabbing desks, talking nonstop. The noise level surged. "This class is huge!"

Kayla shrugged. "It's about the same size as the classes in my last school."

"I never had more than twelve girls in any class at Laurel."

"Only twelve? Only girls?"

Caroline nodded.

The bell blared and thirty kids scrambled for their seats. Ten quiet seconds, then conversations resumed. Summer jobs, hairstyles, outfits. Girls hugged, boys gave each other high fives, a few couples kissed passionately. A stocky boy with blond-turning-brown hair jogged to the front.

"Teacher's late. Shut up and listen. Behind the gym after school. Mexican, Hawaiian, whatever you want, I've got it."

Caroline and Kayla exchanged looks of utter incomprehension. The room filled with hisses, boos, and scattered applause. The boy bowed.

"Most of you know me from ninth grade, and I expect your vote for class president. But I see two mysterious ladies. I'm Kurt." He lifted Caroline's hand to his lips, then reached for Kayla.

"No, thank you," she murmured, withdrawing her clenched fist. "But a pleasure to make your acquaintance."

"A shy damsel!" Kurt leaped back, and the class burst into laughter, which immediately hushed as the teacher walked in.

"Hello, Sir." Kurt bowed again. "I was leading the class in the Pledge of Allegiance."

The man pointed to Kurt's empty seat. "I'm Mr. Cohen. Welcome to Hollywood High School. This is Honors Sophomore English. Anybody think they're in the wrong class?" Two girls and a boy raised their hands, and Mr. Cohen motioned them to the front. "The rest of you, fill out these information cards for the administration." He handed a stack to Kayla. "Take one and pass it on."

The three wrong-class students worked their way from the last row to Mr. Cohen's desk. As the boy walked by, he accidentally brushed against Caroline's arm. She looked up, and up again. He was tall, around six feet, string bean thin. He wore pink lipstick and black mascara. Their eyes met for an instant and she caught her breath, shocked at the depth of sadness and longing that radiated into her core. Then he continued forward. She stared at his hair, light blond, thick and shiny, brushing his hips as he walked.

"I need a pencil," called a boy from the third row.

A girl with brown braids handed him a shiny new #2 pencil, perfectly sharpened.

"Thanks," he smiled.

"Grow up." She shot him a withering look, tossed her braids, and turned her back.

"What's the date?" called a voice from the left of the classroom. In spite of the ninety-degree heat, the girl wore a thick black turtleneck and tight black jeans along with black lipstick, black eye shadow, and long black hair.

"September 4," said a boy with light brown dreadlocks down his back.

"I mean the year," the girl cracked her gum.

"What are you, stupid?" Dreadlocks smirked.

"No, moron, I'm a poetry aficionado. I'm organizing Poetry Night. I'll recite Sylvia Plath, and you can recite the calendar." She blew an impressive bubble that exploded in her face.

"Both of you, lose the gum and the attitude." Mr. Cohen spoke evenly from the front of the room where he filled out hall passes for the three students.

"Nice shot, and 1973." Kurt grinned as the girl fired her gum into the trash can. "Want to see a movie on Saturday?"

She flipped him the bird, and the class laughed.

I can't believe . . . in front of a teacher! Caroline's green eyes darted from student to student, gauging the classroom. Her hair caught the light, turning from wheat to sandy to gold. She moved her head slightly, scanning each person, a two-second emotional x-ray. *Edgy . . . staccato . . . angry . . . live wire . . .* she landed on Kayla *. . . scared like me . . .* and Mr. Cohen *. . . calm, in absolute control.* Caroline's anxiety dropped a few notches.

Mr. Cohen completed the hall passes, and the three students left for the administrative offices to sort out their schedules. The blond boy towered over the two girls, and Caroline couldn't tear her eyes away from him. As the door closed behind them, Mr. Cohen zeroed in on Kurt to begin roll call.

"What's your name?"

"Kurt Christianson."

"And you?" nodding at Brown Braids.

"Sharon Greenberg."

"You?" he glanced at Dreadlocks.

"Victor Sherwood. People call me Dreads."

"Dreads it is." Mr. Cohen checked off his name and looked at the girl in black.

"Elvia."

The class broke into laughter.

"Her name's Andrea Krause."

"She only wore blue in ninth grade."

"She changes her name every summer."

"Last year she was Picasso."

Caroline gripped the edge of her desk, steadying herself from the onslaught of names.

"Settle down." Although Mr. Cohen didn't yell, the room was instantly under his control. "How is it you all know this girl's name?" He pointed at Pencil Boy.

"We've been in school together since kindergarten. Except for the two girls in front. And I'm Mort Holloway."

"Glad to meet you, Mort." Mr. Cohen turned to Poetry Girl. "How'd you pick the name Elvia?"

The kids snickered and she glowered.

Mr. Cohen looked over the group. "It's her name. Her choice. Everyone will call her Elvia." He addressed the girl. "You don't have to answer my question."

She shrugged, her tone deliberately rude. "Elvia is a combination of Sylvia and Emily, for Plath and Dickinson. I'm wearing black because my Blue Period is over, and Picasso doesn't work anymore."

Dreads raised his hand. "I have an announcement. Presto placed seventh in the state surfing competition."

"Presto . . ." Mr Cohen scanned his class roster and looked up, puzzled.

"Egbert Petrovich." A short, muscular boy with a spectacular tan and bushy sun-bleached hair spoke up.

"You prefer Presto." Mr. Cohen made a note.

"Wouldn't you prefer Presto if you were named Egbert?"

Mr. Cohen grinned. "Point taken. You must be an impressive surfer, Presto. Congratulations. Take a bow."

The boy jumped up and raised his fists as though acknowledging a crowd at the beach. The kids clapped.

"Really mature," Sharon muttered, tossing her braids.

Mr. Cohen finished roll call. "When the bell rings, leave your information cards on my desk. Once I have them, you're officially enrolled in this class. This is your last chance to speak up if you think you're in the wrong class." He paused, then wrote on the board: The nondescript man turned out to be a lion in the classroom. "Let's start with grammar, everyone's favorite." A long beat. "Folks, get it out of your systems. Let's hear some objections!" The room filled with hisses and boos, while Caroline and Kayla exchanged a mortified glance. "Excellent," said Mr. Cohen to an immediate silence. "Now, who can find the adjective?"

Four hands shot up.

"I think I'm in the wrong class," Kayla whispered to Caroline.

"I think I'm in the wrong galaxy."

CHAPTER 2

Caroline and Kayla sat ramrod straight through English with Mr. Cohen, then moved on to Introductory Latin with Miss Orville. They suffered, polite and attentive, through Trigonometry and Honors Biology. They huddled together at lunch, wide eyed in the surrounding pandemonium.

Three girls walked by in tube tops, chatting in rapid Spanish. Caroline blushed.

"What's wrong?" asked Kayla.

"At my last school, not wearing a bra was an automatic suspension."

"That doesn't seem to be the case here."

"What do you think we'd have to do to get suspended?" Caroline wondered.

"I don't know, but I'll bet it has nothing to do with proper undergarments." Kayla smiled wickedly. "I'm sure you were suspended from your old school …"—Caroline's smile froze—"… for not wearing a bra."

"Of course. More times than I can count. I … look! That's him!"

"Who?"

"The Blond! The tall thin blond boy who was in the wrong English class. He's walking toward the quad."

"I don't remember him. Those three kids left after about five minutes, and I don't have classes with any of them. Do you know him?"

Caroline shook her head.

"Then why . . ."

The bell blared and they parted nervously, forced to unglue for the first time. Their schedules were identical except for fifth period Monday, Wednesday, and Friday. Kayla had Choral Singing and Caroline had a free period. Caroline lugged her books across the quad, over the crumbling asphalt, to the library. She stopped short and checked her map.

The paint was peeling in chunks. Gang graffiti clambered across the building, a message both incomprehensible and disturbing. From the outside, a sorry sight — then a swift pang of guilt over her privileged background. Caroline pushed the door open.

The sound slammed her like a fist. A familiar inner voice of caution urged her to run. But as she turned numb with shock, a deeper magnetic force pulled her forward into a mob of screaming students.

Several languages ricocheted around the room, a maelstrom of sharp sounds. In the middle, a violent upheaval. Kids jumped on chairs for a better view. The librarian, grey hair in a bun, screamed into the phone for the police. On her desk, a supermarket tabloid pictured a baby hippo, IQ two hundred, performing calculus.

"They have knives!" the librarian shrieked, clutching the receiver. "Tom from The Duke's gang and I don't know the other one. He looks older than high school."

Thought became a discontinuous series of freeze frames as Caroline noted apropos of nothing that the floor was sticky, and most bookshelves were empty. Smells of mold, dust, and adrenaline swirled thickly. In a trance, she backed into a wall and glanced up at the school flag, red with a round, white seal. Above the banner, the Hollywood High motto was painted in giant peeling letters: ACHIEVE THE HONORABLE.

A huge boy leaped onto a desk. "The Duke! The Duke!" he bellowed.

The room took up the chant.

Suddenly, a roar from the epicenter, then groaning and a different kind of screaming.

The guy on the desk jabbed a massive fist at someone below. "I'll kill you!" he shouted hoarsely, stomping with each syllable. "I'll kill Drake!" The desk cracked.

"Tom's cut! He's bleeding!" The librarian's eyes were wild. "Where are the cops?"

The door crashed open. Four officers charged the library, converging on a muscular teen, hands against his cheek, dripping blood. Caroline sidled along the wall then ducked outside, shaking and struggling to breathe, marshaling every ounce of self-control to walk away before she dropped on all fours behind a hedge and waited for the nausea to subside. After a minute, she decided she wasn't going to vomit and sat up.

A crowd surged out of the building, students talking excitedly in several languages. Caroline recognized Spanish, Italian, and French. She couldn't identify the rest. Her breathing steadied as two police officers led out a man in handcuffs. A third officer helped the bleeding teen to a bench. "Sit still and don't move! We've called an ambulance. We have your knife and we'll take your statement at the hospital!"

From the ground by the hedge, Caroline saw the fourth policeman march out next to the huge boy who broke the desk.

"Duke, if there's trouble, you're always in the middle of it! I'm bringing you down to the station!"

"I didn't do anything!"

"Yeah, right. You're always innocent."

Duke glanced toward the hedge and blinked. Caroline froze, trying to disappear into the leaves. "Hey, how you doin'?" he smirked. "Come here often?"

"C'mon, keep moving!" The officer took Duke's arm and propelled him forward. They disappeared around a corner.

Caroline stood slowly, testing her limbs. The bell rang and she moved toward her next class, counting the minutes until she could go home and lose herself in a novel.

CHAPTER 3

Next time Kayla headed to choral singing, Caroline crossed the quad to a small dry patch of lawn at the opposite end of campus from the library. So far, not much homework. If she plowed through four trig problems, she could lounge all evening in her bedroom with her books.

"Hi, new girl!"

She glanced up.

"I forgot your name." Presto smiled.

"Caroline."

"I'm Dreads," and "I'm Presto," they said in unison. Dreads carried a tennis racket.

"Yeah, I remember." She smiled back.

"So," Presto continued, "I surf, and Dreads is number one on the tennis team. Which do you think is cooler?"

"I couldn't possibly choose." Absolutely serious, Caroline was startled when they laughed.

"See you around." Dreads grinned over his shoulder as they walked to their classes.

What was . . . did they . . . was I flirting with boys?

The tall blond boy rushed across the street to campus, hurrying toward the largest building of classrooms. The Los Angeles sun turned his hair into a shimmering river. Their eyes met and Caroline immediately felt his sadness, longing, and . . . was that grit? The Blond looked through her, no recognition from his few minutes in Mr. Cohen's English class. She watched him disappear into the sea of students shouting in forty-plus languages.

Caroline opened her math book. Halfway through her homework, two men in their mid-twenties stepped out of the International House of Pancakes diagonally across the street and zeroed in. One wore a polyester suit of moss green with a yellow satin shirt. A large, jeweled cross hung around his neck. Sensing their laser stares, she raised her eyes and was momentarily riveted by Polyester's shaved head, sweaty through a skull and cross bones tattoo. Then his friend stepped forward and Caroline's jaw dropped.

The man wore a silver lamé three-piece suit. His dark brown skin clashed against the metallic glitter, an effect both stunning and bizarre. His wavy hair, slick with tonic, grazed his shoulders. His fingers flashed with jeweled rings. Gold chains circled an open collar, bursting with curly chest hair. His eyes were sharp, his body rail thin. His left arm was wrapped in an ace bandage, as though recently out of a cast. He walked to a palpable beat. The two men stood over her, then sat uninvited.

"Hi, Honey," Silver Lamé spoke. "Never seen you before."

Caroline said nothing, noticed his beeper, idiotically thought of a doctor on call.

"You new, Honey?"

She nodded.

To his friend, "She's pretty."

"You scared her," the friend noted, amused.

"Don't be scared, Honey," Silver Lamé said. "You got a name?"

"Caroline Black," she said, amazed that her voice worked.

"Pretty name for a pretty girl."

Through her astonishment, she began to bristle.

"You work, Caroline?" asked Silver Lamé, leaning forward.

"I go to school."

"Numbers." Silver Lamé glanced at her math homework. "Smart. You ever think of a job for a smart girl, pretty Caroline?"

She didn't get it, but she heard too many "pretty"s. She grabbed her backpack and shot to her feet.

"It's okay, Honey, sit back down," Silver Lamé soothed.

"I'm Caroline! Not Honey!" Baffled by her own rage, she stormed toward the nearest building.

Caroline couldn't explain why, but she was unraveling, and she still had twenty minutes left in her free period. Out of options, she found her way to the administrative offices and nearly cried with relief when her guidance counselor's door stood open.

She recognized Mrs. Richardson from their one meeting during the summer to register. She was a short, stumpy woman, around forty. In August, her hair had been a spiked metallic red. Now it shone neon blonde. Her parents had glanced uneasily at the hair but grew increasingly impressed as Mrs. Richardson offered the syllabus for Hollywood High's Latin class. She asked politely about Leah's training at the Psychoanalytic Institute, stared awestruck at Geoff's show business credentials, then beamed at Caroline with the predictable, "Do you want to be an actress? Our drama program is excellent!" Seeing the girl's frostbite smile, she switched gears, casually mentioning her optometrist husband and two grown sons, a music teacher and a pediatric dentist. Just enough personal information to convey commitment to education. Geoff offered that their son was an undergraduate at Harvard, his own alma mater, where he had met Leah at Radcliffe. Mrs. Richardson pointed to her special metal cabinet reserved for files of the college bound students and suggested an "academic honors track."

"May I ask a question?" Caroline spoke for the first time.

"Of course." Mrs. Richardson nodded.

"I've been taking French and I'd like to continue. I'd also like to begin learning Latin. Is that possible, or do I need to choose?"

"No problem." Her counselor made a notation, quickly looking over Caroline's transcript from Laurel. "We'll place you in Introductory Latin and, since you've had three years of French at your previous school, we'll put you in Advanced French as your elective."

Her parents smiled, reluctantly convinced that their daughter's leaving Laurel Academy for Girls might be something beyond intellectual suicide.

Now, one month later, Caroline glanced at the wall above Mrs. Richardson's desk. A poster dominated the space, new since their August meeting, stark white print on a solid black background: *Whatever you can do, or dream you can, begin it. Boldness has genius, power, and magic in it.*

"Goethe," the girl said quietly.

"You've read Goethe?"

"I've read all kinds of things. Last night I finished Rita Mae Brown's *Rubyfruit Jungle*, and I started Ernest Hemingway's *A Farewell to Arms*. I also collect *Doonesbury* comics, and I read them when I need perspective."

Caroline was confused when Mrs. Richardson chuckled.

"How's your first week?" her guidance counselor asked.

A confused mess, a massive mistake. "Fine, thank you."

Both turned as Elvia tapped on the open door. "Oh, sorry, I can come back later."

"It's okay." Mrs. Richardson waved her in, and Elvia held out a sheet of paper.

"Five possible dates. I checked it against the team schedules, the county cheerleading competition, the drama department, and every music and dance performance." She turned to Caroline. "Scheduling poetry night. We have English together. You're one of the new girls. I'm—"

"Elvia," Caroline smiled. "You're into poetry, your Blue Period is over, and you don't like calendars."

"November 5 will work." Mrs. Richardson handed back the list.

"Thanks, I'll put it on the main schedule." She turned to Caroline. "Calendars are okay. I said that to annoy Dreads." She grinned and walked out.

Mrs. Richardson turned to Caroline. "Did you stop by to say hello, or did you want to discuss something in particular?"

"How do your students fill free time? I have Monday, Wednesday, and Friday, fifth period." *I have no clue what happened, but shiny clothes and hair tonic and gold chains were involved, and I'll never sit on the lawn again.*

Mrs. Richardson unfolded an enormous grid. "This is the master course schedule. Let's see . . . there's an opening in drama."

"NO!" Caroline blushed and Mrs. Richardson looked up in surprise. "I mean . . . I'm sorr—"

"Quite all right," she paused. "Now I'm remembering our summer meeting in detail. You were definitely not interested in drama. My mistake. Let's discuss alternatives. On this campus, it's best to have a specific place to go, an office or a classroom." Caroline nodded in extreme agreement. "You can work for the administration. Elvia keeps the master schedule of extracurricular activities. We have stacks of filing. Spreadsheets that need organizing and balancing ledgers. You'll get five community service credits. Or you can tutor."

"Tutor whom?"

Mrs. Richardson stifled a smile at the *whom* and handed Caroline a single sheet. "Take a look at this. He's a senior, for the second year in a row. He failed basic math and English last year. He had another tutor, but she wasn't able to help."

Caroline glanced at the page: D. Hunter, mother requests math tutor.

"Does he want a tutor, or is it just his mom?"

"Good question. I'm not sure. I know he wants to graduate this year."

"Okay, I'll try."

"By the way, D is for Duke."

Caroline's polite smile congealed.

"What's the matter . . . oh, I'll bet you went to the library on Wednesday, didn't you?"

Silence.

"How about the administrative office?"

"I . . ." The girl cleared her throat. "Duke's last tutor, where is she now?"

Mrs. Richardson burst out laughing. "She's in good health and attending Valley Junior College."

"I beg your pardon." Caroline turned brick red. "I didn't mean—"

"The gang members have codes of honor," Mrs. Richardson interrupted gently. "They may be different from anything you know, but they make sense in their own ways. Your style will be as strange to Duke as his is to you. So, what's it to be, the administration or tutoring?"

Caroline suddenly found herself fighting tears.

"Do you want to talk about it?" her counselor asked softly.

"Hollywood High seems like . . . it's . . . I mean . . . churning out A's . . . it's not enough. I'm not sure I have what it takes."

"What do you think it takes?"

"Courage," the girl answered immediately.

"It's okay to be scared."

"I'm not sure what I'm scared of."

"I'm sure the knife fight in the library was frightening."

"I've never seen anything like it. But if I'm totally honest, something scared me even more than the violence." *Something from inside myself.*

"That's important to figure out, but you can work on it as you go along. You don't have to solve every puzzle before you move forward."

"Then I'll try tutoring Duke." Caroline caught her breath. *I didn't mean to say it out loud.*

"Do you want some time to think it over?"

Yes, I want to think it over forever, while we discuss Goethe. "Definitely not."

Mrs. Richardson laughed. "A sense of humor might be your biggest asset here."

"At this point, I'll take any asset, big or small."

"If you stay here this year, I bet you'll discover strengths you never knew you had."

"I hope you're right." Caroline took a deep breath. "Okay, what happens next?"

"Welcome to Hollywood High."

CHAPTER 4

Caroline knew her way to her classes. She opened her gym locker on the first try. And she couldn't eat lunch, anticipating fifth period.

"Break a leg!" Kayla gave her a little push.

Caroline recognized Duke immediately. Six-four, two-twenty. His features were chiseled, eyes a rich brown, skin a clear mocha. She offered her hand, which he slapped away.

He's a foot taller than I am, his hands are the size of turkey platters, his feet are bigger than . . . wait a second, OH CRAP! Please please please don't let him remember me from the knife fight, hiding behind a hedge, trying not to puke . . .

Duke marched to two empty desks in the back of Miss Orville's Latin classroom, with Caroline cringing after him. She slid in and steeled herself for the next insult. Instead, he shifted, self-conscious. His legs didn't fit under the desk. He shot her a look of pure arrogance. She shrugged and half-smiled.

"Shall we try the floor instead?" *Please don't kill me, please don't kill me, please don't . . .*

They settled in a corner. Miss Orville glanced over and raised an eyebrow. Caroline nodded, barely perceptible. Duke scowled.

"So, what do you do in your free time when you're not hiding under hedges?"

Caroline's palms broke with sweat.

"Ever seen a knife fight before?"

She shook her head and Duke smirked.

"You're not gonna last five minutes at this school." He waited for her to answer, but she remained frozen. He rolled his eyes. "Are we gonna just sit here?"

Caroline cleared her throat. "You want to go over multiplication?" Her voice was barely above a whisper. She clutched a zero-to-twelve multiplication grid like a life preserver.

"Say what?"

"Multiplication. Mrs. Richardson said you want to learn it."

"Nope."

"Does this look familiar?" She offered him the paper, which he knocked out of her hand.

"My last tutor gave me that. Don't mean shit."

"Duke . . ."

"*The* Duke." A hard stare.

"Perhaps I've misunderstood. How can I assist you?"

"How can I assist you," he mimicked her. "I can't believe they think you can teach me anything."

"I'm sorry," she blushed.

"I'm sorry, too. I'm sorry they saddled me with a moron like you."

Caroline's anger began to stir. "I'm not just any moron. I'm the lucky moron assigned to be your tutor. That means you have a choice. You want my assistance, or shall I crawl back to my hedge?"

"Your *assistance*? What for? Your words are too long."

"I'll attempt to speak in fewer syllables, but it's possible I'll be unable—"

"Girl, you sound like a fucking dictionary!"

The words slashed through the tamed recitation of Latin declensions. But as Miss Orville turned to banish him in disgrace, Caroline broke into laughter. He glared, then he began to laugh as well.

"Can you teach me to do multiplication in my math class?" The Duke finally choked out.

"Can you teach me to say *'fuck'* in my Latin class?"

They buried their heads in their hands.

"Girl, you just did say it."

"Then I guess we're launched."

The Duke picked up his multiplication grid. He squinted, holding it at arm's length. He slanted his left eye towards the page, his head at an awkward angle. He stared, adjusted the paper.

Caroline contained her annoyance, kept her tone even. "If you don't want a tutor, then tell me. You don't have to make a big deal out of it."

"No, it's . . ." He trailed off, brought the sheet a few inches closer, blinked hard.

Enough drama over the multiplication grid. "Okay, I get it, you like jerking people around. Congratulations, you've got talent."

"Huh?"

"Let's call it a day."

The Duke looked at her, surprised. "Is it time to go? I didn't hear the bell." He automatically glanced at his wristwatch, shook his head slightly, craned to see across the room, the wall clock above Miss Orville's desk. "We have ten more minutes . . . how come you're looking at me like that?"

"You can see the clock at the front of the room, but you can't see your wristwatch," she spoke quietly.

"So what?"

"Forget the math for a minute. Read the numbers on the page."

He glared at her.

"When you looked at the clock, did you work from the numbers or from the position of the hands?"

"Say what?"

"Do you know letters and numbers?" she asked gently. "Can you read?"

The arrogance melted and he nodded miserably.

Caroline stood. "Come with me. Please."

"What you doing now, girl?"

"We're going to see Mrs. Richardson."

"No way!" He stopped in his tracks.

"Why not?"

"She's the counselor for people like you. Smart. Maybe even college. She don't talk to me."

"She will now."

He crossed his arms. "If you're wrong, if she shows me any disrespect, you have to tell that tight ass bitch Miss Orville to fuck a mule!"

"Deal." Caroline's lips twitched.

They walked slowly, and Caroline tapped on her counselor's open door. Mrs. Richardson's smile turned forced as The Duke trailed in.

"Mrs. Richardson, I don't know if you've met Duke Hunter."

They reluctantly shook hands.

"Caroline, you don't have to give me a progress report. I don't need to be involved in your tutoring."

"I apologize for the intrusion, but we have a problem. Can the school nurse do eye exams?"

"Are your eyes troubling you?"

"No. I think The Duke needs glasses."

"What makes you think so?"

"He was straining to read numbers on a page. He couldn't tell time from looking at his wristwatch, but he had no problem seeing the clock on the wall across the room."

"Farsighted." Mrs. Richardson turned to The Duke. "You never noticed your vision was blurry when you tried to read?"

He said nothing.

"Okay, I get it." Their guidance counselor shook her head sadly. "You noticed, but you didn't think anyone would care. You were dealing with so much in your life that blurry vision was the least of your concerns."

The Duke stared.

To the kids' astonishment, Mrs. Richardson's eyes misted over. "If that's the case, then this school owes you a big apology."

The Duke eyed her warily, still silent.

"My husband is an eye doctor, an optometrist." She picked up the phone and paused. "With your permission . . ."

He hesitated, then nodded.

She tapped seven buttons. They heard ringing and a click. Their counselor identified herself as "Dr. Richardson's wife" and explained that "a student needs a pro bono eye exam, probably glasses." Ten minutes later, the appointment was set, the arrangements in place.

The bell rang.

As the two kids left for their next class, The Duke covered his astonishment with his signature arrogance. Mrs. Richardson concealed her anger at the system that had failed to meet The Duke's basic needs, setting him back so far in his education. Caroline hid her relief that she wouldn't have to honor her deal with The Duke and order Miss Orville to commit bestiality with a mule.

CHAPTER 5

Caroline and her parents strolled across the courtyard of the Los Angeles Music Center toward the theatre. She surprised them by volunteering to go. Usually, she avoided entertainment industry events like hazardous waste.

"Tough week?" Leah asked.

"Yeah," her daughter nodded. "I feel like a 1492 sailor. I don't know whether I'm going to fall off the edge of the earth or discover a new world."

"Maybe both," answered her mother.

"You can always . . ." her father began.

"Call Laurel Academy and beg." Caroline rolled her eyes and Leah chuckled.

"Not beg." Geoff glared at his wife. "She was one of their top students. I'm sure if she spoke to them, she could . . ."

"Of course she could," Leah cut in, smiling at her daughter. "The point is, she can't."

Her father shrugged irritably. He held the door to the theatre's lobby, and they walked into the expected onslaught.

"Turn down the volume," Caroline muttered, and Leah hugged her shoulders. Geoff, an Oscar winning cinematographer, was immediately surrounded.

Electric magenta, neon turquoise, slinky black, shimmering white. Sequins, jewels, and crystal chandeliers. Except for her parents, no gray hair. The men, jet black or ruddy bronze. The women, perky blonde or sassy red. Face lifts, boob jobs, hair implants. Haute couture on the rampage. The opening of a musical, *Make Mine Music.*

Openings and premiers loomed with overwhelming glitz, while Caroline felt smaller than life. Surrounded by the golden and the glittery, the famous and the beautiful, she shrank. Voices trained to project rang out incessantly, leaving her increasingly aphasic.

"Leah, you're more beautiful than ever!" A colleague of Geoff's, a 47-year-old producer, kissed both of her cheeks and turned to Caroline. "And who's this?"

"Our daughter, Caroline."

"Nice to meet you." Caroline offered her hand to shake. Instead, he bowed before her, turned her hand and kissed her palm.

"You're a very pretty girl."

She said nothing.

He smiled rakishly. "Will you marry me?"

"No."

"Why not? I'm rich, successful, famous, charming. I'll take you to dinner anywhere you want. Your wish is my command."

"You sound like a boy in my English class. His name's Kurt and he's obsessed with my friend Kayla."

Leah watched, amused at the man's antics, impressed that her daughter could fend for herself, looking forward to telling her friends that her daughter's attractiveness was noticed by a mega-producer.

"I'm not obsessed." The producer's eyes were locked on Caroline, only on her, in the crowded room. "I just appreciate beauty."

"Then it's your lucky day. This room is filled with beautiful people who would love to give you a blow job. Unfortunately, I'm not among them." She turned her back and walked away.

"Caroline!" Leah hurried to follow her daughter, laughing in spite of herself. "Blow jobs? Was that really necessary?"

"Yes, that was really necessary. What a total loser! Your wish is my command? Seriously?"

"He's charming." Leah tried to guide her daughter toward reason.

"He's a barf-inducing emetic!"

"He's one of the most sought after producers in the industry."

"If he's so sought after, then why's he trying to do it with a high school girl?"

"Because you're beautiful!"

"No, Mom. Because there's something wrong with him."

He was now speaking to a gorgeous young actress, around nineteen, eyes on her, only on her. Above the noise of the crowd, Caroline and Leah heard him say, "Your wish is my command."

"I told you," Caroline smirked. "His lucky day."

Through the hailstorm of "Hi Darlings" and "Don't You Look Ravishings," the final bell chimed tastefully, and Geoff joined his wife and daughter.

"Hello Leah, darling!" gushed Millie Charlemagne, an actress Geoff had worked with a decade ago. "Caroline, dear, what a lovely dress. Sea green to match your eyes. You simply scintillate! Wherever did you find it?"

"Beverly Hills. Rodeo Drive. A boutique called Hades Haute Couture. They specialize in fashion for the terminally neutral."

"Caroline!" yelped Geoff, as Leah shook with laughter.

Millie charged off to greet another actress. "You've lost weight! Don't you look ravishing!"

Make Mine Music had opened in New York to stellar reviews. A friend of Geoff's wrote, directed, and produced this Broadway extravaganza, which now moved west to California. The story featured three kids — a tap dancer, ballerina, and singer — struggling for stardom. Scenes with their parents in their living rooms doing the casual performance; scenes with their teachers, sweating pure grit; finally, scenes of getting the big break and exiting in triumph. One fabulous song and dance number after the next.

Casting, Geoff's friend had described over an early dinner, had proved nearly impossible: to find kids who were rip roaring talented, uncomplaining work horses, calm in the face of mayhem, and parents who would stay out of the way. "It made auditions a nightmare. Ogre stage mothers, fascist stage fathers, bratty stage children. I had to turn down a fantastically gifted girl because of her mother. The she-shark actually handed me the mandated lunch menu for her 'picky eater' daughter. Ground chateaubriand burger, julienne fries, and a box of Godiva chocolates. I ordered her a bucket of raw tofu."

Throughout her childhood, Caroline puzzled over the paparazzi. Cinematography was her father's profession, and his colleagues were their friends. She never thought of his pals as "movie stars." They were actors and costume designers, writers and producers. A girl with a successful lawyer parent doesn't think of her mom as an "attorney star." These people had careers and some even had talent. Like any other business.

Or maybe not.

As they took their seats, Leah smiled at a thirty-something actress from Geoff's last picture. The young woman gaily waved from two rows down, her shiny skin surgically stretched so tightly she could barely close her mouth. An aging star, blindingly blonde in a sleeveless silver gown, beamed from four seats to their right. She'd recently returned from a secret operation in France. She had to sign a truckload of waivers before the surgeon would cut since she was eighty-two, had a serious heart condition, and wheezed like an asthmatic moose. All for "the upper arms of a teenager! Isn't it simply marvelous!"

The lights dimmed, the red velvet curtain rose, and the three children took off — tapping, singing, pirouetting. The beat penetrated Caroline's internal rhythms in a pulsating rush. Scene one ended to wild applause. Scene two began, overlapping with the last of the cheers to keep the endorphins pumping.

The dancer ripped through soft shoe routines, the singer burst with lyrics, the ballerina twirled, puppets drained of their own essence. These kids were too good, and Caroline knew too much to sit back and enjoy the show. Rehearsals were grueling, pitiless marathons. The children sang until they soundlessly cried from exhaustion, throats raw from hours of yelling on key, loud enough to fill the hall. They danced until their young feet bled. They limped home, soaked their cuts, flesh torn open, blisters rubbed raw. Ointment, bandages, and up the next morning to do it again.

Caroline began to cry.

The play ended, the bows taken, the final curtain call. Staggering under their heavy bouquets, the kids beamed. Slowly the Black family waded through the overdressed gridlock.

"Wasn't it wonderful!" Millie Charlemagne trilled as the crowd shoved them together. She peered at Caroline. "You're terribly blotchy! Whatever's the matter?"

"Leprosy," Caroline stage whispered.

"Where's poor Millie running off to?" Geoff glared at his daughter. "What did you say this time?"

"I'm ready to make the change," Caroline answered quietly.

Her parents turned, both with identical smiles of pride, relief, admiration.

"You're ready to call Laurel Academy." Geoff patted her shoulder. "You've come to your senses."

"No, Geoff." Leah held her daughter's eyes. "She's ready for Hollywood High."

A long beat, then Geoff put a hand to his forehead. "Congratulations, Caroline. Let's get out of here. I need a double scotch and an I.V."

On the ride home, Leah and Geoff admired the tightly woven dialogue, the talent of the performers, the exhilarating musical score. Caroline sat silently in the back seat. After a few minutes, Leah turned and asked if she liked the production.

Caroline shrugged. "I agree with you. The music was great. Same with the singing and dancing. But it was predictable."

"What do you mean?" Geoff glanced at his daughter in the rearview mirror.

"It was good light entertainment, nothing more. The story wasn't interesting."

"Why not?" Leah was surprised. "I thought it was terrific."

"Terrific light entertainment." Caroline held her ground. "Each of the three kids was born with a gift. Tap, ballet, singing. But nowhere in the entire play were the kids ever asked what they wanted to do with their gifts. It was like the gifts owned the kids instead of the kids' owning the gifts. From the opening scene, they were destined for stardom and that's what happened. The story would have been more interesting if one of the kids decided to take a different path."

"Would that have worked with the plot line?" Geoff asked.

"Not the way it was written. It could have been written much better."

"How?" Geoff asked. "I'm curious what you would have done with it."

"If I had been the writer, I would have chosen one of the kids — probably the ballet dancer — and written her character as having another gift along with ballet. I'd make her smart. Maybe she'd get sick of the ballet world, the constant competition, the pressure to be anorexic so your partner can lift you easily, the stress on your body, the expectation that you'll take diet pills. I'd write a scene where she realizes she's good at science. I'd add another scene where she has a difficult talk with her parents. They've invested a ton of time and money in ballet lessons, and she tells them she wants to dance, but not professionally, only for fun. She's decided she wants to study biology. When her costars hit the stage lights to sing and tap, she'd begin college, on her way to becoming a biologist."

"Caroline," her father said patiently, "your story might have been more interesting, but it wouldn't have been as successful."

"You mean it wouldn't have raked in as many millions," Caroline said evenly. "I know, it's so true, an immutable fact of life. Nothing's more annoying than a girl who's too smart, who's more interested in reading than in makeup, who talks about science instead of boys. I mean, if she wants to drop ballet, she should at least have the good sense to become a cheerleader, not a biologist."

"Well, girls like that are . . ." Geoff trailed off.

"Nerds? Boring? Like me?"

Geoff clamped his mouth shut, shaking his head. *Adolescents! They're impossible!*

"I think you should become a playwright." Leah tried to diffuse the tension.

"No way! When I grow up, I'm going to work nowhere near the entertainment industry. I'm going to be a psychologist."

"You'll be a great psychologist. You'll—" Leah paused, blinked. "Wait a moment . . . hold on. How'd you know about diet pills and anorexia in the ballet world? Did you run into that when you took ballet lessons back in elementary school?"

"Of course I ran into it," Caroline answered. "It's impossible to avoid it."

Her parents waited, but their daughter said nothing more.

"What do you mean?" Leah finally asked.

"At first, I loved my ballet classes. I liked the other girls, and they liked me. Then our teacher decided I was her next-in-line. If I stayed thin, if my feet could deal with *en pointe*, if I had the temperament, then I could audition for a ballet company, which would make her look great. She jumped me two classes ahead, with a bunch of teenagers. I was ten. When we danced in pairs, nobody wanted to be my partner. Nobody wanted to be my friend."

"I didn't realize . . ." Leah trailed off.

"It got worse," Caroline said bluntly. "After a few weeks, the teacher brought in a high school boy to dance with me, the only boy in the class. He was really cute, and the other girls wanted to be his partner. What they really wanted was to be his girlfriend, but the teacher always paired him with me. She said we were her girl and boy candidates to make the cut and turn pro. Then the other girls hated me even more. The only good thing was that the boy was nice. I was surprised that he always wanted to talk to me during the breaks. He was five years older, and I thought he'd rather be with the other girls. Then he told me he was gay, and he was glad I wasn't interested in going out with him. I became his shield from the girls who were constantly in his face, throwing themselves at him."

"I had no idea," Leah said.

"Mom, how could you have missed it? You used to watch class sometimes. Looking back, you might have missed that my partner was gay, but you couldn't have missed that the girls hated me."

"I thought they were jealous."

"Of what?"

"That you were better than they were at ballet," Leah said.

"Or that you were so beautiful," Geoff added.

Caroline rolled her eyes. "Dad, you need a jail break. You're locked in the industry's mindset about how people look. You think everything's about being pretty. There's a big world outside of industry bullshit." She took a deep breath. "Back to your question, Mom, the girls were always obsessing about diet pills, losing weight, making themselves throw up. I remember you were watching the class one day when they were talking about it. Didn't you hear?"

"Where'd they get the diet pills?" Leah evaded her daughter's question.

"From our teacher." Caroline paused, waiting for her parents to connect the dots, to realize *they* should have asked what *she* wanted, like the ballet dancer in her revision of the play. Instead, they were quiet. She shrugged. "It's no big deal. Doesn't matter anymore."

"You were adamant that you weren't going back to ballet, but you never said why. If you had told me about the diet pills, I could have talked to the teacher and helped you stay."

"Mom, you're being clueless."

"What do you mean?"

"I didn't want you to help me stay. I don't belong in that world. That world doesn't belong in me. I wanted to get out."

CHAPTER 6

Caroline survived dissecting a worm and aced her first math quiz. Kurt proposed to Kayla, who cringed as he shoved a fake diamond the size of a walnut onto her right thumb. When the bell rang, on her way out of the classroom, Kayla threw the ring into the trash.

Worse than Kayla's engagement, Caroline had to pee. Toward the end of morning recess, she breezed into the main girls' bathroom in the central hall. In the split second before she realized what she had walked into, she flashed on the library. Her intellect urged her to run, but the same clammy numbness took hold, and she stood mesmerized.

Nellie, a junior in her P.E. class, lay on the floor. Three girls surrounded her. The tallest, Della, also in P.E., kicked her hard. As the door banged shut behind Caroline, the three girls wheeled around to face her. Nellie curled into a fetal position.

"What are you doing?" Caroline asked from far away.

"Bitch messed with my boyfriend," Della fired back.

"You gonna tell?" The second girl advanced.

Caroline's breathing turned shallow. Della made a sudden move toward her, and she jumped back, smacking her head against the bathroom wall.

"Aww. She's scared!"

"Think she's good in a fight?"

"Yeah! Like my grandma!"

They jeered.

The door swung open again. Elvia and Sharon walked in, chatting about Sharon's next-door neighbor who had written her a love poem.

"Do you like him?" Elvia asked.

"He's adorable. He's in third grade."

The two girls stopped short as they took in the situation. Sharon clutched her braids and backed against the farthest wall. Elvia tossed her backpack into a corner, eyes sharp.

"Hi," Elvia said to Caroline. "Hey, congratulations, I heard you made varsity soccer," to Della. Then she turned to Nellie. "I'm glad I found you. I'm supposed to tell you that Mrs. Richardson wants to see you. You got the worst grade in the class on your math test."

A thud of silence, then the three girls howled.

"How dumb can you get!"

"Total idiot!"

"What's one plus one . . ."

The bathroom door slammed behind them.

Elvia dropped to her knees next to Nellie. "Are you okay?"

"I haven't taken a math test," she whispered in shock.

"I made that up to get rid of them." Elvia looked at Caroline who was sheet white, trying not to hyperventilate. "It's okay. These things happen here. You'll get used to it."

Sharon shook out her braids, combed her hair with her fingers and expertly began rebraiding. She stared at Nellie as her fingers worked.

"Let's go to the school nurse." Caroline found her voice.

"I can't." Nellie wiped blood from her mouth.

"Why not?"

"She'll ask what happened. If I tell, they'll kill me."

"Tell her I beat you up."

Caroline was confused when Elvia and Nellie laughed.

"Really mature," Sharon muttered, finishing the first braid and starting on the second.

The door opened again. Caroline tensed, then flooded with relief as Kayla hurried in. "Those girls are bragging that they beat up Nellie and you walked in." She looked at Nellie. "Are you injured?"

"They're total wimps." Nellie struggled to her feet, rolled her shoulders. "I'm gonna kill them, first chance I get!" She glared at Elvia. "Thanks. Not that it mattered. I don't need anyone's help. I screwed her boyfriend, gave him the best blow job he's ever had, and I'm gonna do it again!" She marched out.

"Typical Hollywood High girl-fight over a loser guy." Elvia shrugged, going to one of the sinks. "Need to wash my hands." She looked for soap, but the dispenser was dry. She checked the paper towel holder, found nothing, wiped her hands on her black jeans, shouldered her backpack. "See you around." She left, and Sharon followed.

Caroline and Kayla stared at each other.

"I was afraid you got hurt," Kayla's voice broke.

"You came in because of me?"

Kayla nodded.

"They might have come back. Do you know how to fight?"

Kayla shook her head.

Caroline took her by the shoulders. "You're the bravest girl I've ever met."

They moved into each other's arms, regrouping in the deserted bathroom. A faucet leaked with a rhythmic drip, the steady tap gentle and calming.

"My last school was nothing like this," Kayla murmured into her friend's hair.

"Same with mine." Caroline rested her head on Kayla's shoulder.

"I guess we should go to class." Kayla didn't let go.

"I just remembered," Caroline said, "I have to pee."

"I'll never pee again."

CHAPTER 7

Period five brought P.E. on Tuesdays and Thursdays, and this week it was basketball. Caroline was shooting baskets while Kayla tried an awkward dribble.

Their teacher jogged over. "You're both new," she stated. "I teach ninth grade on Fridays. You would have been in my class last year, and I don't recognize you."

They introduced themselves, and the teacher turned to Caroline. "You've got a nice touch."

I've got a what?

The woman took the ball and aimed at the backboard yelling, "Rebound!"

Caroline leaped, jumped, scored.

"Ever think of the basketball team?"

"Wha—, you mean—, I beg your pardon, I'm not adequately following."

"After school, go to the indoor basketball court. Ask for Mrs. Cuthbertson. They need girls. They're looking for more players. They'll be glad to have you."

Caroline nodded courteously. "Thank you."

Seriously? A sports team?

In seventh grade at Laurel, she wrote a history report on the first women's baseball league in the United States. For her term paper in ninth grade science, she studied the muscular development of Olga Korbut, the darling of the summer's Olympic gymnasts. But the basketball team?

Maybe . . . forget it . . . I could try . . . no way . . .

This ridiculous idea was oddly compelling. Even more strange, her P.E. teacher seemed confident she'd make the cut. Before she could think herself into a mental constrictor knot, Caroline called her parents from a pay phone and explained that she'd be home late. When the final bell rang, she gathered her courage and found her way to the indoor basketball court.

"Excuse me," Caroline addressed the woman's back. "Can you please direct me to Mrs. Cuthbertson?"

The woman stepped from behind a table and turned. She was around fifty, five feet even, one-sixty, freckles, blue eyes. She wore glittery silver ballet slippers, white tights and a sparkling pink tutu. Her face was painted in multicolored stripes, her lips a cheery magenta.

She nodded appraisingly. "We need a point guard."

"My P.E. teacher sent me." Caroline tried not to stare. "Is the bas-ketball coach here?"

"Yes dear, grab a ball."

Caroline obeyed automatically.

"Take a shot."

She dribbled twice, bent her knees and straightened from her toes to her fingertips. The ball circled the rim and clanged through.

"Okay sweetie, there's Irene, the team captain," pointing to a tall, lanky redhead.

"I beg your pardon, but when are tryouts?"

"Sugar," the woman chuckled, "this is Hollywood High, not U.C.L.A. You just tried out. Congratulations, you made the team and . . ." she pirouetted, ending in a deep curtsy, ". . . I'm Mrs. Cuthbertson, your coach."

Now an official member of the Girls Varsity Basketball Team, Caroline looked around. Her teammates were joking with each other, shooting hoops. Three were Black, one Korean, one Chinese, one Mexican, and two white including Irene, the captain. Caroline walked shyly toward the redhead.

"Hi, I'm Irene," the girl said, catching her breath. "You must be Caroline. Your gym teacher told Mrs. Cuthbertson you'd be here."

"Pleasure to meet you." Caroline offered her hand.

Irene raised an eyebrow.

Suddenly Caroline's hand felt gawky. "I shouldn't have done that."

"Your manners need some work," Irene grinned. "Take it down a notch."

"Are you a senior?" Caroline asked, astounded by her easy self-assurance.

"Junior," Irene answered, "and you're a sophomore."

"It's that obvious?"

Caroline scanned the large room and saw nothing familiar. The hoops had no nets. The court's surface was splintery. Each girl held a basketball, shooting and dribbling, shouting and joking.

Two girls jumped for a rebound and accidentally knocked each other to the ground. Instead of getting up slowly and examining their fingernails, they began to wrestle playfully. The others formed a friendly ring, shouting "Go, Lureen!" and "Get her, Shawna!"

"What number do you want?" asked Irene, as Lureen and Shawna hopped up. "Hey, Caroline, your mouth's hanging open. Focus over here." She held a red felt rectangle, a pair of scissors, and a white folded something wrapped in plastic.

"Fifteen." Caroline quickly chose her age.

Irene flattened the rectangle and cut out a one and a five. She handed them over. "Got two dollars?"

"Sure," Caroline was utterly lost.

Irene pulled a white t-shirt from the plastic package, three for six dollars. "Here you go," she said, handing Caroline a needle and red thread. "Sew the numbers on the back of the shirt tonight. Wear your red gym shorts."

Caroline didn't move, and her captain asked curiously, "Where'd you go to school before this?"

"Laurel Academy for Girls."

"Why'd you leave?"

"I . . ." *Brush it off, answer like it's no big deal.* "It's . . ." *She seems like she'd understand.* "Um . . ." *Don't be stupid, keep your mouth shut.* Caroline shrugged, excessively nonchalant. "I needed a change."

Irene shot her a look. A Laurel girl who "needed a change" transferred to Choate or St. Paul's. But Caroline offered nothing more.

"People at Laurel have lots of money, huh?" Irene felt her way, trying to figure out why she liked this odd girl.

"Yeah, I guess."

"Lots of the kids here don't have much," she explained. "Food stamps, clothes from church. Some live on the streets." She nodded at the red felt and thin white shirt. "That's your team uniform. If you didn't have two dollars, Mrs. Cuthbertson would have paid."

Caroline thought of Laurel's school colors, white and gold. Every team had trim white outfits with gold clover emblems. Gold and white warmups, gold and white zippered jackets, gold and white swimsuits, gold and white customized tennis shoes, white socks with gold pom-poms for the cheerleaders.

"Okay. Thanks." She gathered up the clothes, then glanced at their coach. "Does Mrs. Cuthbertson always dress like . . . I mean, in a tutu . . . and the makeup . . . for practice and games . . ."

"Yeah, she wears her tutu and paints her face every day. She's the dance teacher and she likes ballet shoes with sparkles. She doesn't know anything about basketball. We coach ourselves and she's totally behind us. Without a faculty coach, we couldn't have a team."

Caroline nodded politely.

"She graduated from Laurel, y'know." Caroline stared and Irene shrugged. "She owns a big house in Venice Beach. Lives with her husband and a bunch of people. They grow a lot of their own food. She always brings fruit for us after practice. Oranges and apples from her trees." Irene grinned. "Once she brought grapes, and I had a fit. I thought they were from the store. I started yelling . . ."

"Hold on. You boycott grapes?"

Irene turned on her heel. "You know about the boycott?"

"Haven't eaten grapes in ages. Most people at Laurel have never heard of Cesar Chavez. If they have, they think he's a threat to our excessively white nation."

"I donate half of my allowance to the United Farm Workers," Irene spoke quietly.

"I give half of mine to a food bank in Watts."

"The food bank near Watts Towers?" Irene asked, and Caroline nodded. "I volunteer there on Sundays, serving meals."

"Ladies, center court!" Mrs. Cuthbertson's tutu shimmered as she clapped for order.

Irene watched Caroline size up their coach. "Y'know," she broke in, "Mrs. Cuthbertson may be a fashion disaster, but she doesn't need to work. She's here 'cause she feels like it."

"I just figured out why I left Laurel."

"Why's that?"

"To follow Mrs. Cuthbertson to Hollywood High."

Irene grinned. "Where do you eat lunch?"

"In the quad next to the tree that's dying."

"Tomorrow, can I join you with a few friends?"

CHAPTER 8

"Hi." Irene dropped to the ground, legs crossed easily. "This is Vincent Takayama and Gary Mulligan."

"Hello," Caroline extended her hand, then remembered. "Oops."

"No problem," Irene grinned. "I warned them you were pathologically polite."

"This is Kayla Davidson," Caroline grinned back. "She suffers from a similar affliction."

"Sorry." Gary caught Kayla's orange juice with his elbow and quickly steadied the carton.

"Gary's my favorite football player. He suffers from excessive largeness," Irene laughed.

"You mean klutziness," Gary shot back.

"You play football?" Kayla was impressed.

"Second string," Gary answered matter of factly. "I've got good size and I'm strong, but I'm a total klutz."

Good size was an understatement. Gary was humongous. Six-three and muscular. He had bright blond hair, freckles, and green eyes. He pulled from a paper sack three sandwiches, an apple, a banana, two bags of chips, eight cookies, and a quart of milk. He looked from Caroline to Kayla. "We have English, history, and science together."

"How'd we miss you?" Caroline blurted, then blushed as the group broke out laughing. "I beg your pardon, I . . ."

"It's fine," Gary grinned. "I always sit in the back. Anyone who gets stuck behind me is a lost cause."

"How come you're not in our math class?" Kayla conversationally.

Gary hesitated and Irene stepped in. "He's got a brain to match his brawn. They booted him into calculus."

Gary studied his apple.

"That's cool," Kayla said.

"No problem," Caroline added, and Gary smiled. She turned to Vincent. "Are you a junior?"

"Senior," he answered. "Irene and I met in art class. I met Gary through football."

Caroline and Kayla exchanged a confused look. Vincent was five-foot-three and slim.

"He manages the team," Gary explained.

"Most of them think I'm weird," Vincent shrugged.

"Y'know, they could be right," Irene laughed, and he slugged her arm.

"What's weird about you?" Kayla looked at him.

"I'm into painting and I'm small. Even worse, I founded the Poetry Club last year. We meet at lunch on Thursdays, talk about our favorite poets. By football standards, that's three strikes against me."

"Do you know Elvia?" Caroline asked him.

"She's in Poetry Club. We had our first meeting last week. She's taking over Poetry Night. I was in charge of organizing it last year, but they cancelled it because the gangs were threatening to turn it into a cage fight. I'm glad it's back. Elvia seems like she'll do a good job."

"Elvia and Dreads are always fighting," Gary said. "They really need to admit they've been in love since the third grade, when he gave her a lollipop for Valentine's Day and she gave him a bloody nose. I was an eyewitness. I was on the swings, and they were standing next to the handball court."

Caroline finished her tuna sandwich and turned to Vincent. "Why'd you decide to manage the football team?"

"I thought it would be fun. I like trying different things."

"So does Caroline," Irene offered. "Otherwise, why would you go to Laurel Academy and then come here?"

"Yeah, I like trying different things." Caroline began to shred her napkin.

"You went to Laurel Academy?" Gary was amused. "I read about that place last year in the newspaper. The two girls they tossed out for smoking pot . . ."

"That was a huge mess," Caroline grinned "The students loved every minute of it."

"The article said it was some kind of a scandal, because the third girl wasn't expelled . . ."

Caroline nodded.

"Did you know them?" Irene asked

"They were in my grade. The first two were expendable. They paid their tuition and gave a decent donation each year, nothing remarkable by Laurel standards. The third girl presented a problem. Her parents own half the real estate in downtown Los Angeles. They had pledged four million. They told the Laurel Board of Trustees that if they kicked out their daughter, they'd lose the money. So the Board changed the bylaws. Drugs on campus became a two-day suspension, and the disobedient Laurel Clovers were un-expelled. They—"

"Laurel Clovers?" Vincent interrupted.

"A gold three-leaf clover is the school emblem. That's what they call the students. Laurel Clovers."

"I need a barf bag," Irene flatly.

"Four million," Kayla shook her head.

"Yep," Caroline nodded, "for a greenhouse to study plant biology, a team to take care of the plants, a cutting-edge lab, a new teacher with a double doctorate in botany and biology, and an army of guest lecturers. Turns out it was money well spent. Laurel Academy was written up in several publications as a role model educational institution. The number of applications tripled. Donations broke records."

"Any farm workers on the list of guest lecturers?" Irene asked.

"At Laurel Academy for Girls?" Caroline raised an eyebrow. "It would be unseemly to invite people who actually use their hands to work the land. They might incite sedition, or worse, they might offer the Clovers an alternative perspective."

"Four million can buy a lot of tropical plants and petrie dishes." Gary opened his quart of milk.

"They probably wanted to clone themselves," Caroline said dryly, and the group broke into laughter. "Hollywood High is very different, and I'm not sure why I'm here. But I know exactly why I'm not there." *Not even close to exactly, couldn't explain if I wanted to, which I absolutely don't.*

Vincent turned to Kayla. "Are you from Los Angeles?"

She shook her head. "We moved from Boston because of my dad's work."

"Do you miss it?" Caroline asked.

"Yeah, I miss my friends, and I miss . . ." Kayla took a deep breath. "I miss the community theater. I auditioned in elementary school. Got in when I was eight. Been doing musical theater ever since. *The Sound of Music* goes up in October. I was going to play Liesl, the oldest von Trapp daughter. Then we moved."

"That's rough," Caroline sympathetically.

"Do you want to keep acting?" Irene asked. "They do a lot of plays here."

Kayla nodded. "I'll audition if they do musical theater. I like acting okay, but singing is what matters to me."

Two boys walked by, and Caroline stared. The Blond and a friend. Their hair flowed down their backs, gold and black. They wore white clothes, platform heels, gold tasseled belts. The Blond wore a bright scarf, shades of orange in a geometric pattern. Caroline wondered why he was always off campus at lunch. He said something to his friend, who nodded and handed him half a sandwich. They both ate ravenously. Caroline continued to stare.

"You know him?" Irene asked.

"Who? That guy? No." Caroline couldn't tear her eyes away, watching them cross the quad and join a small group of boys, similarly dressed, all with long hair.

Kayla punched her arm gently. "I guess you wouldn't see that kind of . . . um . . . diversity at Laurel."

Caroline forced her eyes back to her friends.

"Not many Japanese like me, I bet," Vincent said.

"Or my type," Gary added. "I'm a guy."

"Laurel's very predictable." Caroline balled up her napkin shreds. "It's prep school, then Ivy League, then Junior League, and meanwhile you marry a purebred of excellent pedigree and proper astronomical income."

"Yes!" Gary punched the air. "I'm pure Irish. I can marry a Laurel girl."

"Trust fund, Gary, don't forget the trust fund." Irene bit into an enormous chocolate chip cookie. "Anyway, they have a height requirement. You're too big to be an investment banker."

"Don't worry, Gary, you're not alone," Vincent smiled. "I'm too Asian to marry a Laurel girl."

"I'm too African," said Kayla.

"I'm too socialist," said Irene.

"I tried, but I couldn't hack it," Caroline said truthfully and was surprised by their friendly laughter.

"I have to pee," Irene announced, and Kayla froze. "What's wrong with you?" Irene asked. "Don't the fine folks in Boston pee?"

"Irene," Kayla cleared her throat, "do you know a girl named Nellie?"

"Oh, I heard about that. She got beat up. A word of advice. It's a bad idea to give another girl's boyfriend a blow job and then brag about it. I suggest—"

"Wait!" Caroline interrupted. "Let me write that down."

Irene laughed. "Anyway, the little hall leading to the principal's office, on the left there's a small girls' bathroom. There's usually no trouble, y'know, with the administration next door. So, ladies, shall we leave the gentlemen and embark upon a female excursion?"

"You're talking like Caroline," Gary grinned.

"For the record," Caroline tossed over her shoulder, "the girls at Laurel don't pee. They urinate."

CHAPTER 9

Caroline arrived at school and dodged through the crowded hallway. As she approached Mr. Cohen's classroom, a commotion erupted. A pack of athletes surrounded a boy. He wore white pants, a gauzy white shirt, a striped scarf, platform shoes, light makeup. His black hair was wavy, past his shoulders but not down his back like The Blond. The pack began chanting "FAG! FAG! FAG!" The boy backed into a wall as the pack closed in. The chanting grew louder. A hand reached from the crowd and shoved him. His head hit the wall and he dropped his backpack.

Caroline stood paralyzed. Suddenly the door to Mr. Cohen's classroom flew open and he stormed out. He showed no hesitation as he strode into the group and shouted, "That's enough!" The pack immediately ran for the nearest exit, scattering into the quad.

The boy sank to the ground. Mr. Cohen knelt next to him. The bell rang and the hall emptied. Mr. Cohen didn't move. In a few minutes, the boy's breathing regulated. He remained crouched on the ground next to his backpack. He hugged his knees to his chest.

"I'm Mr. Cohen. What's your name?"

"Carlos."

"Do you have a class now?" Mr. Cohen asked.

The boy shook his head.

"You have a free period?"

The boy nodded.

"What grade are you in?"

"Junior."

"Are you physically hurt? Do you want to see the school nurse?"

Carlos shook his head.

"Would you like to come into my classroom? I can use an assistant. You'll record grades and absences. Or you can do your homework. You'll get community service credit. Interested?"

Carlos nodded.

Mr. Cohen stood, and the boy rose slowly. At the same time, they both noticed Caroline against the opposite wall. She was visibly shaking. Mr. Cohen held the door to his classroom for the two kids. Caroline walked through, clutching her backpack to steady her hands. Carlos hesitated at the threshold and Caroline turned to face him.

"I didn't know what to do. I'm sorry. I'm so sorry—" her voice broke.

"It's not your fault," Carlos huskily.

"I should have stood next to you."

"They were surrounding me. You couldn't have reached me."

"I should have done something."

Mr. Cohen continued to hold the door, watching the two kids closely.

Carlos stood rooted at the threshold, not moving forward.

"You can come in," Caroline's voice was still shaking. "Nothing like that happens in Mr. Cohen's classroom."

"She's right," Mr. Cohen said. "I'd never allow it."

Carlos walked in slowly. The students were immediately quiet.

Mr. Cohen announced simply, "This is Carlos. He's my new assistant."

"Hi Carlos!" The class laughed at their own dorky chorus.

"Hi," Carlos softly.

Mr. Cohen pointed to the chair by his desk for student conferences and Carlos sank down on the wooden seat.

Kayla shot Caroline a quizzical look, sensing that something was wrong.

Caroline said nothing.

When the bell rang, Mr. Cohen stood at his desk, collecting their first assigned essays. Caroline gave him three hand-written pages, stapled together. Walking to their next class, Gary and Kayla chatted about the assignment. Gary had written about winning the state science fair in ninth grade, Kayla about leaving her friends in Massachusetts. Caroline listened silently.

It took her until lunch to be able to speak.

"What happened with Carlos this morning?" Kayla asked, as the five friends sat in a circle eating their sandwiches.

In a careful monotone, measuring every syllable, Caroline told them.

"That's awful." Gary put down his carton of milk.

"Some people in this school have their heads up their asses." Irene shook her head angrily.

"Do you think Carlos is really gay?" Kayla asked.

Vincent shrugged. "*Gay* is just an insult people use around here. Doesn't mean anything. Carlos is probably a normal guy."

Caroline and Gary froze.

Irene glared at Kayla and Vincent. "Like I said, some people have their heads up their asses."

"What's your problem?" Vincent glared back at Irene.

The bell blared, ending the conversation.

In his classroom during the lunch break, waiting for his next group of students, Mr. Cohen glanced at Caroline's essay resting on top of the pile. The title caught his eye, and he began to read.

Caroline Black
Honors Sophomore English
September 16, 1973

Assignment #1
Creative Writing
Autobiography or Fiction
Describe an experience that involves a change.

Rona Finds Religion

Quiet on the set! Never look at the camera. Smile. (I'm thirsty.) Don't smile. (I'm sweating.) Hold your places. (I'm hungry.) Kids, act scared. Cry, if you can. Hey, Rona can cry on cue! (I'm bored.) We should be done in five minutes. (Or ten, or thirty, or . . .) And once more — lights, camera, action . . . wait, the lighting's wrong. Cut!

Growing up in the film industry.

Her father, a cinematographer with two nominations and one Oscar to his name.

Blonde, green eyed, and a legacy, Rona understood that the acting world belonged to her. Age nine, on location in Madrid for the summer, she took the plunge and signed on as an extra, an orphan on a ship in a typhoon. She arrived at the studio at 6AM, shrugged off her clothes, and stepped into a costume of rags. She closed her eyes as the makeup artist wiped down her face, slapped on rouge, slashed her lips crimson. Next stop, the wig lady, who speedily pinned on a long albino tangle. Finally, on to the set, where she sat watchful and silent while technicians fixed lights, adjusted microphones, through takes and retakes. Rona became fluent in Spanish, opened her first bank account, and would have considered her acting career launched except the experience left her tormented. The heartbreaking poverty of the Spanish extras, the frantic competition among the actors for attention, the quivering hope of the bit parts for the big break. Too much raw need on the set. Rona decided to let acting go.

But that turned out to be more difficult than expected.

Windy Canyon Elementary Education, 1960s private school of the arts in Los Angeles. For years, Rona had been the oddball, out of step with the Age of Aquarius, fascinated by the structure and balance of math, devouring literature with "unhealthy enjoyment" (sic Moonbeam Jackson, her third grade teacher). "Half-geek-half-human" to her peers, "creatively blocked" to her teachers . . . until that summer, when everything turned golden. Back from filming in Spain, she suddenly rocketed to ultra-cool, even surpassing two popular girls who landed modeling contracts. This was too good to give up, and Rona decided to take on a speaking role, her next step on the path to stardom.

For two glorious months, Rona lived a gilded existence. She was picked first for every team. Boys fought to be her partner in their weekly square dancing class. She topped the guest list for every slumber party. Best of all, an agent called with promises surpassing her finest daydreams.

Then, without even granting her the courtesy of a consultation, her body went haywire.

Her face carried an oily sheen no matter how many times she washed. A horrid rash appeared. Diagnosis: acne. Her odor took an appalling turn. Hair sprouted in impossible places and her chest hurt when she caught a football. Just when she thought things hit rock bottom, she awoke one Tuesday feeling unplugged. She stayed home with chills and stomach cramps, but instead of culminating in a good fit of barfing, she found a pink discharge in her underwear.

In the bathrooms at Windy Canyon, the toilet paper came not in rolls, but in separate squares. The trashcan was clear plastic. The quandary kept her up at night — how to get rid of her bloody menstrual pads? Finally, inspiration struck. During the dreaded five days of her monthly cycle, she carried brown paper lunch bags to school, sneaked her used sanitary napkins inside, and smuggled the evidence home in her backpack.

She was the only girl in the entire school who was menstruating. The only one with breasts, or zits, or deodorant.

But her body wasn't finished. Rona began to expand, contract, lengthen, harden, soften.

"Try cutting out carbs," an actress suggested sympathetically, but her body's trajectory was unstoppable. Six inches and nineteen pounds later, her movie career was in shambles. She was no longer child star material.

The agent disappeared.

"You're beautiful," she'd been told. But she didn't feel beautiful. She felt like a woolly mammoth.

Banned from the world of her father, her career snuffed out before it began. How could she face their actor friends? She wracked her brain for a solution and arrived at a notion of pure genius. She'd tell her parents she was finished with the industry. She now had loftier goals. She was devoting her heart and soul to her intellect. Whenever anyone said, "You're beautiful," she'd fire back, "I'm smart. That's what matters to me." A "young women's libber," the adults proclaimed proudly, and Rona allowed the deception to grow until she herself fell for it. She achieved to the max, tossed out le bon mot, startled people with her agile mind. By the time she entered seventh grade, Rona was primed for the ranks of the geeks, on her knees before the intellectual icon — a convert, parishioner, and missionary.

A canonized nerd.

Mr. Cohen finished Caroline's assignment. He wondered how a girl from a film industry family, who had gone to a private elementary school, ended up at Hollywood High. He thought of her reaction to Carlos. Most students walked by and didn't give that sort of violence a thought, shrugging it off because it didn't affect them. But Caroline's reaction seemed strangely aligned with Carlos's reaction. Even more odd, as a child of the industry, why was she writing about bloody menstrual pads rather than bragging about red carpet glitz? Mr. Cohen picked up his pen. As always, he took a moment to choose his words, tailoring his comments to the student's academic needs and personal growth.

Dear Caroline,

You followed the creative writing assignment with humor and sensitivity. You showed growth and change in your main character. I liked Rona and sympathized with her dilemma.

My criticism: Rona is extremely influenced by the undertow of her environment. For a girl who demonstrates thoughtfulness, creativity, and brains to this degree, her choices are too contingent on how others define her. I would have liked to see her begin to define herself on her own terms. I also wonder why she didn't pursue adult roles in acting after her body blocked her from the child roles. That was the only piece of your short story that didn't make sense.

I hope you continue to write fiction, although in this class, the rest of the papers will be analyzing other writers.

Good job.
Mr. Cohen
Grade: A-

CHAPTER 10

Through the basketball team's drills, Caroline's thoughts circled back to ninth grade. Riding the public bus home, she retraced her final year at Laurel. Lounging in her bedroom, between chapters of John Steinbeck's *The Grapes of Wrath*, she transported to her previous school. Bouncing back and forth between her *then* and her *now*, she struggled to find a new equilibrium.

Ninth grade.

Ironically, when the academic year began, Caroline was relieved to return to school. During the summer, a girl in her eighth grade math class landed a supporting role in a sitcom and checked out of Laurel to be tutored at Burbank Studios. Her next-door neighbor dropped out of his private Catholic school when he was cast as the lead in a feature film. Nails bitten to the quick, Caroline craved texts, exams, and A's. The stage was set for her to remain "bookish," the ultimate Laurel insult, and continue her reign as the class grind.

Had it not been for the May Queen and her court.

Every May Day, Laurel hosted a festival complete with burgers and ice cream, a ring toss for stuffed animals and, best of all, tennis balls to hurl at a target, to throw a switch, to flip their headmaster Mr. Hammer into a vat of cold water. The girls hovered in clumps, whispering about his copious chest hair, cheering wildly as he splashed down. Students, parents, faculty, and administration turned out for the annual May Day fundraiser. The adults gathered under massive gold and white striped tents, buying overpriced flutes of champagne that they had previously donated. A silent auction would bring in a mint.

Valerie Hartnet, Grand Poobah of the class's top echelon clique, displayed her newest boyfriend. She and her airbrushed friends formed their lunchtime circle, "The Platinum Ring," as Caroline called them. Flanked by slickly handsome dates, they spoke only to each other, confident that nobody except the most popular upperclass girls would cross the invisible barrier separating them from Laurel's ordinary mortals.

Lelia Dane, the grade's self-appointed rebel, arrived with her two Shar Peis named Andover and Exeter. The entire school applauded as she entered campus in a tux, top hat, tails, and a leash in each hand for her wrinkled, wheezing, four-legged companions.

In seventh and eighth grades, Caroline enjoyed the extravaganza, hanging out with her Clover friends Vicki, Maren, and Tory. But one piece of Laurel's May Day tradition bothered her: the election of the senior class May Queen and her five princesses, one from each of the lower grades. An unabashed beauty pageant.

It would be years before Caroline understood how *bothered her* in seventh and eighth grades escalated into *outraged her* in ninth grade. She didn't connect the dots because Laurel Academy did absolutely nothing to set the shift in motion. Like many of Caroline's upheavals, the problem was rooted in her father's profession.

Four weeks before the May Court election, Caroline stood with her parents in the enormous lobby of the Academy of Motion Picture Arts and Sciences. Waiting for the film to begin, Leah and Geoff mingled, and Caroline found herself talking to three young actresses. They complimented each other's beauty, exchanging tips for losing weight. To Caroline's surprise, they invited her to sit with them during the movie. The following week, the tabloids exploded. One of the women, often photographed as a style icon and praised for her emaciated body, was hospitalized for drug addiction, trying to speed her way through the hunger. The next day, another in the group fainted from malnutrition, cracked her head, and sustained a concussion. Twenty-four hours later, the third girl dropped dead from heart failure, her electrolytes so depleted from anorexia that conduction failed.

When she heard the news, Caroline closed the door to her bedroom. She stripped and stared at her body in her full-length mirror. Five-four, one-hundred-twelve pounds. As she grew through the years, her metabolism burned whatever she ate, and she rarely gave calories a thought. She took rebellious pleasure in eating anything she wanted, knowing that everyone looks 10-15 pounds heavier on-screen, glad that she didn't want to act so she didn't have to care . . . which she reminded herself several times each day. Now she studied the mirror. Her belly was not quite flat. Her breasts had grown. Her muscles were defined and strong. Compared to those three actresses, she looked thick, lumpy, hefty.

Sitting in the plush seats before the film began, one of the young women had turned to Caroline. "I like your jeans. I like your natural hair. I like that you don't wear makeup."

"Why?" Caroline honestly wanted to know.

The three actresses exchanged knowing glances. "Because you're so pretty and you're breaking all the industry rules about how you're supposed to look."

Caroline grinned and shrugged. "Sorry."

"Don't be sorry. Be you." Spoken by a talented actress, age twenty, now dead.

Caroline pulled her clothes back on. By the time she zipped her jeans, she was no longer bothered by Laurel's beauty pageant. She was livid.

As the May Court election drew closer, even the highest score on two consecutive math tests couldn't redirect Caroline's course of action. She drafted a petition to cancel the pageant, outlining the dangers of society's emphasis on underweight beauty. She cited statistics, listed medical risks, and added a few photos of teenagers in comas. To her surprise, every girl in the school signed, including Royal-Debutante-Baked-To-Perfection Valerie Hartnet.

Then the Board of Trustees caught a whiff of rebellion and demanded a recant. Tradition, they insisted, must be upheld. For a week, Laurel stood at an impasse. Mr. Hammer attempted to negotiate, bouncing between the girls and the Board. The faculty and administration largely supported the students but had to tread lightly to protect their jobs. Caroline's rebellion took on a pulse of its own, pounding through the ranks, wreaking havoc.

Finally, a compromise was reached. Each class would elect its princess for both looks and achievement, with votes cast by the students, faculty, and administration. Caroline knew the election would still boil down to a popularity contest, but at least it wasn't a human Best in Show. Eager to return to bookish obscurity, she quickly scored 103% on a science midterm, 99% on a history portfolio, and forgot about the May Court.

Two days before the ninth grade princess election, Caroline woke up with a fever. Diagnosis: strep throat. She wasn't surprised. She had spent the previous weekend with Vicki, Maren, and Tory, who were already absent from school with raw throats. The four friends would be home all week. They joked on the phone about how happy they were to miss the ninth grade princess election.

This post-petition election, however, took on a curious character. One by one, the class's mega-achievers and most popular girls were nominated. Each politely declined. Slowly, the difficulty clarified itself. Winning this vote of the faculty and administration was a social kiss of death, a tepid nod to intelligence, a joke regarding attractiveness — viewed with open contempt by every girl. Then someone snapped her manicured nails with an inspired solution — nominate Caroline. She's at home with strep throat and can't turn it down. What's more, the petition was her idea. This mess was her fault. The votes were cast, and Caroline won by a landslide, unopposed and ringing in with 100% of the vote. A deal signed, sealed, and delivered when she returned to school the following Monday.

Mr. Hammer summoned Caroline before the first bell rang. She had never before visited the headmaster's office and couldn't imagine why he wanted to speak to her. Like all the faculty and administration, he was an unpredictable mix of astoundingly intuitive and spectacularly dense. Now, he had no clue that this was anything other than the highest of accolades and claimed for himself the privilege of breaking the grand news.

A May Princess! Caroline's tears spilled, and Mr. Hammer stumbled to get a tissue.

"Caroline, please stop crying. This is an honor."

"What are you honoring?" She blew her dripping nose. "I'd accept an award for an achievement. But this is a popularity contest, and I'm not popular! It's a joke! And this," gesturing to her blotchy face, "is a genetic roll of the dice!"

He stared blankly.

"Don't you get it?"

Mr. Hammer blinked in confusion. Even with her anti-beauty-contest petition, Caroline was still considered one of the school's most composed, steady, and polite students. What in the world was going on?

"It's wrong!" she almost shouted.

He spoke soothingly. "Caroline, you're smart. You've done well here." Situation salvageable had he shut up. Instead, he blundered into the ultimate negation of her soul. "And you're beautiful."

An accidental incantation.

"You're beautiful," Mr. Hammer repeated.

Something nameless surged.

"A beautiful girl," he tried to calm her.

Caroline toppled over the edge. She found her voice, or it found her, and she heard herself yelling, "Fuck you!"

In that moment, she made history—the first Clover to speak that precise epithet to the headmaster.

Mr. Hammer dialed the phone grimly and ordered Leah to pick up her daughter, instantaneously. Caroline had suffered a seizure of excessive rudeness and was suspended for a week. On the spot, he revoked her princess tiara, her vocabulary unsuitable for royalty.

The gossip circuit quivered. The F-bomb! To the headmaster! The girls were delighted.

An emergency class meeting was convened, and Valerie Hartnet was quickly voted the ninth grade princess. In the initial election, Valerie had been the first girl nominated and the first to politely say no, which set the stage for Caroline's victory. Now, Valerie's classmates were so grateful to her for bailing them out of this fiasco that she was happy to gracefully accept. Mr. Hammer ushered her into his office, thanked her profusely, and intimated that she was now the front runner for the coveted Clover of the Year Award.

From house arrest, Caroline wrote a proper apology to Mr. Hammer, every word found in Webster's Dictionary. He handled the aftermath with statesmanlike calm and had only one additional requirement to complete her atonement. She had to attend the May Day Festival.

As the date approached, something deep within Caroline began to stir — something boundlessly sad and spitting-nails furious — something fed up with speaking softly, treading lightly, and getting A's on every test. Her fall from grace in Mr. Hammer's office was entirely wrong, but it felt entirely right. If she could have avoided the May Day Festival, she might have retreated quietly. But as she anticipated being forced to watch the May Court Clovers, their hair braided with white baby roses, gold streamers down their backs, everyone applauding — this felt to Caroline like her final defeat. Deep within her core, a tremor vibrated. A notion took hold, a slowly swirling haze which clarified into digital precision. The faces of three beautiful young actresses hovered before her. She heard a clear voice: "Don't be sorry. Be you."

Caroline had no idea how to navigate what was about to unfold, but she knew with absolute certainty that doing nothing was no longer an option.

CHAPTER 11

Monday, week four.

The Duke swaggered into Miss Orville's classroom and gave her a crisp salute. Mrs. Richardson had driven him to her husband's optometry practice, where the doctor's quiet respect rendered The Duke nearly speechless. After his exam, the assistants showed him a room, wall-to-wall shelves of frames.

"Take your time choosing," the staff encouraged him, bringing a gigantic triple decker corned beef sandwich from Lev's Delicatessen next door. He spent an hour deciding on a crossbreed of aviator goggles and wrap around glasses. The vote was unanimous. He looked terrific.

The faculty grapevine hummed, and overnight The Duke evolved into Hollywood High's alpha underdog. A team of teachers stepped forward to help. Mr. Cohen, at his own request, taught basic English to the roughest of the rough. He was medium height, with medium brown hair, medium even features. But when he taught, there was nothing medium about him. His classroom was his domain, and he maintained stringent requirements. Class began with each student's reading one sentence out loud. If the student didn't know how to pronounce a word, then his neighbors, even if they were rival gang members, were required to help. Their weekly essays must never contain the words "a lot" or "very," and sentences must never begin with "And." Cursing meant an automatic lunch hour in Mr. Cohen's classroom, doing homework and cleaning the blackboard. Absolutely no disruptions were tolerated. If the class behaved well, he rewarded them with a vignette about Edna St. Vincent Millay's social life, Sylvia Plath's taking the Women's Liberation world by storm, Catherine of Russia's aerobic exercise. Every Friday, he gave a quiz. If the class averaged at least 75%, he read a passage from Anaïs Nin, Geoffrey Chaucer, Walt Whitman. The kids held themselves in check, rival gang members attentive and quiet. In the world of hormonal reign, the mind electric stood hand in hand with the body electric.

Now, Mr. Cohen recognized an intellect awakening and drafted The Duke into his third period class. The other gang members glared as he strutted in. Mr. Cohen calmly announced that they had a new student, introduced The Duke, and congratulated the class on its eighty-three percent average on Friday's quiz. By the time he finished reading the opening paragraphs of Vladimir Nabokov's *Lolita*, The Duke sat rapt with everyone else, and they were off to business as usual.

Miss Orville, too, heard the news. As The Duke and Caroline staked out their floor space, she approached. Caught off guard, The Duke shot to his feet and Caroline scrambled up as well. Next to him, Miss Orville looked tiny, with lovely black hair and huge brown eyes.

"Hello, Duke. I wanted to properly introduce myself." She extended her hand.

Oh, Lord. She said his name wrong. And split an infinitive.

The Duke didn't correct her. He took her hand gently. "Thank you for letting us use your classroom."

"You can use this room any time." Miss Orville smiled warmly. "You can catch up on studying during any free period. If I'm here, you're welcome."

"Thanks. Yeah, right, well . . . thanks a lot." She walked away and he whispered, "Well, fuck me hard. I thought she was a total jerk."

"No," Caroline's lips twitched, "just an uptight Catholic girl."

"How do you know she's Catholic?"

"Her necklace is a small cross. She keeps rosary beads in her desk. She takes them out when the class is quiet during a test."

"Are you an uptight Catholic girl?"

"I'm an uptight Jewish girl," testing her ability to banter with a boy.

"You're Jewish?"

"Yes," rummaging through her backpack for The Duke's math lesson.

He whistled softly. "No wonder you're smart."

Caroline looked up sharply. She never expected to find anti-Semitism at Hollywood High with its sixty-one percent immigrant population, forty-four languages among the students, and heaven knows how many religions. She glared at The Duke, forgetting that every beat cop in the Hollywood precinct knew his name.

"Some day I'll broaden your horizons and introduce you to some stupid Jews."

"You don't look Jewish."

"Why not?"

"Blonde hair, green eyes, normal nose. Shit, you're pretty."

"Thanks a bunch," she glared, appalled at how pleased she was that The Duke thought she was pretty. "I'll make a deal with you. I won't jump to any bigoted conclusions because you're Black, and you lose the Jewish stereotypes."

"Girl, you're talking crazy! I said you were smart and pretty, and you're saying I'm prejudiced?"

"It's a stereotype. It's based on my religion. It's not a compliment."

"Okay, whatever. Didn't mean no insult."

He had no idea why she was upset, and she had no idea how to explain why calling her smart and pretty was obnoxious and insulting.

She shrugged and held out a new multiplication grid. "Let's do some math."

"I can see the numbers now. But I don't get it."

The Duke could multiply anything by zero, one, or two. Then he became confused. Caroline went back to the beginning and carefully explained the relationship between addition and multiplication. They went over it several times, using different numbers. He listened with a charged focus. Suddenly, he grabbed the grid. He understood every bit of it. She handed him a worksheet, which he finished in five minutes, one hundred percent correct.

"I did good!" he grinned.

"Better than good."

"Hey professor," he lightly punched her shoulder, "let's not get carried away."

"Listen," she answered, "I think you're really smart."

"That's bullshit."

"You learned two months of lessons in thirty minutes. You can't be dumb."

"Teachers been saying I was dumb for years."

"How many years?"

"Maybe seven."

"When did your vision start to change?"

The moment lengthened.

Caroline shrugged. "Bad news. You have to redefine yourself."

"Say what?"

"Do over the way you think about yourself."

"I don't like to think about myself too much," he said quietly.

"Okay, do it your way. But don't ever let anyone call you dumb."

The Duke sat back, looked at her appraisingly. "You're a very strange girl."

Caroline broke into laughter. "Thank you so much."

"No, really," he persisted. "You figured out I needed glasses. Nobody's ever told me I was smart. Now you're saying I have to do over how I look at myself. Last year, Mrs. Richardson gave me another tutor. Snotty piece of shit. Couldn't stand her. She thought she was so superior. You talk fancy, but you're not snotty, even though you're white."

Even though I'm white? "Your point is . . ."

"You don't see things like most people."

Caroline turned still. They held each other's eyes for a long beat. Slowly they both smiled.

The Duke fisted his hands, held them up and punched the air. "I need a good workout. Maybe I'll go kick somebody's butt!"

"Please, I'm a Laurel girl. Talk of violence does not become me."

"What the fuck's a Laurel girl?"

"My old school. Laurel Academy. They called us Laurel Clovers."

He snorted with laughter. The bell rang and he jumped to his feet. Caroline gathered her papers. The Duke waited, watching her curiously.

"What now?" she asked.

"You got nervous when I said you were pretty." She turned arctic and he held up his hands. "I'm not hitting on you. It's just . . . you're the only girl I've ever met who doesn't like being told she's pretty."

"We'll be late to class," she answered stiffly. She turned her back and moved toward the door. The Duke shrugged and loped out. Caroline was past Miss Orville when her Latin teacher spoke.

"You're right."

Caroline turned. "About what?"

"Duke. I couldn't help overhearing some of your conversation. He's quite bright. He's been treated unfairly. I'll have to give it some thought."

Caroline couldn't figure out what anyone could do about it, but she nodded politely and headed to her next class, profoundly grateful that Miss Orville had overheard only some of their conversation.

CHAPTER 12

A Laurel Girl. A Laurel Clover. The Duke snorting with laughter. Eating lunch with her friends, taking notes in her afternoon classes, relaxing in her bedroom with Ralph Ellison's *Invisible Man* — Caroline found herself thinking about her final day at Laurel Academy, which was also the day she committed to Hollywood High School and, without realizing it, to The Duke.

The dreaded May Day Festival had arrived, five weeks from completing ninth grade. As was mandated, Caroline attended.

"How was it?" Leah asked as she passed the garlic bread to her daughter, across the table eating dinner.

"Fine." Caroline's eyes never left her spaghetti.

"There seemed to be something going on when we picked you up," Leah continued conversationally, "but we couldn't really see from the car."

Caroline shrugged and speared a forkful of salad.

"Glad that's behind you?" Geoff smiled at his daughter.

"I guess." Caroline put down her fork and folded her napkin.

Her parents exchanged glances of mild exasperation.

They moved to the living room to relax. Caroline's older brother studied Russian at Harvard. With her parents' diplomas also from Harvard and

Radcliffe, they basked in their family's Ivy League Dynasty. Geoff lounged in his armchair, happily immersed in the "L" section of his favorite book, *The Random House Dictionary*. Leah, an anthropology major in college, thumbed through an article on mental health in New Guinea.

"Mom, Dad, I need to talk."

They looked up.

Caroline gripped the arms of her chair. *Please listen. Please hear me. Please let me do what I need to do.*

"What's on your mind?" Leah was puzzled by the sudden surge in tension.

"I'm going to Hollywood High for tenth grade."

"What the hell are you talking about?" demanded Geoff, the former Marine Corps Lieutenant.

"I'm leaving Laurel. I can't stay there."

"Did something happen?" asked Leah, trained at the Psychoanalytic Institute to find the precipitating event.

"It's boring. Everybody's the same."

"How the hell did you come up with Hollywood High?" Geoff growled. "Was it that damned article?"

The previous week, they had discussed over dinner a series of articles in the *Los Angeles Times* featuring different public high schools. The first article was about Beverly Hills High. The second piece focused on Hollywood High.

"Partly the article," Caroline answered. "I've been thinking about it for a long time. I don't want to stay at Laurel. I want something completely different."

Geoff, who led troops in Okinawa, who kept a restless platoon of hairy testosterone in line, sat slack-jawed. "The newspaper article," he finally managed. "It said Hollywood High ranks in the nation's thirty-fifth percentile for academics." He swallowed dryly. "They have gangs."

"Do you remember the second part of the article?" his daughter fired back. "They talked about diversity. No single race is a majority. The kids can study a lot of things. They teach auto mechanics and print shop."

"You want to walk away from Laurel so you can take classes in auto mechanics and print shop?" Leah was incredulous.

"Hello, have we met?" Caroline glared. "I want to take Latin, which they also teach at Hollywood High, which they also *don't* teach at Laurel! I want to meet students who take all kinds of classes, including print shop and auto mechanics."

"Why?" Geoff demanded.

"Why not? Two weeks ago, when your car broke down, you said your auto mechanic saved your ass. Now he's not good enough for you?"

"Of course he's good enough for me!" Geoff exploded. "But you don't have to go to high school with people like him!"

"People like him? Oh, I get it. He didn't go to Harvard like you. If he's married, his wife probably didn't go to Radcliffe like Mom. Maybe he didn't go to college. He's definitely not good enough for your daughter. Thank the Goddesses you've helped me see the light!"

"I never said—"

"Let's stay on track," Leah interrupted Geoff. "College is important, and Laurel opens many more doors than Hollywood High."

"College is important to me, too." Caroline tried to regain a semblance of calm. "Hollywood High's guidance counselor . . . I'm trying to remember her name—"

"Mrs. Richardson." Geoff's photographic memory kicked in, even as he prepared for spontaneous combustion.

"You both said Mrs. Richardson sounded extraordinary. The guidance counselor at Laurel is nowhere near extraordinary. She's the most proper, predictable person I've ever met."

"It doesn't matter if Miss MacIsaac is proper and predictable! She has an excellent record helping students get into the nation's top colleges!" Leah's frustration broke through her years of training in analytic neutrality.

"You're caught in Laurel's Ivy League acceptances, and in Hollywood High's thirty-fifth percent academic rank. You're forgetting some important parts of the article. Mrs. Richardson sent two people to Columbia last year, one to Barnard, one to Dartmouth and two to MIT!"

"Out of a class of twelve-hundred!" her father exploded. "The article said only forty-six percent go on to any further education, including the kids who drop out of community college after a week! Some of the students live on the streets!"

"You're judging students for running away from dangerous homes and not being able to move into nice houses with yards?"

"I'm not judging anyone!" Her father glared.

"You're not judging them, but you don't want me sitting next to them in my English class?"

"I'm saying Hollywood High is no academy!" Geoff shouted.

"I don't want an academy! I want to meet different people with different ideas!"

"Hollywood High's not your only option. You've always gone to private schools. What about Obelisk?" Leah tried to redirect her daughter. Obelisk was an alternative high school whose curriculum revolved around mandatory community service.

"No way," Caroline flatly. "Obelisk has more of a social conscience, but it's still wealthy and wealthier, white and whiter. I'm going to Hollywood High."

"There are Blacks in your grade at Laurel. Asians, too." Geoff sounded like a drowning man.

"One Eurasian. Her name's Arabella Mayflower. Two Blacks. And ninety-seven very white Clovers."

"I'm sure some of them are interesting," Leah said, trying not to sound like she was grasping at straws.

"Interesting, bound for the Ivy League, or the Seven Sisters if there's a matriarchy legacy. Stanford might be acceptable if you're an athlete, or Juilliard if you're a musical genius. But you need a good reason for such radical choices. Then off you go to marry someone headed for wealth, preferably inherited, and on to the board of the opera and the symphony. Align the family name with a worthy cause, as long as it doesn't involve an unsightly disease."

"Let's think together," Leah's voice began to shake. "A Laurel education isn't something to throw away."

"I'm not throwing away my education. I'm trading it for a different kind of education."

"Trading traditional academic excellence for a place that's question-able, at best!" The doctor was growing desperate.

"Like when you auditioned for Martha Graham's modern dance troupe? Without telling your parents?" Leah froze. "You've always said your mother and father pitched a fit and stole a priceless opportunity."

Seeing his wife speechless, Geoff leaped in. "This is different."

"You're right. I'm not doing anything behind your back, like when you ran away to be a merchant seaman."

Geoff's turn to freeze.

"Your father did that to earn money—" Leah began weakly.

"—for his education," Caroline broke in, reciting from family folklore. "But his story doesn't quite hang together, because he was working as a plumber's helper. Had most of his tuition saved when the ship sailed. He joined the merchant seamen for the adventure, like you and Martha Graham, because being a part of her groundbreaking dance troupe would have been incredible. But your parents threw such a supreme tantrum that you pulled out of your audition and went to Radcliffe College and UCLA med school."

"Those were good decisions!" Leah protested angrily.

"Of course they were good decisions!" Caroline countered. "Joining

Martha Graham's dancers would have been a good decision, too. The issue isn't whether it was a good or bad decision. The issue is that your parents didn't let you make the decision."

That stopped Leah and Geoff in their tracks.

"I'm one of the only people I know who actually likes academics," Caroline pleaded. "Our family treats education like a religion, and we're total believers. I always think of it as our Intellectual Icon. I'm not trying to turn my back on our religion." Her eyes filled with tears. "Let's call Mrs. Richardson. I'll take Latin, and I promise I'll go to college. I just . . . I can't go back to Laurel."

They sat still for a several minutes, sifting through their inner sandstorms.

"Okay," Geoff sighed, and Leah nodded. "Tomorrow we'll make the call and set up the appointment. We'll go with you to register."

Before Caroline could feel relieved, the phone rang. Leah reached out her hand.

"Wait!" Caroline cried. "That's probably Mr. Hammer. No! Don't answer it!"

"What's the matter?" Leah shot a glance at Geoff.

"Mom, Dad, there's something else I need to tell you. It's about the May Festival."

CHAPTER 13

Caroline tapped on Mrs. Richardson's open door.

Her guidance counselor smiled. "Come in. Take a seat."

"Thank you. I got a summons to see you." She placed the square of yellow paper on Mrs. Richardson's desk.

To: Caroline Black

From: Mrs. Richardson

Message: See me immediately. Ask your teacher for a hall pass.

"I need to schedule you for a practical art. Today's the last day to register. It's a four-week class required for graduation. You can take it during your free period or during P.E."

"I had no idea. Thank you. My last school didn't have that require-ment. I don't know what it is."

"What *what* is?"

"A practical art."

"A useful skill in later life," her counselor explained. "Let's see what fits into your schedule."

"I tutor The Duke during my free period, so I'd rather schedule the class during P.E."

"Exercise is important."

Not as important as The Duke. "I'm getting a lot of exercise after school. I'm on the basketball team."

Mrs. Richardson raised her eyebrows in surprise. "Good for you! Let's look at the options. How about cooking?"

"Oh . . . it's . . ." Caroline cleared her throat. "It might be gossip, but I heard that three girls were suspended last year because they got mad at the teacher and tried to . . . um . . . stuff her in the oven."

"Yep. That happened."

"I think I'd prefer a different class," Caroline in a tiny voice.

"Sewing fits into your schedule as well."

Caroline swallowed hard. "I don't mean to be difficult, but one of the girls in my P.E. class showed me the skin graft on her arm. She said last spring in sewing, she and her best friend used the needles, tried to give each other tattoos, botched it, ended up in the emergency room with infections."

"True again." Her guidance counselor gave her a sympathetic look. "I'm sure this must be a lot to process after Laurel Academy."

"I'm okay with it." Caroline shrugged. "The girls at Laurel could use some practical art in their lives."

Mrs. Richardson smiled. "Do you ever miss it?"

"Yes, but I like it here."

"What do you like about Hollywood High?"

"I like that it's a lot to process after Laurel Academy."

Mrs. Richardson laughed. "If I'm understanding you correctly, you prefer a class with no ovens and no botched tattoos. How about Power Ace Presentation?"

"I beg your pardon?"

"Job interviewing."

Power Ace Presentation was a parade of impulses running amok. Rival gang members threatened each other, posturing and cussing. One girl flipped her tits to impress a boy. Mrs. McCann ignored the floorshow and was welcoming her students when Caroline heard a loud creaking from the direction of the door. She glanced up, but the door rested closed and silent. The sound came from a seat in the second row near the entrance. The girl stared intently at her own fist, her forearm flat on her desk. Slowly, as though rusty, she raised her fist to a ninety-degree angle, her elbow on the table, her creaking loud enough to reverberate throughout the room. She examined her fist carefully then with the same *cr-eee-eak*, she lowered her hand. She repeated this ritual through four weeks of classes, through her faux job interview as Mrs. McCann attempted to excavate scraps of teaching.

"It's best to make eye contact."

"Cr-eee-eak!"

"Repetitive sounds create an unprofessional atmosphere."

"Cr-eee-eak!"

"Perhaps you'd prefer a different line of work."

Moving on, Mrs. McCann gratefully called her next interviewee, Toni. A tall, slim, girl with deep brown skin rose, self-conscious and slinky. She wore slacks, a loose glittery sweater, platform shoes, long curly hair, thick makeup. Caroline looked at the hands, looked at the girl, looked at Mrs. McCann. She watched their teacher register something, then go forward without hesitation, not wanting to draw extra attention to Toni. Caroline glanced around. Most kids stared out the window. A few were obviously stoned. A handful watched Toni, some comfortably bored, others uneasy without knowing why.

Caroline understood, but knew to keep her mouth shut, or Toni wouldn't last the day. It was the hands. The knuckles, to be precise. The slacks hid the knees, the scarf hid the Adam's apple. Toni was a trans girl at Hollywood High, and the trans kids lived in fear every moment. Their eyes locked and Toni saw that Caroline knew.

If the athletes figured it out, Toni would be beaten without mercy. Caroline watched her classmate struggle to fight down the panic of being revealed. Then looking around, Caroline realized she was effectively invisible, of interest to absolutely nobody. She gave Toni a tiny nod, a tiny shrug, a tiny smile, and mouthed, "It's okay."

Toni gave no acknowledgement, but focused on Mrs. McCann, her "prospective employer." When she returned to her desk, she passed Caroline and whispered, "Thanks." Caroline nodded almost imperceptibly.

When the bell rang, the two girls walked into the hallway at the same time.

"I'm Caroline."

"I'm Toni."

"You did a good interview."

"Thanks."

They hesitated a moment, smiled shyly, then hurried in opposite directions to their next class. When Power Ace Presentation met again a week later, the two girls moved to empty seats in the back, so they could sit together for the remainder of their practical art education.

CHAPTER 14

Thursday, November 8, 10:15AM.

Caroline waited anxiously in the fourteenth row of Hollywood High's auditorium. Next to her towered Gary. On Gary's other side sat Irene and Vincent.

Caroline stared at the curtain, willing invisible waves of strength to reach Kayla backstage. The sounds swelled as more students pushed their way in for the Fall Music and Dance Recital, an ordeal Kayla had been dreading for weeks. Her name listed last on the program, singing the only solo, a Schubert Lieder in German. Classical music of all things. She didn't stand a chance.

Caroline and Kayla had attended one assembly during the first week of school, and it was not a pretty sight. Students shouted at each other, launching fleets of paper airplanes, yelling insults. The auditorium reverberated with volume so loud that Caroline felt mildly dizzy. The principal tried a Welcome to School speech, unheard beyond the second row. She edited out the last two-thirds and abruptly sat down. The dean took the mic and launched into a detailed description of the school's English Second Language curriculum, irrelevant to anyone with enough English to understand her. Suddenly a deep cry of "TAKE COVER!" boomed from the fifth row, and the dean ducked, nearly decapitated by a basketball.

The cheerleaders bravely took the stage. White leotards with a big red H, short red skirts, white tennis shoes with red socks, huge red and white pom-poms in their hands, fuzzy red and white pom-poms on their shoes. They bounced and kicked, threw their hips and tossed their hair. Caroline stared, unable to take her eyes off one of the girls, clearly the head cheerleader. She was tall and slim. Her thick chestnut hair hung below her waist, catching the lights with every move. They launched into a new routine and Caroline swallowed dryly. Every September, Laurel Academy elected a limber group of cheerleaders. Their routines pulsed with gymnastic enthusiasm, nothing like this pony sexuality.

The noise swelled louder. The girls broke into the school song. Caroline only heard the roar. She found the Laurel Alma Mater incongruously playing like a tape in her head, powerful in its plagiarism of "America the Beautiful."

Oh beautiful for spacious minds,
For colors white and gold,
For girls into young ladies grow,
With lives we strive to mold!

Oh Laurel girls, our Clover girls,
God bless thee in thy ways!
And proud we stand with outstretched hand,
To guide thee through thy days!

Caroline snapped into focus as a bulky history text, *Peace Impossible: The Colonies and King George*, hurtled toward the cheerleaders. The girls shrieked and scurried off stage left. Their boyfriends pounced and a brawl erupted. Caroline and Kayla cowered as the teachers tried to quell the riot. Eventually four police officers stormed the auditorium and herded the students out. Three boys left in handcuffs, two on stretchers.

One week later, Caroline and Kayla relaxed in the quad at lunch, sitting under a dying tree.

Kayla couldn't hold back a grin. "November's the first choral concert. I got the solo."

Caroline flashed on countless performers declaring, "I'd sell my soul for that role!" But Kayla's soul wasn't for sale.

"That's fantastic!"

"It's the only solo in the show. I can't believe I got it."

"I'll be there, front and center, for your debut," Caroline smiled. "I promise not to throw anything."

"Oh, gosh!" Kayla bit her lip. "Assemblies are war zones."

"What are you going to do?"

"Go to rehearsals. Learn to dodge unidentified flying objects."

Now, six weeks later, two cops stood at the auditorium exit doors, annoyed to waste their time at a high school assembly. Gary gripped the arms of his chair. On the floor by his feet lay an introductory Latin syllabus for college. Over the summer, he had read several textbooks for fun and qualified for an A.P. Latin tutorial with Miss Orville. He was sheet white with concern for Kayla.

Sharon and Elvia took the seats in front of Vincent and Irene. As always, Elvia wore black clothes, black lipstick, and smudged black around both eyes. From the aisle, Presto and Dreads smiled at the two girls, but Elvia shot Dreads such a severe look that they quickly moved back several rows. Sharon tossed her braids, whipping Vincent in the eyes. She turned and glared as though he had smacked her hair with his face.

Moving toward the back, Mort called to Sharon, "Hey, save a sharp pencil for me!"

"Grow up," she hissed.

"Kayla was nervous this morning," Caroline told her friends. "It might have been about performing, or it might have been because that idiot Kurt won the election for class president. In English class, he shoved a crown on Kayla's head and announced that she was his first lady."

Carlos walked by wearing his usual white pants, gauzy white shirt, platform shoes, light makeup. He was with another boy who wore jeans, a t-shirt, no makeup. He smiled at Caroline and Gary, who smiled back.

"Kurt's a pain in the ass." Irene picked him out, four rows back.

Kurt stood on the arms of his chair, shouting. "Now that I'm president, I promise free ice cream every Tuesday and no school on Thursdays and . . ."

Vincent watched Kurt with the same distaste you'd watch someone vomit. "My European History class can't afford enough books. We're sharing the texts, taking them home on alternate days. President McMoron wants to spend money on ice cream. Can one of you muzzle him?"

"He's always yelling at the top of his lungs about something, usually himself," Irene rolled her eyes. "Y'know, the only reason he won is he's been passing out joints to anyone who promised to vote for him."

"Total schlemiel," Caroline said.

"Total what?" Gary asked.

"Yiddish," Caroline grinned. "The language of my ancestors. It means a complete douchebag."

Her friends laughed.

Toni smiled at Caroline as she walked down the aisle and found a seat toward the middle of the auditorium. Toni was with a friend—lean, short dark hair, angular features, caramel skin. The friend wore blue jeans and a bright t-shirt that said MEXICO. Caroline blinked, unsure if Toni's friend was a boy or a girl.

The curtain opened, and the two police officers exchanged a resigned glance. Hollywood High's musical director took the stage, surveyed the bedlam, and realized the futility of an opening speech. Without a word, he signaled for the first act, a mercifully short ballet sequence set to Curtis Mayfield's "Superfly." Next, a rousing dance by a big, athletic boy from The Duke's gang. He moved to the pounding rhythm of Stevie Wonder's "Living for the City," his partner a basketball. He dribbled, tossed, caught, feinted, dodged — in perfect time. During the routine, The Duke and his boys leaped on their chairs, bellowing support. The cops glared, but wisely chose to stand down. They yawned through the next offering, an inaudible four-part harmony rendition of a colonial Thanksgiving prayer, sung by the entire chorus.

Then, zero hour. Kayla took center stage, alone. She wore a simple black dress, her hair tied back. She looked poised and focused, serene and lovely, but so small. Over the shouts and whistles, Caroline faintly heard the strains of the taped classical orchestra. Kayla's chest expanded hugely as she inhaled. Her first notes sailed through the auditorium, clear and pure, gossamer laced with steel. She moved her head slightly, locking onto the loudest groups. She met each person's eyes, singing to him, to her, reaching out to them. One by one they began to listen.

Simultaneously, Caroline and Gary realized they were witnessing something wondrous. Irene and Vincent stared reverently. As a child of the industry, Caroline knew she was hearing a performance of professional quality. Even more extraordinary was Kayla's effect on the audience. The undercurrent of violence crackled, sputtered, and receded into nothing. Her music embraced, eiderdown, a gentle wave of peace and calm. The rowdiness tapered to a buzz, to a hum, then silence.

Kayla finished. The last strains of the orchestra faded. Everyone waited, breathless, wanting the moment to last forever.

The room exploded. The students, the teachers, even the police officers rose to their feet, screaming and stomping and clapping. The entire room felt a transformation, an incredible high. The cheers continued for a full five minutes while Kayla stood tiny and proud and somehow towering.

The clapping didn't stop but metamorphosed back into the din. Shouts and paper airplanes crossed mid-air, and the students filed out to their fourth period classes.

CHAPTER 15

The newspaper article Caroline's family had read painted an intriguing picture of Hollywood High School. The wide spectrum of economic backgrounds, racial heritages, religions, languages. The students in harsh circumstances, the deprivation, the rage at having been dealt such lousy cards, the need for a sense of protection. All of these factors led to the formation of gangs. The journalist portrayed Mrs. Richardson, her vision, her commitment to educate students from every conceivable circumstance.

The name itself created an unusual challenge. When adolescents run away, they need a destination. What better place than Hollywood? Looking at tabloid photos of haute couture, stretch limos, lavish events — a teen from a damaged home would never imagine that these people ever experienced pain, fear, deprivation. Hollywood High had a significant population of runaways from every corner of the United States, and Mrs. Richardson realized that in order to absorb knowledge, certain basic needs must be met. She instigated a breakfast program where showing a Hollywood High ID card got the kid a scrambled egg, hashed browns, and a carton of orange juice. At lunch, an ID bought a peanut butter sandwich, an apple, and a carton of milk. She required showers after gym class, with soap and towels provided. All students were given mandatory physical exams by the school nurse. However, the extreme needs of the street population sometimes outdistanced the school's resources. Some students were forced to make a dangerous choice to survive, undiscussed in this otherwise informative article.

The Hollywood High district was defined by a semicircle of hills. At the base, the flats converged on its hub, the famed Hollywood Boulevard. The sidewalks were crowded with dilapidated shops. Giant Slice (a gargantuan triangle of soggy pizza), Super Slush (enough soda to water a camel), Solar Sound (second hand scratchy records). Madras and tie-dyed clothing hung on racks next to tube tops and miniskirts. The old Chinese Theatre, with its sidewalk of stars, was mostly for tourists. But the food, clothing, and entertainment merely provided the backdrop for the main commerce of the boulevard: sex workers. Located a block away sat Hollywood High School, a convenient holding pen with roughly three thousand potential candidates for hire.

A crew of pimps, mainly drug dealers in their twenties and thirties, trolled the campus for recruits. Runaways — the kids who slept between cardboard boxes in back alleys — were prime targets. For them, the opportunity provided something as close to security as they had ever known. They spoke of their pimps with awe, described beatings as therapeutic spankings, solemnly thankful for doctor bills paid, pleased when given an allowance for a new pair of shoes.

The price list, though not advertised through the channels of conventional retail, was explicit and well understood. Pretty, handsome, or cute drew a large billing. But the most coveted were virgins. If a teen could hold out long enough to qualify, the experience would earn enough to keep the kid for months. Then the pimps looked after them, gently feeding a drug habit and the kids responded — traumatized, loyal, fiercely dependent. It was a harsh world, tough and sleazy, lost and lonely. But for a desperate adolescent, it was the only deal available, and it allowed them to pursue the holiest of American grails, an education.

Equally important, Hollywood High provided a community of runaways, an unofficial network of peer foster care. Although disappointed in the gritty reality that replaced the red-carpet dream, their school became their social services center. They signed each other's field trip permission slips, shared clothing, kept a running discourse on available jobs. But if circumstances required a guaranteed hire for quick cash, the student could walk across the street into unlisted recruitment headquarters, the International House of Pancakes.

This information, essential to every student whether for the purpose of joining or avoiding the ranks, was conspicuously missing from the Black family's introductory meeting with Mrs. Richardson. As a guidance counselor, she could cut through the red tape and enroll Caroline in honors classes without the mandatory placement test given at the public middle schools. She could reassure Leah and Geoff that gang violence targeted specific rivals, not random wrong-place-at-wrong-time victims. The gangs existed not for turf control in the sale of hard drugs (few could afford them), but to offer some element of identity through a language, a racial heritage, a religion, a place of birth. While extremely forthcoming about certain issues, Mrs. Richardson's position prevented her from talking about the vital statistics of Sex Workers 101.

Six weeks into the semester, Caroline, Kayla, and Gary made a mistake: They met at the International House of Pancakes for coffee. They chose a booth by the window, entirely unaware that they had entered prime hunting ground for Pimps, Inc. Unspoken etiquette dictated that if you ordered coffee to go, you were there just for coffee. If you chose a table, you were offering yourself. Blissfully clueless, the three friends were sized up from all directions. Although Gary's athletic build drew attention at school, his ruggedness greatly lessened his price tag. Male patrons of the trade generally preferred an androgynous look. Kayla was lovely, and her beauty might have racked up serious billing. Most eyes, however, were on Caroline. At that time, in that place, the most coveted look for a girl in the profession was blonde and virginal. Caroline was a sitting duck, and Silver Lamé viewed her as *his* sitting duck.

Ordering her coffee, Caroline had no idea that she wore her virginity like a neon sign. Her un-deflowered state felt so natural she was barely aware of it. Silver Lamé, a seasoned pro, pegged her sexual status with sonar accuracy. She was uncomfortably conscious of his staking a claim, but the crucial element of the chase eluded her.

The three friends chatted about Elvia's poetry night, ruined when the Puerto Rican and Bolivian gangs burst in, knives drawn, followed by a storm of cops. The next morning in English class, when Dreads asked why she was dressed head to toe in magenta, Elvia glared, "Duh, I'm in mourning."

Carlos rushed into the restaurant and ordered black coffee to go. He scanned the place. His eyes rested for a puzzled moment on Caroline, Kayla, and Gary. He quickly looked away, paid for his coffee, and left without saying hi.

Kayla and Gary were laughing about Elvia's foray into magenta when Caroline noticed Silver Lamé in the opposite booth. Her palms broke with sweat. Then she blinked. He sat across from The Blond, the tall thin boy who was in her English class on the first day of school. *What the hell?*

"Give me your book!" Caroline grabbed Kayla's hard cover text and opened it in her own face. She cowered, peeking around the edges of *Music Theory for the Young Mozart.* Music theory wasn't in Hollywood High's curriculum, but Kayla's choral singing teacher was so impressed with her talent that he arranged an independent study. Now Caroline found herself staring at a sketch of Wolfgang Amadeus playing a harpsichord.

Kayla and Gary exchanged an appalled glance.

Caroline peered at The Blond. "I wonder what his name is."

"Who?" Gary asked.

Caroline shook her head. She hadn't meant to say it out loud.

Silver Lamé faced away from her. He wore a satiny lizard-colored jacket. When The Blond spoke, Silver Lamé listened closely. To Caroline's astonishment, Silver Lamé reached to pat his hand. Their food arrived. Orange juice for Silver Lamé, and an enormous plate of pancakes and eggs for The Blond. Caroline couldn't drag her eyes away.

"What's the matter with you?" Gary hissed.

"You're acting, um, improper." Kayla tried to quell her embarrassment.

Caroline saw herself through their eyes and blushed. "I can explain. Well, maybe I can't. I don't know."

Another bewildered exchange of glances.

"She can explain," Kayla told Gary.

"Well, maybe she can't," Gary fired back at her.

"Is this good?" Kayla.

"I don't think so." Gary.

Caroline cautiously lowered Kayla's book. "That man. He talked to me the first week of school. He was watching me. He wants something."

"What in the world could he want?" Kayla was as confused as Caroline.

Gary glanced over, took in The Blond and Silver Lamé, and turned brick red. As a tenth grader, he didn't know that walking into the House of Pancakes was like wearing a "For Hire" sign. Still, he was savvy enough to understand the transaction at the next table.

"I think I get it," he squirmed.

"What's your problem?" Kayla frowned at Gary.

"Um . . . it's . . ."

At that moment, Silver Lamé turned. His eyes locked on Caroline. She clutched Kayla's textbook and he chuckled.

"Well, well, well. Hello, Honey. No, it's Caroline. Definitely not Honey."

Caroline clung to Mozart like a gladiator's shield. Gary and Kayla were deer in headlights. The Blond watched calmly.

"Want to introduce me to your friends, Hon—, Caroline?" He glanced at his watch and looked pointedly at The Blond, who rose.

"Thanks," he murmured to Silver Lamé.

"In front of Super Slush, red convertible, five minutes," he murmured back. "Bye, Honey."

Caroline blinked. *Another Honey?*

Silver Lamé no longer wore an ace bandage on his left arm, but his right arm was in a cast. Lounging comfortably in the booth, his eyes pinned Caroline.

"Let's go!" Gary jumped to his feet. He dug into his pocket and threw some crumpled dollar bills on the table to cover their untouched cups of coffee.

"Don't be in a hurry," Silver Lamé raised his voice. "We've got lots to talk about."

Gary held the girls' arms, propelling them toward the door. "We've got nothing to talk about!" He glared back at Silver Lamé. "Stay away from her!"

He topped Silver Lamé by four inches and outweighed him by sixty pounds. But Silver Lamé somehow loomed monster-sized. He grinned, knowing Gary with his awkward height was no match. Then he pointed at Caroline.

"That one's mine!"

The other customers took a brief break from their waffles to watch, curious but not alarmed. Nothing unusual for this particular House of Pancakes.

The three kids hurried out. Caroline was shaking and Kayla was crying. Gary urged them across the street and into an empty hallway.

From their tight huddle, Caroline located her voice.

"What just happened?"

Kayla wiped her eyes. "I don't know."

The girls turned to Gary, who steeled himself. "Caroline, our career counselor would be proud. You got your first job offer."

CHAPTER 16

On a Beverly Hills verandah the size of a soccer field, overlooking spectacular terraced gardens, Caroline studied the calligraphy on her name plate. She wore a sleeveless lace dress, low-heeled white sandals, a simple gold chain. Four tables of baking guests daintily dehydrated in the late November heat wave. Conversation at Caroline's table revolved around clothes, diets, concerts, and boys. They drank a revolting mixture of grapefruit juice, crushed strawberries, and ginger ale, the dreaded champagne substitute. Maids in starched uniforms served foie gras, then salmon soufflé, predictably followed by a sorbet trio and Belgian chocolate. Mrs. Hartnet had pulled out all the stops for Valerie's sweet sixteen.

Through the fall term of ninth grade, Caroline had tracked Valerie with veiled fascination. She envied Valerie not for her popularity, but for her unshakable composure. Nothing rattled her, with her Mona Lisa calm, her almost-smile implying the secret to life. Throughout Laurel's ranks, Valerie was widely admired for her beauty. Her black hair hung in a sheath, a striking contrast to her creamy skin and grey eyes. What's more, she had talent. Her oil paintings and metal sculptures surpassed her own looks in stunning originality. Caroline's straight A's seemed bland in comparison, and she regarded Valerie's perfect life with carefully concealed jealousy.

Then, one evening at dinner, Valerie's father suddenly looked startled and pitched forward into his filet mignon. Paramedics pronounced him dead of a massive coronary.

Caroline's envy dissolved on the spot. The students whispered about how well Valerie handled her personal tragedy, her presentation unblemished as always. But Caroline couldn't ignore the contrast between the haunted look in Valerie's eyes and her cultivated poise. She wrote a heartfelt condolence letter and although Valerie never acknowledged the note, when they shared a science class, she passed over several popular girls and asked Caroline to be her lab partner. As a grieving fifteen-year-old, she suffered through anxiety, depression, and insomnia. Leah offered suggestions to ease Valerie through the worst, as Caroline helped with her homework. The two girls stayed in their different circles, but they became unlikely friends. When Caroline left Laurel for Hollywood High, she never expected to hear from Valerie and was surprised to be on her birthday party guest list.

The invitation hurtled Caroline into seizures of ambivalence. On the one hand, her life at Laurel was history, and she had moved on, thank you very much. On the other hand, she and Valerie had forged a friendship, and seeing her would be nice. But she'd have to face The Platinum Ring, the mega-popular girls who always treated her with a perfected disdain, making sure she remembered her inferior social status. Still, this was her once in a lifetime opportunity to experience a Laurel A-List event and, although she hated to admit it mattered, scoring this invitation was a gigantic coup. Caroline bounced from pro to con until she was dizzy. Finally, she mailed her reply card with an X in the little box by *accept*.

Surrounded by Hartnet grandeur, Caroline missed her Laurel cadre. Tory would have shot off a catalogue of unprintable observations by now, comparing each flawless guest to a new species of hyena. Vicki would be listening courteously, memorizing every word, and would entertain them for weeks imitating the society ladies. Maren would be cursing in gutter French. But they hadn't been invited.

Legs properly crossed, napkin correctly folded, Caroline clenched sweaty fists under the embroidered tablecloth. Valerie, more beautiful by the minute, reigned supreme at the table of Hartnet cousins. Next, the Hartnet aunts; then the octet of debutantes, including her best friend Celia, a Manhattan socialite, flown in for the grand occasion on her father's private jet. Finally, Caroline, miraculously included in the Laurel elite.

Caroline was surprised to find the girls oddly friendly, going out of their way to include her in their conversation. Having dispensed with concerts, outfits, and diets over the hors d'oeuvres, talk now revolved around a spectacular gaffe committed by two new Laurel teachers, Mr. Dexter and Miss Goodwin, who arrived after Caroline left for Hollywood High. Breathless with red hot gossip, the girls interrupted each other, tripping over their eagerness to tell the tale.

"Mr. Dexter—"

"Teaches art—"

"He has a mustache—"

"And a ponytail—"

"I want to marry him!" That drew ecstatic shrieks.

"I just want his body!" Hysteria in the high registers.

So far, typical Clover banter about a male teacher.

"Miss Goodwin's cool, too." To Caroline, "Teaches physics."

A portrait emerged of a beaded, flowered pair of ex-hippies who, in their sheer contrast to the starched majority, became immediately idealized among the students. Young and attractive, they established themselves as friends, then a couple, and finally unofficial co-chairs of the limited cool faction among the faculty. Mr. Hammer watched carefully but had to admit they helped keep in line the more problematic Clovers. When a pile of cigarette butts was discovered behind the locker room —

"Is it possible to be that stupid . . ."

"Leaving your ashes outside for the world to see . . ."

"Gross . . ."

They described Mr. Hammer's ranting before the student body as he waved the evidence of evil, preserved for posterity in a sandwich bag.

"You know how he can overreact," Nicole said breezily, then bit her lip.

The others froze.

"Caroline," Angela shot Nicole a look, "she didn't mean . . ."

"It's okay," Caroline managed to smile. "He does overreact."

"Anyway," Trisha leaped in, "he was a maniac, spit flying—"

"I was sitting right in front of him," Bronwyn interrupted. "I had to, like, duck. He still caught me in the face. Gag me out!"

The girls laughed and the tension dissipated.

Punishment, Mr. Hammer bellowed, would commence immediately. Proctored study halls during recess and lunch. All would suffer until the criminals confessed. Working in shifts, the teachers paced the auditorium aisles as six hundred glowering Clovers completed homework assignments while munching on sandwiches and chips.

"I've never been so bored . . ."

"My parents filed a formal complaint . . ."

"My dad thinks it might be illegal . . ."

After a three-day eternity, the culprits slunk out of hiding, wisely not to Mr. Hammer. Instead, they tearfully admitted their guilt to The Cool Couple, who mediated a week's suspension rather than the promised banishment.

"You won't believe who it was . . ."

"Lelia Dane?" Caroline guessed. Lelia's message to the world was an ongoing up-yours.

"Brittany Mansfield and Lark Fielding." Two of Laurel's second-tier hell raisers.

"Why mediate?" Caroline grinned. "No way those two would be expelled."

The girls laughed. Brittany's family, philanthropists (i.e. Herculean inherited wealth), had donated two new tennis courts, and the Fieldings, who owned a diamond mine, had added a swimming pool the size of the Red Sea.

At that point, the episode would have concluded had the Dynamic Duo not been compelled to push beyond the limits of reason. They hosted a party in their Venice Beach bungalow, blasting the Grateful Dead, The Band, and Jimi Hendrix. The table included an expected array of vegetarian hors d'oeuvres and an unexpected platter of beef hot dogs. The problem was they also offered home-grown pot and home-brewed beer to their extremely cool guests — which included a chosen few Laurel students, gorgeous and under legal age. The junior class president, a stunning brunette, accepted an alcoholic drink, a few hits from a bong, and Mr. Dexter's hand in a slow dance where he held her against his unmistakable erection. She freaked, her parents freaked, and her father sped his chrome Bentley straight to the Hammer residence. He pounded on the door, interrupted Mrs. Hammer's bedtime cleansing ritual, and all hell broke loose. A scathing series of phone calls, frantic emergency meetings, flurries of abject apologies, to no avail. The Terrible Twosome got the boot, kicked off campus, never to return.

"So anyway, Caroline, how do you like Hollywood High?" Nicole, Valerie's sidekick, asked as the laughter faded.

"It's different from Laurel, but I like it."

"Any cute guys?" asked Bronwyn, Laurel's go-to authority on eligible boys, trying to expand her inventory.

"Sure, I guess." The Duke and Cute didn't belong in the same sentence. He was show-stopper handsome, high-voltage charismatic, continuously simmering, ready to detonate. Vincent was attractive, talented, articulate, and Asian, the last attribute disqualifying him from Bronwyn's private Social Register. As for Gary, he was just Gary. Girls followed him around, but he always gravitated back to their quintet.

"Valerie said you tutored," Katie sampled her soufflé. "Is she, like, really dumb?"

Katie's family had hosted the eighth grade holiday party. She lived on twelve lacquered acres, in a Beverly Hills castle where visitors signed the guest book, then removed their shoes to preserve the white Parisian carpet and priceless Oriental rugs. The furniture, uncomfortable and invaluable, had been shipped from palaces of fallen European royalty and was covered in fitted, clear plastic.

"It's a he," Caroline answered evenly. "And no, he's not dumb."

"Is he cute?" Bronwyn again.

"Six-four," Caroline grinned wickedly. "Built like Michelangelo sculpted him."

"What's his name?" Katie asked.

"The Duke."

The girls giggled.

"Does he have a girlfriend?" Bronwyn on a mission.

"He's got an entourage of girls. He's incredibly smart. He's the leader of a gang. Carries a switchblade." Smugly, Caroline sipped her faux drink. *Ladies, you can shove 'bookish' in a dark place.*

"Cool!" said Bronwyn.

"Totally cool!" echoed Angela.

"Is his hair long?" asked Katie. "I love guys with long hair."

"Please tell me he's blond!" said Trisha.

"He's Black."

Bronwyn's smile faded. Nixed from the Social Register.

A circle of sparkling eyes. Then Nicole whispered the forbidden question.

"Have you slept with him?"

Caroline shook her head, speechless that they'd consider her cool enough for sex.

"C'mon, this guy can't be smart and be in a gang," Katie stated.

"Yes, he can," Caroline turned flinty.

"Are all of your friends Black?" Angela asked.

Caroline's anger took root, and she gave in to the rush. "No. My friend Gary is blond and plays football. His father paints houses. His mother's a seamstress. They're Irish immigrants. He's a Latin scholar. He's one of my best friends. Then there's Kayla. She sings like a muse. And yes, she's Black." Caroline filled her lungs, ready to launch into Irene and Vincent, when Angela cut in.

"What's her genre, jazz?" No awareness of the racially motivated assumptions she comfortably carried.

A wave of loneliness caught Caroline off guard, and she was suddenly fighting tears. "No," she managed to whisper.

"Blues?" Angela back for another try.

"Classical."

"How does a Black girl know about classical?" Trisha was puzzled.

"The same way you do." Caroline felt her throat close. She knew that for the remainder of the party, she'd sit silent, unable to speak.

But help was on the way. Mrs. Hartnet entered singing cheerfully, carrying an enormous birthday cake, and attention shifted to Valerie.

CHAPTER 17

"This is Ray."

Gary, Vincent, and Irene shook Ray's hand. Caroline nodded politely, her hands off limits. Even relaxing with her friends, her hands broke with sweat. From the moment she set foot on campus until she arrived back home, her palms leaked.

Ray was five-nine, with broader shoulders than the average teenager. Dark brown skin, short black hair, round face. Cute, not handsome. Most impressive, he needed a shave. He shook hands firmly, more like an adult than an eleventh grader. He and Kayla dropped to the ground, and her friends tried not to stare at Kayla's first boyfriend.

Three weeks before, Kayla emerged late from Choral Singing looking dazed. She'd just met a junior, a transfer student with a surprisingly mature baritone. Mr. Chung suggested that Ray and Kayla try a duet, and the chorus gave them a standing ovation.

Ray lived with his mother and grandmother. His father had disappeared when he was a baby. Originally from Minnesota, his family faced a crisis when his grandmother's arthritis worsened and the prairie winters threatened to cripple her for life. They flipped a coin, California versus Florida, and headed for the sun.

The kids calmly took in Ray's family constellation. A trinity of grandmother, mother, and son was hardly Apple Pie America. But the students at Hollywood High came from such diverse backgrounds that *conventional* lost its meaning. Monday through Friday, they showed up as representatives of an unpolished, undignified, un-United Nations, and it never occurred to them to question family circumstances.

"Where'd you live in Minnesota?" Gary conversationally.

"Minneapolis," Ray smiled. "Great city. Freezing winters."

"Do you miss your friends?" Caroline asked.

"Yeah, a lot." He and Kayla shared a smile.

"I know how that feels," she said. "I can't say I miss the cold in Massachusetts. The winters can feel like forever. I—"

A collective shout erupted in the quad. Ray jumped to his feet, radiating an intense alertness. Instead of the expected gang fight, a boy ran by stark naked, wearing a gorilla mask.

"A streaker!" Irene laughed.

Thirty seconds later, the campus cop raced in hot pursuit.

Ray shook his head, laughing with Irene. Gary and Vincent grinned. Caroline and Kayla exchanged looks of abject mortification.

On the far side of the quad, they saw the streaker dash into the street and jump into a waiting car. They sped off and disappeared around a corner as the bell rang to end the lunch break.

"Call you tonight?" Kayla said quietly to Caroline as they separated.

"Sure."

At 7PM, the phone rang.

"It's me."

"Everything okay?" Caroline asked.

"Yeah, well no, not really. It's Ray. I couldn't say this in front of him today and . . . well . . . I don't know what to think."

"What's going on?"

"It's his mother."

"What about her?"

"Ray's sixteen. She's twenty-nine." Kayla's voice dropped so her parents wouldn't overhear.

"Okay, so what's the problem . . . wait . . . she was only thirteen when Ray was born?"

"Yeah. She's totally paranoid that Ray will get a girl pregnant. She's super strict."

"Super strict how?"

"Super strict like no dating until he's eighteen."

"Eighteen?" Caroline was shocked. "Seriously?"

"Ray says he can't tell her about me. We can't ever go out on a date. We can't see each other outside of school."

"Ray's okay with that?"

"He doesn't like it, but he says he has no choice."

"That will change," Caroline stated flatly. "After a while, he'll introduce you to his mother and grandmother. You're the dream girlfriend. They'll love you."

"You think so?"

"Kayla, seriously, you're what every parent hopes for. You're smart, talented, nice, beautiful, polite. You're everything."

"Really?"

"Definitely really. They'll meet you and everything will be fine."

Kayla smiled over the phone. "Thanks, Caroline. I hope you're right."

"I'm sure I'm right."

But Caroline wasn't right.

In the beginning, the secrecy was intriguing, which made the situation tolerable. As the weeks went on, Kayla grew increasingly frustrated. She and Ray couldn't see a movie, get a burger, go to a concert. They barely had time to grab a quick ice cream cone after school. Most difficult, Kayla was discovering sexuality, and she longed for more than kisses tailored for an audience of three thousand omnipresent kids. Still, Ray refused to defy his mother.

Caroline watched closely as Kayla navigated this rich terrain. Every time she thought about boys, her shoulders tightened, and her thoughts turned to Latin vocabulary. Kayla's new frontier was too alluring, too physical, too sensual. Caroline was frightened that once she took that first step, there would be no turning back. Her buff intellectual musculature would ring in worthless, and her head would devolve into a vapid state of breathlessness.

She thought back to Windy Canyon Elementary Education and her introduction to sex. Through the years, the kids repeated ad nauseam renditions of songs from the movie du jour. Loud and heartfelt for Elsa the lovable lioness, "*Born free, as free as the wind blows.*" For Oliver the golden waif, "*Consider yourself at home!*" But Broadway threw a curve ball with *Hair*. Overnight, the kids abandoned the orphaned cub and the heart-melting boy and moved on to a lilted, lisped — *sodomy, masturbation, orgy.*

A flurry of emergency faculty meetings. Debates on freedom of speech versus censorship. In spite of the love-in zeitgeist, the song was banned with no explanation ... which backfired. The kids were drawn to the lyrics like forbidden fruit. Most of the children had nowhere to turn for this sort of information, but Caroline's family had a pact. Any questions, no matter what the subject matter, would be answered honestly. Leah and Geoff swallowed hard and defined every word. For a few weeks, Caroline was a school celebrity, the only kid who could explain the lyrics. Reactions were limited in variety. Shrieks of *eeyuck!* accompanied by ecstatically crossed eyes and delighted gagging motions. Caroline strutted, Windy Canyon's expert on sex.

More accurately, on dictionary definitions of sex. Looking at Kayla and Ray, Caroline realized her days of keeping sex in her head were numbered. Then, a new thought began to take shape. Until that point, sex meant creepy older men in the industry hitting on her. Now, it struck her that sex could be something entirely different. Maybe it could even be nice. At fifteen, Caroline was already well versed in saying no. Suddenly, the idea of saying yes became a possibility. She knew she wasn't there yet, but some day . . .

Kayla's *some day* had arrived. She waited to speak privately to Caroline as the two girls walked home on a Friday afternoon. Usually, they took a grimy public bus down Ventura Boulevard, got off at Broadlawn Drive, and separated. Caroline hiked into the hills, Kayla straight ahead to her tract house in the valley. But this was a rare, smogless day, and they decided to carry their backpacks and stroll, leaving school at the same time because the basketball team didn't practice on Fridays. In her peripheral vision, Caroline saw Silver Lamé watching from across the street. She tensed, but he didn't approach. The girls worked their way through the exiting throngs before Kayla began.

"Something about Ray I haven't told you. I think he does a lot of drugs. When we first met, he asked if I had any good connections. I didn't know what to say."

"What's he take?"

"I think anything he can get."

Their eyes locked. Many kids at Hollywood High smoked pot. Cocaine and hashish were far too expensive. There was, however, another alternative, much more risky. Twitchy men and women stood at every street corner selling pills, baggies with multicolored tablets looking like misshapen M&Ms. Some of the pushers were walleyed and some were wild, all emaciated and pallid. A few dealers had contacts at school, sex workers whose pimps also had them selling. But this particular recreational option was peddled mainly on the streets, and you never knew what you were buying. It could be painkillers, Play-Doh, or rat poison, and users regularly ended up in the emergency room. If Ray was choosing that option, he was playing Russian roulette.

"It's bad," Kayla said, "but everything else about him is good . . . except that we can't see each other outside of school. That's bad . . . but that's his Mom's fault. Everything else . . . I mean, he's . . ."

"Yeah," Caroline nodded. "He's . . . yeah."

There was something about Ray that was hard to define, something simultaneously charismatic and disarming. Everybody liked him. During lunch, he'd sling his guitar off his back and sing. He took average academic classes, excelled in gym, made no attempt to play team sports. He was pleasant and funny. To everyone's astonishment, he broke up a few lunch hour gang fights before the cops arrived, his presence surprisingly commanding. Best of all, as the masses settled down after the first brawl, Kayla saw Kurt staring from the sidelines. Since then, although he continued to gawk at her through their classes, he watched from a distance.

"Does Ray take drugs when you're with him?" Caroline asked.

Kayla thought carefully. "He's shown me the pills and the pot he bought, but I've never seen him take anything. I told him I don't do drugs."

"Maybe he's keeping it away from you. If he really likes you, he won't get you involved."

"I guess. He says it gets him through the weekends taking care of his grandmother."

"If you stay together, maybe you can get him off drugs."

"I'm sure I can."

Kayla and Caroline smiled at each other, confidence built on a foundation of ignorance. Not the slightest clue that they didn't have a clue.

CHAPTER 18

Saturday night, Irene's apartment.

Gary had turned sixteen the previous Tuesday and now flashed his driver's license. He almost flunked the test due to a nine-point turn, which his friends found hilarious. He picked up Caroline and Kayla, driving exactly the speed limit, stopping at every intersection, even when he had the right of way. Sitting in front, Caroline watched Gary's hands. Big hands for a boy, knuckles defined and strong, nails ragged, blond tufts on the backs of his fingers. She studied her own hands, small and smooth in comparison, then back to his, transfixed.

This gathering had become a weekly event, moving easily from one home to another. Gary was the most reluctant to host and when he finally invited them, his friends understood. Caroline lived in a spacious home with stunning views. Kayla and Vincent's parents owned small, pretty valley houses. Irene lived in an apartment complex with a pool. Gary's circumstances were different. He lived in a tiny flat in the heart of Hollywood. His building rose up like an afterthought in the middle of a parking lot. But as long as the kids were together, they didn't mind.

This Saturday was Irene's turn, and they sprawled around her room. Sitting comfortably on the floor, Caroline related the sweet sixteen debacle. With Jimmy Cliff's *The Harder They Come* blaring on the stereo, the others strained to hear.

"Caroline, will you ever learn to speak up?" Irene complained.

"No."

Gary smiled fondly. "You talk way too soft."

Caroline shook her head. "Everyone else talks way too loud."

"Not me," Vincent sipped soda. "I only paint loud."

"Deep, deep, from the diaphragm," Kayla imitated her voice teacher.

"I can't hear you over the music," Irene shot an annoyed look at Caroline.

"Then tell Jimmy Cliff to tone it down."

"Give it up Irene," Gary laughed with the rest. "She's hopeless."

Caroline described the five-strand natural pearl necklace from Valerie's aunt and the vanilla slice with frothy pink icing that a new maid dropped on one of the debutantes, plopping a thick splotch of rose colored gunk in her sleek blonde French braid. Caroline finessed the searing loneliness, transformed the event into a joke, momentarily at the top of the adolescent food chain.

Her Hollywood cadre had smoothed out the tension at home from transferring schools. After the Fall Music and Dance Recital, Kayla's parents threw a party to celebrate. Leah and Geoff couldn't help being impressed by their daughter's new friends. Ironically, their fears about Hollywood High calmed as Caroline's skyrocketed. How could she tell them she was being stalked by Silver Lamé? How could she explain her narrowing sphere of existence — the lawn, the library, and the House of Pancakes now strictly off limits? At this rate, every building on campus would be forbidden by the end of the semester, and if Leah and Geoff found out, they'd haul her back to Laurel within the hour. Frightened as Caroline was of Hollywood High, the idea of three more years of social events chez Hartnet loomed scarier.

The Duke unknowingly helped bolster her confidence. His progress in math was slam dunk terrific. He scored one-hundred percent on every exam and continued to surge forward. Like his body, his mind had an athletic style of spotlight intensity. Discovering his brainpower caused layers of tectonic shifts. His confidence soared, and Caroline felt oddly valuable, her intellect put to practical use at last. Maybe she wouldn't make a career of gathering cobwebs.

Then another surprise. The Duke introduced Caroline to his friends, calling her "The Professor," a nickname that would stick through graduation. She introduced her friends and Ray walked up to put his arm around Kayla. To Caroline's amazement, she liked The Duke's gang. They were loud and brash, also warm and funny. They had a rugged, relentless charisma that reminded Caroline of her basketball teammates. They accepted her without question, and her rabid dog gang stereotype disintegrated.

Six boys orbited The Duke, eager for his approval. They were all Black, dressed in identical blue jeans, white sleeveless undershirts, combs stuck in their afros, black hightop athletic shoes. Two stocky kids, Jay and Tom, strutted tough. Caroline fought down a wave of queasiness at the shiny pink scar running down Tom's cheek. The knife fight in the library.

Three girls circled The Duke. He was offhand with two and clearly favored the third, Doraine. The Duke and Doraine were a commanding team, both tall and striking. Doraine radiated a coltish beauty, half woman half child, lean with a baby-fat thick waist.

Tom and Jay launched into a percussive, nonverbal reenactment of a screaming fight between their French and Government teachers, who had accidentally been assigned the same fourth period classroom. Through the hysteria, The Duke offered that Caroline had "walked out on Laurel Academy," and the group applauded.

"What's it like?" Doraine asked.

"It's clean." Their laughter surprised Caroline. "The girls wear uniforms. Gray pleated skirt, white Oxford shirt, white knee socks, penny loafers, gold cotton cardigan." The kids looked horrified. "Everyone gets a Jaguar for her sixteenth birthday." An astounded silence. "Actually, there's a girl you'd like. Her name's Lelia." Caroline transported the group back three years to seventh grade, a classroom referred to as "the carousel" for its circular shape, furnished not with desks but with round tables hosting six carved dining room chairs. Velvet curtains with sashes hung on the floor-to-ceiling windows. Mandatory training in Social Graces, monthly meetings taught by the school's guidance counselor, Miss MacIsaac.

As they walked into the third meeting, the girls unknowingly entered the class that would rocket Lelia to stardom. Each girl was assigned to bring something worthy of a socially graced household. Caroline's friend Vicki brought a fabulous Steuben glass sculpture; Maren, an antique English tea set; Tory, an embroidered bag of seventeenth century Venetian trading beads. Valerie Hartnet tacked on the bulletin board (concealed behind a faux Renaissance portrait) photographs of several Tiffany lamps. Caroline offered a crystal bowl her grandmother somehow carried on the boat from Russia near the turn of the century. Miss MacIsaac regretfully informed the students that although the cut was magnificent, the unknown maker fell short of the refined.

Then Lelia's turn. Hard work and consistent performance had earned her the unofficial title of Laurel's Supreme Bad Clover. The entire school reveled in her naughty pranks, carried out with shameless panache. Lelia was nearing the end of a productive semester. For her debut in September, she spiked the cafeteria's orange juice with a fifth of vodka. She wore edible underwear, which she daintily munched through several morning recess breaks and once onstage during a rainy day lunch in the auditorium. But it seemed Lelia had succumbed when she brought a Waterford crystal decanter full of lemonade and twelve champagne flutes. The girls sighed, both relieved and disappointed. Miss MacIsaac gushed her approval, sufficiently pleased to deviate from the lesson plan and demonstrate proper pouring technique. She hoisted the heavy crystal, held it at the correct angle and turned rigid. The girls began to scream. The liquid poured in a controlled stream. It was pale yellow, and it was unmistakably not lemonade.

Caroline's Hollywood friends howled.

"You give Lelia a message!" The Duke shouted. "Tell her she can eat my edible shorts any time!"

Now, Caroline relaxed in Irene's room, mulling over the week. The Duke gave her more than he'd ever realize, the pride of having her own student outdistance her teaching abilities. The previous Monday, Caroline arrived at a difficult decision. The Duke needed a pro, not a sophomore hack. Caroline talked to Miss Orville, who talked to Mr. Cohen, who talked to Mrs. Richardson, who talked to The Duke —"Never had so many meetings with teachers in my life, at least not without a cop!"

Academic placement defied an obvious solution. A senior, talented in math, performing at a fourth-grade level. Miss Orville broke the brief impasse, offering her lunch hour twice each week. The Duke transferred out of remedial math into an independent study.

He stared as Mrs. Richardson signed the schedule change, lifted his file, and opened her metal COLLEGE cabinet.

"Congratulations," she said quietly.

Through the process, Caroline barely contained her anxiety over losing The Duke. Although she admitted it only to herself, she needed him for what little security she had.

"I guess we won't meet anymore." Caroline spoke in a careful monotone.

"Girl, what you talkin' about?"

"You'll have Miss Orville. She's a real teacher."

"So you'll tutor me in English or history or whatever. She's the teacher. You're The Professor."

Caroline understood. She was his guide as he navigated the academic white waters.

"Girl," The Duke cocked his head, "why you care so much about me?"

"I don't like to see potential go to waste."

"Potential. Another fancy-ass word. What kind of tenth grader thinks about potential? You're strange."

"I thought that was already established," she said, smiling slightly.

"Do you like it?"

"What?"

"You ask different questions. You see different things. You're different. You like it?"

Like it? Are you kidding? I say things nobody else says. I see things nobody else sees. Everyone thinks I'm weird. Sometimes they like me anyway, sometimes they don't. Either way, I'm still weird. What exactly am I supposed to like about it?

Caroline said nothing.

"Hey, I get it," The Duke read her perfectly. "I'm head of a gang, don't mess with me. The teachers always hated me. Same with the administration. Now all my teachers like me, and Mrs. Richardson thinks I'm going to college."

"Do you want to go to college?"

"Yeah, right, college. Where every member of my family goes, and every member of my gang goes. I won't last five minutes."

"When we first met, you said I wouldn't last five minutes at Holly-wood High."

"Okay, whatever. I was wrong about you."

"And now you're wrong about you. If you want to go to college, I'm betting on you."

A long beat. Then The Duke lightly punched her shoulder. "I'm not betting on you! Everyone knows you're stupid!"

Relaxing in Irene's bedroom, thinking about The Duke's words, Caroline smiled. A strange feeling of strength stirred and coalesced. She looked around her circle of friends.

Suddenly she snapped to attention. Friends. Gary was no match for Silver Lamé. He was street smart and muscular. But at the core he was a gentle boy. Vincent's paintbrush was his sword, the art room was his arena, and physically he was small. Caroline needed someone with size and brawn, someone who didn't mind hurting another person. A friend who was savvy and tough.

It was right in front of her all along. She'd talk to him next week. The Duke would know what to do.

CHAPTER 19

Caroline took one bite and pushed her lunch aside. Gary and Irene didn't bother to open their paper sacks. Only Vincent and Kayla ate.

"I don't get it," Gary dropped his head into his hands.

Caroline could sense his anguish, literally feel it. A surge of tenderness coursed through her bloodstream. She wanted to reach out, take him in her arms, offer comfort. She clenched her fists in her lap to control such a bizarre and inappropriate urge.

"Is he going to be okay?" Irene asked.

Gary shrugged. "I don't know."

The day before, the last drills ended, and the football team scattered. Outside the locker room, two linemen, one defensive back, and the punter hung around talking. Then a student walked by, late on his way home from finishing a midterm project. Instinctively, the athletes retreated into the shadows, snickering at his long hair, white laced sailor pants, teal scarf, platform heels. Suddenly they lunged. They grabbed him from behind, threw a towel over his head, dragged him into the empty locker room, and beat him. A broken nose, a dislocated shoulder, two cracked ribs, three smashed fingers, a fractured wrist, a twisted ankle, several cuts, bruises all over, and a concussion. The janitor found him crying and unable to walk, lying on the cold tile floor of the showers.

Caroline's upbringing had left her stunningly naive about the sexual spectrum, though not in the usual style of stars and stripes America. In their teens, long before they met, her parents separately thought over homosexuality. At that time, being gay was not only considered unsavory, but was also illegal. Leah and Geoff each concluded that hating gays simply made no sense. One of Leah's closest friends in college was a lesbian, which bothered her not in the slightest. Geoff, fighting in World War II with his heterosexual credentials in order, pulled Marines out of the brig at every opportunity, men who had been caught with another man. Hatching a creative array of reasons why he needed each person's suddenly discovered expertise for his platoon, he refused to stand by while good Marines rotted in confinement. Another Marine challenged him to a fight over his infidel beliefs, and Geoff knocked him cold. No other challenges followed.

Caroline's earliest family memories included her parents' LGBTQ friends. Introduced to the notion from the cradle, she barely gave it a thought. Over time, when she learned that LGBTQ was considered synonymous with perversion, she was incredulous. It never struck her as odd that some couples were two men or two women. It was part of her natural order.

At Laurel, it was clear to Caroline that a small group of girls were lesbians. It was equally clear that a few were dating. They never spoke openly of their girlfriends, never bragged about their sexual conquests. Mired in misconceptions, Caroline thought they were unusually understated and mature.

Hollywood High's style was much more colorful. Many of the lesbians and bi girls presented themselves in a loud alliance. Years before punk rock crossed the Atlantic to America, these girls dyed their short hair rust, green, blue, or all three. Alternatively, they shaved their heads and sometimes tattooed their skulls.

Some of the openly gay and bi boys chose to dress like the male sex workers, wearing white pants, gauzy white shirts, tasseled belts, colorful scarves, platform shoes. Unlike the sex workers, they had the option to choose different clothes, the length of their hair, and whether or not they wore makeup. All of the kids, Caroline included, assumed the male sex workers were gay. They had no comprehension of the difference between having gay sex and being gay. If you were a boy trying to stay alive by selling your body, your patrons consisted of men. Whatever your sexuality might be, identity took a back seat to survival.

There were other gay, lesbian, and bi students who chose not to advertise their sexuality. Again, Caroline thought their discretion indicated maturity. She was clueless regarding the dilemma they faced.

Convinced that the world would enlighten her soon enough, Geoff and Leah never spoke of the collective phobia so many felt regarding anyone who wasn't cisgender and straight. Her parents lived their acceptance, brought it into their daily life, and Caroline picked it up effortlessly. Now she was rocked to the core, facing the hatred and violence directed at gay, lesbian, bi, nonbinary, and trans folks, simply because they're gay, lesbian, bi, nonbinary, and trans — no other reason.

"Do you know the guy?" Caroline asked.

Gary shook his head. "Name's Jeremy, never met him."

"I heard he's good at print shop and auto mechanics," Vincent offered. "Seems strange."

"Why's print shop strange?" Irene looked up.

"Not print shop," Vincent shifted. "It's just not what I'd expect from . . ."

Irene turned steely. "From what?"

"From a homosexual. I mean—"

"You expected he'd major in flamenco dance with a minor in flower arrangement?"

"Irene, give him a break," Kayla spoke softly. "It's not like he's saying it was right to beat up Jeremy."

"Nobody deserves that," Vincent nodded at Kayla. "Not even homosexuals."

"The word is gay," Irene glared. "And when did you turn stupid?"

An uncomfortable pause.

"I don't understand the administration." Caroline's friends looked at her, confused. "When I was at Laurel, our star tennis player slapped another girl in the face. She was suspended from school for a week. The administration called an assembly to talk about it, and the next two P.E. classes were about nonviolent ways to express anger. How come nothing's being done here?"

"This is Hollywood High, not a college prep academy," Irene explained impatiently. "Gangs are always fighting. Y'know, if they called an assembly every time someone got hurt, we'd never have any time in the classroom."

Caroline shook her head. "There's got to be another way."

"I agree," Irene nodded. "When you figure it out, be sure to let the rest of us know."

Ray sauntered up, lifted his guitar out of its case, and dropped next to Kayla. He formed a chord. She reached out and covered his hand.

"What?" he asked, and Kayla told him. Ray turned intent and serious.

"You should hear the team talk. They think it's funny, or they act like it's a time-honored tradition to beat up a gay boy, like a fox hunt." Gary's eyes filled. "One of my uncles is gay. Dad's younger brother. Uncle James."

"Really?" Kayla curiously. "I don't know anyone who's gay."

"How's that possible, not to know any gay people?" Caroline asked.

"You know homosexuals?" Vincent put down his food.

"GAYS!" Irene bellowed and "Of course," Caroline said at the precise same moment.

"Some of my family freaked out when Uncle James broke the news. The Irish Catholic sinner thing. But then they settled down. Judge not others and all that." He shrugged. "Thing is, nobody would have guessed. Uncle James is big, six-six. He's a Ph.D. in physics. Really smart. Good basketball player, too. Almost made the pros. That helped everyone get used to it. Far outside the stereotype." Gary paused, losing himself in a memory. "Once, when my parents were away in Ireland, I got chicken pox. I was five. I was staying with Uncle James. I don't think he slept for three days in a row. I was running fevers, blisters driving me crazy. I kept crying for my mom. Uncle James held me the whole time, even when I slept. He didn't leave me for a second. His partner took care of me, too. Phil. They're still together. It's like they're married, except they can't legally marry. All I would eat was one type of orange popsicle, mashed up. Phil must have bought ten boxes."

The group turned quiet, imagining Gary, tiny and miserable, cradled in the arms of this huge, kind man.

"And everything was okay? When you were with your uncle, did he . . . ? I mean . . ." Vincent trailed off.

"No, it was awful. I had chicken pox."

"I mean . . ."

"He's asking if your uncle molested you." Irene tore open her lunch sack and took a savage bite of her roast beef sandwich.

Gary and Caroline stared at each other for an astounded moment. Then Gary turned flinty as he faced Vincent. "Listen very closely. Gay men. Lesbian women. Bisexual. Trans. There's probably more on the spectrum that we don't have words for yet. Being straight is one way to be normal. There are lots of ways to be normal. Get used to it. And the answer is no. Being gay and being a pedophile are not the same. Uncle James didn't molest me. Phil didn't molest me. They took care of me."

"Does your coach know what the team is doing?" Caroline broke the awkward silence.

"Yeah." Gary looked nauseated as The Who's "Teenage Wasteland" blared over the quad's loudspeakers. "He says he understands what it means to be a growing American boy." He lowered his voice in imitation. "Do what you have to do, guys."

"That's disgusting," Caroline snapped. "What do they think they're doing?"

"Achieving the honorable," Irene snarled. "Living up to our school motto."

Carlos was suddenly standing over them with two friends. One boy dressed like Carlos, in white with a tasseled belt, light makeup. The other boy wore jeans and a t-shirt, no makeup.

"Hi." Carlos shifted uncertainly, not sure if he'd be welcome.

"Hi," Caroline answered.

"Want to sit?" Gary asked, and the three boys dropped to the ground. "This is Irene, Vincent, and Ray. You know Caroline and Kayla from English class."

Caroline, Irene, and Ray smiled. Kayla and Vincent held their discomfort in check.

Carlos introduced his friends. "You heard about Jeremy?"

They nodded, and Carlos bit his lip.

"Are you okay?" Gary asked.

"Everyone's talking about it," Carlos said. "Everyone who's gay is scared and . . ." — indicating the boy in jeans —". . . this is my boyfriend. If those guys knew, they'd . . ." he trailed off. "Like I said, everyone's scared."

"That's understandable," said Gary quietly.

Caroline and Irene nodded.

"Some guys are changing how they dress," Carlos continued. "Cutting their hair. No makeup. Jeans."

"Why aren't you . . ." Vincent began.

"Because he shouldn't have to!" Irene spoke fiercely. "He should be able to dress in whatever way he wants! He should be able to wear makeup or not! He should be able to choose! Like you choose, Vincent!"

"I don't wear makeup!"

"You *choose* not to wear makeup!" Irene snapped. "It's your *choice*. And you don't have to worry about getting beaten up for *choosing* not to wear makeup!"

"It's who I am," Carlos said. "I could be next. Nobody knows what to do." A long pause. "Anyway, see you around."

The three boys stood and walked over to a few other friends. They huddled together, speaking softly.

"I never realized . . ." Kayla trailed off.

"Never realized what?" Caroline asked.

"How brave they are to show up at school every day."

"This is really messed up!" Gary's voice rose. "Someone has to do something!"

"I know what to do." Everyone turned to Caroline. "We need to tell Mrs. Richardson what Gary knows."

"Right. Let's go." Gary started to rise.

"Wait," Kayla pulled him back down. "You can't make that call. If anyone finds out, you're dead."

"I have to."

"What those guys did was wrong, but we don't have to get involved."

"Shut up, Vincent," Irene growled.

"When something like this happens, everyone should get involved." Caroline put her uneaten lunch in her backpack.

"I'll do it—" Gary began.

"I'm doing it!" Kayla insisted. "What is it, Caroline?"

"I'm sorry, I didn't mean to stare, it's . . ."

"What?" Kayla demanded.

"You're a soldier."

"Me? I'm a soprano, not a soldier. I just have a busy week, and I don't have time to go to Gary's funeral."

"Kayla's right," Irene nodded at Gary. "We'll take over on this one."

"No. I have to do it. They can't beat me up worse than Jeremy." Gary's voice broke. "For Uncle James and Phil. I have to do it."

"But . . ."

"Kayla, you need to back down."

The gentleness in Gary's tone stopped Kayla.

"Okay," Gary took a deep breath. "Let's go."

With an absurd show of studied carelessness, they walked to a pay phone off campus. As they passed the House of Pancakes, Caroline saw Silver Lamé leering from his window seat. Kurt walked by, saw Kayla, and turned on his heel.

"Hey, Kayla! I haven't talked to you in a while, but I'm always thinking about you. You look really pretty today."

Instinctively, Ray put his arm around Kayla's shoulders and the group formed a blockade, pushing Kayla and Ray behind them.

"Leave her alone!" Vincent stepped forward and Kurt, taller and heavier, backed away. From Ray's arms, Kayla smiled at Vincent.

They surrounded Gary as he called Mrs. Richardson and identified the four assailants. Their counselor never revealed Gary's name. The boys were questioned by her, the high school's campus cop, and the Hollywood police department. The athletes had no trouble lying, being perfectly at ease with what they had done. Jeremy could identify nobody, which left Mrs. Richardson no choice but to drop it.

Life picked up, business as usual. Jeremy's wounds healed and he returned. The four Neanderthals received boisterous congratulations from their teammates and strutted as though they had scored the winning touchdown.

Gary had nightmares for a week, Carlos for a month.

Every day, Caroline arrived at school and anxiously looked around until she saw The Blond was unharmed. She couldn't explain her obsession and she told nobody. *What's wrong with me?* she asked herself every morning as she compulsively performed her safety check. *Why can't I get him out of my head?*

CHAPTER 20

"Caroline, it's for you!" her mother called down the hall.

Caroline closed J.D. Salinger's *The Catcher in the Rye* and lifted the phone's extension in Geoff's study.

"Hello?"

"Hi. It's Valerie."

"Oh, um, hi."

Three weeks had passed since Valerie Hartnet's birthday brunch. She sent a proper note of thanks, and Caroline expected never to hear from her again.

"How's life at sixteen?" Caroline cringed. How idiotic could she sound? But after the party, she vowed to keep it short and shallow.

"Well, fine, well . . ."

She sounds . . . no, it's not possible . . . she sounds more uncomfortable than I am. "Valerie, what's wrong?"

"This is so embarrassing."

"What happened?"

"Nothing. I mean, all right, here goes. At my party . . ."

"Did something offend you?"

"Yes!"

"I know what it was," Caroline's voice was heavy.

"You do?"

"It was my gift. I'm sorry. I thought you'd like art supplies. I know I was supposed to give you a friendship ring. Everyone else did and it's the traditional present. I wasn't trying to hurt your feelings. I was—"

"No!" Valerie cut in. "I loved your gift. I don't know what I'm supposed to do with all those ridiculous rings. I only have ten fingers. No, it's . . . I overheard the talk at your table. About Hollywood High. About your friends and being Black and who was dumb. I was so embarrassed."

Caroline couldn't have been more surprised if Valerie had pulled out an uzi. "It's okay. I mean, it isn't okay, but it's not your fault."

"My friends are fucking morons."

Caroline played it back in her head to make sure she heard it right.

"Honestly, Miss Hartnet, *moron* is a rude word, not to be used in polite company." She could hear Valerie smile over the phone.

"It's weird," Valerie said. "We're the cool group at school, and I'm at the top of the pecking order. But I don't even know who I am anymore."

"I know how you feel." *Wow, we're really bonding!*

"I have to act a certain way at Laurel. Our Lady of the Perpetual Poise. I can't stop even when I want to."

"That's why I like Hollywood High. There's more than one way that's right. You can really be yourself." Caroline swelled with pride at her original thinking.

"I kept looking around my party and wondering if I liked my friends. Honestly, they looked like a bunch of douchebags wearing pearl necklaces."

The two girls broke into laughter.

"Valerie . . ." *Whoa, don't say it. Don't get carried away. She's everything and I'm nothing.* "What are you doing Saturday night?" *Oh, shit! I didn't mean to say it out loud. She'll never say yes, and I'll look like a total jerk.*

"There's a small party at my house." *Shut up! Now she'll turn frosty polite and hang up forever.*

"I . . . are you inviting me?"

No, of course not. "Sure, if you want. My new friends from school. Boys and girls. Really informal. Blue jeans."

"Do you think they'll like me?"

"Yeah, and I think you'll like them. Can you drive, got your license yet?" *I sound so extremely totally in control. This is bizarre.*

"Got it as soon as I turned sixteen. I got a Jaguar for my birthday."

"Did you and Nicole plan your colors?"

"No. I went solo. Plain black. Nicole is displeased."

Caroline grinned. Best friends at Laurel usually drove complimentary custom painted cars. Katie and Angela, the first in the group to turn sixteen, chose beige Jaguars with maroon trim. If the twosome suffered a falling out, an emergency paint job was mandated.

"What about Saturday?"

"I'll be there."

"Seven-thirty."

"Caroline, thanks."

"No problem. I . . . I have to tell you something."

"What?"

"They don't know what happened last year."

"Why do they think you switched schools?" Valerie asked quietly.

"I told them about the rich and infamous threesome, and about smoking pot on campus, and being expelled, and being un-expelled, and how four million bucks is the going rate for changing the bylaws."

"They think you left Laurel in a fit of moral outrage over drug use by the offensively rich?"

"Pretty much. Hollywood High has so many different kinds of people. Kids living on their own, barely making it. Lots of immigrants from all over the world. Different customs, different ideas, different everything. When someone does something offbeat, everyone accepts it. It didn't occur to my friends to ask questions."

"Caroline, I don't mean to intrude, but if these are really good friends, sooner or later it's going to come out."

"Over my dead body."

"Okay, it's your choice. I won't say a word."

CHAPTER 21

The Duke graduated from multiplication to grammar, one of Caroline's pet subjects.

"Grammar and math are cousins," she explained. "Both are seeking an equilibrium, one with words, one with numbers."

The Duke liked that idea and wrote a poem about it, which appeared in *The Literary Crimson*, Hollywood High's monthly magazine. When Caroline admitted she'd never written a good poem in her life, he leaped around like a crazed boxer, punching the air. "I'm a smarter poet than The Professor!"

Caroline laughed, deeply unoffended.

Miss Orville invited him to read his poem to the class and when he finished, she led the applause. The students cheered while he bowed, throwing kisses and thanking "my fans. I love you all, every one of you! And I love me, every bit of me!"

He settled down at last and sprinted through transitive verbs. He devoured the rules in ten minutes, ripped through two pages of worksheets and raised his fists in triumph.

Caroline's palms broke with sweat. "Can I ask you something?"

"Sure."

She tried to speak, cleared her throat.

"Girl, what's the matter with you? Spit it out!"

"I don't know how to say this."

"What you mean? I never met anyone with so many words. Go on, make like a dictionary!"

"I've got a problem."

"Someone giving you a hard time. I'll kill him."

"Shh . . ." she whispered, glancing at Miss Orville.

The Duke leaned closer. "Who is he? What grade?"

"He's not in school. He's an adult."

The Duke shot her a puzzled look.

"Duke" — unconsciously dropping the *The* — "this . . . this . . ." Caroline shut her eyes, "this pimp keeps coming after me!"

To her complete shock, The Duke shook with laughter. She glared in haughty outrage, and he laughed harder.

"Tell him you're a Clover from Laurel Academy. That'll scare him off!"

The Duke and Caroline seemed to get through their toughest moments with seizures of hysteria. It was cleansing and exhausting, and when they stopped, she inexplicably felt safer.

"Who is he?" The Duke whispered.

"I don't know his name. Black, wavy hair, really skinny. Weird clothes. The first time I saw him, he was wearing a silver lamé suit."

"It's Drake. He's bad news. He got my cousin to be one of his ladies. Trina. Got her hooked on heroin."

"Can we help her?"

"Nah. She's a lost cause."

But Caroline had grown up in a privileged environment: Problems had solutions. "Listen, my mother can help. She's a psychiatrist. She knows about lots of programs. Your cousin can detox, get therapy, bring in social services."

"It won't work."

"Yes, it will!" Caroline insisted.

"It's too late."

"It's never too late."

"Trina's dead."

Caroline caught her breath.

"She overdosed last summer. Two days after her birthday. Seventeen." The Duke shook off his sadness. "When she died, I beat the shit out of Drake. Broke his arm. He sent a guy after one of my boys. Tom. Knife fight in the library. First week of school. Asshole cut Tom's face. The guy has a long record, and he'll be locked up for a while. Tom got suspended for carrying a knife on school property, but he wasn't arrested. He was cut, so they figured it was self-defense."

Caroline found her voice. "I was there."

The Duke thought a moment. "Right. That was the first time I saw you. Behind your hedge. Looked like you were staying there forever."

"Thought about it."

"Anyway, after he cut Tom, I couldn't let it end there. So I beat Drake up again. Broke his other arm. Now he's terrified of me."

"He says he owns me." Caroline had never before spoken those words and was stunned by the humiliation that saturated every pore.

"Don't let him do that to you. Don't give him that power. You own yourself. But to get him off your case, you got to do what I say."

"I keep thinking about it and I can't figure out how to get him to be reasonable."

"Girl, this isn't about reasonable."

"But ..."

"You're always in your head somefuckingwhere! You can't fix this situation in your head."

"But ..."

"Girl, get out of your head!"

"But ..."

"Listen to me," The Duke's tone turned gentle. "You won't be able to think your way out of this. You'll have to act."

"I don't know how."

"I do."

"I've never been so scared in my life."

"I have."

CHAPTER 22

The lunch break was almost over, and Caroline dashed into the girls' bathroom by the administrative offices. She was about to leave when Toni walked in with the same friend Caroline had seen at Kayla's debut assembly. Toni was striking in a mid-thigh flowered dress, cinched at the waist, and heels that brought her to six feet. Her black hair tumbled down her back, thick and curly. Her friend wore jeans, a t-shirt, athletic shoes. Close up, Caroline still wasn't clear about the friend's gender.

"You look great," Caroline smiled at Toni.

"Thanks. This is Blake, and this is Caroline." Toni introduced her friends.

"Nice to meet you," Caroline lifted her backpack and turned to leave.

"Wait a sec. Do you have a tampon? Blake needs one and amazingly I don't have any." Toni grinned.

Caroline laughed. *Thank you, Toni! Now I know you're trans, Blake knows you're trans, and we each know the other knows. I also know Blake's a girl even though I really can't tell with her very short hair and her lean angular build and her name that doesn't clarify anything. If she has her period, then she's a girl and . . . wait . . . hold on . . . Toni never menstruates and she's a girl. Still, Blake must be a girl, not because she needs a tampon, but because she's choosing the girls' bathroom. Okay, Blake's a girl.*

Caroline emerged from her spinning thoughts and offered a tampon.

"Thanks." Blake disappeared into a stall.

"How you doing?" Toni asked. "Getting used to this school?"

"Yeah, sure. You?"

Toni shrugged and lowered her voice. "Ever since Jeremy got beat up, everyone's nervous. I mean anyone who's gay or trans. Blake's my girlfriend, and they're scared, too."

"Who's they?" Caroline was puzzled.

"Blake. They're my girlfriend. *She* isn't right for Blake. Neither is *he*. Blake's *they*."

Blake emerged from the stall and began to wash their hands. "I heard you talking." They gave Caroline a hard stare. "Most people don't get me. You probably think I'm weird and—"

"I don't think you're weird," Caroline interrupted.

"Yes, you do!"

"No, I don't!"

"She doesn't think you're weird. She doesn't think I'm weird," Toni spoke quietly to Blake. "If anyone's weird, it's Caroline. She's weird because she doesn't think we're weird."

"Then I guess I'm okay being weird," Caroline said.

"You still don't understand," Blake challenged her.

"You're right," Caroline admitted. "I don't know what it means that *she* and *he* don't work for you. I don't know what it means that you prefer *they*. I haven't heard that before. But I'm not judging you, and if you want to explain, I'll listen."

"You think she'll really listen?" Blake asked Toni, who nodded. "Okay. But if she's a douche about it, you have to buy me an ice cream cone after school!"

"Deal," Toni held her grin in check.

Blake turned to Caroline. "*He* and *she* work for most people. Toni's *she*. You're *she*. For some of us, having only two options doesn't cover who we are. Toni's a gay girl. You're a straight girl. For me . . ." Blake trailed off.

Caroline waited. Toni and Blake watched her closely.

"It's hard to explain," Blake continued. "I'm Toni's girlfriend. I'm a girl. But sometimes I feel like a boy and a girl, both at the same time. *They* seems more right for me."

"Okay," Caroline took it in, digesting it slowly. "I can see how that makes sense."

The bell rang.

"C'mon," Toni held the door for her friend and her girlfriend. "Blake and I have History. Our teacher has fits if anyone's tardy. He's kind of uptight."

"Kind of?" Blake raised an eyebrow.

"And boring, the most boring teacher I've ever had. But it's still my favorite class. I love history."

"Toni's a nerd. I love her anyway!" Blake briefly touched their girlfriend's arm.

"People tell me I'm a nerd," Caroline walked into the hallway.

"Shit! I'm surrounded!" Blake laughed. "And I'm mad at you, Caroline! You weren't a douche, so you lost me an ice cream cone!"

"I read history books at home," Toni grinned at Blake. "If you promise not to tell, I'll buy you an ice cream cone, double scoop, bittersweet chocolate and coffee, your favorite flavors."

"Your secret is safe." Blake said to Toni, then turned to Caroline. "Why would anyone read history when they can read fiction?"

"Sorry, Toni. I'm with Blake on that."

"What's your favorite book?" Blake asked Caroline.

"*Fahrenheit 451*. Ray Bradbury. Yours?"

"Same!"

"Seriously?"

"Hell yeah! I wish they taught it in my English class. It would be perfect for papers and discussions, because it's really about people who are afraid of ideas."

"That's why it's my favorite book," Caroline agreed.

"My English teacher is almost as boring as our history teacher, and studying literature should never be boring. They teach it wrong."

"They teach history wrong, too," Toni said. "It's so one-sided that it's totally inaccurate."

"How?" Caroline was curious.

Toni glanced at her wristwatch. "Gotta go to class. Don't want our teacher to have a coronary because we're late." She rushed down the hall with Blake hurrying to keep up.

CHAPTER 23

Caroline jerked awake, sweating, gasping for air, clutching a soft, unidentified handful. In the dim light, she scanned for something to orient herself. Her desk, her chair, her comforter scrunched in her fists. The dream crouched low during the day, ready to pounce at night, leaving her afraid to sleep. She tried hugging an extra pillow, a sheet pulled over her head, her favorite stuffed animal gripped tightly. But the nightmare slithered through the cracks.

The dream always started innocently. Walking down a sidewalk, seeing a blonde woman smooth her hair. Then a blond man. Then blonds everywhere, too many people, crowded and jostling. Caroline reaches to smooth her own blonde hair. She struggles to stay calm as the voices escalate in volume. Eduardo! Doris! Eric! Anna! Christopher! Men and women urgently shouting, as though trying to locate lost children. Then a screech of brakes. Men in blue shirts, louder voices growing angrier. Through this sensory overload, Caroline spots a small blonde girl, alone in the commotion. The child holds a red lollipop. Her grip slackens and the candy hits the ground with a sound more primal than birth and death. Caroline watches the red, translucent slivers break apart and scatter. She shatters as well.

For three restless nights, the dream shredded her sleep, and Caroline knew what had set it off. The previous Friday, walking to the public bus stop after school, Kayla kissed Ray goodbye and joined Caroline.

"I really like Ray, but it's getting ridiculous that we can't see each other outside of school. He still won't introduce me to his family. He refuses to meet my parents. We should be going out on a date tonight and—"

Caroline grabbed Kayla's arm and pulled her into a doorway. "It's him!"

"Who?"

"The boy who was with Drake!"

The Blond strolled down the opposite sidewalk, lost in thought, holding a gigantic red lollipop. He looked absurdly tall, an overgrown kid happily licking his candy. He wore his usual white clothes, tasseled belt, platform shoes, with a bright orange scarf. Ambling, he stepped into the intersection as a car pulled out of its parking space. The Blond jumped back and fleetingly glared at the offending Mustang. Absently he raised his middle finger, shot the driver the bird, and walked on. He didn't see the car skid to a stop or the driver leap out, bright blue shirt stretched with bulging muscles.

The man grabbed The Blond's shoulder and spun him around, chest to chest.

"Who the fuck you flippin' off, asshole! Don't you ever get in my way! Happens again, I'll run you down! Understand, you piece of shit?"

The Blond tried to speak, but his voice failed. His eyes filled with tears. His hands went limp and his lollipop fell and shattered. It was the lollipop that cut into Blue Shirt's anger. Because of The Blond's height, he looked like an adult from the back. Blue Shirt suddenly realized he was facing a boy. He put his arm around The Blond's shoulders and led him back to the sidewalk. He spoke, tough but earnest.

"Kid, do yourself a favor. Never flip off a stranger. You're gonna get yourself killed. I'm a nice guy and I'll let it go this time. But if you ever do that to me again, I'll beat you up so bad your mama won't recognize you."

"I don't have a mama." The Blond, in shock.

"Fine. Your daddy."

"I don't have a daddy."

"Are you an idiot? I didn't ask for your family tree! Do you get what I'm saying?"

The Blond nodded, staring down at his ruined lollipop. Blue Shirt slapped his face gently, trotted to his Mustang, and drove off. Caroline, Kayla, and The Blond stood rooted in place. The girls watched him breathe deeply, smooth his hair, and recover. Finally, he looked carefully to the right, then the left, and walked for the second time into the intersection. He disappeared around a corner.

Caroline and Kayla got off at their bus stop and separated without speaking. Caroline had seen The Blond with his group of friends at school, all boys, all sex workers. She flashed to Drake patting his hand at the House of Pancakes, calling him Honey. Walking up the hill to her house, she began to cry. She wiped a rough hand across her eyes and pushed the front door open. Caroline breathed deeply and sat in her favorite corner chair, with a full view of the living room. The stone floors gleamed a shiny deep maroon. The walls, an unfinished dark wood with huge windows overlooking the valley and distant mountains. The ceiling beams crossed, also deep brown, supporting six skylights. A Steinway concert grand stood majestic in one corner next to a collection of soapstone sculptures and a bright metal Roman vendor's ice cream sign. From two beams hung a sixteenth century Sicilian cart. A Spanish crucifix, Israeli menorah, and two complete sets of the Britannica grouped around the huge brick fireplace. The eccentric balance always calmed Caroline.

The dream began that night.

Now, three nights later, she reached for her bedside lamp. She'd been informally supervised in the workings of the mind since the cradle, as Leah's colleagues debated theories and analyzed dreams over dinner. She knew she felt a kinship with The Blond. She knew the red lollipop represented a splintered childhood. She knew this somehow connected to lost innocence. "But I'm fine," she whispered. "I'm fine," she repeated, weighing the words as her anxiety tightened its grip.

It was youth stolen at emotional gunpoint. Caroline hated the entertainment industry and her parents' aggressive cluelessness about its pitfalls. Still, Leah and Geoff made sure she had a childhood, a home, and a base of security. Sometimes Caroline rested comfortably in their care. Other times, she fought them hard. Sometimes she fought for the sake of fighting. Other times her reasons were solid. Either way, with or without her consent, her mother and father provided a safe harbor, which allowed her an invaluable privilege. Caroline belonged to her own self.

The Blond had no mother, no father. He belonged to Drake, tormenting Caroline with guilt that she had watched while his lollipop splintered, while Blue Shirt knocked him around.

Then came the most frightening realization: There was nothing she could have done. Caroline was powerless to fix The Blond's world. She cried with helplessness and relief. No sense in drowning in guilt over something so far outside her jurisdiction.

She turned out her light, floating warm and sleepy. She pictured her living room, full of character and eccentricity.

Then another image pushed aside the menorah, the Sicilian cart, the ice cream sign. Age nine, at an opening for one of Geoff's films. Breezing into the ladies' room and finding two women leaning over lines of white powder. Caroline recognized the lead actress and the director's young girlfriend. They turned to Caroline and dissolved in hysterics. Caroline knew they were doing drugs, although she didn't know which drugs. She also knew their hysteria was drug induced. So far, nothing she hadn't seen before. But Caroline found herself in new territory when the two women offered her a rolled $100 bill and invited her to "join the party." With a poise developed from years of dealing with the industry, she simply said "No, thanks," and walked out.

On the ride home, she told her parents. Leah and Geoff were outraged.

The next weekend, the actress, her boyfriend, the director, and his young girlfriend sat at Leah and Geoff's dining room table, invited to a "spontaneous, spur-of-the-moment gathering" (Leah). Caroline watched them laughing together, having a lovely evening. Nobody mentioned white powder or $100 bills or hysterics.

A familiar chill crept into Caroline's limbs, lungs, fingertips. She didn't understand why the feeling was invading her at this moment, but she knew how to reverse the process. With a firm discipline, she conjured up the view from the living room of the valley and mountains. She pictured sunlight and moonlight as she looked up through the towering trees surrounding the house. She summoned the sensation from childhood of lying on the stone floor, cool and soothing in the summer's heat.

The next thing she knew, it was morning.

CHAPTER 24

In the living room waiting for Valerie, Caroline stood with Gary, Irene, Vincent, and Kayla. Leah and Geoff had invited another couple to dinner, Gretchen and Janet.

The kids wished Ray could join them, but he remained adamant. Kayla was running out of patience, wondering why Ray didn't have the backbone to stand up to his mother. New to this frontier, she was confused. Was she being too demanding? Was she disrespecting Ray's family? Were her sexual feelings too much, too fast? Did he like her as a friend but wasn't attracted to her?

Mingling with the adults until Valerie arrived, Kayla and Irene devoured the olives, brie, paté, and crackers Leah had set out for her own guests. Gretchen, a professor of linguistics, and Janet, a poet, chatted with Vincent about the personalities of different languages. Gary spoke animatedly to Leah and Geoff about his latest science project, an electronic device to improve hearing aids. Caroline watched the clock, unable to believe that Laurel's most popular Clover would show up. Their phone call had been astonishing, and she assumed that Valerie had regained her senses and was on a date with a rich, handsome, totally cool guy.

At 7:45, they heard the clank of the iron gargoyle knocker, and Caroline hid her relief. She and Valerie hugged automatically, and the six kids trailed back to her room. Valerie radiated raw nerves. She wore designer jeans with a gray silk blouse that mirrored the color of her eyes. Its black stripes matched her hair. As always, her beauty was riveting.

"What's the latest, Valerie?" Caroline tried to set her at ease. "A sculpture or a painting?"

"You're into art?" Vincent leaped on it.

Caroline mentioned a metal sculpture of Valerie's from the annual Laurel Art Show, and everyone listened as Valerie described her work. She relaxed a bit, still much more nervous than a new social situation should warrant.

At Laurel, parties with boys were always for the explicit purpose of finding dates. Perhaps a group of boys and girls, good friends, was new to Valerie. Caroline watched her react to Gary's size. He clearly enjoyed the attention, but both were understated, not openly flirting. Sensing he wasn't going to hit on her, Valerie stopped tossing her hair every few moments.

Caroline glanced at Gary. His shoulders stretched massive. He caught her staring and she blushed. Quickly, she busied herself putting *Abbey Road* on the stereo.

"Do you have every Beatles album?" Kayla asked.

"Yes."

"What else do you have?" Irene glanced at Caroline's record collection.

"Nothing."

"'The Long and Winding Road' is my favorite song," Gary smiled at Caroline.

"The Beatles are great, but don't you think you should move into this decade?" Irene raised an eyebrow.

"Why should I? Everyone else is moving into this decade for me."

The group laughed. Irene shook her head, mildly annoyed.

"Really, Caroline, how can you be so uncool?" Kayla joked.

"I was cool once, for five minutes," Caroline grinned.

"How in the world did it happen?" Vincent asked.

"Elementary school. *Hair* moved from Broadway to Los Angeles, and I was the only kid who could define cunnilingus."

The group dissolved in laughter, even Valerie, although she looked mildly scandalized.

"There was one other time," Caroline still laughing. "I was super cool for about two months, after I was in a movie and everyone thought I'd be an actress. It was like this perfect life unfolded with me in the center, but then—"

A knock on the door. Leah carried a platter heaped with sandwiches in one hand and a gigantic bowl of potato chips in the other. Gretchen lugged a bucket of sodas submerged in ice. Valerie tensed as soon as she saw Gretchen, and Caroline was confused. Her mother had met Gretchen when they were working on their graduate degrees at UCLA. She was bright, funny, hilariously playful with words. She and Janet had lived together as long as Caroline could remember.

The moment they left the room, Valerie turned to Caroline, previous conversation forgotten. "Do you always have people like Gretchen and Janet at your house?"

"My parents know other poets like Janet, but Gretchen's their only friend who's a linguistics professor."

"No, I mean . . ." Valerie blushed.

"She means gay," Irene held her temper in check. "She wants to know if your parents always invite people to your house who are gay."

"My parents have lots of friends. Some are gay, some straight, some—"

"Gretchen and Janet are gay?" Vincent interrupted.

"They're a couple?" Kayla was surprised. "I assumed they were just good friends."

"Good friends who own a home and share a bedroom," Caroline smiled.

"We've never had people like that to our house." Valerie bit her lip. "Gretchen and Janet seem so normal."

"That's because they are," Caroline evenly.

"Nobody at Laurel talks about this stuff. It's like nobody's gay."

"Sure they are," Irene turned flinty. "Y'know, maybe they're choosing not to tell you."

Valerie visibly startled and Irene rolled her eyes.

"Irene, take it easy," Kayla said softly.

"You could have warned us, Caroline." Vincent opened a can of Ginger Ale.

"Warned you about what?"

"You want a warning? Are you kidding?" Gary chopped his hand in an angry arc, squashing his turkey sandwich.

Irene boiled over. "What do you want, Vincent? A billboard with flashing lights, like in Times Square? A sign like when you're driving into a dangerous construction zone? A siren like you hear before an air raid? Red alert! Gay person in the vicinity! Proceed at your own risk!"

Caroline glanced at Valerie, who looked panicked.

"You're being ridiculous!" Vincent glared at Irene. "I mean that Caroline could have . . . if she . . ." he trailed off.

"If she what?" Gary put down his sandwich. "Exactly what kind of a warning do you want? Maybe the same warning Valerie wants about the girls at Laurel who are lesbians!"

Valerie shook her head, close to tears. "It's not like that. I know—"

"I don't think you know anything!" Gary overrode her. "Here's a news flash. My uncle's gay. Think he's a pervert?"

Caroline shifted uneasily. Her party was going down in flames, her friends were splintering, and Valerie was turning out to be a big mistake.

"Don't get mad at me," Valerie almost pleaded.

"Why not?" Gary barreled forward. "You're being a total jerk! Every time Gretchen comes near you, it's like you study her. It's so rude! She's a lesbian! Deal with it!"

"I am dealing with it," Valerie in a tiny voice. "It's just—"

"It's just what?" Gary was furious. "What's your problem? Are you worried Gretchen and Janet can't control themselves in the presence of other females? Do you think you're so irresistibly pretty that every lesbian on the planet will glom onto you like a magnet and you'll never escape? Are you scared that before you know what's happening, Janet and Gretchen will jump on you? Are you worried that if they get too close, you'll catch the virus? Why would you look at Gretchen like that?"

"Because," Valerie blurted, "I'm gay, too!"

Absolute silence among the guests.

"*Bang, bang, Maxwell's silver hammer came down upon her head!*" Paul McCartney sang cluelessly.

Vincent's mouth hung open.

"Wow," Kayla breathed.

Caroline scooted forward and gently kicked Valerie's shoe. "It's okay," she said softly. "It's fine."

Valerie dragged her eyes from the floor, tears on her cheeks.

Sprawled on Caroline's bed, Irene recovered from her surprise. She picked up Claire-Bear, the softest stuffed animal ever, and tossed her to Valerie.

"I'm sorry," Gary said. "I . . ."

"It's okay." Valerie hugged the bear. "I don't blame you."

"Does your family know?" Irene asked.

Valerie shook her head.

"What about The Platinum Ring?" Caroline spoke without thinking, then clapped a hand over her mouth. She'd told the others about the coveted Laurel clique, and they stared mortified.

"The what? Who . . . wait a sec . . ." Valerie's eyes widened, and she started to laugh. "That's perfect!"

The group dissolved in hysterics.

Finally composed, Valerie turned to Caroline. "What would your parents say if they knew one of your friends was gay?"

"Pop quiz," Caroline shot back. "Who's sitting in the living room?"

"You're really gay?" Vincent taking it in. "You're serious?"

"Ignore him," Irene ordered. "He's a card-carrying bonehead!"

"Irene, back down," Kayla met Vincent's eyes.

"I . . ." Everyone looked at Vincent, who turned to Valerie. "You seem nice. I just need a minute to get used to the idea."

"You've got to be kidding!" Irene punched the bed.

"It's okay," Valerie cut into Irene's frustration. "I need to get used to it, too."

"Do you . . . never mind, not my business," Kayla stopped herself.

"What do you want to know?" Valerie asked her.

"Do you have a girlfriend?"

Valerie hesitated. "I need a drink."

Caroline handed her an ice cold can of 7-Up as Gary took a gigantic bite of his dented sandwich.

"Okay, Valerie," Irene grinned, "tell us about her."

"I . . . well . . ." Valerie faltered.

"You don't have to talk about it," said Caroline, the polite hostess.

"I've wanted to tell someone for a long time," Valerie's black hair shimmered. "It's weird, finally saying it."

The past three Augusts, her family summered on the Riviera. They became close to a family from Manhattan with a daughter Valerie's age, Celia Compston. The girls were immediately inseparable.

"Was she at your birthday party?" Caroline pictured the table of debutantes, the flawlessly poised girl with styled brown hair who traveled on her family's private jet.

Valerie nodded. "Mr. and Mrs. Compston move mountains to support the friendship. They think it's the social coup of the century." She ran her fingers through her hair. "They have no idea—"

"You met Valerie's girlfriend?" Vincent interrupted, turning to Caroline. "What does she look like?"

"Very pretty—"

"A lovely girl," Irene talked over Caroline. "Exceptionally engaging and attractive, especially when she was bench pressing meat lockers. Her favorite food is chocolate-covered thumbtacks. It's so sweet that she gave Valerie a tractor for her birthday and—"

"That's enough!" Kayla faced Irene. "You have to give Vincent a chance! This is a new idea for him, for me, and I guess for Valerie, too. He's asking the questions lots of people are afraid to ask. We're his friends. He should be able to turn to us. If he gets his answers and he's still holding on to his stereotypes, then you can call him an asshole. But you have to give him a chance!"

An awkward moment.

Then Gary shook his head. "Did Kayla say the word *asshole*?"

"It must be bizarre at school," Caroline thought out loud, turning to Valerie. "I mean, everyone sees you in a certain way, like you're some kind of icon. Even the older girls look up to you. They wouldn't know how to fit *gay* into that picture."

"It's strange," Valerie nodded. "Sometimes I write to Celia to remind myself who I am." But the widening gap between who Valerie was and how she presented herself, along with Laurel's mandatory boy crazy stance, wore her down. "Your friends," Valerie nodded at Caroline, "Vicki, Maren, and Tory. They're not so caught up in the popularity race. They're not so obsessed with boys. But my cool crowd, they're maniacs."

"I didn't realize there was so much pressure at Laurel to act like having a cute boyfriend is the ultimate goal in life," Irene said. "I thought the point was to empower the girls to be more than someone's girlfriend."

"Apparently most of the Clovers missed that memo," Valerie's lips twitched.

"Hormones are hormones, wherever you go to school." Caroline turned to Valerie. "In my first few weeks at Hollywood High, a girl got beaten up for having sex with another girl's boyfriend."

"I can't imagine the Clovers beating each other up, even over a guy with a yacht," Valerie smirked. "Bronwyn's always setting me up with a new boy, each more social register than the last. If I have to listen to one more discourse on polo ponies, I swear I'll buy a new pair of proper white gloves and commit my first strangulation. Then there's Katie, the definition of a bottom feeder. Nicole is a porcelain doll, looks perfect, hollow inside. Trisha belongs in a wax museum. Angela carries an emergency supply of epinephrine, in case of accidental exposure to an original thought. And I'm the leader of the pack. If they only knew."

The group laughed except for Vincent, who stared at Valerie.

"Am I making you uncomfortable?" she asked quietly.

"No . . . it's . . . I've never met someone who was gay."

"Congratulations. Now you've met a gay person. Your life is complete." Irene sarcastically.

"Wait, hold on," Valerie to Irene. "If there's something Vincent wants to know . . ."

Vincent hesitated. "I have questions, but I don't want you to think I'm a shithead."

"I'm okay with questions," Valerie outwardly calm. "If you're asking because you're honestly trying to understand, that's a good thing."

"Okay," Vincent took a deep breath. "I guess I'm surprised because you don't look like a lesbian."

"What do you think lesbians look like?" Irene exploded. "Sumo wrestlers? Built like a steamer trunk? Favorite outfit is combat gear? Rocks for brains—"

"Let him ask his questions!" Valerie with surprising authority.

Irene shut her mouth with extreme difficulty.

Valerie took a moment to think. She knew what she wanted to say. How to say it was the challenge. "People have a lot of stereotypes about lesbians and how they look. I know I don't match the stereotype. The stereotypes for most groups of people are usually wrong. There are lots of ways to look, different features, different body types, different styles of dress. Because of their personal likes and dislikes, some are closer to the stereotype than others." Valerie waited and Vincent nodded. "It might be better to think of it another way. I look like me. And I'm a lesbian." "Okay," Vincent nodded again. "Can I ask another question?"

"Sure."

"How did you decide to be gay?"

"Hang on, Irene," Kayla said as Irene turned an alarming shade of vermillion.

They all turned to Valerie, curious how she'd answer.

"I decided to be gay the same way you decided to be straight."

"I didn't decide," Vincent said. "It's just how I am."

"Exactly."

"Oh! Okay. That makes sense. I . . ." Vincent searched for the right words. "I've never had a gay friend before. You're not what I expected."

"I'm not what I expected, either."

"I . . ." Vincent looked down, then met Valerie's eyes. "I can see why Caroline thought you'd fit in with us. If the whole gay thing hadn't come up, nobody would have felt weird."

"Speak for yourself!" Irene jumped in. "I don't feel weird about this!"

"Same with me," Caroline and Gary almost in unison.

"Does it have to be weird?" Valerie asked Vincent. He hesitated to answer, so she continued. "You and I both love art."

He nodded.

"I can't wait to go to college, knock the distribution requirements out of the way and major in art, because that's what I want to do for the rest of my life."

Vincent smiled.

"We're both attracted to girls, not boys, because that's who we are and—"

"And that's where it gets weird," Vincent stepped in.

"That's my point," Valerie said. "Does it have to get weird? We have a lot in common. You have to decide how much our differences matter to you. You have to decide how weird this has to be. You have to decide."

Valerie tried not to hold her breath. Her expression was calm, her posture relaxed. Inside, invisible to the rest, her entire body clenched.

Vincent took a long moment. "I think maybe the differences don't matter to me."

A pause, then Irene jumped to her feet. "Good! Problem solved! Vincent has decided to end his career as a steaming bag of douche! Throw me the stuffed animal!"

Valerie tossed Claire-Bear to Irene, who shot her across at Caroline.

"Hike!" Gary was ready for a scrimmage.

Vincent lunged as Gary lobbed the bear to Kayla. She sprinted down the hall with the rest charging after her. Finally, they collapsed in the living room.

Geoff carried from the kitchen a gargantuan pitcher of lemonade. Leah and Gretchen followed with trays of food, leftovers from dinner. Salad, scalloped potatoes, asparagus, sliced filet mignon, assorted cookies, and chocolate truffles. Kayla and Irene immediately began to devour everything except the green vegetables.

Claire-Bear rested in Caroline's arms after her busy evening.

Talk turned to sports. Geoff, a college running back, told the kids his favorite Harvard football story. Playing against Cornell on a frozen field in upstate New York, Harvard's quarterback lay flat on his back at the thirty yard line, kicked unconscious by a horrified cheerleader.

Irene pulled Marx and Engels' *The Communist Manifesto* from a bookshelf and ordered everyone to place a hand on the document. Swearing the crew to secrecy, she divulged Hollywood's classified basketball catastrophe. Last year, the regional finals. Hollywood was ahead by one point when a teammate, dizzy with pumping adrenaline, broke from the pack and scored a basket as the buzzer sounded — a basket for the wrong team. Mrs. Cuthbertson wore a plain white tutu for two weeks before she reverted to her usual pink sparkles.

Caroline sidled over to Valerie. "You okay?"

"I'm good. You?"

"I'm fine. I'm glad you came."

"Me too."

"I'm glad Gretchen and Janet came," Caroline said. "Otherwise you'd never—"

Valerie nodded.

It was 11:15 and everyone had a midnight curfew. People gathered coats and thanked Leah and Geoff.

"I . . . um . . ." Vincent cleared his throat and turned to Valerie. "Next week's at my house. Want to come?"

The kids stopped short. Caroline had never seen her friend smile like that.

"Thank you," Valerie said to Vincent, then to Caroline, a resonance implying worlds unspoken.

Wordlessly, Irene brushed past Caroline and went to Vincent. She took his shoulders, then hugged him tightly. Gary wrapped his gigantic arms around them both, lifting them off the ground.

The adults watched closely, knowing to keep their mouths shut.

As Caroline lay in bed, her parents came in to say good night. They asked how the evening went. Caroline yawned sleepily and they let it go. She was too tired to go into it and she slept easy, no nightmares, to honor Valerie's courage.

CHAPTER 25

Caroline's morning bus usually arrived at school fifteen minutes before the first bell. While she waited for her friends to arrive, she walked alone in slow circles around the perimeter of the quad. She didn't mind being by herself as she mentally prepared for whatever fireworks Hollywood High might bring.

"Hey, Caroline!"

She turned. Toni and Blake were a few steps behind her.

"How you doing?" Caroline smiled.

"Okay," Blake shrugged.

"What's wrong?"

"Jeremy." Toni tersely.

"Did something happen? Was someone else hurt?" Caroline asked.

"Not yet," Blake grimly, "but someone else is going to get hurt. It's only a matter of time and it could be me or Toni. They've beaten up gay students before and they'll keep doing it. Trans students, too. And people like me. This time with Jeremy, it was worse than it's ever been. He had to spend a night in the hospital under observation for internal bleeding and a brain injury. He'll recover, no permanent damage, but he just got lucky." Blake heard their own words and grimaced. "Lucky. Yeah, right."

Toni nodded. "People give me and Blake shit all the time. The locker rooms and the bathrooms are the worst. I'm always afraid the wrong person will figure out who I am. If that happens, I'll get beaten up. They broke Jeremy's bones, gave him a concussion. These assholes get so amped up, it's like they stop being human and turn into animals, tearing up their prey."

"You can take a day or two at home if you need a break." Blake touched Toni's arm for a quick second. "I'll call in sick, too. We can hang out at my house while my parents are at work."

"No way!" Toni's eyes flashed. "I'm showing up every day! I won't let them stop me! My parents didn't go to college. They had to work, help support their families. I'm going to graduate from Hollywood High. I'm going to college, and I'm going to major in history. I'm going to get a job teaching history, and I'm going to teach it right!"

Caroline stared at her friend. *Wow . . . she's . . . wow.* "How do they teach history wrong?"

"They teach it like the only people who matter are straight white men. There are no women in the history books. Nobody's trans, or a lesbian, or gay, or bi, or like Blake. Nothing about how Black and brown and gold people built this country. Nothing about the way everything is set up for all people NOT to be created equal. The inequality is woven into our self-evident truths, and people don't even realize. History teachers should tell the truth."

"You're right," Caroline quietly. "You need to go to college and teach history."

"My girlfriend is a badass!" Blake grinned.

"I'm glad you're not letting them stop you from going to school," Caroline said. "And I like your earrings." Deep green beads threaded through dangly steel, bright and silvery against Toni's dark brown skin.

Toni smiled. "Blake made the earrings in their jewelry class."

"Reading and art. My favorite subjects and—" Blake's words were drowned out as the bell blared.

The three friends separated.

From that day, Caroline met Toni and Blake every morning before classes began, and the girls walked in circles around the quad, together.

CHAPTER 26

As a young nerd hitting her stride, Caroline never expected the girls' basketball team would become a profound influence on her Hollywood High experience. She was by far the worst player and was surprised that her teammates were unfailingly kind. She looked forward to their practices, unbothered by her sub-par athleticism, a liberating contrast to her drive to achieve in academics.

Two weeks into the season, a new girl joined the team. At practice that afternoon, she approached Caroline, introduced herself, and helpfully explained the meaning of a "zone defense." She missed the next three practices and was kicked off the team. When Caroline ran into her in the hall between classes, she said she had taken a job after school. Her family needed money for food. Caroline remembered her P.E. teacher saying the team was looking for players. Now she understood why.

Some of the team's behavior was startling to a prep school escapee. They cursed with impressive fluency, percussive and unprintable in several languages, brazenly uninhibited in front of Mrs. Cuthbertson. They crashed into each other as they scrimmaged and pounded forward with no apology. Caroline obediently did the drills, barely speaking, watching and listening. Her teammates were hilariously unholy and the adolescent in her, hidden under layers of mannerly convention and astronomic grades, began to shake off the shackles.

Through the first few weeks, Caroline tiptoed through their scrimmages. Then at the beginning of week three, one of the outstanding athletes knocked into her. After the girl scored a basket, she came straight back, hand raised for a high five as she mouthed, "Sorry." In that moment, Caroline realized her teammates understood their physicality was new to her. She also realized that in spite of her fair skin, blonde hair, and polished exterior, she was much tougher than she looked.

Caroline often spent entire games on the bench. She understood that the girls valued her presence because without her, they wouldn't have enough members to qualify as a team. They'd lose their practice time on the court and their funding for busses to games at other schools. Caroline didn't mind being needed for the team's survival. Still, she couldn't help feeling like an outsider.

The game against Palm Tree High, a school known for its violence, changed Caroline's relationship to the team. Hollywood won by one point, and the Palm Tree girls were livid. Their coach took Mrs. Cuthbertson aside and warned her not to walk to their bus until a police escort arrived. The team banded together, ready for a brawl, each girl picking her target.

"Who wants the tall asshole with the ugly hair?" Shawna whispered.

"I got her," Lureen bared her teeth. "She looks like a coward! And shit, her hair! I'll do her a favor and rip it out!"

"I'll take the redhead holding the basketball." Shawna punched one hand into the other with a fierce clap. "Total coward!"

Caroline began to shake uncontrollably. She wanted the team's acceptance so much she could taste it, but she had never thrown a punch in her life. She looked at her hands and wondered if she could use her fists as weapons. She clenched her right hand into a tight fist and looked at the enemy team. She picked out a girl who had played a ferocious game and imagined punching her in the face, her soft tissue crushing, her cheekbones cracking. In that instant, Caroline knew that she couldn't fight, and she broke into a full body sweat. She was about to let down her teammates in their moment of crisis, no doubt while suffering a terrible injury at best and an excruciating death at worst. She was a coward.

Lureen and Shawna glanced at Caroline standing slightly apart from the group. The two athletes shared a knowing grin and Lureen strutted over.

"Hey girl, we got your back!"

Caroline stared, uncomprehending.

"We get it. You're not used to this sort of thing." Lureen hit her shoulder lightly. "It's okay. Take some deep breaths. Don't pass out. Don't barf. We'll be a human shield. We got your back!"

Lureen turned to the other girls. "Who wants to take the skinny idiot with the stupid braid?"

"She fouled out in the first half. Spent the game screaming from the bench." Shawna rolled her eyes. "She's harmless!"

"I got her," their center spoke up. "Squash her like a bug! She's a coward! It—"

Both teams shut their mouths as the door to the gym burst open and a police officer strode onto the court. With no hesitation, he motioned Hollywood's team to walk ahead of him and escorted them outside. No violence broke out.

"Thank you," Caroline murmured as she reached the bus.

The officer tipped his cap.

Mrs. Cuthbertson smiled at the girl. "It's nice that you're so polite, even under stress."

"I don't mean to be," Caroline answered.

The team swaggered onboard, radiating a macho high. Caroline and Irene shared a seat, and the commentary began instantly.

"We kicked their butts!"

Caroline glanced at Irene, who stifled a grin.

"Those girls were too scared to throw a punch!"

"Did you see the redhead's face? Poor baby! She was ready to cry!"

I was ready to cry. I was scared. Me, not them, just me. Suddenly Caroline caught her breath.

"What?" Irene quietly.

Caroline shook her head as a flash of clarity hit. *They were scared! All of them! Every girl! I'm not the only one!*

They pulled out of the parking lot and to her teammates' surprise, Caroline spoke loudly enough to reach the entire bus.

"Hey, thanks. I wouldn't have known what to do. I would have been killed!"

The girls burst into laughter.

"What happened when the kids fought at your last school?" Lureen asked from the front of the bus.

"There were no fights."

"The boys never fought?" A point guard sitting across the aisle from Caroline and Irene.

"No boys. Only girls."

A thud of silence.

"No boys? That sucks! What'd you do when you needed to get laid between classes?" Shawna yelled.

Raucous laughter.

"Ask Caroline about their uniforms," Irene called out.

"White button-down shirt, gray skirt, white knee socks, penny loafers, gold cotton cardigan sweater."

"I'm going to puke!" Their center, from the back of the bus.

A storm of laughter, gagging motions, barfing noises.

"Did you ever visit them? See their houses?" Lureen was curious.

"Some of the girls lived on acres of land with swimming pools and tennis courts. Mansions filled with furniture covered in plastic. They made guests take off their shoes because the rugs were worth a fortune."

An exchange of incredulous glances. Then Lureen shook her head. "That's no fun."

"That's no home," Shawna added. "That's a museum."

"Why'd you leave?" The point guard.

"I felt like the walls were closing in on me. And I was terrified I'd spill a soda on the priceless rugs."

More howling. Irene gave Caroline a high five.

"Do you ever wish you could go back?" Lureen asked.

Of course I wish I could go back! A few minutes ago, we dodged a melée and barely escaped with our limbs intact!

Caroline glanced around the bus. Young faces, different shades of brown, gold, pink. Hair long, short and one shaved head. Mrs. Cuthbertson lounged in the tutu she wore to every practice and game. All eyes were on Caroline, waiting to hear what she'd say. She began to formulate a polite response to hide her urge to charge back to Cloverville. She opened her mouth and her words caught in her throat. She turned still.

I don't want to go back. I like it here. I never liked Laurel. I never fit in there. Hollywood High is my school.

"Do you miss it?" Lureen again.

"I'm okay at Hollywood High."

The girls were moved, bonded. The moment lasted two seconds. Then Shawna began singing at the top of her lungs, a song of her own creation, about a series of X-rated acts by "Blow Job Jillian" and "Bang Bang Boris." The team shouted approval, tossed in their own verses, hormone driven improv.

Caroline grinned. She knew that her teammates thought she was beaming her approval of their raunchy lyrics. But they were wrong. She smiled because something deep within her stirred and reached for the light. A quiet confidence, a core validation. She felt protected. She belonged.

That night, 1:30AM, Caroline sat bolt upright. Blonds. Lollipops. Blue shirts. Eduardo, Doris, Eric, Anna, Christopher.

She lay down, rolled over, and was falling back to sleep when a fuzzy question floated across her vision like a scripted dream. *Who protects The Blond? Where does he belong?*

CHAPTER 27

"Dad, it's me."

"What's wrong?"

"I'm fine. It's Kayla. Can you pick us up from school? Her parents aren't home."

"Ten minutes."

Caroline could picture her father grabbing his keys and sprinting for the car.

The problem had begun that morning, but Caroline didn't put the pieces together. She first heard about it on the radio, driving to school with her father. It was a stormy December day, so she accepted her father's offer to give her a ride. The rain pelted and the radio crackled, reception fighting through the erratic winds. They strained to sift words through the static. An enormous drug bust at Beverly Hills High School. Undercover narcotics agents had posed as students and infiltrated the gilded and the glamorous. The Beverly Hills kids had money to burn and could afford heavy drugs. The previous day, a truckload of students had been arrested. Several well-dressed dealers sweated in the district's police station before their parents stormed in, outraged at the "false accusations," and effortlessly wrote checks to cover bail.

Caroline wondered about Hollywood High. Not enough disposable income for a real shakedown. But…she tried to squelch the thought…Ray.

As the hours passed uneventfully, she relaxed. Then, in American History, their last class of the day, Kayla received the nausea-green hall pass that meant a summons from their principal. The two friends smiled. Kayla had auditioned for a community workshop for artists during the holiday break, sponsored by the school district. She had run into Elvia, who was applying to the poetry workshop. Kayla arrived in time to see Elvia storm out when the judges insisted that her application list Andrea Krause as her legal name. Official word for Kayla would arrive in the next few days through the principal. This had to be it.

"Bye, I'll miss you," Kurt blew a kiss as Kayla left the room.

Presto shook his head. "Dude, take up surfing. You need a hobby."

"He needs more than a hobby," Elvia shot a disgusted look at Kurt. "He needs a brain transplant!"

Caroline vaguely heard the teacher drone on about colonial America. Her thoughts wandered back to her history class at Laurel. The battle campaigns they diagrammed to win the Revolutionary War, the diaries of indentured servants they composed, the world maps they created based on views of geography in the 1400s. She adored her history teacher at Laurel, known for his riveting lectures and wacky sense of humor. Caroline stifled a smile, remembering their final seventh grade assignment, a term paper tracing the history of any essential piece of American culture …and the resulting furor when Lelia turned in (complete with several glossy photos) a meticulous chronicle of American pornography.

Suddenly, Caroline was wide awake, listening to every word. At Hollywood High and at Laurel Academy, history was taught the same way. Straight white men filled the pages of their textbooks. Nobody else mattered. The dominance of male over every other gender, the oppression of white over every other color, the assumption that all people are created straight.

Toni's right. It's messed up here, and it was messed up at Laurel. It's taught wrong everywhere, and I never realized. Maybe Toni gets it because she's Black and gay and trans.

The Duke's words from their second meeting circled back to Caroline. *"You talk fancy, but you're not snotty, even though you're white."* At the time, she was insulted. Now she began to wonder if he had a valid point. *How much do I miss because I'm white? Do I miss more because I'm straight?*

The bell blared. Kayla hadn't returned from her summons, so Caroline shouldered her backpack and headed for the administrative offices. She spotted her friend and hurried over, anticipating the good news.

"Hey, how'd it go . . . what's wrong?"

Kayla's expression was glazed with shock. Caroline grabbed her shoulders and Kayla melted into her arms. Final-bell-dismissal-mania swirled around them. Kayla stood dazed, Caroline's shoulder sticky from her tears.

Mrs. Richardson spotted the girls through her open door and wrapped her arms around Kayla. "Come into my office."

Caroline followed, frightened.

"How about if I call your parents to give you a ride home?" Mrs. Richardson asked, her hand on Kayla's shoulder.

"They're at work until five," Kayla sobbed.

"I'll skip basketball practice. My father's working at home today, thinking about a new project. I'll call him."

Mrs. Richardson offered Caroline the phone on her desk. As she hung up, Kayla held out a folded piece of paper.

Dear Kayla,

I'm sorry it has to end this way. You're a beautiful girl, inside and out. I'll always remember our time together. Now, I have to go.

Ray

"The drug bust?" Caroline asked, and Mrs. Richardson nodded. "How many arrested?"

"A few." Their guidance counselor shrugged angrily. "There's not much here for this kind of haul. Waste of police resources."

"He wrote it just before the police car left," Kayla wept.

"I hope he gets help," Caroline shook her head. "He's a good guy with a bad problem."

Mrs. Richardson and Kayla exchanged glances. Kayla hoisted her backpack. "Let's go meet your dad. I'll explain the rest."

The girls hit Sunset Boulevard as the Aston Martin pulled up. Geoff opened the door for Kayla, gently helping her into the backseat. He knew not to ask.

"We'll go to our place," he soothed her. "Your parents can pick you up later." He turned on the radio and The Eagles' "Desperado" filled the car.

As soon as they arrived at the house, Kayla headed for the powder room. Geoff grabbed two root beer cans, a few apples, a block of cheddar, and a box of crackers. As he brought the snack to Caroline's room, he raised an eyebrow.

"Later," she whispered.

The girls barricaded themselves. Kayla burst into tears again and filled in the missing pieces. Nobody saw it coming. The administration learned of it only that morning. The principal was speaking to the faculty this minute.

Kayla's worried mother arrived a few hours later and hugged her daughter protectively. As the front door closed behind them, Caroline turned to her father.

"Ray's gone."

"The drug bust?" he asked, and she nodded. "Shit! What'd they get him for?"

"No, you've got it backwards."

"Fuck! Screw! Crap!"

Thoroughly out of context, it dawned on Caroline why The Duke's language never rattled her.

"Dad . . ."

"Drug users. They lie. They cheat. Anything for a fix."

"He lied, but . . ."

"I hate to see how he hurt that terrific girl."

"He hurt her but . . ."

"Can his family make bail?"

"No!" Caroline cried out. "You don't understand! He's not in jail!"

Geoff stopped, chilled as his daughter's words caught up with him. He suddenly knew what was coming. He shook his head almost in wonder. "I'll be damned."

"I can't believe this is happening to Kayla."

"Are you sure?"

She nodded, struggling to assimilate it.

"So there's no doubt . . ." Geoff trailed off.

"His name's not Ray. Phone's disconnected. Address unknown. His mother and grandmother don't exist." Caroline shut her eyes, forcing herself to accept the truth. "He's an undercover narc."

CHAPTER 28

Caroline returned to the International House of Pancakes for the second and final time in her career at Hollywood High. She nervously clutched The Duke's arm, as he instructed. He strutted, tall and arrogant, glancing down like he owned her. Jay and Tom followed, pit bulls primed for battle.

Toward the back, Drake sat in deep conversation with a second thug. Mr. Number Two was shorter, more muscular, still too thin. Hair greased, gold cross in his left ear, gaudy gold chain and — Caroline blinked — a chest toupee. The Duke also noticed the man's over-endowed chest, and his eyes met Caroline's. They pushed it down hard. No time for one of their hysterical fits.

Then Drake saw them, and a look of pure panic crossed his face. The kids marched smack up to his table. The Duke stared stonily.

They'd practiced for this moment during several lunch breaks. The Duke was a typecast, but Caroline wasn't. She was having so much trouble playing her role that Irene announced she was "the most sorry-ass actress in the known universe." They were ready to give up when The Duke's favorite girlfriend Doraine stepped in. She taught Caroline to swing her nonexistent hips, to simper, to look up at The Duke with a mixture of fear and adoration.

"It's just acting, pretending to be a different person." Doraine's sandal dipped into a small pothole and she reached down to dislodge a pebble. "Didn't you dream about being an actress when you were little?"

"Yeah, sure. I was in a film and for a few months everything was perf— I mean no, absolutely not, no way! I live in that world, my dad's a cinematographer, and I wouldn't want to act for anything! It's insane! You have to be rail thin on screen, but everyone photographs at least ten pounds heavier, so you're supposed to starve, and people act like beauty is the holy grail, and if you're not in the club they treat you like you're worth nothing, and I never was in the club and I don't care, I don't care at all, but actually I was in the club for a while, and—"

"Whoa, girl, say what?" The Duke cut in and Caroline froze.

The entire group stared.

Doraine began to laugh. "You're talking crazy. Watch and learn."

Caroline blushed. *Don't speak, hold still, get in control.*

"Oh, no!" The group turned to Kayla, who gestured to her left. Kurt stood to the side gazing at her. "Why's he still here? He's always talking about selling drugs. Remember when he was giving everyone joints and telling them to vote for him in the election for class president? Why isn't he locked up after the drug bust?"

"You haven't heard?" Irene grinned. "He was the first student in handcuffs. They brought him to the police station, searched him, emptied his backpack. They confiscated five candy bars and a pack of gum. Then they questioned him. Turns out the joints he handed out were tobacco. The arresting officer gave him a stern talk about lung cancer and sent him home."

"That's pathetic!" Kayla shook her head. "He can't even get arrested without screwing it up!"

The Duke and Doraine modeled how to hang on his arm as though Caroline needed his touch to feel complete. They taught her to squint mean and tough. Doraine warned her that in the showdown with Drake, if the point needed highlighting, The Duke might toss an order her way, snap his fingers, and Caroline's job was to obey.

"Hey, Professor, gotta act stupid," Doraine punched Caroline's arm sympathetically. "Save the smarts for college."

Doraine was so fiercely committed that Caroline was puzzled until she explained. Drake had approached her and she "hated his sorry guts." When she declined his offer of employment, he hassled her for a solid year. "Watch his face, Professor. He'll get scared and it'll be fun."

In bits and pieces, Caroline allowed herself to be swept away. She began to enjoy herself, which appalled her. At unexpected moments, she felt ambushed by longing for the Laurel days of privileged predictability. Sometimes her thoughts would jump from a trig lesson to the approaching confrontation with Drake, and she'd be dizzy with fear and loneliness. Her Clover friends — Vicki, Maren, and Tory — extremely openminded by Laurel's Spode china and finger bowl standards, would find this situation incomprehensible.

Even now, as Caroline followed The Duke's battle plan, she didn't fully get it, caught in a Clover mindset. "Why can't I tell him I'm not interested?"

Her friends burst out laughing.

"What are you going to say?" Kayla hugged her friend's shoulders. "Thank you kindly, Mr. Drake, but I'm too busy translating Virgil to turn tricks."

"Yeah, I guess I'd say something like that."

"You've got to get into his head," Irene explained with uncharacteristic patience. "In Drake's mind, you're his property. He doesn't understand why you're not cooperating. He won't back down unless he has no choice."

Caroline swallowed dryly.

Doraine patted her arm. "It'll be okay. The Duke's gonna scare the shit out of him!"

As Caroline embarked on the climactic scene of her acting career, she noted that Drake indeed looked scared and, for a fleeting moment, it was fun. Then The Duke hit Drake with a bullet stare, Drake's buddy shifted in his seat, and Jay immediately put his hand inside his jacket. Tom, next to Jay, turned his head, flaunting his scar from the library knife fight. He ran a finger down his cheek, the length of the scar, then shook his head slightly at Drake's buddy. Mr. Chest Toupee returned to his original position. The Duke's eyes never left Drake.

Doraine had warned Caroline there would be some posturing. Advance notice duly noted, this drama had barely begun, and she was nearing a heart attack.

Apparently, she wasn't alone. Drake broke the silence. "What you come here for? What you want?"

Even to Caroline's untrained ear, he sounded pathetic.

The Duke continued to stare, granite in his fury. Drake's nervousness overtook him again and he started to rise. Tom and Jay both shifted, reaching under their jackets. Drake dropped back in his seat and The Duke spoke dangerously low.

"My girl here tells me you've got your eye on her."

This was Caroline's cue. She squinted balefully at Drake.

Silver Lamé began to sweat through his purple satin jacket. "I'm sorry. I'm so sorry." Lines of perspiration ran down the pimp's face. "I didn't know she was yours."

The Duke continued as though he hadn't heard. "She tells me you pointed at her and said '*That one's mine.*'"

"I'm sorry. I didn't know. I didn't know she was yours. I'm so sorry."

"Shut up!" The Duke commanded. "Apologize to my lady! You showed her disrespect. Apologize!"

Caroline looked up. This was a gift from The Duke, not a part of the script. She began to feel moved, then she remembered the character she was playing. She simpered, then eyes back on the enemy.

Although taken aback, Drake obeyed. "Honey, I apologize, I . . ."

"What you call her?" The Duke growled.

"I'm sorry. I'm so sorr—"

"You call her Professor."

Desperately baffled, Silver Lamé tried again. "I'm sorry, Professor."

Without another word, The Duke turned and Caroline followed. She knew to keep her mouth shut, not to accept his apology. Then The Duke pivoted, pointing at a target between Drake's eyes.

"Don't go near The Professor!"

They strutted out, flanked by Tom and Jay. Caroline remembered Doraine's instructions. *Don't look back. Don't break stride until you're out of sight.* They stalked across the street, over the lawn where Drake first found Caroline and safely into the quad. Surrounded by buildings, they shrieked, hugging each other, giddy and triumphant. Caroline's friends waited with the rest of The Duke's gang. Doraine and Caroline ran into each other's arms. Irene and Gary piled on in a bear hug. Tom and Jay brayed in victory. Kayla and Vincent jumped with excitement. The Duke repeated every word, imitating Drake, and they howled their celebration.

From around the quad, students watched in astonishment. In one corner, Elvia and Sharon exchanged an incredulous glance.

"Are they friends?" Sharon stared.

"Of course not!" Elvia snorted. "That would be ridiculous!"

Toni and Blake burst into giggles.

Presto muttered, "What the hell?" and Dreads answered, "No idea."

Carlos and his boyfriend blinked hard. "Does she know about The Duke, who he is, what he does?" the boyfriend wondered.

Carlos shrugged. "She's nice, but kind of clueless. One time, I saw her at a table with her friends at the International House of Pancakes."

His boyfriend grinned.

Two girls from from the basketball team walked by. "The Duke and Caroline?" their center gaped.

"No way! She'd never . . ." their point guard trailed off as Caroline disentangled herself from Irene and Gary, and moved into The Duke's arms.

Caroline's teammates dissolved in laughter.

The Duke was always aware of eyes following him and played to his audience. Caroline, entirely unaware, would have been mortified. The rest didn't care one whit.

In the midst of the pandemonium, Caroline turned to Doraine. She stood stunning, with her slim legs that wouldn't quit. Caroline noticed she'd put on a few pounds since September, but she remained graceful as a fawn.

"Hey, Doraine," Caroline spoke softly. "Thanks."

"This is cool," Doraine smiled. "I taught The Professor."

"More than you'll ever know." Their eyes held for an instant before The Duke leaped over.

"Thanks so much," Caroline said to him.

"My lady," he joked, bowing before her.

"The Duke only likes beautiful girls," Doraine punched his arm. "What's wrong?" she asked, as Caroline tensed.

"She doesn't like being told she's pretty." The Duke shrugged.

"Huh?" Doraine shook her head.

"Caroline's weird," Irene grinned. "That's old news."

"You did great," The Duke said to her. "You did what you had to do. Now you can go back to being a nerd."

But Caroline knew that one more girl had to be acknowledged, someone she'd never be able to thank in person. She had no idea how to approach this territory, and her etiquette training was useless. Then The Duke gave her an opening. Gary passed out Cokes to celebrate, and The Duke raised his can of soda.

"To all of us," he toasted.

"To your cousin," Caroline said clearly.

Everyone turned, shocked silent. She held The Duke's eyes. In slow motion, he touched his Coke to hers.

"To Trina," his voice steady and strong.

"To Trina," eleven young voices echoed, raised in solidarity for a girl lost before her time.

They sipped carefully and for Caroline, the taste of Coke became the taste of Trina's memory.

CHAPTER 29

Hammering at the front door.

Caroline fumbled for the clock. Midnight.

The gargoyle knocker banged urgently. Then soft padding, Leah's slippers hurrying through the house.

"Wait!" Geoff called out. "Don't open the door until I get there!"

"I can hear someone crying," Leah said.

Buttoning her bathrobe, Caroline stumbled down the hallway. She blinked at the living room lights as her father threw the bolt and barely caught Valerie as she hurtled herself into Caroline's arms.

A few hours before, Valerie had gathered her courage. Once she came out at Caroline's Saturday gathering, she couldn't turn back. Supported by her new friends, tormented by the shame of secrecy, she told her mother and older brother Lincoln that she was gay.

A heavy silence followed.

Lincoln stared, wordless.

Her mother's eyes filled with tears. "How can you do this to me?"

"Mom, I'm not doing this to you. It's about me."

"First, I lost my husband! Now, I've lost my daughter!"

"You haven't lost me!"

"You'll never lead a normal life!"

"That's not true! I met a couple at Caroline's house. Friends of her parents, two women, Gretchen and Janet. They're totally normal!"

Mrs. Hartnet cried into her embroidered handkerchief.

Lincoln remained speechless.

"That's it?" Valerie demanded of her mother. "That's all you've got to say?" She glared at her brother. "And you have nothing to say? Not a single word?"

Her mother continued to cry. Her brother sat wide eyed and mute.

"Seriously? That's all you've got for me?"

More crying. More silence.

"Say something! Say anything!"

Valerie lost hold of her surreal composure and shot to her feet. Through a torrent of tears, she grabbed the keys to her black Jaguar and stormed out. She drove recklessly to Caroline's house, pounded on the door, and burst in sobbing.

The girls talked through most of the night. Over Valerie's angry objections, Leah insisted on calling Mrs. Hartnet to let her know her daughter was safe. The next day, with Valerie's exhausted permission, Leah invited her mother to brunch. Mrs. Hartnet stared at the menu, glazed and unseeing, and Leah realized she was too distraught to make even a simple decision.

"May I?" Leah asked, when their server returned for their order. Mrs. Hartnet nodded, and Leah ordered for them both — scrambled eggs, bacon, wheat toast, fresh fruit, coffee.

"If you want to talk, I'm glad to listen," Leah said.

"I thought I knew my daughter. Now I think I don't know her at all."

Their food arrived and they talked about the gap between Mrs. Hartnet's vision of Valerie and her actual daughter.

"Did you ever consider," Leah suggested gently, "that your real daughter might surpass your fantasy daughter?"

Mrs. Hartnet set down her cup of coffee. "How is that possible?"

"Let's go home." Leah signaled for the check. "You can talk to Valerie and find out."

When the two women walked in, the girls had fallen asleep. Valerie was curled on the floor, clutching Claire-Bear. Caroline burrowed under her comforter on the bed.

Caroline opened her eyes and sat up. "Hi Mom, Mrs. Hartnet."

Valerie jerked awake and turned her back on her mother. Mrs Hartnet began to cry.

"Girls, take five minutes," Leah said. "Then meet us in the living room."

"Dr. Black, I don't think—" Valerie began.

"Five minutes," Leah repeated and walked out.

Shortly, an icy Valerie, a tremulous Mrs. Hartnet, a wide-eyed Caroline, and a perfectly calm Leah gathered next to a Roman ice cream sign, across from a crucifix, under a Sicilian cart.

"When you're ready, I'm here to help," Leah broke the silence.

"Maybe I should go . . ." Caroline began to rise.

"You stay!" Valerie ordered.

"I don't know what to say." Mrs. Hartnet reached for a tissue. Her daughter stared stonily at the floor. "I want to help you. I . . ."

"Help me with what?" Valerie interrupted.

"First, with your manners," Mrs. Hartnet turned frosty.

"For now, let's not worry about manners." Leah shot down that diversion.

"Help me with what?" Valerie repeated. "Help me not be gay? Help me not be a lesbian? Help me be someone I'm not?"

"What kind of help do you want?" Leah asked the girl.

"I don't know."

"I'd like help," Mrs. Hartnet spoke up.

"With what?" Leah turned to the woman.

"With bringing my daughter home."

"How can I go home when you don't love me?" Tears rolled down Valerie's cheeks.

"I do love you."

"How can you love me when you don't know me?"

"I'd like to get to know you."

A long pause.

"I'd like to get to know me, too," Valerie said softly.

"That's your starting point." Everyone looked at Leah. "That's your common ground. Getting to know Valerie. Can you both work together to get to know Valerie?"

Another long pause.

Mrs. Hartnet stood. "Come with me, Valerie. We both have a long way to go. Let's start by going home."

Slowly, Valerie stood. They didn't touch each other. Caroline and Leah followed quietly.

At the front door, Mrs. Hartnet turned. "I beg your pardon, this is quite impolite. Thank you . . ."

Leah held up a hand. "Remember, for now, don't worry about manners."

Mrs. Hartnet's lips twitched. "Ignoring manners is as strange for me as having a gay daughter."

Valerie stifled a grin. They moved closer, still not touching.

The door closed gently.

CHAPTER 30

Caroline and her parents were in the kitchen cleaning up a dinner of chicken, corn bread, and salad.

"Mom, Dad, I need to talk."

Leah and Geoff froze.

Slowly, her mother closed the refrigerator. Her father deliberately turned off the faucet. They sat back down around the table.

"Um . . ." Caroline shifted in her chair.

Geoff threw up his hands. "Don't tell me you're changing schools again!"

Leah braced herself. "Okay, let's have it."

"I want to learn to fight."

They stared blankly.

"What are you fighting?" her mother asked. "You mean another petition? Like the Laurel beauty contest? Considering how that turned out, I don't think—"

"No," Caroline interrupted. "I mean physical fighting."

"You don't mean like real fighting? Boxing?" Her father was incredulous.

"Self-defense," Caroline explained.

Leah was suddenly frightened. "Honey, are you in danger?"

Honey. How could two people speak the same word and sound so different?

"No, nothing like that," she reassured them, amazed that she lied so sincerely. "It's just that the neighborhood around school isn't great. Walking to the bus after basketball practice, it's getting dark. I'd feel safer if I knew how to protect myself."

Until that point, Caroline had carried a sense of invulnerability around physical safety and had managed to ignore several red flags. A girl in her Latin class was mugged walking home from school, shoved to the ground as two men grabbed her purse. A boy in trig had his wallet taken at knife point when two students mistook him for a rival gang member. Caroline carried mental snapshots of Nellie curled on the floor of the girls' bathroom, of the fear in Toni and Blake's eyes, of Carlos surrounded by a bloodthirsty pack. And Jeremy.

Although Caroline had lied to her parents before by omission, she'd never looked them straight in the eye and told an irrefutable whopper. But she couldn't tell them the truth. She was in danger. Doraine had accidentally let the cat out of the bag, and two weeks after Drake's apology, Caroline topped his I'm Going To Nail You list.

The problem started innocently. Doraine and Duke's connection to buy pot moved to San Diego. Doraine smoked occasionally, although lately she had lost interest. The Duke smoked regularly, and Doraine told him she'd find another source. Following the logical course, she asked a perennially stoned girl in her drama class, Kelsey, for her dealer's name. At that point, things became complicated.

Until Caroline signed up for the multifaceted education of Hollywood High, she assumed sex workers were a particular breed. Cheap, stupid, easily recognizable by their neon sleaze factor. At fifteen, she was only beginning to grapple with the nuanced layers that resulted in any career decision. A therapist friend of her mother's once said, "Scratch the surface of a psychiatrist and you'll find a doctor trying to heal from their own emotional wounds." On Career Day at Laurel, an attorney told the room of buffed and polished Clovers, "Under the skin of every lawyer is someone who feels the victim of injustice." People's motivations were idiosyncratic, complex, and largely about personal experiences. When Caroline found the girl who sat to her right in Honors History and the boy to her left in Latin were both in the trade, she began to question her simplistic ideas. At Hollywood High, sex workers were anywhere and everywhere. Some were smart, others weren't. Some were decent to the bone, others not so much. The boy next door, the girl across the street, the student in geometry class — all in emotional or financial circumstances converging on someone like Drake.

When Doraine asked Kelsey for pharmaceutical advice, she had no idea that Kelsey turned tricks. Kelsey suggested Doraine go to her source, Drake. Pimps invariably supplied drugs, so Kelsey's mentioning Drake was no surprise. Given the circumstances, Doraine should have stopped and asked for Kelsey's relationship to Drake. Instead, she snarled, "I wouldn't ask that sorry son of a bitch for shit!"

"Why?" Kelsey wondered hazily. "He's a good connection."

"He wouldn't leave me alone for a whole year. Had to get three of my cousins to make him back off." Doraine burst out laughing. "But I got even. It was the perfect revenge!"

"What'd you do?"

If Kelsey's eyes hadn't been dulled by a layer of smoke, Doraine might have noticed a sharp spike in her interest. Instead, she carelessly related the entire saga. The Duke terrorized Drake. The Duke pretended to be Caroline's boyfriend and The Professor, a "total bimbo." Best of all, "Drake made a complete jerk of himself. Anyway, I'll score drugs somewhere else."

Doraine was missing two crucial pieces of information. First, Kelsey's best friend worked for Drake. Second, Kelsey was a sex worker with a heroin habit. Kelsey's ex-pimp had begun withholding chemicals as a work incentive program, while Drake offered an unending supply. When her ex-pimp beat her up, she joined Drake's ranks. She was petrified of losing her medicinal source and would trade any information for the promise of a fix. In short, Kelsey told Drake everything. To regain his pride, he gave Kelsey a black eye, making her angry enough to report back to Doraine in their next class.

Doraine broke into a cold sweat and confessed to The Duke, who tracked Caroline down at lunch. Doraine was tearful and apologetic, but Caroline couldn't blame her. The kids struggled to think clearly as Tom and Jay punched the air and threatened to "crush Drake, ream him, torch him!" A part of Caroline wanted The Duke to give the order, which horrified her. With a sweet nostalgia that disgusted her, she felt a pang for the era of Clover ignorance.

Gradually, they regained their ability to think. Nothing changed immediately. Drake still knew The Duke protected Caroline, although he was puzzled by the nature of the connection. However, this turn of events brought the obvious reality home to Caroline. The Duke would graduate in June. Caroline would remain, and so would Drake.

Caroline took the bus home in a daze. It was time to cash in a slice of innocence, and she knew what to do. Three weeks before, girls' P.E. classes were suspended for a self-defense demonstration given by two police officers — one gargantuan man in his twenties, easily six-five, and a tiny, middle-aged woman, a petite five-one. As the girls sat side by side on the gym floor, the officers showed a few moves, highlighting the woman's ability to defend herself in spite of the difference in size and age. They warned the kids, "Look to the right" (Caroline smiled at Irene). "Look to the left" (she grinned at Kayla). "Someone will try to rape one of you in your lifetime." Then the two officers put on pads and showed the girls how to knock an assailant unconscious.

Caroline knew she had the option to change schools, clearly the most straightforward solution with the least hassle. A phone call to Mr. Hammer from her contrite parents, a meeting where she cried and apologized (and begged, if needed), a few timely comments from Leah and Geoff about their Harvard/Radcliffe legacy — Caroline would be welcomed back into Laurel's open arms. If that failed against all odds, she could transfer to a different private school. The problem was that she was happier at Hollywood High than she'd ever been. Nope, she was staying. The tricky part would be presenting it to her parents. She needed to be convincing, but if she overplayed the danger, they'd send her back to Cloverville in a heartbeat.

"Okay," Geoff broke the silence. "No problem. I'll teach you to fight."

"Dad, thanks," his daughter answered calmly, "but this isn't about boxing in a ring. I need a self-defense class for girls. I'm strong in my head. I want to be equally strong in my body." Caroline silently congratulated herself on coming up with that gem.

Unfortunately, her father pulled out a gem of his own. "I know what to do. I'll drop you at school every morning and pick you up every afternoon."

Caroline's face registered pure horror. Daddy hovering protectively by her side. How embarrassing! Didn't he realize how low his profile needed to be? At Laurel, parents were regularly on campus for committees organizing events, volunteering in classrooms, conferencing with teachers, kissing the administration's butt. At Hollywood High, any time a parent showed up, the kid was ridiculed for days. Luckily, when Geoff picked up Caroline and Kayla after the Ray debacle, he was gone so quickly that nobody noticed. But every day, Daddy the dutiful chauffeur? At Laurel, some of the Clovers were dropped off and picked up by real chauffeurs. If the car was cool (Bentleys were greatly admired), the girls viewed it as high status. At Hollywood High, *cool* and *high status* were viewed through a different lens.

"Dad, you can't. This isn't Laurel. Things don't work like that at Hollywood High."

"Why not?"

Caroline rolled her eyes.

"What?" Geoff sharply. "I'm offering a good solution to a problem!"

Caroline shrugged helplessly, and Leah stepped in.

"Geoff, I think this is something Caroline needs to do on her own."

"She needs to fight?" he shouted.

"If necessary." Leah had moved past her initial shock and was catching on. "Self-defense is something every girl should know."

First Lieutenant Commanding Officer Geoffrey Black stood stock still as he slowly, reluctantly digested the notion that what every woman needs, instead of a man by her side, is a good self-defense class. This was not only a generational issue, but also a Dad coming of age, a father realizing that he can't always protect his daughter. Caroline and Leah waited respectfully as he struggled. Then he turned to his wife.

"Where would we find a class for her?"

"I'll call the Rape Crisis Center, ask about self-defense for teen girls. I know their chief psychologist."

"Rape! Who's talking about rape?"

"Geoff," Leah said firmly, "this keeps girls from getting raped. It doesn't make it more likely." She nodded at her daughter. "This is a good idea. Give me a day to do some research."

Caroline looked down, humbled. Her father crossed the room and gently took her shoulders. When she saw his tears, she began to cry. They stood still for several moments, giving Geoff time to find his voice.

"Caroline, anyone comes near you, just give them hell!"

She moved into his arms, allowing herself to be cradled. Leah stepped forward and they held each other in a world of safety and oneness, a world where nobody needs to know how to fight.

CHAPTER 31

The Hartnet home exuded grandeur in every sunny room, down every paneled hallway, from every domed ceiling. Comfortable furniture loaded with oversized cushions counterbalanced the antiques and original art, narrowly holding pretentiousness at bay. Four sets of French doors opened onto the verandah of the infamous sweet sixteen. The previous afternoon, Caroline's family had joined the Hartnets to decorate their tree. Then Caroline stayed overnight to brave the annual Laurel Holiday Party the following evening.

The weekend before, sprawled around Kayla's bedroom, Valerie had invited the girls to attend.

Irene and Kayla looked at each other, then at Valerie.

"You're sure it's okay for us to be there?" Irene asked. "I don't think I can pretend to be a Clover."

"In case you haven't noticed, I'm Black," Kayla added. "I won't exactly blend in."

"It's at my house," Valerie said firmly. "I can invite my friends, as long as they're female. The only male specimens are Laurel faculty and administration, and the dads." She turned to Gary and Vincent. "Sorry."

Kayla looked at Caroline. "You're going, aren't you?"

"I . . . I don't know." *Mr. Hammer and every girl in my grade and all my teachers and that's a lot of Laurel Academy packed into one night.*

"I'll be there," Irene smiled at Valerie. "Kayla and I will hang out together. We'll be the oddities. Caroline will fit right in. She can show us how to act like good Clovers."

"I . . ." Caroline's voice failed.

Irene shrugged impatiently. "I'm sure you're not the first girl to transfer schools. What's the big deal?"

"It's . . ." Caroline trailed off. She and Valerie locked eyes for a long moment. "I . . ." *It's okay. They'd understand. I can . . . no, I can't. They'd never look at me the same again.* Caroline clamped her mouth shut.

Over the next few days, Caroline remained torn. She wanted to see her old friends and to support Valerie, who was still closeted to her Laurel classmates. On the other hand, she dreaded the stares, feeling like an alien, snubbed by The Platinum Ring assuming they reverted to their pre-sweet-sixteen behavior. Eventually, she decided to buck up.

The Clovers began to arrive. Settled in a craftsman chair, Caroline was pleased to find her palms dry and her breathing steady. She sat with Kayla, Irene, and her old Laurel cadre — Vicki, Tory, and Maren. Valerie greeted people at the door. She wore a designer black velvet dress with elaborate white lace trim.

"She's beautiful," Kayla whispered to Irene.

"She looks like a hybrid crossbreed of a fashion model and a 17th century British lord," Irene whispered back.

Mrs. Hartnet moved among the adults, the perfect hostess. Valerie had told her Hollywood friends that her mother hadn't talked more about The Topic, but the tension was lifting. Caroline watched as Mrs. Hartnet walked by and paused to smooth her daughter's hair. They smiled at each other.

Lelia made a grand entrance in red knickers and a green pointy cap. A sign hung from her back, blue script on silver: "Hi! I'm a Chanukah

Elf!" From a huge sack, she handed out jawbreakers with notes reading "Happy Kwanzaa!" She spotted Caroline from across the room and jogged over. The two girls hugged. Lelia shook hands with Kayla and Irene, introducing herself as "Caroline's evil twin." She then turned to Caroline. "Let's catch up."

Caroline glanced at Irene and Kayla.

"Go ahead," Kayla smiled.

"We're fine," Irene nodded.

Caroline and Lelia chose a window seat in the adjoining parlor, which was empty of guests.

"How are you?" Lelia asked, oddly earnest.

"Good. Great, actually."

"Really?"

"Really."

"You're not just saying that?"

"No, it's true. How are you?"

"I'm having my best year yet. You're going to be proud." Lelia dropped her voice. "I broke into school at 4AM last month and replaced the light bulbs with strobe lights. Then I hooked them into a sound system, so whenever anyone threw a switch, the Looney Tunes cartoon theme song blasted and the lights went crazy. Being a responsible citizen, I first tapped into the top-secret files, to make sure nobody had epilepsy."

"You're so considerate," Caroline laughed. "A Good Samaritan."

"Of course they knew I did it, but they couldn't prove a thing."

"They're lucky to have you. Otherwise they'd bore themselves to death."

"They found the cabinet's lock broken and the files scattered. They acted like the CIA was infiltrated. It was the most boring crap I've ever read. I was hoping someone was a protected witness or a secret rock star in disguise. The most interesting things were a few allergies. For a week, the administration was in a state of apoplexy over the breach of confidentiality. A few of the parents registered formal complaints that their daughters' peanut and shellfish allergies were no longer classified. Now they keep everyone's medical records in a safe. A brand new, shiny steel, massive pirate booty locker takes up half of Miss MacIsaac's office." Caroline was still laughing when Lelia turned serious. "You know that any time, any place, you say the word, and I'll do the right thing."

"We're both where we belong. I think we should let it go."

"You're sure?"

"Totally sure. I . . ."

"What?" Lelia asked.

Caroline hesitated. She knew what she was going to say, but she had no idea why she was going to say it. "I'm not sure when or how, but I think I might want to write about it some day. If I do, I'll change your name."

"What will you call me?"

Caroline thought carefully. "Genevieve."

"Who's Genevieve?"

"My next-door neighbor's parakeet."

Lelia laughed. "Named after a warm-blooded egg-laying vertebrate. Such an honor." She rummaged through her sack and pulled out two purple balls the size of large marbles. She popped one in her mouth and offered the other. "Want a jawbreaker?"

When Caroline returned to Kayla and Irene, the Platinum Ring mingled, going out of their way to be friendly. Nicole chatted about her holiday plans (Bermuda), Angela about her boyfriend (mainly about his family's Kentucky Derby racehorse). Trisha described her recent coming out party and its pink baby roses in every conceivable arrangement. Bronwyn, widely viewed as Laurel's ultimate authority on boys, bragged about her dating exploits (scheduling two guys to arrive simultaneously on a Saturday night and the ensuing fistfight). Katie had taken up a new gardening hobby, growing pot in her family's greenhouse, telling her parents it was a rare species of orchid called Himalayan Haze.

Caroline glanced at Irene who grinned, and at Kayla who smiled gently. The three friends moved to a quiet corner. They looked around the room. In a sea of white, two Clovers were Black and one was Asian.

"Is it my imagination or are a lot of people staring at you?" Irene asked Caroline.

Nope. Not your imagination.

"I thought they were staring at me," Kayla said. "In this crowd, I kind of stand out."

"How're you doing?" Caroline asked her.

"Okay," Kayla shrugged. "It's a different planet from Hollywood High."

"This room doesn't have enough color," Irene spoke quietly.

Kayla nodded. "I lived in Boston all my life until last summer. In the Northeast, it's called a whiteout. So much snow covers the landmarks that nobody can find their way. Everyone gets lost. Too much white. Not good for anyone."

Her friends laughed.

Laurel's most talented pianist, who would join the ranks of Juilliard a few years down the road, went to the Steinway concert grand and a sweet disharmony of Christmas carols filled the room. Caroline listened silently. She never sang in public. Even "Happy Birthday" filled her with crawly self-consciousness. She swayed happily between Irene and Kayla. Irene hit the notes, sort of. Kayla sang beautifully, blending with the lesser voices, harmonizing with Irene. Caroline smiled at her softness.

Her parents had thrown their own annual holiday party the week before. They invited both friends and business associates. The guest list was tricky since Leah's therapist friends had analyzed Geoff's industry friends for decades. The party's patient/therapist ratio was astronomical.

A fleet of bartenders served oceans of booze, and waiters circulated with trays of canapés, cheese puffs, barbecued meatballs, marinated shrimp, lobster tartlets, gourmet chocolates. Caroline dressed in her usual faded jeans and drab t-shirt. She spoke when spoken to, listened and watched, playing her role of the rapt audience.

Predictably, with the third round of martinis, the need for applause infiltrated like a wicked spell. Skye, a popular singer, belted out her latest hit while holding her white toy poodle, Cotton Ball. As her final note faded, before anyone else could grab center stage, another guest launched into a tap routine that covered the entire living room. As Ned danced, the undercurrent changed. With each step, he became more proprietary, radiating ownership, as though his birthright included a notarized entitlement to the spotlight.

Caroline retreated to a corner where Gretchen and Janet stood together.

"This isn't going to end well," Janet narrowed her eyes.

"It feels like something's about to erupt," Gretchen said.

Caroline watched tightlipped.

Her parents stood against the opposite wall, enjoying the show, unaware of the atmospheric shift.

A surge of excitement coursed through the room as Tray, also a dancer and unable to tolerate another second of his rival's solo performance, leaped onto the hearth to begin his own soft shoe number.

The crowd shouted approval.

Ned, however, was in no mood to tolerate competition. He catapulted up on the hearth, landed in front of Tray and the two men locked horns. Ned, bigger and stronger, shoved Tray, who tripped and SMASH! A flurry of white fur, the high-pitched bleats of a crying dog, and Skye's sultry alto gave way to husky screams. Tray had bombed on Cotton Ball's head.

Skye dropped to the floor by her dog, who lay trembling and bloody under the Roman ice cream sign. "DO SOMETHING!" she yelled at Ned and Tray.

Off the three went, carrying Cotton Ball in a large shoe box, to the twenty-four hour veterinary clinic for emergency surgery. Skye wept in the waiting room, flanked by a contrite Ned and Tray. Finally, the surgeon emerged with the verdict. Cotton Ball would live, minus vision in her right eye.

Caroline barely slept that night, haunted by the Napalm-The-Village drive for center stage. Put out an eye if that's what it takes! Don't let anyone push you out of the spotlight! Don't let anyone steal your dreams!

"You have to be one of us to understand," Caroline had been told by countless performers.

But Cotton Ball only knew she was hit with a 160-pound boulder and left maimed.

"Something's wrong with your friends," Caroline said to her parents, adding fresh strawberries to her bowl of cereal the next morning.

"It was an accident," Geoff defensively. "Nobody meant to hurt that dog."

"You're correct. Cotton Ball got caught in the crossfire. Ned and Tray only meant to hurt each other."

"She's got a point," Leah overrode Geoff's retort.

"Why was everyone at our party white?"

"What?" Leah scrambled to keep up.

"Why. Is. Everyone. In. The. Industry. White?" Caroline exaggerated each word.

"Are you referring to Sidney Poitier?" Geoff sarcastically.

"Of course not! I know he's Black! He's every white person's answer when someone challenges the industry's unwritten, unspoken racial quotas. There should be more people of all racial heritages. Not just the actors, everyone behind the scenes, too. The industry is a landscape of white. And it's not just racial bigotry. How many woman directors do you know? If you're gay, then you have to hide it. If you're—"

"For goodness sakes, Caroline! What about . . ." Geoff interrupted and launched into a list of names.

"Yeah, they're gay," Caroline cut in. "They're also not actors. They're also white. You and Mom have told me over and over that if I know an actor is gay, I can't talk about it, because if the press got hold of it, the actor would never work again. And don't worry, I won't talk about it. But that's totally messed up!"

"Be realistic. Who's going to watch a romantic lead if they know the actor is gay?" Geoff attempted to convince his daughter to be reasonable.

"I'm sorry. My mistake. All this time I thought the actors and actresses were playing roles. I didn't realize it was real. Those stories were actually documentaries. The spy thrillers with guns and explosions — people really died. They were snuff films."

"Of course they're not documentaries and snuff films!" Geoff tried not to explode.

"Then why does it matter if the lead is gay?"

"It's not about bigotry," Geoff explained patiently. "It's what sells. If you can't sell tickets, your show dies before it has a chance."

"It's about money. What a relief! That makes it perfectly fine."

With extreme discipline, Geoff managed to not roll his eyes. "You can't cast a gay man as a romantic lead! You can't cast too many Blacks in one film! Nobody will watch. It's how things are."

Caroline glared at her father. "You and Mom talk about how much you support Civil Rights. Are you defending the industry's pledge of allegiance to its club, white members only? Oops, my mistake again. I mean white members only except Sidney Poitier. Do you think that's right?"

"I didn't say it was right! I said it's reality!" Geoff hit his limit.

"Does it have to be reality? People in the industry are always congratulating themselves on their creativity. Why do they follow the herd on this convention? It's wrong!"

Leah put a hand on her daughter's arm. "Calm down. Give your father a break."

"Why? Nobody should get a break if they're excluding people because they're Black, or gay, or whatever! That's what you both raised me to believe. Are you arguing against me or against your own beliefs?"

Geoff shot to his feet and stormed into the next room. Leah glared at her daughter and followed her husband. Caroline heard Geoff ranting. "If her adolescent bullshit doesn't fix itself soon, I'll send her to boarding school in the Antarctic!"

Leah's response was inaudible.

"Okay, fine!" her father shouted. "If you won't let me send her away, then *I'll* go to the Antarctic! I'm sure I can convince the producer to set up the entire production on an ice floe! It'll be a helluva lot easier than dealing with her!"

Now, at Valerie's home, Caroline realized she'd take a Laurel party over the entertainers any day. Then an idea struck. She didn't have to take either. Kayla, Irene, Gary, Vincent, Valerie. They had their jokes, their support, their pride, their genuine interest in each other. Everyone had an equal voice. Everyone mattered.

Caroline smiled at Kayla, companionably singing with Irene. Kayla softly harmonized until Irene lost her way. Then Kayla joined her, guiding Irene back to the melody. Valerie walked over and the girls linked arms.

Before Caroline could think and analyze and lose the moment, she began to sing.

CHAPTER 32

Caroline, Toni, and Blake were walking in their morning circles.

"What's wrong?" Blake saw Toni looking uncomfortable.

"I have to pee."

Blake stopped in their tracks. "Okay, let's go."

"Why do you both sound worried?" Caroline asked.

"The bathrooms aren't safe for someone like me," Toni said.

"Or me," Blake added. "It was bad before, but it's worse since Jeremy got beat up."

Caroline didn't hesitate. "I'll go with you."

Her friends stared.

"C'mon." Caroline took a few steps toward the nearest building, then turned back. Toni and Blake hesitated to follow. "We're sticking together. I'm not leaving you." *Did I say that? What am I doing?*

"You're the strangest nerd I've ever met," Toni gently punched her shoulder.

Blake and Caroline waited by the sinks. As Toni joined them to wash her hands, three girls came in, chatting about their hairstyles. They saw Toni and Blake, stopped talking, exchanged smug glances.

"What are you?" Girl #1 smirked at Blake. "A girl or a boy?"

Blake was silent.

"She asked you a question!" Girl #2 raised her voice. "What are you?"

"They're my friend," Caroline clearly. "That's what they are."

"Are you lost?" Girl #3 glared at Blake. "This is the girls' bathroom. The boys' bathroom is down the hall."

Her friends sneered.

"You're very tall." Girl #3 said to Toni.

Toni said nothing.

Caroline's breathing turned shallow. *No no no! This is the small restroom by the administration. Nothing bad is supposed to happen here. Shit! I don't know what to do! I . . . wait . . . hold on.* She forced herself to take a deep breath. She thought of the basketball team. *I need to act like Shawna and Lureen.*

In a fraction of a moment, Caroline entered a zone of intense focus. She evaluated the threat through a new lens. Girl #3 was clearly the leader of the pack. Every time the others spoke, they glanced at her for approval. Caroline shrugged off her backpack and handed it to Blake. She took a step to her left, placing her body between her friends and the three girls.

"You're so pretty," Girl #2 said to Toni, sending her friends into a round of smirks.

"Aren't you going to say thank you for the compliment?" Girl #3, an open challenge.

"Thank you," Toni said softly.

"Why's your voice so low?" Girl #1 wasn't backing down.

The posse laughed.

"I like your ponytail." Girl #3 reached to grab Toni's hair.

"BACK OFF!" Caroline catapulted forward. Her voice bounced off the tile walls, a sharp echo. She bodychecked Girl #3, a skill acquired during basketball scrimmages. She stormed toward Girls #1 and #2, smacking the ground so hard with her athletic shoes that the sound reverberated. "DO NOT TOUCH MY FRIENDS!"

The three girls froze.

Caroline glared at Girl #3, who quickly retreated to the far wall. Her friends scurried after her.

Toni and Blake huddled by the sink.

"We're going to leave and you're going to stay out of our way." Caroline now dangerously quiet. "If you ever see us again on campus, you're going to walk in the opposite direction. You will not approach us. You will not speak to us. Do you understand?"

Silence.

"DO YOU UNDERSTAND?"

"Take it easy."

"We understand."

"We didn't mean anything."

Caroline motioned Blake and Toni through the door, following them closely. An unfamiliar adrenaline rush surged through her bloodstream. She grabbed her backpack from Blake, strutting with power. *I can't believe I did that! I feel fantastic! I'm—* then she noticed her friends' expressions. "Are you both okay?"

"Those three assholes are in our P.E. class. In the locker room, they always ask if I'm a girl or a boy. This is the first time they tried to get physical." Blake tried to shrug it off. "Happens all the time."

"Like Blake said, it's getting worse." Toni glanced at Caroline. "How'd you know what to do? I'd never have thought you'd . . ."

"I acted like some of the girls on the basketball team. I didn't think. I just reacted." *I didn't think? I just reacted? Did I say that?* Caroline looked back and forth between Blake and Toni. Both girls' hands trembled. "Take some deep breaths. It's okay." But even as she spoke, she knew it was nowhere close to okay.

"So many people . . . they look at me . . . they look at Blake . . . and . . ." Toni lost her voice.

"And what?" Blake shakily.

"And it's hunting season."

Caroline stopped walking. Blake closed their eyes, fighting for composure. Toni dropped her head into her hands and silently cried.

CHAPTER 33

Caroline reached the classroom as Dreads and Presto walked up.

"Hi," Presto smiled at her. He gave Dreads a pointed look and slipped inside, closing the door behind him.

"I . . ." Dreads cleared his throat. "I was wondering, do you want to see a movie on Saturday?"

Caroline stared. They had barely exchanged a word beyond "hi" as they passed each other in the halls.

"Or we could get pizza," Dreads offered.

For the first time, Caroline took in Dreads' trim, muscular build. He carried his tennis racket like a natural extension of his athletic frame. His dreadlocks hung down his back, different shades of brown in the overhead lights. *His hair is amazing. I can see the muscles in his arms. He's . . .* before any more thoughts could materialize, she flashed on a Latin vocabulary quiz and turned completely uninterested.

"You're asking out the wrong girl." Her tone was matter of fact.

"What do you mean?"

"Would you take a punch for the girl you love?"

"Of course."

"Even if it meant a bloody nose?"

"Sure, but why . . ."

"Think about it." She smiled over her shoulder as she walked through the door.

"A swing and a miss," Elvia smirked as she brushed past.

Then the day turned sour. Walking into English class, Caroline automatically said hi to Carlos, then did a double take. He wore jeans, a Rolling Stones t-shirt, athletic shoes, no makeup.

"Don't say anything," he whispered.

"Okay," she whispered back.

"It's not safe here. Something bad's gonna happen."

"I get it."

"You don't get it. You don't know what it's like. You're not gay."

"What can I do to help?" she asked quietly.

"I don't know."

Caroline took her seat and it occurred to her that The Blond and his friends continued to wear their usual white pants, platform heels, gold tasseled belts, colorful scarves, makeup. Since Jeremy was assaulted, they huddled together, spoke in hushed tones, hurrying on and off campus, meeting nobody's eyes. For a moment she wondered why they didn't change their appearance. Then it made sense. Carlos chose how he dressed. The Blond and his friends worked for Drake, who told them what to wear. They had no choice.

Kurt entered the classroom carrying a guitar. Intimidated by Ray's presence, he had backed off. With Ray gone, he resurfaced. In the few minutes before Mr. Cohen arrived, he launched into a lusty rendition of Don McLean's "Everybody Loves Me Baby (What's the Matter with You)."

"Bad move," Presto frowned at Kurt.

Elvia reapplied her black lipstick, radiating disapproval.

"Really mature," Sharon tossed her braids.

Gary glowered from the back row.

Kayla looked ready to sink into a hole.

As Kurt belted out his finale, Mr. Cohen strode in.

"Keep your day job," he said dryly, lifting Kurt's guitar. He turned to Kayla. "Some unsolicited advice. First, as long as you're intimidated, you're a target. Second, if you're angry, then own it. Fight back. Third, this classroom appears to be your arena." A pause while Kayla stared. Then, as though nothing had happened, Mr. Cohen reached for his text. "Everyone, please take out your copies of *Macbeth*. Turn to Act Two, scene one."

They opened their books as Mort called out, "Someone throw me a pencil."

Lunch was uneventful for five minutes. Then a vicious fistfight erupted between the Mexican and Chilean gangs. The campus cop was hit in the face trying to break it up. He fell hard, his left eye closed and discolored. The gangs ran off, momentarily united over whacking a police officer.

Caroline couldn't eat another bite.

Now, she took one look at The Duke and knew something was extremely wrong. His confident strut was more of an ungainly stomp. He smirked at the classroom, reverting to his original arrogance, and grimaced at the three typed pages Caroline offered. *Metaphor and Simile: A Poet's Introduction to Poetry.*

"What's going on?" she asked.

"Nothing."

"Okay, whatever you say, but you look like you're going to rupture a nutsack."

He laughed in spite of himself. "You're a very rude nerd!"

"Duly noted. What's wrong?"

He patted her head, radiating condescension. "Nothing you'd understand."

"Try me."

"Above your pay grade."

She shrugged and turned to the xeroxed pages. "Metaphors and similes are the building blocks of poetry. A simile incorporates either the word *like* or *as*. A metaphor does not, but implies the comparison. Tell me what's wrong."

"I got arrested."

She caught her breath. "What'd you do?"

"I didn't do shit! I hate cops! I was out. I was thirsty. I was at Dudley's, y'know that little market?" She nodded. "So, I took a Coke and drank it. I guess it's a crime to be thirsty."

"They arrested you for buying a Coke?"

"I didn't say I bought it."

"You were arrested for shoplifting? You stole a can of Coke? Are you an idiot?"

"Caroline!" Miss Orville cut in. "Please lower your voice."

The girl blushed. "I beg your pardon."

"I don't blame you," Miss Orville said kindly. "Perhaps you two should continue your discussion elsewhere."

The Duke sized up their teacher. "You know about this?"

"Of course I know," Miss Orville didn't flinch. "Mrs. Richardson and Mr. Cohen know as well. We're extremely angry at you, but we don't scare easily, and you can't get rid of us. We're still on your team." She grasped both kids' shoulders and shoved them out the door.

They hesitated in the hallway. Caroline shrugged. "Let's go for a walk."

They moved outside, past the International House of Pancakes, into the heart of Hollywood Boulevard. Caroline was thinking up a storm. The Duke was as intelligent as anyone she knew. He had a group of administrative heavyweights putting him at the top of their A list. And he was willing to throw it away for twelve fluid ounces. She flashed on the Coke commercial of the 1960s, young adults on a hill, under glorious blue skies, the many racial heritages of the United States bonded in major chords, conduits for the voices of angels. *"I'd like to teach the world to sing in perfect harmony."* Harmony, hell. She wanted to throttle him.

Finally, his anxiety broke their standoff. "You mad at me?"

"Yes," she sighed, "but I still think the world of you."

He reached to pat her head tenderly. "Back at you."

They strolled quietly past Super Slush toward a rack of clothes.

"What's going to happen?" she asked.

The Duke stared at a hideous gold paisley tank top. "They arrested me, put me in jail. I called my Mom. She started screaming her head off. She called my uncle. He pitched a fit, bailed me out, drove me home, yelled at me the whole ride. I have to see a judge in a few months who'll tell me how long they'll lock me up." The Duke cleared his throat. "I'm eighteen. I've been arrested before. My first stint in Juvenile Hall was a week after my eleventh birthday. They may be so mad that I have to do time."

Something bothered Caroline. "You didn't have money for a Coke?"

"I didn't say that."

She halted in her tracks. "You had the money and you stole it anyway? I don't get it."

"It's not rocket science!" The Duke's eyes were frantic. "I went to the store owned by Mr. Jerk Off, who lives two doors down from me. He's hated me since I was born and told me a million times I'd come to no good. So I decided to make his day and show him he was right for the first time in his lousy life. I walked in, took the Coke, shot Mr. Jerk Off the bird, walked home. The cops came within an hour."

"How could you do something so irresponsible?" she demanded, sounding like an anal-retentive aristocrat.

The Duke wheeled on her. "Maybe I'm tired of being responsible! Maybe you should leave me alone! Fuck you all! Fuck math, fuck

English, fuck Mrs. Richardson, fuck Miss Orville, fuck Mr. Cohen, and fuck you!"

Caroline blinked. Subtract out the bark and the bite, there was a message here.

"Lots of fucking going on," she said quietly.

The Duke looked at his shoes and finally came out with it. "Doraine's pregnant."

Caroline felt sick. She pictured Doraine with her thickening waist contrasting to her whiplash body.

"She told me at school yesterday. I took the Coke on the way home. My life's coming apart."

"You displayed poor judgment. You should have left the Coke and taken a pack of Trojans."

"Say wh—" Then he saw her lips twitch and off they went, falling to their knees in hysterics on the sidewalk.

Finally, they staggered to their feet. They strolled back toward school, companionably silent.

"Can I ask you something?" The Duke smiled down at her.

"Sure."

"Don't get mad, but … I can say *fuck* ten times in one sentence, and you're totally calm. But if I say you're pretty, you turn into an ice queen."

"Is there a question in there somewhere?"

"Do you get that's very strange?"

You don't understand. You've never had a parade of men in the industry, in their forties and older, hitting on you, staring at your breasts, trying to get you to have sex with them. They always start by telling me I'm pretty. So no, my "strange" reaction actually isn't strange at all.

"Yes, I get that's very strange."

"Okay," he grinned. "Glad we agree."

Automatically, Caroline dodged a volley of nonsense from a manic pusher, a bag of colorful pills shoved in her face. The Duke waved him off like a gnat. She barely registered Drake's bottomless eyes tracking them from across the street. She glanced up at The Duke.

"Will Doraine keep the baby?"

"Definitely. She wants to get married."

"Do you want to marry her?"

"I don't know."

"How many months along is she?"

"She went to Planned Parenthood. They think four months. She didn't want to tell me. She was afraid I'd want her to get an abortion."

They crossed the campus perimeter as the bell jangled. Following the same impulse, they hugged tightly.

"Sorry we ditched metaphors and similes," he smiled sadly.

"Doesn't matter. We can cover them next time."

They separated. Caroline wondered how Mrs. Richardson, Miss Orville, and Mr. Cohen tolerated the uncertainty. They could knock themselves out helping the students, but ultimately the kid either would do their part or not. The teachers and administrators held steady as their students flew in their faces with one adolescent impulse after another. Caroline measured her pace, squared her shoulders, renewed her vows to The Intellectual Icon. She would never succumb to any teenage urge. She would stay aggressively loyal to her mind, to her books, to her platonic friendships.

Proudly, she continued toward her locker, having no notion, not the slightest clue, how adolescent her vow to ignore her adolescence was.

CHAPTER 34

A beat up West Hollywood gym.

Caroline steeled herself and walked through the door. A young woman, mid-twenties, stepped forward to greet her.

"Hi. I'm Linda, your instructor."

"Pleasure to meet you." Behind her polite veneer, Caroline's hopes deflated. Linda was five feet even, ninety pounds tops, with fluffy blonde hair and a button nose. *This bleached elf is going to teach me to roar like a lion, fight like a tiger? Seriously?*

A curious place to spend Christmas vacation. Kayla was enrolled in the community music program Caroline thought had accepted her the day Ray disappeared. Irene prepared holiday meals at a food bank near Watts Towers. Gary and Vincent lounged with no structured plans. Valerie surfed in Maui with her mother and brother, and Caroline signed up for self-defense.

Her nightmare had quieted for a week, and she hoped it wouldn't return. But the night she mailed her tuition, she woke up terrified. Blonds, blue shirts, shouting, shattering. Eduardo, Doris, Eric, Anna, Christopher. Through the years, she listened to her mother's psychoanalyst colleagues talk about dreams, and she knew that several layers underlie a recurring nightmare. With each uncovered layer, the dream would stop temporarily. To put it to rest, she'd need to unearth the root. She considered it from every angle, wondering why a boy she'd never spoken to had such a powerful grip on her.

Now, in an aging gym with thick tumbling mats covering the floor, Caroline joined seven other adolescent girls, sitting in an anxious circle. Linda dropped next to them, her legs crossed easily. They all wore sweatpants, hair tied back, no makeup or jewelry.

Linda welcomed them and carefully explained the difference between violence and self-defense. They were never to use their knowledge in anger, never to show off. Only to protect themselves or someone else from injury. "The ability to fight, to hurt another person, is serious business."

Linda asked each girl's reasons for enrolling. Some had been assaulted. Some had a friend or relative who'd been raped. Caroline's turn arrived, and she hesitated. How could she explain Drake, The Blond, the blue shirt, and the broken lollipop? Then she heard her own voice coming from a deep pocket of truth.

"I grew up in the film industry. Everything about me is wrong. No glitz. No glamour. I've never owned a tube of lipstick, and I have no clue how to put on mascara. I was told I was too fat by more people than I can count. I was offered cocaine for the first time when I was nine. Men in the industry started hitting on me as soon as my body developed. I . . . it's not like I was assaulted, and I know it's not nearly as bad as what lots of you have gone through. It's just . . . it felt . . ."

"Even though it wasn't an assault, it felt assaultive?" Linda asked.

"Like something was crouching around every corner, ready to jump on me."

A pause, then Linda spoke. "Each of you has a different reason for being here. Even if your reasons sound the same, we're each unique.

Every person's reasons and every person's experiences are important. Every person's feelings are valid."

The next girl was speaking, but Caroline barely heard her. In a flash, behind enemy lines, a new clarity of insight took hold. The current trauma with Silver Lamé was scary and dangerous. But Hollywood High's jagged edges weren't the real enemy. Caroline found her school's immediacy oddly bracing and affirming. She was here to kick through the remnants of her childhood that believed she was plain and boring, inside and out, an entertainment industry castoff, a plaything for men desperate to recapture their youth.

Another girl was crying as she described being repeatedly molested by a neighbor. She had told her parents, but they didn't believe her.

"I believe you," Linda said and the circle of girls nodded. "After class, anyone who wants can stay for a few minutes. I'm going to give you the names and phone numbers for some community resources, clinics with therapy at sliding scale fees, rape crisis counselors. You don't have to go through this alone."

Caroline felt a wave of gratitude that her parents had always believed her when she told them about men trying to sleep with her, about being offered drugs. But something clenched in her core. The tension built, shoving her thankfulness aside. *Mom and Dad always believed me. So, what's my problem? What's the big deal?*

Caroline snapped to attention as Linda called in her co-instructor, their "mugger." Quincy entered, his movements carefully measured. He smiled, and the class nervously smiled back. Linda explained that in his cut-offs and T-shirt, with his brown eyes and black hair, he was Quincy, on their team, a soldier in the war against violence. He showed them the protective gear he'd wear for their muggings. Once his mask was on, he'd become the "assailant." When he took off the mask, he'd be Quincy again.

Linda and Quincy explained the format. They'd demonstrate the full sequence, breaking it into individual moves. Then Quincy would "attack" the girls, one at a time. Linda would always be at her student's side, coaching, shouting instructions, while the rest of the class shouted with her. In each class, every girl fought three times and yelled instructions twenty-one times.

Quincy then disappeared into the locker room. Although prepared intellectually, when he emerged fifteen minutes later the girls gasped. From head to toe, he wore heavy, metallic padding, from his enormous shoes thick enough for them to stomp without hurting him, to his huge bubble headed hockey mask. Shiny from top to bottom, reinforced with duct tape, he looked like a futuristic cyber monster. He waited for their response to peak, then he removed the mask.

"The suit is for my protection," he explained, "so you can fight without hurting me."

They'd be told this many times. Still, the notion of pounding him required a hefty leap, jumping over social, cultural, and personal prohibitions. In the second class, when they learned how to knee a man in the groin, Caroline obediently slammed him, then caught his shoulders and asked if he was okay. Cracking a man in the balls. Whatever would the Laurel Clovers say?

"This is the beginning," Quincy spoke to their doubt. "Trust me and Linda, you'll feel different at the end. For now, keep this in mind. I'm normally six-one, one-eighty-five. In this costume, I'm six-seven, two-fifty. You learn to take me down, you can take down anyone." He waited a beat. "Everyone ready?" The girls nodded and he replaced the mask.

Without preamble, Quincy grabbed Linda from behind, threw her to the mat and pinned her. They crashed down, lying on their left sides like enemy spoons, Quincy behind her, his right hand snaking around her upper arms to her throat. Caroline clutched the girl next to her. Before anyone could hyperventilate, Linda yelled "NO!" in a deep voice of rage and power. She bit his forearm to loosen his grip, slammed her elbow into his solar plexus and rolled free. Staying prone, she anchored herself on the floor with her hands, drew back her leg and crashed her foot into his face. Knock out.

Linda, nimble and unharmed, hopped to her feet. The class stood frozen, staring at Quincy who lay immobile. Caroline mentally shook herself, ready to call an ambulance. Before she could speak, he clambered up, removed his mask and began to clap for Linda. The class broke into wild applause.

"Ladies," Linda grinned wickedly, "it's not the size of the woman in the fight, it's the size of the fight in the woman."

Over the next two weeks, the girls learned to fight from standing, sitting, or lying down. They learned to use fists, knees, elbows, feet, and teeth. Pinned on their backs, stomachs, sides, from behind, or in front, they learned to break free. They learned to yell constantly because, Linda explained, some assailants are scared off by the noise.

"Don't let anyone take your voice away," Linda said. "Your voice belongs to you, now and always, in here and everywhere."

To her surprise, Caroline learned that most challenging to her was not hitting, biting, or kicking. Her biggest hurdle was yelling. Surrounded from birth by thespians trained to take over theaters, outshouted repeatedly, her speech devolved. She talked early, in full sentences. Over time, her words became increasingly silent. In her head, she heard her own voice loud and clear. Sharing her voice was another matter. Now, Linda and Quincy had a meager two weeks to rewire Caroline's relationship to her own voice. *I can't . . . it won't work . . . wait . . . hold on. The girls on the basketball team. Always loud with no apology. I need to copy Shawna and Lureen.* In her next fight, Caroline's voice broke free.

Class by class, step by step, the girls began to feel stronger, more confident. Every fight left Quincy crumpled in defeat, and the rush was like nothing Caroline had ever known — high on adrenaline, intoxicating and dangerous. Standing tall, with her "attacker" crumpled at her feet, with Linda by her side and an entire class cheering, Caroline learned the allure of physical power.

In the fourth class, she also learned something not as clear to define, but equally life changing. Quincy, wearing jeans and a sweatshirt, sat next to Linda on the mat in their opening circle. Linda spoke to the girls about "unwanted and intrusive physical touch, something girls and women deal with much too often."

She nodded at Quincy, who cupped his hand over her knee, drumming his fingers against her sweatpants.

Linda began a monologue. "I don't want his hand on my knee, but I don't know what to do. Quincy's a friend, and I don't want to hurt his feelings. Maybe I'm overreacting. It's not really sexual, but it is crossing a boundary. He might think I'm a prude if I tell him to move his hand. He might get mad. Maybe he'll get the message if I change positions."

She uncrossed her legs and nodded at Quincy, who shifted his hand to her shoulder, continuing to drum his fingers.

"Shit!" Linda continued. "He's not getting the message." She waited a long moment. "Thank you, Quincy."

He immediately withdrew his hand.

"Okay," said Linda, "here's the point. If someone touches you in a way that makes you uncomfortable, then respect your own feelings. You don't have to justify it or defend it. It's your absolute right to draw a boundary." She paused to let that sink in. "If you say no or tell a guy to stop, if he's a good person, he'll react exactly how Quincy did when I told him to stop our demonstration."

"If he doesn't respect your boundaries," Quincy added, "then he doesn't deserve your respect or your friendship. And he absolutely doesn't deserve a piece of your body, whether the piece is big or small."

Caroline breathed in their words, knowing something had shifted, not quite able to define it.

For the last class, the girls brought gifts. One girl gave everyone a sketch of her favorite tree in her parents' back yard. Linda distributed a Native American prayer for peace. Quincy handed out seeds to grow impatiens, his favorite flower. Caroline brought shiny red lollipops. They celebrated their strength and promised to stay in touch.

Caroline never saw any of them again.

Her dream burrowed into a place of downy quiet, covered in newly discovered bodily confidence. Its core remained hidden, pulsating, waiting to resurface.

The following weekend at the next industry party, a producer in his fifties approached and bowed before Caroline. "I'm humbled in the face of your beauty."

Geoff and Leah exchanged a smile.

The man took Caroline's hand, then leaned in to kiss her lips. She stepped back and held him at bay. "Nope. That's not gonna happen."

He froze, along with her parents.

"Sweetheart," the man smirked, "you'll never make it in the industry with that attitude."

"What did I say or do that made you think I wanted to make it in the industry? Or that I wanted to make it with you?"

"I'm sorry," Leah apologized. "She's just a kid."

"We clearly raised her wrong," Geoff tried to joke.

The man glared at them, then looked Caroline over from head to toe. "You might want to drop a few pounds. You're not nearly as pretty as you think you are."

"More to the point, I'm not nearly as pretty as you think I am."

"I don't think you're pretty!" he fired back. "I was trying to be nice because I thought you'd be nice!"

"I guess you got that wrong, which makes us even, because I don't think you're nice, either."

He stalked away.

Caroline turned on her parents, fists clenched. "Seriously? You apologized for me? You said you raised me wrong because I stopped someone your age from sliming all over me?"

Her mother and father were incredulous.

"It's the industry," Leah tried to explain. "You have to learn to deal with people like that."

"I did deal with it!"

"You have to just go with it. It's how the industry works," Geoff stepped in. "You need a sense of humor!"

"Thanks, but I've already got one. By the way, there's nothing funny about a man in his fifties trying to make it with a teenager!"

"He wasn't—"

"Of course he was!" Caroline interrupted her father. "And you want me to 'just go with it'? You want me to let that sleazeball kiss me on the lips? That's okay with you?"

"It isn't okay with me," said Leah and Geoff, in unison.

"I'm sure that's not true!"

"What do you mean?" Leah was startled.

"You knew! I told you! You saw it! Over and over again! You did nothing to stop it! You kept bringing me back for more!"

"What are you talking about?" Geoff angrily.

"I don't understand why you're so upset and . . ." Leah began.

Caroline stormed out.

CHAPTER 35

"Follow me!" Lincoln ran into the water, diving onto his surfboard. He glanced over his shoulder at his mother and sister. "Come on!"

Valerie and Mrs. Hartnet ran in after him. They skimmed through the warm sea, but Lincoln didn't stop with the other surfers. He paddled beyond the breakers, where the world turned still.

Mrs. Hartnet sat on her board and looked back at the Maui shore. "It's beautiful here." The water was a sheath of sun-drenched blues.

After a moment, Valerie spoke up. "Are we going to surf?"

"In a minute," Lincoln answered. "First we talk."

"About what?" Valerie's hair reflected the heat like onyx.

"About it." Lincoln looked at his mother. "We all maneuver around it. Time to talk."

"Okay, where do we start?" Valerie asked.

"Some of my friends want to ask you out. What should I say?"

"Who?" Valerie grinned.

"They swore me to secrecy. What should I tell them?"

"Tell them . . . Mom, fasten your seatbelt . . . tell them I'm seeing someone."

Mrs. Hartnet smiled. "That's nice of you. Then it won't hurt their feelings and . . ." her smile congealed. "You're not actually . . . oh, dear, you are actually seeing someone."

Valerie nodded.

"May I ask who?"

"Not yet," Valerie quietly. "Soon, but not yet."

"Do I know her?" Mrs. Hartnet asked.

"Yes."

"Do I like her?"

"Yes."

"Oh, shit," Mrs. Hartnet said so primly that both of her children burst out laughing.

A long pause.

"I thought I was getting more comfortable with a gay daughter. It seems I have work to do."

"Mom, it's like me with my girlfriend," Lincoln shot his sister a supportive glance. "Valerie and her girlfriend do the same stuff I do with—"

"Thank you for that image I shall try mightily to forget," Mrs. Hartnet interrupted, and her children laughed again.

"Substitute the word gay for straight and she's the exact same pain in the neck kid sister she was before she told us." Lincoln closely watched the swells. "Gotta go. Surfing calls. Good talk." He paddled furiously and caught the next wave.

"That was enlightening," Mrs. Hartnet's lips twitched. Then she turned serious. "It's healthy that you have a girlfriend. I apologize for being taken aback. I'll do better."

"It's okay, Mom. I get where you're coming from. I'm still not totally comfortable being gay."

"Can I help in any way?"

Valerie's eyes filled. "Thanks, Mom, you just did help."

"I'm getting used to the idea."

"Me too, It's getting better."

Her mother tightened her grip on her surfboard. "May I ask a difficult question?"

"Absolutely yes, ask it, whatever it is."

"Did I do something wrong? Or is it because your father died?"

"No, it's nothing like that. I don't understand where it comes from. I've known since I was twelve, even though I didn't know the words gay or lesbian."

"That makes me feel a lot better," her mother smiled. "It's not about something going wrong."

"I'm not sure what it's about."

"It's about your becoming who you're meant to be."

CHAPTER 36

Ceramics. Caroline's art requirement, six weeks, every Monday, chosen for its convenient fit in her free fifth period slot. Slim choices were available at that time, each with its own drawbacks. Wood shop would have worked, but last semester a boy severed a finger, and although enrollment skyrocketed with the morbidly curious, Caroline decided to pass. She could have signed up for modern dance with Mrs. Cuthbertson, but that entailed wearing a leotard and performing in front of the entire school — yeah, like that was going to happen. Auto mechanics was a possibility, but she would have been the only girl — no way. Beyond stick figures, drawing was far beyond her capabilities. Which left her with ceramics, taught by Mr. Warren "Call-Me-War" Lock.

"You're taking ceramics?" Toni and Blake stood at the door to their drawing class, across the hall.

"My art requirement," Caroline nodded. "You're both taking drawing?"

"Blake's really good. I'm really not," Toni shrugged. "I'm getting the art requirement out of the way so I can take more history classes."

"At least our teacher won't . . ." Blake trailed off.

"That's what I've heard," Caroline dryly.

"Have fun!" Toni wickedly.

The bell rang and the three girls quickly entered their classrooms.

Caroline surveyed the ceramics domain, a large space with a kiln at one end and two wheels at the other. In the middle stood four high tables, each with six stools, but only seventeen kids enrolled due to wood shop's spike in popularity. At the helm stood Captain Warlock. A tall man, dressed in a muscle t-shirt, arms bulging with his daily gym regimen, and a shaved head. Irene and Vincent had warned Caroline of a well-known undocumented fact. Each semester, War chose one girl to receive special favors culminating in an A+. The queen's reign lasted exactly the duration of the course. He then moved on to the new crop.

"For our kick-off project," War instructed, "you'll create an asymmetrical container." His eyes slid over table number one. "Begin with one shape on the bottom and end with another on top." He skimmed table two, evaluated and passed over. "And please," a naughty smile, "if you make a bong, call it a flower pot or an avant garde bowl. My boss says I have to report any bongs." Laughter as he measured the girls at table three.

Caroline forced herself to grin with the rest, as her palms broke with sweat. *Bongs . . . he's talking about bongs . . . what kind of a teacher . . . !* She scanned the room, gauging everyone's reaction. *Amused . . . relaxed . . . stoned . . . I'm the only one who's completely mortified.*

The Warlock's gaze slithered to table number four. He surveyed the pickings and landed on Caroline. The search stopped. He smiled, a confident invitation.

As the kids received their lumps of clay, he glided onto the empty stool next to her. His aftershave cologne smelled sickly sweet.

"Ever worked with clay before?" Words for her alone.

She couldn't turn her head toward him, or their lips would be only inches apart. She studied her clay intently, put her hands around it, beginning to form a shape. She shook her head.

"I'll show you," a beckoning tone. "You're going to do great."

He placed his hands over hers. "This is the right amount of pressure." His fingers were thick and damp from handling the clay. He kneaded her hands and Caroline fought back the urge to slam him in the solar plexus.

"Thanks," she said quietly. "I got it. You can move on to someone else."

A bit perplexed, but still in the game, he countered in a low baritone. "I'm fine here with you."

"It's okay," shooting for Olympic caliber obtuse, "you have a classroom full of new students. I don't want to take too much of your time."

He leaned back and smiled. "Wouldn't you like me to teach you?"

Caroline's table watched closely, puzzled by her reaction. Did she really not get what was going on?

After two classes of failed attempts, War gave her up as irrevocably clueless. His new chosen was Dawn, a sweet girl who eagerly filled the position. The Warlock set up her throne, a stool beside his in the front of the room. Nobody snickered, respecting Dawn's elevated status as she reigned, benign toward her subjects. Dawn was five-seven, skinny in her slacks and tube top, brown curls past her shoulders. She wore heavy makeup, purple hair ribbons, sparkling nail polish and multiple bracelets. The Warlock's proud cupcake. In class, they never touched beyond his guiding her hands over the clay. He allowed her to dole out grades and her lowest was an A-. The students liked her, and Caroline was especially grateful since she took War off her hands.

With The Warlock otherwise occupied, Caroline was free to concentrate on her table. Across from her sat one of the school's most popular girls, Lacey Tract. Five-ten, a beautiful face, doe-brown eyes, and bodacious chestnut hair almost to her butt. Caroline recognized her from the assembly at the beginning of the year, Hollywood High's head cheerleader, her routine interrupted when the brawl broke out. Caroline expected to ignore her, but quickly realized that she was truly nice. Lacey spoke to everyone, assuming the role of table leader and, in spite of War's sleaze factor, Caroline looked forward to her six weeks of ceramics classes.

To Lacey's left sat Moishe and to her right Manny. Across the table, Caroline sat between an empty stool and Elton.

As they began to sculpt anything but a bong, Lacey turned to Moishe. He was painfully shy, answered her questions in monosyllables, bowled over by her beauty. Although Lacey radiated sexuality with boys lined up at all times, she showed no disdain for his social awkwardness.

"I've never seen a hat like yours," Manny said to Moishe.

"It's a kippah," Lacey answered for Moishe, who looked like a deer in headlights. "My boyfriend is Jewish. I went to synagogue with him last weekend. It was cool." She peered at her blob of clay. "I have no idea how to sculpt anything. I hope I don't create a piece of crap!"

Moishe muttered a few words, barely audible.

"What'd you say?" Lacey asked.

Moishe repeated the words. "It means *piece of crap* in Yiddish."

The table burst out laughing.

Lacey then turned to Manny. She sympathized with his confusion, only three weeks in the United States. At the following lunch, she introduced him to a cheerleader friend who was fluent in Spanish. Her friend showed him the bathroom where fights didn't occur and told him which gangs to avoid.

"Your Hollywood High Survival Manual," Lacey smiled.

Manny thanked the girls and offered to share the churros his mother had made for his lunch. "Why do you both look surprised?"

"Most guys are always telling us how cute we are because we're thin," Lacey's friend explained. "They don't want us to eat too much."

"You should eat," Manny answered earnestly.

A week later, they were a couple.

In the next ceramics class, Lacey turned her attention to Caroline, scrunched her forehead, then lit up. "You're the tutor!" she announced.

"Anyone need help with a test, go to Caroline. She's really smart."

Lacey beamed and Caroline was floored. Never would those words have been spoken at Laurel with such heartfelt acceptance.

As she worked on her clay, Caroline absently watched Dawn joke with one of the boys. Then Caroline caught the expression on War's face. Her hands turned still, and she stared. *He's jealous! He's a pathetic, insecure jerk! What a loser!*

Lacey was telling a story about last year's championship football game, when one of the cheerleaders lost her balance and knocked the entire squad down like ninepins. The table was laughing, and Caroline saw War's eyes flicker toward them. Initially, she had been puzzled how he had passed Lacey over, but now it made sense. Lacey was too popular, too beautiful, too radiant, too focused on her acting career. When she landed an appearance in a commercial and disappeared for a week's filming, everyone missed her, and if she had sat in Dawn's chair, The Warlock would have been a wreck.

During her absence, Elton stepped forward as substitute table leader. Caroline had never before met one of the Eltons, five in total, famous on campus. They carried boom boxes with tapes of every Elton John song. They copied his glittery outfits, scrounged up the cash for his concerts, and eventually achieved full Elton status by legally changing their first names.

With War's permission, Elton played his idol's tapes through every class and, for a solid decade, Caroline couldn't hear "Daniel" or "Goodbye Yellow Brick Road" without instant transport back to the gleam in Lacey's kind eyes, Moishe's Yiddish lessons, the feel of moist clay, the sickly sweet smell of War's aftershave cologne.

The following Monday, Lacey returned triumphant. She'd become good friends ("I mean *very* good friends") with the commercial's star, Cobra, the lead guitarist in the wildly popular band PowerFire. PowerFire had been around, and Cobra was thirty-five if he was a day.

Still, with his new (and soon to be extinct) acting career, the band's popularity spiked, with Cobra precariously perched at the pinnacle.

"Will you see him again?" Caroline asked, knowing the answer, curious what Lacey would say.

"He flew to England for an audition the day the shoot ended. Our paths won't cross again."

"Are you glad you did it?"

"For sure!" Lacey's eyes flashed as she reached for her own hair, thick and reassuring.

When the class ended, Caroline had produced a lopsided toothbrush holder, three muddy green mugs that leaked, an elephant that collapsed under its own weight, and a cracked vase. She stood in line for Dawn's final evaluation. Lacey and Elton received A's. Moishe, who turned out to have talent, an A+. Caroline wondered if she'd receive her first B or heaven forbid, worse. Dawn, generous to the end, studied the exhibit respectfully.

"Good for a yellow rose," setting aside the vase. "Interesting shape," to the subsided elephant. Smiling shyly, with The Warlock looking intently away, she awarded Caroline top honors.

"You didn't want to sit there?" Lacey jerked her head in Dawn's direction, whispering to Caroline as they walked out of the ceramics classroom for the final time.

"That's a definite no."

Lacey grinned. "So, you knew what he wanted? The rest of us weren't sure you got it. I was going to tell you. Then he got together with Dawn, so it didn't matter."

"I got it. It's . . . I mean . . . yccch!"

"Yeah, yccch! Or *oy vey*, as my boyfriend's parents would say!"

"That's what my ancestors would say, too."

"You're Jewish?" Caroline nodded, and Lacey was suddenly fighting tears. "My boyfriend broke up with me when I told him about Cobra. I guess I don't blame him, but I thought he'd understand. I mean, Cobra's famous, and he was so nice to me, and—" her voice broke.

"Are you okay?"

Lacey nodded bravely. "There's always another guy, right?"

"I'm sure lots of guys want to go out with you."

The two girls smiled and went in their separate directions. When Caroline glanced back, Lacey was surrounded by four boys.

CHAPTER 37

Oblivious to the roar of the lunch hour, Caroline and her friends sat in a trance. The same foursome had attacked another gay student. Along with three cracked ribs and multiple contusions, this boy suffered two broken arms and a shattered kneecap. Worse, when he finally fainted, his head cracked against the tile steps leading from the showers to the lockers. In a frenzied encore, the four athletes delivered a series of kicks to the unconscious boy. With each blow, his skull crashed into the edge of the step. As the assailants ran off to celebrate, he lay too still.

Early January, 1974, back from the holidays. The weather was sunny, clear, and brisk. Caroline was pleased to reunite with her friends. They looked forward to Saturday night at Valerie's house, swimming in her heated, trapezoid shaped pool (photographed by *Garden Estate Magazine*, then dumped for an Oscar winner's star shaped watering hole).

Valerie had called Caroline as soon as she returned from Maui and reported every detail of the surfboard conversation. The girls celebrated over the phone and Valerie said she couldn't wait to tell the others. Best of all, she promised a gargantuan supply of Hawaiian chocolate and macadamia nuts from her holiday.

Then another lynching.

"Who is he?" Irene asked.

"Nobody knows his name," Vincent shrugged.

"Someone must know something," Kayla insisted.

"It's kind of strange. Nobody knows anything." Gary shook his head. "It's like he's been flying under the radar."

"I feel sick." Vincent pushed his food aside. "I didn't get it at the beginning of the year, so it didn't matter to me when Jeremy was hurt. Now it matters a lot. I mean, it could have been Valerie. Some people hate Blacks, hunt them like animals, kill them. That could be Kayla. Lots of people think Jews are dangerous and evil. That's Caroline. The Irish stereotype is a falling down drunk with a subzero IQ. That's Gary, who's smarter than the rest of us put together. My parents were in the Japanese internment camps when they were kids. At Hollywood High, it's okay to beat up gays. It's just an excuse to hate someone, do awful things and feel fine about it."

"Trans, too," Caroline said. Her friends looked at her, confused. "At Hollywood High, it's okay to beat up people who are trans."

"Can I ask you guys something?" They nodded at Vincent. "What's trans? What does it mean?"

"How can you not know—"

"Irene, let him ask questions," Caroline cut in before Irene could launch into a full rant. "He asked Valerie what it meant to be gay, not because he wanted to be a douche, but because he wanted to understand. I wish everyone wanted to understand."

Irene looked down.

"Can you explain it to me?" Vincent asked Caroline. "I want to get this, and I don't know who to ask."

"Me. You can always ask me. If I don't have the answer, I'll find someone who knows more." Caroline took a moment to gather her thoughts. "I'm sure someone who is trans would have a better way of explaining, but here goes. When you're born, the doctor looks at your body and writes on your birth certificate, male or female. That's when the world starts treating you like you're a boy or a girl. It works well for a lot of kids because as they grow older, they know that the gender the doctor wrote is the right match for who they are. It worked for me because I know I'm female. It worked for you because you know you're male."

Caroline paused and Vincent nodded.

"But it doesn't work for everyone. There are people who have *male* or *female* on their birth certificates, but it really isn't who they are. For those people, the doctor got it wrong. They have a body that people assume means a specific gender, but that's not always the right assumption. Someone can have a body where people assume *girl*, but in his head and in his heart, he knows he's a boy. Or someone can have a body where people assume *boy*, but in her head and in her heart, she knows she's a girl."

She waited, and Vincent nodded again.

"That's called trans," Caroline finished.

Vincent looked puzzled. "You make it sound so normal, no big deal."

"It is normal, and it shouldn't be a big deal."

"If you're gay, then are you also trans?" Vincent asked.

"Oh for God's sake—"

Caroline shot Irene a *shut up* look and turned back to Vincent. "Gay and trans are different. Trans is about defining your gender. Gay is about whether you're sexually attracted to people who are your gender or a different gender."

"Can I ask a question?" Everyone turned to Kayla. "It seems . . . I don't know how to say this . . . it seems limited that there are only two genders. Male and female. I mean, everything else about people is much more complicated, more than two choices. I . . . I know that what I just said is really strange. But have any of you ever thought about it?"

"Yeah," Gary nodded. "I mean, it's the beginning of 1974, and we're just teenagers. I'll bet that when we're adults, somewhere along the way, people will realize there are more than two choices."

"What you said isn't strange," Caroline looked at Kayla. "A friend of mine feels like *she* or *he* is too narrow. *They* works better. My friend told me they're a girl, but they also feel like a boy and a girl at the same time."

"Is she—"

"They," Irene interrupted Vincent. "Caroline said her friend is *they*, not *she* or *he*."

"Are they … well … kind of … not normal?" Vincent steeled himself for Irene's outrage. To everyone's surprise, Irene held herself in check.

"They're very normal," Caroline answered. "They have a girlfriend, who's also a friend of mine. They like to read as much as I do."

"Oh no no no! Not another nerd!" Irene raised her hands to the heavens.

"So the guy who was beaten up, he's gay but he's not trans. He's a guy who likes guys." Vincent circled back.

Caroline, Gary, and Irene nodded.

"I wish we knew the boy's name, so we could send a card or flowers," Kayla finished her lunch.

"Hold on," Vincent remembered, "I heard one of the jerks on the football team saying it was too bad to wreck the guy's hairdo, such a pretty blond."

Caroline caught her breath, along with Kayla and Gary. They jumped to their feet.

"Where are you going?" Irene scrambled after her friends. "Do you know who he is?"

"I hope not." Caroline's palms broke with sweat.

"We might know who he is," Gary grimly. "Caroline pointed him out to me and Kayla months ago, when we were at the House of Pancakes. He was with Drake."

"Wait, I'm coming," Vincent hurried to catch up.

They moved towards a corner of the administration building. Though unspoken and unwritten, certain territory in the quad was allotted to the more powerful gangs and the most visible student groups. The cheerleaders owned the one thriving oak tree and whatever shade it offered. The jocks sat at the quad's center table, a permanently sticky surface covered with graffiti. The performing artists clustered on the library steps. The Duke's gang owned a patch of gravelly asphalt, raised slightly above the rest. The west side stairs of the administration building were the domain of the male sex workers.

Caroline studied the stairs from a distance. A handful of boys huddled together, bony and angular, hair down their backs.

"I don't see him," Gary tried to pick out faces.

"Me neither," Kayla squinted.

Caroline bit her lip. He could be with a client. *Please let him be with a client.* Since her self-defense class, The Blond mattered more and more, which she understood less and less. Every time she thought of him, a snapshot from her dream jumped into her head and her emotions spiked. Now from ten yards away, she peered at his friends dressed in their white uniforms, tasseled belts, pink lipstick, signature hair. Curly, straight, frizzy, wavy. Brown, black, red, palomino. None as lustrous and flowing as The Blond's.

"I'm going to talk to them," Irene decided.

"Hold on," Vincent grabbed her arm. "You can't do that."

By the standards of Hollywood High etiquette, one clique did not invade another's turf without an invitation, registering on the same politeness meter as crashing a wedding. But Irene shook Vincent off.

"You two stay here," she tossed over her shoulder at the boys. "You're the football team. Y'know, you'll scare them." To Kayla and Caroline, "C'mon."

They approached cautiously, aware they were trespassing. One by one, the boys noticed the girls. The group quieted, incredulous.

Five boys. Five haunted faces. Five pairs of sad, hungry eyes. Each boy's hair beckoned, a powerful invitation, so beautiful Caroline had to stop herself from reaching out. She tucked her hands in the pockets of her jeans.

"Please excuse our intrusion," she began. "We mean no lack of respect."

The boys exchanged quizzical glances.

"Huh?" A boy with long brown curls.

"I apologize for arriving uninvited," Caroline tried again. "We're—"

"We're looking for one of your friends," Irene cut in. "Tall and thin, blond hair."

The group froze.

"J.D.," a boy with shimmering black hair. His lashes held tears.

"Beg pardon?" Kayla stepped closer.

"That's his name," the boy said softly. "J.D."

"That's a very nice nickname," said Irene, carefully respectful. "What's his real name?"

The boys looked at each other blankly.

"J.D.'s his real name," Red Hair said.

"I'm Irene," she said to the redhead. "This is Caroline and Kayla. What's your name?"

"Johnston." He followed her lead. "This is Billy (wet lashes), Gren (brown curls), Stephan (almost albino), Hal (astounding lavender eyes)."

Everybody nodded politely.

"What do the teachers call J.D.?" Irene asked.

"He's in my math class," Gren answered. "Everyone calls him J.D."

"Same in English and History," Billy added.

"Doesn't matter what they call him now," Johnston said bitterly.

"He's the boy the football players hurt yesterday." Irene was grim.

J.D.'s friends nodded. Through the surge in tension, Caroline sank down on the steps, dropping her head in her hands.

"Where'd they take him? What hospital?" Kayla asked.

"Cedars-Sinai." Johnston glumly. "They won't let us visit. Only relatives."

"We're his brothers!" Hal fiercely.

"Did Drake visit him?" Gren asked Billy.

"Not a chance," Billy's voice hitched. "Drake already sold J.D.'s stuff to his newest boy. Twenty bucks. J.D.'s face is messed up. No use to Drake anymore."

"We were hoping to send him a card, or maybe flowers," Irene offered, "but we don't know his name. Cedars-Sinai won't register him as J.D."

If the boys thought it odd that the girls would send their friend flowers, they kept quiet.

Then Gren had an idea. "Let's go to the administration."

From a distance, Vincent and Gary stared as three virgins and five sex workers climbed the stairs. Once inside, they hesitated. Caroline looked around and spotted Mrs. Richardson. Their guidance counselor was grave as she ushered the group into her office. The boys scattered on the floor, unexpectedly offering the three extra chairs to the girls. They surveyed the modest, windowless room with undisguised curiosity. Their first time in a college counselor's office.

"There are times," Mrs. Richardson began, "when I do things outside the book, because the official options fall short of someone's needs." She sighed. "You know Drake?" Caroline nodded and the boys exchanged surprised glances. "Drake found J.D. on the streets when he was nine. He was malnourished, lice, rat bites, boils and infections covering his body. Drake took him in, paid his doctor bills in exchange for certain services."

The five boys nodded, nothing remarkable to them. Caroline gripped the arms of her chair. Nine years old. Fourth grade. Baking cookies, slumber parties, jumping rope.

"What set J.D. apart from the rest of you," Mrs. Richardson

continued, "was he had no name, no birth certificate, no county records, no memories except of the streets. Drake called him J.D., and that became his name. Officially, J.D. doesn't exist."

Hal raised his hand, not realizing that formality was for the class-room only. Nobody smirked as Mrs. Richardson acknowledged him.

"Why'd he go to Hollywood High? Lots of Drake's boys don't go to school."

"He wanted an education." Mrs. Richardson steadied her voice. "Drake let him take classes, as long as his work schedule wasn't interrupted. J.D. audits Basic Math, English, Science, and History. Nothing on paper. He gets no grades. He's scheduled to take the high school equivalency exam in three weeks."

"I don't mean to be disrespectful, but you've done so much for him," Johnston was puzzled. "Why didn't you get him a birth certificate?"

"Fair question," Mrs. Richardson answered evenly. "Drake wouldn't allow it. I think it kept J.D.—"

"Under Drake's thumb," Irene finished the sentence.

The five boys nodded. They knew Drake well.

"What's being done about it?" Everyone looked at Caroline. "Has someone contacted the police? Or the press? Is the school going to call a mandatory assembly, at least say that it's wrong? I mean, he's in a coma. He has no voice. Someone needs to speak for him."

"I agree," Mrs. Richardson nodded. "We certainly filed a police report. However, it's tricky to call an emergency assembly at a school he doesn't officially attend. I'd like to contact the press, but it will be difficult to find a journalist who's willing to write about a boy who doesn't exist on paper."

"I'm the press."

All eyes turned to Irene.

"I'm on the school newspaper. The paper comes out every Monday. I'll write an article for the next issue."

"You can interview us," Stephan said, and his friends nodded.

"I'll be glad to give you a quote to use," Mrs. Richardson added.

"Thank you very much." As always, Irene was courteous to her sources. "I can use your names, or you can be anonymous. You can choose."

"You'd keep our names secret if we wanted?" Hal double checked.

"I'd die before I betrayed a source!" Irene's ferocity didn't surprise her two friends, but Mrs. Richardson and the boys blinked. "I know it's not safe at this school to be openly gay. It makes me sick!"

"That's something I hope to change," Mrs. Richardson said quietly.

Johnston raised his hand. "Is J.D. going to die?"

Mrs. Richardson forced herself to answer honestly. "I hope not, but it's quite possible. He suffered severe head trauma. Even if he lives, there may be permanent brain damage. The doctors can't assess the situation until J.D. comes out of his coma."

Billy bit his lip hard, fighting for control. His shoulders collapsed, and he cried into his hands. "I'm sorry," he choked out. "I'm so sorry."

Johnston, sitting next to him, reached out, then quickly pulled his hand back.

Caroline felt a wave of anger. The baffling culture of The Land of the Free forbids two gay boys from touching, even in sorrow, if heterosexuals are present. Before she knew what she was doing, she reached down with complete lack of finesse, grabbed Johnston's hand and thumped it on Billy's shoulder. Everyone stared, and Caroline blushed. Johnston shifted, unsure what to do with his awkward hand. Then Mrs. Richardson nodded, and Billy melted into Johnston, crying on his shoulder. Caroline watched closely, and something clicked into place. Billy and J.D. were a couple. They waited in deference to Billy's grief. Finally, when he lapsed into a dejected silence, Irene remembered her mission.

"What name did they use at the hospital for registration?" she asked Mrs. Richardson.

Their guidance counselor opened her mouth to answer, but Caroline beat her to the punch.

"The name for people without a name."

From the quad's speakers, Cat Stevens' plaintive "Moonshadow" filled the room. Mrs. Richardson's eyes held tears. She nodded at Caroline.

"His name's John Doe."

CHAPTER 38

The following Monday, Caroline joined Toni and Blake to walk in their morning circles.

Toni smiled, then caught her breath. Moving toward them, walking in their own circles, were the three girls from the bathroom.

"Oh, shit!" Blake whispered. "We should go—"

"Keep walking!" Caroline hissed. "Don't drop your eyes!"

The girls suddenly recognized Toni and Blake. They started to smirk when they noticed Caroline. A look of panic crossed their faces.

"Good morning," Caroline said evenly as she walked past.

"G'morning," the three girls muttered, moving away as fast as their platform shoes allowed.

A few more steps and Toni glanced back. She burst out laughing. "They're running into the nearest building!"

"They're scared of you!" Blake punched Caroline's shoulder.

"It was a pleasure to meet them. I was hoping they'd hide in a toilet for the rest of the semester." Caroline remembered the rush of power as Girl #3 retreated to the far wall of the bathroom, followed by her posse.

"Since then, in P.E., they point at us and whisper, but they don't talk to us." Blake shrugged. "Fine with me. I'm glad to never speak to them again."

"You heard about that guy who got beat up?" Toni turned grim.

"Yeah," said Caroline.

"I heard he's unconscious," said Blake.

"I heard he might die," said Toni.

Caroline nodded.

"The whole campus is talking about it," Blake continued. "Most of the kids think it's no big deal. A gay guy who turns tricks. So what."

"It happens all the time." Toni spoke softly, not wanting to be overheard as more students arrived and the quad grew crowded. "It's always *so what* when the person is gay or trans."

Blake shook their head. "If a straight white kid is attacked, it's front page news. If the kid is gay or trans or Black or like me, lots of times you don't even hear about it. If you do, it's on the last page of the newspaper, hidden between a movie review and a recipe for vanilla cupcakes."

"My friends and I were talking to J.D.'s friends yesterday. They're really upset. That's his name. J.D."

Toni and Blake stopped in their tracks.

"You and your friends were talking to his friends?" Blake stared. "What were you talking about?"

"We wanted to bring J.D. a card and flowers. We didn't know where he was. His friends told us he's at Cedars-Sinai Hospital."

"You wanted to bring him flowers?" Blake was incredulous.

"Do you have a problem with that?" Caroline was surprised.

"Of course not!" Blake said defensively. "It's just . . . you're probably the only one who will bring him flowers or a card or anything. He'll be forgotten in a few minutes."

"Not by me," Caroline firmly. "I'll always remember him."

"How'd you and your friends end up talking to J.D.'s friends?" Blake was curious.

"Walked up and introduced ourselves."

"Just like that?" Toni raised an eyebrow.

"Just like that."

"You really are weird," Blake smiled.

"At my old school, a lot of the girls would think I'm weird because my friends here aren't all white and straight. My dad's a cinematographer, and lots my parents' friends in the industry think I'm weird because I read too much and I don't wear makeup." Caroline thought for a moment. "I'm used to being seen as different. But nobody's going to beat me up over it."

"You're lucky," Blake said sadly.

"All *different* is not created equal." Toni said quietly.

Irene emerged from the main building with two other journalism students. Each carried a huge stack of *Hollywood Crimson* newspapers, fresh off the press from the print shop classroom. They placed their bundles on the center table in the quad and hurried back inside for another load.

Caroline walked to the table, lifted a paper, and scanned the front page. She pointed to the lead article. "My friend wrote that."

Toni and Blake took copies, and the three girls began to read.

Hollywood Crimson Newspaper
January 14, 1974

Our Community
By Irene Gibb

On the first day back at school after the holiday break, a student was attacked on campus. He was minding his own business when he was assaulted by a group of students. He's in a coma, in the Intensive Care Unit, with several broken bones and a serious head injury. He might not live. His name is J.D.

"He's one of my closest friends," said an anonymous source. "He's a really nice guy."

"I've known J.D. for two years. He's a good friend," said another anonymous source.

Why would someone attack a really nice guy who is a good friend? Because he's gay.

Hollywood High School has several big problems. Gangs fight each other. Sometimes our classes don't have enough books. Some of our students live on the streets and don't have enough food. Gay and trans students are singled out and attacked verbally and physically. Now, one of those students might die.

"We have an extremely diverse community," said our guidance counselor, Mrs. Richardson. "Our students speak forty-four languages. We have students with different talents, many lifestyles, several racial heritages, a range of sexuality. If people choose to be accepting, supportive, and respectful of each other, our school will be unsurpassed. When students turn against each other, it's dangerous. Now J.D. is fighting for his life. That's not what Hollywood High should be. We're better than this. We should live up to our school's motto, Achieve the Honorable."

Like Mrs. Richardson said, our school motto is Achieve the Honorable. Attacking J.D. (or anyone else) for looking different, being different — that dishonors our entire community. Hollywood High's colors are crimson and white. But crimson shouldn't be blood, and white (or straight) shouldn't be supremacy. Our community should include all, and I mean ALL, of our people. Our differences can make us stronger. Our school should be about inclusion, not marginalization, and definitely not about violence against our own people.

I hope students, faculty, administration, and support staff will come together, uniting in our good wishes for J.D. to recover fully and return to our community soon. I'll be first in line to welcome him back. I hope you'll join me.

That evening, Leah and Geoff overheard Caroline reading Irene's article to Valerie over the phone. When she hung up, they asked what was going on. Caroline didn't talk about her recurring nightmare or her inexplicable obsession with J.D. Instead, she described the violence targeting the gay and trans students at school.

"Your friend Irene wrote a helluva piece," Geoff said admiringly.

"Irene's going to change the world."

"I just remembered something. Give me a moment." Leah rushed to the hall closet, filled with storage. She rummaged around and came up with a faded yellow notebook. She handed it to her daughter. "You put this together when you were eight years old."

Caroline opened the notebook, and a puff of silver glitter floated to the floor.

"I remember that glitter!" Geoff began to laugh. "You designed an observational research study. You set out to prove, scientifically, that there was no difference between gay love and straight love. You interviewed our friends."

"Look at that! The first page is about pizza!" Caroline grinned. "It's coming back to me. A boy at school said a word I had never heard. It was during a kickball game, and he was mad because his team was losing. I thought he yelled *You're Facts!* to the other team. He was famous for his talent at cursing, but I was confused why calling someone a *fact* was bad. The teachers pulled the boy from the game, which was normal when he'd shoot his mouth off. Then he was taken to the principal's office and sent home for the rest of the day. That wasn't normal, and the kids had no clue what had happened."

Leah nodded. "When I picked you up after school, you told me about it. You were baffled. I explained the word, told you it was a rude insult for a gay man. You said, *what's gay?*"

Caroline brushed silver glitter from her t-shirt. "I had forgotten about that conversation. Now I remember. You told me what *gay* meant, and I couldn't understand why it was a big deal. I said something about how much I liked Gretchen and Janet because they were nice and funny and baked caramel cupcakes on my birthday."

"That's right." Leah thought through the conversation from years before. "Then you said they were great wives in a great marriage. So I explained that they weren't allowed to get married legally."

"You were outraged. You kept saying *it doesn't make sense*," Geoff smiled at his daughter. "We agreed with you. Then you pulled out your favorite yellow notebook, a bottle of silver glitter, and set out to prove that the law was wrong."

Caroline turned the pages and burst out laughing. "The questions I asked are extremely scientific. What's your favorite pizza? What's your favorite color? Favorite ice cream, favorite song?" She flipped through the pages to the end. "I wrote a conclusion. I spelled conclusion with a K! I couldn't find any significant differences between gay love and straight love. Proven scientifically because Gretchen and Janet both picked mushroom pizza and strawberry ice cream, the foundation for any successful relationship."

"I still can't find any significant differences," Leah said.

"Me neither," Geoff agreed.

Leah hugged Caroline's shoulders. "It's funny and cute, but I'm actually very proud of you for that notebook."

"I am, too," Geoff nodded.

"When your father was in the Marine Corps in charge of his platoon, he'd pull as many men as he could out of the brig, in confinement for being caught with another man." Leah smiled at her husband.

Geoff smiled back. "Did your mother ever tell you that she got in a lot of trouble when she was a psychiatric resident, because she was always arguing with the attending physicians, insisting that homosexuality wasn't a disease?"

"I wish more people had listened to you both," said Caroline.

"I wish they had, too," said Geoff.

"I wish they'd listen now," said Leah.

"I hope J.D. is okay." Caroline closed the notebook gently. She began to walk toward her bedroom, then stopped and turned. "It's not safe to be gay or trans at Hollywood High. Was it always this bad?"

Her parents nodded.

"Will it ever get better?"

Leah and Geoff didn't answer.

CHAPTER 39

Caroline had been on enough movie sets to know that fights on camera are choreographed down to the last detail. The actors rehearse until they achieve a thundering dance sequence, often accompanied by pounding background music to feed an adrenaline rush. A fight in real time is different. The thud of fist on meat, except the meat is a human body. The cries, grunts, torn flesh, blood. People slip, stumble, flail. They heave as they struggle to breathe.

At Hollywood High, gang violence was common during lunch and recess. In her first semester, Caroline had seen numerous fistfights. Most kids gathered in a circle to yell and applaud, while Caroline backed away. She'd always remember the first broken nose she saw, the boy's face shiny red with blood, her surprise at the brightness of the color, with The Moody Blues' dreamy "Nights in White Satin" flowing through the quad's loudspeakers. Though more of a veteran four months later, the violence still left her sickened for hours.

When the school year began, in spite of their boisterous physicality, the girls on the basketball team were deeply respectful of each other's safety. Shawna and Lureen were by far the team's best athletes, and Caroline could pinpoint the moment when their friendly competition turned mean. During the sixth week of school, they fell for boys in rival gangs. Since then, the two girls had gone after each other at every basketball practice. At this point, the team was impatient, and even Caroline found their moves predictable and annoying.

The season's end approached. The team had just played their archrival in the city's quarterfinals. Before each game, both captains and coaches gathered at the midcourt line with the ref, while the rest of the team waited on opposite sidelines. The official's message was always the same: No brawls. This time, the other captain, a go-to-hell six-foot bleached blonde Asian girl, brought with her a simultaneous interpreter. To Irene's surprise, she spoke fluent English. Dripping condescension, she stated that Irene was an inferior creature, unworthy of direct address. Her interpreter repeated her words, daring Irene to pounce. Irene remained calm, and Hollywood creamed them while Caroline sat comfortably on the bench with a pencil, keeping track of every girls' stats — shots hit, shots missed, shots blocked, assists, rebounds, fouls, turnovers, free throws.

Now, the team had five practices before the semifinals (where they'd make history, the only team in Los Angeles County to lose a playoff basketball game by shutout). Twelve minutes into the workout, Shawna pounced on Lureen. True to their boyfriends, their open warfare was obligatory. Still, respect for gang etiquette notwithstanding, the situation had escalated beyond reason. Cussing, insults, fists, then streaks of red (Irene's gym uniform) and shimmering pink (Mrs. Cuthbertson's tutu) sweeping in to separate the gladiators.

One by one, the team members complained to Irene, who urged tolerance of the violence inherent in gang protocol. But stressed with their vigil of J.D. who remained unconscious, Irene lost patience and discussed the problem with Mrs. Cuthbertson, who gathered the team. Usually Irene took charge of their practices. This time, their coach took the whistle. Without mentioning individuals, Mrs. Cuthbertson stated that no further disruptions would be tolerated and signaled to begin a one-on-one drill.

First Caroline versus Irene. The group cheered for both girls, although Irene's athletic abilities left Caroline in the dust. Next, Mrs. Cuthbertson pointed to Lureen and Shawna. The team exchanged nervous glances, but Caroline locked onto their tutu clad leader. Intent and shrewd, their coach had a plan.

Lureen and Shawna strutted to center court. Irene threw a sharp pass to Lureen, who faced Shawna, defending the basket. Lureen dribbled, faked, feinted, caught Shawna off balance and charged for the lay up. Shawna tackled her football style. On cue, Irene and Mrs. Cuthbertson charged in. This time, Mrs. Cuthbertson surprised them.

"You want to fight? Fine. Let's try something new." She stomped over to the bench and rummaged through her gym bag. She tossed out two pink tutus, three tubes of lipstick, an extra pair of sparkling ballet slippers. "Here we go!" She held up four huge, fire-red boxing gloves. Mrs. Cuthbertson marched to Lureen and Shawna, and shoved the gloves on their hands. "Carry on!" she barked.

The team perched on the bleachers. Suddenly, Shawna threw a right hook, catching Lureen flatfooted. Lureen countered, snarling, and the battle was on. They punched in swift flurries. They rolled, leaped, kicked. Caroline clenched her dripping palms, riveted with horror, fascination, and something she couldn't identify. She'd have to figure out the unidentified something later, because both girls were now bleeding from their lips and noses.

Mrs. Cuthbertson shot to her feet. "Follow me!" she ordered, leaving no room for questions. The team filed out of the gym, with Caroline last in line. As the door slammed behind her, she saw Lureen and Shawna glance up. Mrs. Cuthbertson seated the team out of sight for thirty seconds, then she tiptoed to the tiny window in the door. The boxers shifted awkwardly, unsure of their next move. Their coach didn't hesitate. She stormed back, her team in tow. She marched up to Lureen and Shawna, ballet shoes sparkling with rage.

"How dare you! As soon as you lost your audience, you lost your fight! How dare you use us in this way!"

Shawna and Lureen blushed, but their irate teacher barreled onward. "I'm your coach, not your personal boxing referee! These girls are your teammates, not your bloodthirsty fans! And this is basketball, not roller derby!" She glared at the two girls, staring them down.

Finally, Shawna whispered, "I'm sorry" and Lureen, "Me, too."

Mrs. Cuthbertson paced for a long minute, then faced the students. She spoke with an intensity the girls had never heard. "Basketball is a team sport. The most important word is *team*. You don't have to like each other. You don't have to be friends with each other. But as soon as you enter a practice, as soon as you put on your uniform for a game, you're bonded as teammates, and you work as a team. Got it?"

The girls nodded.

"I have some new rules. Listen carefully, because I'm saying this only once. Any physical violence against each other, you're off the team. Any verbal discourtesies, you're benched five minutes. Any second transgressions, you sit out the practice or the game. Three strikes, you wear my tutu for a solid week." The girls smiled nervously, and their coach glared. "Think I'm kidding? Try me." A long beat. "Questions?"

Silence.

"We have a game to prepare for. Ladies, on the court!" Once again, she dove into her gym bag. This time, she pulled out a tambourine. She handed the whistle back to Irene and parked herself on the bench. "If I hit the tambourine, you stop. It means someone broke a rule."

Slowly, Irene walked to center court and the team followed.

Caroline's horror calmed. Her fascination settled. She ignored her unidentified something.

That night, 2AM, she jerked awake in a sweat, clutching Claire-Bear.

Blond hair, red lollipop. Eduardo, Doris, Eric, Anna, Christopher. It took her over an hour to fall back to sleep.

Bleary, she arrived at practice the next day.

"Good afternoon, ladies!" Mrs. Cuthbertson greeted them with a perfect pirouette. "Are we clear that we're basketball players, not mud wrestlers?"

The girls laughed and no further fights broke out.

True to her word, their coach banged the tambourine when Shawna called Lureen a "turd on rye" for missing a shot. Five minutes on the bench for Shawna. She rejoined the game, grabbed the ball, lost control, and Lureen shouted, "You're a sweaty tool!" Five minutes on the bench for Lureen.

Practice calmed, but Caroline's sleep remained turbulent.

Then a shocker. Mrs. Cuthbertson benched Caroline. Always outwardly reserved, Caroline expressed appreciation for her teammates as though a polite spectator at Wimbledon. Restrained applause, certainly never raising her voice to a shout. She'd just blocked a shot, her only successful block of the season. She swelled with pride. Lureen, on her team, grabbed the ball and scored. Irene and Shawna yelled lustily, and Caroline nodded her congratulations.

The tambourine jangled and the girls stopped their four-on-four scrimmage.

"Caroline, you've got to yell," their coach said earnestly.

The girls exchanged confused glances.

"If your teammates can't hear your support, you're not fully on the team."

Caroline still didn't get it.

"Your voice, Caroline. I want it loud during every play. That courteous nod of yours won't do." By this time, the girls were laughing, but Mrs. Cuthbertson remained serious. "Get off the court!" she commanded. Caroline blushed as Mrs. Cuthbertson pointed toward the bleachers.

"Five minutes on the bench for an inverse technical foul!"

Grinning, the girls resumed play. Dribbling, shooting, shouting.

Caroline sat alone, expression serene, posture perfect, hiding a storm of shame. She thought of her self-defense class, the immense inhibition she overcame to unlock her voice. She breathed deeply, ratchet-like, trying to find the precise place where the sound caught in her throat and tapered to mannerly insignificance. Finally, Mrs. Cuthbertson motioned her to rejoin the group. With no forethought, no time to modulate herself bloodless, Caroline leaped to her feet as Irene clanged the ball through the hoop. Hands fisted, eyes shut, face persimmon, Caroline roared at the top of her lungs, "GOOD SHOT!"

Play suspended another five minutes as everybody, including Mrs. Cuthbertson, rolled on the floor. Lying flat, looking up at the stained ceiling, Caroline knew a piece of her longed to be loud, brash, even violent. Like Shawna and Lureen, with their focused fury, their brazen chutzpah, muscles sleek through sweat, long hair whipping. Dangerous.

The unidentified something. Caroline longed to be dangerous.

That night, she slept peacefully.

CHAPTER 40

Caroline dodged her way through the packed hallway to Miss Orville's classroom. She reached the door when she saw Toni huddled against the opposite wall. She walked over to her friend.

"Blake and I didn't see you this morning," Caroline said.

"I didn't want to walk around. Too visible, too out in the open." Toni's eyes darted, sizing up every student near her.

"Where's Blake?"

"They're taking an extra art class. Sculpture from Scraps."

"My friend Vincent signed up for that class. He likes it a lot."

"Blake likes it, too." Toni bit her lip.

"What's wrong?"

"I have a free period. I need a place to go. It's not safe to just hang out in the quad anymore. Not after what happened to Jeremy and to J.D."

Caroline didn't hesitate. "Come with me." She opened the door to her Latin classroom and motioned Toni to the front of the room. "Miss Orville, this is my friend Toni. She has a free period. Is there any chance you need an assistant?"

Miss Orville glanced at Toni and immediately understood. "Actually, I'd find an assistant extremely helpful. If you're interested, I can fill out the form now. You can stay here this period and do your homework. If you're caught up, you can relax and observe the way I run my classroom. I'll turn in the paperwork at lunch so it goes through right away. You'll be official tomorrow. You'll get community service credit. Does that sound like a good plan?"

"Yes, please. Thank you."

Miss Orville introduced Toni to the class as Caroline joined The Duke on the floor in the back corner of the room.

"That's a very tall girl," The Duke glanced at Toni.

"You're a very tall guy."

"That's the truth!" He grinned and pulled a copy of *To Kill a Mockingbird* from his backpack. In whispers, careful not to disturb Miss Orville's game of Latin Jeopardy, they discussed The Duke's paper, due in a week. "We can make up our own topic. I want to write about names. Boo Radley's real name is Arthur. It matters when the reader learns his real name. It makes him human, gives him respect. He's not just the town weirdo anymore." He watched Caroline anxiously. "I don't want to look like an idiot. Is that a good topic?"

"It's a great topic. Think about the significance of having a name and the impact of not having a name."

"Damn, girl, it's an even better topic than I realized. I'm a genius!"

Caroline began to show The Duke different ways to include quotations in a paragraph, how to reference the page in the text without interrupting the flow of his writing. Ten minutes into class, they were bent over his notebook when there was a tentative knock and the door cracked open.

"Can I help you?" Miss Orville asked the small group of students. She didn't recognize any of them.

Caroline gaped as her ceramics table filed in.

"I'm sorry to interrupt," Lacey's beauty held the room spellbound. "We're here because we have tests we're about to bomb."

The class laughed.

"That certainly is regrettable," Miss Orville chuckled. "However, I'm not sure how I can help with your misfortune."

Toni was wide-eyed. This was the strangest classroom she'd ever set foot in. First, Miss Orville accepted her without question. Then Caroline disappeared into the back of the room with the most notorious gang leader in the school. And now this, whatever *this* was.

Caroline was equally wide-eyed, staring from her spot on the floor.

"Do you know them?" The Duke whispered.

She nodded.

"Who are they?"

"My ceramics class."

"You took ceramics?" The Duke grinned. "Did War hit on you?"

"Of course. I'm female and I have a pulse, although I really don't think the pulse mattered."

"Did you . . ."

"His unsurpassed skill. His poetic declarations of love. His prodigious size. Such pleasure happens only once in a lifetime and—"

"Okay, okay, I get it." The Duke laughed.

Standing by the chalkboard, Miss Orville remained puzzled. "Are you looking for something specific?" she asked, as Lacey scanned the room.

"Actually," Lacey explained, "we heard The Professor was here."

Caroline shot to her feet and Elton waved.

"I'm sorry," Caroline blushed, as the group walked back to her corner without Miss Orville's permission.

"I think it's quite wonderful," their teacher smiled. "Take those open desks in the last row. You can run your own classroom."

The group pushed the chairs into a circle while Caroline sorted out the academics. Manny had a history test. Elton, a Spanish quiz. Moishe, a spelling test. Lacey, a retake of a multiplication quiz.

The Duke hunched in a corner, eyes moving from Lacey in her cheerleader outfit, to Elton in a gold sequined cape, to Manny in a rival gang, to Moishe in a kippah.

"Let's get organized," Caroline took control. "Miss Orville, since Toni's observing today, can she tutor Manny? He needs help with a history test, and Toni's good at history."

"Absolutely," their teacher nodded at a surprised Toni, who worked her way to an empty seat in their circle.

"Manny," Caroline continued, "can you help Elton with Spanish? When you're done, Toni can help you with history."

"Thanks," Manny smiled at Toni.

"You're welcome," she said softly.

"Moishe," Caroline continued, "bring me your spelling list. Lacey, this is The Duke. He can help with your math."

The Duke clambered up, and the ceramics class froze.

"I'm gonna teach?" The Duke was incredulous.

"You're good at multiplication. You can show Lacey what she needs to pass her test."

"But I've never taught . . ."

"Oh, my God!" Lacey clutched her notebook. "You're The Duke!"

He looked her over with the old arrogance. "You've got to be kidding. Your shoes have pom-poms."

Lacey swallowed hard. "Caroline, I'm not sure this is a good idea. I mean, I thought . . ."

"That I'd beat you up?" The Duke said, dangerously quiet. "That I'm too stupid to teach you?"

"Something like that," Lacey whispered. "Maybe I should go—"

"Hold on!" Caroline cut in. "The Duke's smart and he's good at math."

"And he won't . . ." Lacey looked petrified.

"He can kill us all with one hand tied behind his back. But that's not scheduled until tomorrow."

"Caroline, honestly!" called Miss Orville, and the Latin students broke into laughter. "However," she turned to Hollywood High's head cheerleader, "in this classroom, everyone is treated with equal respect."

Lacey took a deep breath. "I'm a moron," she shook her gorgeous chestnut mane. "Sorry for being a . . ."

"Douchebag?" The Duke offered helpfully.

"Duke!" Miss Orville couldn't help laughing. "I'm extremely close to making you and Caroline recite Latin declensions!"

"Let's not resort to weapons," The Duke grinned. "I apologize for my rude vocabulary." He faced Lacey. "I won't disrespect your pom-poms again."

"The pom-poms aren't my favorite," she smiled shyly.

"Let me see your math." The Duke sat on top of one of the desks, ignoring the chair.

"I get mixed up multiplying when the numbers get too big."

"I used to have that problem. Then The Professor drew columns so I could see where the numbers go. I'll show you."

Lacey sat next to The Duke, on top of the desk, and they began to work.

Caroline studied Moishe's list of words and realized that the goal of his test was to learn *I Before E Except After* C. She explained the rule to Moishe.

Two seats to her left, Manny immediately figured out the source of Elton's confusion.

While Elton went over a few practice questions from his Spanish textbook, Manny turned to Toni. "Can you explain the Articles of Confederation?"

"No problem," she answered. "If it's okay with you, I'll give you a quick summary of the background. Then the Articles of Confederation will make sense."

"That would be good, because I don't get why it matters that the thirteen colonies became thirteen states. I transferred to Hollywood High in the middle of the semester, and I missed a lot of the background for this test."

"It's an interesting step in our country's history. The reason it matters is ..."

Caroline turned to Moishe and said, "Ceiling."

He nailed it on the first try.

CHAPTER 41

A spectacular stomach flu rampaged through Los Angeles. Gary and Valerie were puking like geysers. Vincent and Kayla were nauseated and feverish. Their Saturday night gathering was canceled. Leah was fighting the bug, so Geoff asked Caroline to a showing at The Academy.

"Dad, you know I don't . . ."

"It's not an opening," he reassured her. "It's viewing a new release on a big screen in comfortable chairs. Much nicer than a theater."

"We wouldn't want to be seen watching a movie with civilians, as you and your friends call the rest of us."

Geoff shifted uncomfortably. "I didn't know you heard that expression."

"I heard it from you."

"I'm sorry. I didn't mean . . ." her father trailed off

"Of course you meant it. You didn't mean for me to call you out on it."

"You're doing that a lot lately." He waited for his daughter to apologize. Instead, she turned silent, so he continued. "Chip Harley has the lead, and people are already talking about an Oscar."

"Chip Harley's an asshole."

"I have to admit that's true. Still, if you'd like to come with me, I'm glad to have you."

"Do I have to get dressed up?"

"Your blue jeans are fine."

"Do I have to be polite if someone acts obnoxious?"

"I've given up on that."

"Let's go."

They arrived at The Academy of Motion Picture Arts and Sciences and entered the plush lobby built for the industry to meet and greet.

Geoff steered her to a quiet corner. Unfortunately, his efforts to avoid trouble amounted to naught.

"Geoff!" boomed Mel Fein, a successful director who had just celebrated his forty-seventh birthday. "How the hell are you?"

"Good to see you. You did terrific work on your last picture."

Mel shrugged modestly, raking his fingers through his thick black toupee. "A man's gotta make a living in this cutthroat world." He flashed a *you sly devil* grin. "Who's the lovely lady?"

"My daughter," Geoff answered dryly.

Seriously? You thought I was my father's date? Is everyone in the film industry a sexual pervert? And after fifteen years, it finally hit her. No, everyone wasn't a pervert but yes, the overall sexual mindset in the industry was twisted into a perverted Gordian knot. Caroline swallowed hard, coming to terms with something she had known for a long time, but didn't want to know.

"Caroline," Geoff continued as though nothing was wrong, "you remember Mel Fein from our holiday party?"

"Of course." Caroline automatically offered her hand. *You left the party early with a torn ligament. A sports injury, dancing a frenzied polka, trying to impress a stunning young actress.*

"Your daughter," Mel muttered. "I thought—"

"Do you really want to say it?" Caroline interrupted, iceberg polite.

Mel laughed. "No, I suppose not." As her father turned to another colleague, Mel began to massage Caroline's fingers.

"Where are you in school?" he asked.

"Hollywood High, and I think we've completed a successful handshake." She reclaimed her hand.

He laughed again. "I like a girl with spirit. Caroline doesn't suit such a beautiful girl. Too formal, three syllables. Callie suits you better."

"Too formal and three syllables are fine with me."

Her father was deep in conversation when she approached. "My daughter, Caroline," he introduced her. "Remember Chip Harley from our holiday party?"

"Certainly," she answered demurely. *You dumped an entire vodka collins all over yourself, refused to borrow dry clothes, and spent the evening strutting shirtless with your state-of-the-art chest hair implant.*

"Geoff," Chip thrust out his torso, "she's gorgeous!"

"She's right here," Caroline countered, overriding Geoff's *please behave yourself* look. "No need to talk about me in front of my back."

Chip laughed as Geoff was greeted by a producer. "I didn't notice you at your parents' party. What were you wearing?"

"Jeans and an old t-shirt. Like I'm wearing today. Like I wear every day."

"How charmingly down to earth. A rarity in the industry. Does a lovely girl like you have many boyfriends?"

"More than I can count."

"I'm not afraid of competition." He smiled his famous smile. "Caroline . . . hmmm . . . I see you more as a Carrie."

Caroline opened her mouth to suggest he style his chest curls into a French braid. Before she could speak, Chip's costar joined them.

"Darling," she slid into his arms and pointedly kissed his lips while glaring at Caroline. "Who's your date?"

"Marcie Carmichael," he introduced the woman without correcting her. "This is Geoff Black's ravishing daughter."

Marcie wore a silver beaded minidress that barely covered her butt. Her spike heels shot her over six feet. Her affair with Chip during filming made the tabloids, as did his dumping her the moment the final scene was a wrap. She looked down on Caroline, who stood at five-foot-four in her athletic shoes. Marcie smirked. "Who does your outfits?"

Caroline smiled gently. "I don't do outfits. I pull on clothes. You look beautiful, and I'm told you were brilliant in this picture."

Marcie raised her perfect eyebrows in surprise. "I didn't catch your name."

"Carrie—" Chip began.

"For the record," the girl talked over him as Mel Fein sauntered up, "I'll be Chip's date when actors stop wearing makeup."

"A wise decision," the woman shot her ex-boyfriend a mean smile. "And your name is . . ."

"Carrie" repeated Chip, and "Callie" said Mel.

Caroline turned extremely still. "So this is what it feels like," she murmured.

"What?" asked Marcie.

"To not have a name."

CHAPTER 42

J.D. remained unconscious, and Hollywood High was on edge.

Campus split into two factions. The vast majority of the students thought beating up someone for being gay was perfectly fine and skimmed past the issue as *not-my-problem-no-big-deal*. The remaining twenty percent were anxious and frightened. Mr. Cohen and Miss Orville took Carlos and Toni aside, quietly inviting them to spend breaks and lunch hours in their classrooms. Carlos remained in jeans and without makeup. Toni startled every time the door opened unexpectedly. Blake's eyes darted continuously during their morning circles.

The school newspaper received an unusually large number of responses to Irene's article, deposited by students in the COMMENT box outside the journalism classroom. The journalists were choosing which pieces to publish, trying to represent diverse perspectives. Suddenly the editor-in-chief turned pale and handed to their teacher an anonymous note written in block letters. *IF IRENE LIKES GAYS, THEN SHE NEEDS TO GET LAID AND FIND OUT WHAT A REAL MAN CAN DO. GIVE ME FIVE MINUTES WITH HER.* In the next edition, the following was published.

In response to the recent article entitled Our Community, *we have received several notes left in the COMMENT box. Most comments are appropriate and thoughtful, and we thank you for sharing your ideas. However, one anonymous note threatened to rape the journalist who wrote the article. This is unacceptable, and the following steps have been taken. For everyone's safety, no responses will be published. The school administration has brought two additional police officers to patrol campus. We are now actively working with the police department, and they are in possession of the anonymous note. No further threats of violence or assaultive actions will be tolerated at Hollywood High School. This includes gang fights as well as attacks on our gay and trans students. Along with consequences at school, legal action will be taken.*

That got everyone's attention.

Ten days after J.D. was found broken and unconscious, Caroline's group huddled under their scraggly tree, trying to eat lunch through the tension. They were deeply shaken that their friend had been threatened, and even Irene admitted that "y'know, this shit is serious."

"Until this calms down, Caroline and I are walking you to every class and to your bus after school." Gary laid down the law. "We've already talked to Mrs. Richardson about it. Our teachers know and they won't mark us tardy."

"That's ridiculous!" Irene objected. "It's . . . wait a second, you and Caroline went to Mrs. Richardson behind my back?"

"Yeah, we did!" Caroline didn't flinch. "We knew you'd pitch a fit, so we went ahead and talked to her."

"You're acting like I'm a damsel in distress!"

"You're not a damsel in distress! You're a macho douchebag!" The group stared as Gary raised his voice. "I'm huge! You know I'm a total klutz, completely useless in a fight. But most of the people here don't know, and I recommend you don't tell them! Caroline knows self-defense. If anyone decides to show you what sex with a real man is like, I'll get in their way, and our ex-Clover friend will beat the crap out of them!"

Suddenly, J.D.'s friends stood over them, blurs of white as Caroline squinted into the sun. Everyone jumped up, and Irene stepped toward Johnston.

"Is he . . ."

"Dead. Cerebral hemorrhage." Johnston's voice broke.

"He never made it out of critical care," Gren wept. "He regained consciousness and talked, so the doctors thought he might be okay."

"Talked for over an hour," Hal added. "But then he got a bad headache and he fell back into a coma."

"I'm so sorry for your loss," Gary said to Billy, both of them crying.

Billy nodded, struggling to identify the big, blond guy. Suddenly he went rigid. "He's on the football team! He's one of them!"

"Hold on," Irene began, but Gary knew what to do. He stepped back, palms up.

"No." His tone was steady. "I mean yes, I play football, but my name is Gary and no, I'm not one of the animals who hurt your friend."

"Killed him," Hal corrected. "He's not hurt anymore. He's dead."

Caroline began to shake. She'd always thought of murderers as another species, easily recognizable by their rolling eyes and foaming mouths. But these boys were scary in their normalcy. They took math exams and spelling tests. They ate breakfast, bought socks. And they beat the life out of an adolescent boy.

There was nothing more to say. Slowly, J.D.'s friends turned away. Caroline watched them, and something seized her.

"Wait!" she cried. "Where's his body?"

"The hospital got rid of it," Stephan answered.

"Was he religious?"

"Christian, I guess," Billy shot her a puzzled look. "He didn't belong to a church."

"We should have a memorial service."

Nine kids stared at Caroline.

"She's right," Billy agreed through tears.

"Where should we do it?" Gren asked.

"J.D. loved the beach, especially at sunset." Billy wiped his eyes. "His favorite color was orange, and sometimes the sunset looked like an orange ball of fire lowering into the ocean."

"I can see it," Vincent barely audible.

"My parents have a beach house," Caroline offered thoughtlessly. "We can go there if you want."

Drake's five boys exchanged glances, and Caroline realized her mistake. Owning one house was rare for a Hollywood High student. Two implied immeasurable riches.

"She can't help it," Gary stepped in. "Her parents have money. She's okay."

"No big deal," Kayla added.

"Caroline's one of us," Vincent said as Irene punched her shoulder.

The boys nodded, although they eyed her with curiosity . . . which threw Caroline even more off balance, because she'd been among the lesser wealthy students at Laurel. The conspicuous display of jewelry, the competition over swimming pools, the boasting over original art, the sweet sixteen Jaguars (although the entire fleet paled when one of the girls sniffed at her shiny silver car and announced that her gazillionaire grandfather had bought her an island).

"Okay, thanks." Johnston halted her flight into the safety of Laurel.

Caroline mentioned it to Valerie in their nightly phone marathon, and she caught Caroline off guard by asking to attend. Nervously, Caroline approached the boys for permission to bring a girl from her old school. Understandably, they balked.

"How's she with gays?" Johnston finally asked.

"She's gay."

A flurry of surprised glances.

"Does she know what we do?" Stephan asked. "How we live?"

Caroline nodded. "She's okay with you, if you're okay with her. Her dad died last year, when I was still at Laurel Academy. I think she's remembering her father."

"She's a Laurel girl?" Billy asked. "Mansion, trust fund, Jaguar?" Caroline nodded, surprised. "One of my regulars lives in Beverly Hills. Huge house, pillars and marble, swimming pool and tennis court. I stayed there with him for a week when his family was out of town. His daughter goes to Laurel. Ever met a tenth grader named Nicole?"

Caroline was stunned speechless. Valerie's Platinum Ring vice president. But even in shock, knowing nothing of this world, Caroline understood that Billy, in his distracted grief, had committed a spectacular indiscretion. She knew she needed to hold her reaction in check and let the moment pass unnoticed. Caroline didn't need to be told that Nicole, her mother, and her sisters had no idea. Over the next few days, the weight of the secret became too burdensome, and she confided in her parents. She told nobody else.

"Okay," Billy agreed. "Your friend can be with us if she wants."

Caroline nodded wordlessly.

Early afternoon on Saturday, Valerie picked up Caroline and Kayla in her sleek black Jag. Gary drove Vincent in his family's third-hand Datsun. J.D.'s five friends insisted on piling into Irene's Volkswagen bug.

As soon as they arrived, Valerie scanned the group and picked out Billy. She expressed condolences and thanked him for allowing her to attend. Both had shimmering black hair, patrician features, same height. They could have been brother and sister, until you saw their eyes.

Everyone began unloading a feast from Irene's trunk. Watermelon, lasagna, cookies, and orange soda. J.D.'s favorites.

The kids sat on the beach in a tight circle. Each of his friends said goodbye and threw a handful of sand into the sea. Kayla pulled out her guitar and sang "Corner of the Sky" from *Pippin,* an adolescent's longing for a meaningful identity.

Billy, leading the ceremony, asked if anyone had more to say, and Caroline raised her voice above the breeze.

"Every country has a tribute to the unknown soldier. He represents the people who died too battered to be identified by name. J.D. had no name of his own, but he can still die with honor." She pulled from her backpack an American flag. With everybody working to shield the flag from the wind, she folded it as her father had shown her, with military precision, and presented it to Billy.

"May he rest in peace," murmured by a circle of bewildered teenagers.

"May his memory be a blessing," whispered Caroline.

Looking toward the horizon, the universe loomed forever. The waves, the indifferent pulse of the earth. The sand cold under their feet.

Silently, the group headed for the house.

Caroline lit the room brightly. She reached for The Beatles' *White Album,* but Irene caught her hand. "Trust me," she said quietly and put *Godspell* on the stereo. Nobody spoke as Caroline set out the food. Absently, Billy picked up a chocolate chip cookie.

"This is exactly how J.D. liked it," grave and heartfelt. "With big nuts."

A moment of disbelief.

Then Billy, laughing and crying, "I can't believe I said that."

They laughed until they collapsed, grateful for Billy's slip.

Grateful to begin healing.

CHAPTER 43

The following Monday, Caroline and her friends remained consumed by J.D.'s death and his memorial. In his advanced art class, Vincent painted J.D. from the back, looking over the ocean, his blond hair flowing. He watched the sunset, a fiery orange ball lowering into the dark sea. Against the bright sunset, Vincent painted J.D. in quiet colors, the beach and the ocean in grey.

An announcement was made that the assailants had been identified and were in police custody. Later that day, Mrs. Richardson called J.D.'s friends and Caroline's group into her office. Months before, armed with Gary's information, she had distributed pictures of the football team to Hollywood High's openly gay students. J.D. had done his homework. Several days into his hospitalization, the afternoon before he died, J.D. awoke. He spoke urgently to a nurse, who paged the doctor, who called police headquarters. J.D. identified the four assailants, who were arrested a few hours later. Now they paced in jail, outraged and self-righteous. They showed no comprehension, not one whit of insight, that their team sport had devolved into murder.

Handcuffed and given their rights, the officer asked the obligatory question, "Do you understand your rights as they have been explained to you?"

"We didn't do anything wrong!"

"We did the school a favor!"

"We even tried to talk some sense into that idiot who wrote the article for the school newspaper!"

"She can't write things that defend those people and upset the rest of us! She's trying to cause trouble!"

"Then they sent our comment to the police, like we were the problem, not her! What a bunch of morons!"

"Give me five minutes with her and—"

"Stop talking!" The arresting officer spoke sternly, looking each boy in the eye. "You're in a load of trouble. Use your right to remain silent."

The four assailants exchanged you've-got-to-be-kidding glances, but shut up.

The next morning, Carlos sat in his chair by Mr. Cohen's desk, ready to mark absences. Caroline, Gary, and Kayla went to him.

"They caught the guys who killed J.D.," Caroline said quietly.

"I heard the announcement," Carlos looked exhausted.

"They confessed to beating up Jeremy a few months ago and two other students last year," Kayla added.

"It's over," Gary softly.

"It's not over," Carlos was grim. "Lots of talk around school. They're looking for their next target. They're out for blood. They're saying they'll avenge their brothers who are going to prison."

"That's why Carlos is still wearing jeans and no makeup," Kayla whispered to Caroline and Gary as they walked to their seats. "What happens if it's never over? What happens if people always hate gays?"

Gary shook his head. "No way. This can't go on. By the time we're adults, hating gays will be history."

"I hope you're right," Kayla said, "but people haven't stopped hating Blacks, so—"

The bell blared, and they moved to their seats.

Through her classes, Caroline barely heard her teachers. Carlos' words echoed in her head, a continuous loop, "It's not over." She treaded the halls on autopilot until her meeting with The Duke. He contained his annoyance as she barely said hello, forgot to ask after Doraine, and fumbled into their lesson.

"The subjunctive. It's when you're saying something hypothetical, something that might be but isn't necessarily, then you use *were* instead of *was*."

"Girl, you on drugs?"

"Of course not!"

He grinned. "Try that again."

"It's that *were* can be plural, or maybe singular, to convey a possible but not definite state."

"Say what?" He peered at her. "What's wrong?"

"It's . . . Oh! I forgot to ask. How'd Mr. Cohen like your paper on names and why they matter?"

The Duke shrugged. "He's still grading the papers on *To Kill a Mockingbird*. Tell me what's wrong."

Caroline bit her lip. "It's that boy, the one who died. I can't get him out of my head."

"The guy the football team beat up?" She nodded, and The Duke gave her a sympathetic look. "I don't blame you. It's awful."

"How can anyone treat people like that?"

"Makes no sense." The Duke shook his head.

"I can't believe this is happening. It's so wrong."

"I agree. They should get medals. Instead, they're going to prison. They—"

Caroline looked up sharply. "Wait! Hold on! What did you say?"

"I know how you feel. It's wrong. Four guys doing the normal thing, standing up for American values, and they get arrested for it."

"You think murdering J.D. is the normal thing? You think killing someone with their bare hands is standing up for American values? You think it's wrong that they were arrested for beating a student to death?"

"What's the big deal? He's only a fa—"

"Don't say that word!" yelled Caroline, not caring if the entire Latin class overheard. Toni's eyes snapped wide from the front of the room. The rest of the students turned to stare.

"Girl, you nuts? He's just one less fa—"

"Don't say that word!" The speaker was Miss Orville. "How dare you!" The Duke and Caroline both froze as their teacher marched from her desk to the back of the room where they sat on the floor. "Stand up when I address you!" The Duke obeyed, and Caroline scrambled up as well. "You have no right to judge that boy!" Miss Orville was formidable as she faced a teenager fourteen inches taller and known for his violence. "That boy harmed nobody! How dare you!"

"With all due respect, why does he matter so much? He wasn't even normal."

"Why was J.D. abnormal? Because he had sex with boys? Because he had sex with men?" The Duke actually blushed, but Miss Orville barreled forward. "Tell me what's wrong with that! You're writing him off because he was gay. The next lynch mob might go after you because you're Black!"

"No way! Nobody gets me!"

"Really? If I'm not mistaken, you lost a fight with a bottle of Coke a short while back. You're prejudiced, Duke, and you of all people should know better!" She took a quaking breath. "You may return for our next scheduled meeting. For now, you may leave my classroom!"

He gathered his books and slunk out. Caroline wasn't sure what to do. Then she saw The Duke at the door, beckoning urgently. She slung her backpack over her shoulder and stomped out. As she closed the door, her eyes locked with Toni's.

Caroline stormed to the lawn at Sunset and Highland, The Duke at her heels. She faced him, absolutely furious. To her horror, she began to cry.

The Duke was equally angry. "Girl, if you think something's wrong with those four football players, then something's wrong with you!"

"That's not news!" Caroline fired back. "You already think something's wrong because I'm Jewish." She roughly brushed tears out of her eyes. "I thought you were different. I thought you had changed."

"That's not fair. I am different than I was before. I have changed. I didn't know any Jews until I met you. I know you now. I know you're okay."

"Then maybe you should get to know some gays so you can see they're okay, too."

"C'mon, get serious," he glared.

"I'm completely serious."

"Forget it."

"Why not?" As she challenged him, she gained control of her tears and stopped crying.

The Duke shot her a *what's wrong with you* look. Caroline was breaking the rules. She was obviously clueless about the wrongness of homosexuality. Even worse, what the hell did she think she was doing? She was standing up to the school's most dangerous gang leader. She was angry and completely unafraid. What the fuck?

"You're being an idiot!" The Duke shouted. "You don't understand anything!"

"You honestly think I'm wrong about J.D.?"

"I don't *think* anything! I *know* you're wrong! Everything you're saying is wrong! Everything you're doing is wrong!"

Caroline stood stock still. "I don't think I want to be friends with you anymore." *Fight for us, argue with me, tell me we can work it out.*

The Duke laughed derisively. "Girl, you really are stupid! We were never friends!"

Caroline caught her breath.

"You thought we were friends? You're pathetic! I'm sick of you, always thinking about what's right! Your head is so fucking perfect! Why don't you stay there forever! The rest of us have a life to live!"

Caroline's face was an icy mask. *Never friends.*

"Goodbye, Caroline. Want to shake hands? Make it polite? Isn't that how it's done at Laurel Academy?"

He reached out to shake, but Caroline knew if they touched hands, she'd break down completely. Instead, she clenched her fists, her voice barely above a whisper. "Go fuck yourself."

"What did you say?" He hit her with the look that sent rival gangs running for cover.

"I said go fuck yourself!" Loud and clear.

"Nobody speaks to me like that!"

"I just did, asshole!"

"Fuck you, too!"

They stormed in opposite directions, determined to show no hesitation, no fear, brash and visible in their breach. Watched with great interest by Drake, who sat in the window of the International House of Pancakes, both arms free of casts at last.

As soon as The Duke was out of sight, Caroline changed direction and walked to the nurse's office. In a careful monotone, she said she had vomited. She was given a pass to leave school immediately. Caroline would have no memory of catching the bus. At home, she went to her room and opened Joseph Heller's *Catch-22.* She stared at the first page for two hours.

The Duke marched to his next class, boiling mad, high on adrenaline. The bell rang, and he was the first to take his seat. As his blood pressure regulated, he realized what he had said. *Never friends.* He rushed to the bathroom and vomited. Then he strutted back to class, radiating arrogance, daring anyone to challenge him.

Nobody did.

CHAPTER 44

That night, Valerie called Caroline in tears.

She took an advanced drawing class with three other girls, and their teacher made an unprecedented decision. She hired a woman to pose nude. The model turned out to be a graduate student in art at UCLA. As the high school students sketched, the more advanced artist offered tips and anecdotes from her own work. The experience was transforming, and the four charcoal sketches reflected the exhilaration. The drawings were displayed in Laurel's entrance hall.

The next morning, the wall was empty. As the artists cried in their teacher's arms, their headmaster called an emergency assembly. Waving the sketches, Mr. Hammer took the stage like a cyclone, vermilion and nearly berserk. Someone had ruined the drawings, adding bright orange nipples and pubic hair. Art desecrated.

"I never knew that violence against my art would feel like violence against my self," Valerie tearfully.

"I'm really sorry that happened to you."

"I feel like a jerk, crying about my sketch when J.D. was murdered."

"You're not a jerk. I know this sounds weird, but . . . I don't know how to say this." Caroline took a moment to formulate her thoughts.

"Students are always attacking each other at Hollywood High. Happens all the time. A lot of them think it's no big deal that J.D. was beaten to death. But wrecking art is unthinkable."

"How do you know?"

"Back in October, we had our fall art show, the best pieces from all the art classes. I was wandering around, and I stopped at one of the paintings. It was amazing. An angel swirling in the wind during a lightning storm. Then I realized this burly Doberman gang member was next to me, staring at the painting. The guy looked so proud that I asked if it was his work. He nodded, and I said it was great. He thanked me, very polite. The next thing I knew, this thug from a rival gang walked over."

"Uh oh. Here comes trouble."

"That's what I thought. I was backing up so I wouldn't get caught in the middle of a gang fight. But then the Thug clapped the Doberman on the back and gruffed out, 'Nice fucking shit, man,' and the Doberman growled, 'Thanks, man, 'preciate it.'"

"Then what happened? Did they dismember each other?"

"No. They walked around looking at paintings together."

"An art truce." Valerie said.

"The same thing happens when Kayla sings. The auditorium is filled with students who never shut up. The gangs yell and curse and throw stuff at each other. Then Kayla takes the stage, and everything turns quiet. When she finishes, it's immediately chaos again. I can't explain it."

"There's something about art and music."

"Yeah," Caroline agreed, "and whatever that *something* is, those two gang members at the art show understood it. And whichever Clover ruined your sketch — she doesn't get it."

CHAPTER 45

Caroline's friends sat in their circle at lunch, amazed that their soft-spoken hyper-academic friend had told The Duke to—

"—go fuck himself? Really? You told The Duke to—"

"Yes, Irene, she really did," Gary interrupted, laughing. "Caroline, you finally achieved what nobody thought possible. You shocked Irene."

"Hell yeah, I'm shocked!" Irene opened her carton of milk. "She called The Duke an asshole!"

"And you're still alive?" Kayla looked at Caroline.

"I believe I am."

Vincent turned to Caroline. "The Duke was probably too stunned to kill you. He'll come out of shock any minute. You should go into protective custody before he recovers."

"He was defending the guys who beat J.D. to death. He said they were patriots." Caroline had told nobody about The Duke's saying they had never been friends. If she spoke those words, she'd start crying and might never stop.

"It's scary how many people agree with him," Gary put down his sandwich. "Most people won't change their minds, no matter what you say. It's like a cult mentality, beyond reason. They're looking for someone to hate, and gays are a convenient target."

"The trans students, too," Caroline crunched her apple.

"You know one of the trans students?" Kayla asked, and Caroline nodded. "Boy or girl?"

"Girl."

"A real girl or a trans girl?" Vincent asked, then shook his head. "I think I said that wrong."

"You sure as shit said that wrong!" Irene gritted her teeth.

"How should I say it?"

Irene rolled her eyes. "Is it possible for you to be more dense? Y'know—"

"Irene, stop!" Caroline's tone was firm. "Like Gary said, most people won't change their minds. Vincent knows he's saying it wrong, and he's asking because he wants to change. Give him a chance!"

"Whatever." Irene muttered. "Sorry."

"Holy shit!" Kayla's eyes widened. "Did Irene say she was sorry?"

"Of course not!" Irene shot back. "Did Kayla say holy shit?"

"Of course not!" Kayla's lips twitched.

"I really want to get this," Vincent said quietly.

"It's not hard to get," Caroline shrugged. "She's a girl. She knows it, feels it, like I know I'm a girl and I feel like a girl. Like you know you're a guy and you feel like a guy. You're a real guy. I'm a real girl. She's a real girl. Trans girls are real girls."

"What's she like?" Vincent asked.

"Nice. Smart. Funny. Pretty."

"Is she, y'know, kind of weird?" Kayla was more curious than judgmental.

"No, she's a normal girl. Except there's one thing about her that's kind of amazing. She knows that if the wrong people figure out she's trans, they'll beat her up. She also knows they could take it too far and kill her, like they killed J.D. She shows up in school anyway, every day. She's the bravest person I've ever met."

"I think . . . look over there!" Kayla interrupted herself.

J.D.'s friends were walking towards them.

"Is it okay if we sit with you?" Johnston brushed his long red hair out of his eyes.

"Please have a seat," and "Sure! Sit!" Caroline and Irene said at the same time.

The ten kids tightened their circle into a huddle.

"We want to do something for J.D.," Billy began.

"Like what?" Gary asked.

"Like leaving things for him, in his memory," Gren explained, his brown curls almost touching the ground as he sat. "Have you ever seen people leave things at a gravesite? Flowers, stuffed animals, notes. There's no gravesite for J.D., so we thought we could do it at school, maybe tomorrow."

Vincent looked at Billy. "On Monday in art class, I painted J.D. watching the sunset over the ocean. It's like you described to us. When you were talking, I could see it. I asked Caroline what he looked like, because I didn't know him. She said he was tall and thin, with long blond hair like a gold river. You said he loved bright orange sunsets, so I painted an orange and yellow ball of fire, lowering into the sea, reflected in the water." Vincent paused. "Can I put the painting with the flowers and notes?"

"That's . . ." Billy's voice broke. He nodded.

The next day, they all arrived early and gathered on the west side stairs of the administration building. Vincent placed his painting on the top step. For a minute, everyone stood still, looking at his work. Caroline, Gary, Kayla, and Irene each put a bouquet of flowers in a cluster, on the step below. Billy placed a small poster in front of the flowers, black print on white paper: FOR J.D. His friends added more flowers, except Hal, who brought a small paper plate of chocolate chip cookies with enormous whole nuts, which made them smile.

Billy untied his own colorful scarf and draped it around the poster.

Mrs. Richardson walked toward the administration building, saw the display, and stopped. She spoke into her walkie-talkie. The campus cop arrived within a minute, quickly joined by three other police officers from the precinct.

"Are they going to kick us out?" Stephan whispered.

The campus cop and one of the officers climbed the steps and stood on either side of the tribute. The other two officers took their places at the bottom of the concrete stairs.

Ten confused kids turned to Mrs. Richardson.

"You've done a beautiful thing," their guidance counselor said. "I'll be in my office all day. Whenever I have a break in meetings, I'll come out here. The officers will keep you safe. Rest in peace, J.D." She shook Billy's hand and disappeared into her office.

"Maybe I should give a speech."

The group turned to Irene.

"Why?" Stephan asked.

"Y'know, so people can see J.D. has allies."

"You're here. People can see. They'll know he has allies." Johnston said. "Thanks for that. I mean it. Thanks."

"No problem. I'll . . ." Irene paused, seeing J.D.'s friends exchange uncomfortable glances. "What's wrong?"

"The problem with giving a speech," Caroline explained to Irene, "is it puts people's attention on you and on us. We need to be here, visible, in solidarity with J.D. But if we start making speeches, then it's like we're making it about ourselves."

"You're always afraid of the spotlight!" Irene impatiently.

"I hate the spotlight," Caroline agreed, "but this isn't about my allergy to attention. It's not about me at all."

"I'm not going to say anything about you or me. I'll talk about J.D., only about him." Irene defended herself.

Gary stepped in. "Irene, you're our unofficial leader. We look up to you. But this one time, you need to follow in Caroline's nerdy footsteps."

Vincent, Kayla, and J.D.'s friends nodded.

"Damn," Irene shook her head. "The apocalypse has arrived."

As the day progressed, several students from J.D.'s classes left notes and flowers. A few added stuffed animals. During the morning break, at lunch and in their free periods, the ten kids gathered on the steps. Caroline saw The Duke across the quad with Doraine, now obviously pregnant. A few of the athletes were clearly not happy, but one stern look from the police officers sent them backing away. To Caroline's surprise, her ceramics class approached at lunch, led by Lacey in her cheerleader outfit.

"We didn't know he was a friend of yours," Lacey said. "We're really sorry."

She placed a white rose with the flowers and hugged Caroline. Moishe, Manny, and Manny's cheerleader girlfriend stood close but didn't speak. Elton placed his boom box on the steps and blasted "Candle in the Wind," cutting through the noise of the quad. Caroline thanked him for the song and he hugged her. When he let go, a cloud of red glitter floated off his shirt.

Carlos stood to the side, next to Toni and Blake, watching from a distance. Caroline hadn't realized they were friends. She nodded to them, and they nodded back. Carlos's boyfriend joined them. The backs of their hands brushed. Then Caroline's eyes widened as the three girls from the bathroom walked up to Toni and Blake. She rushed over and to her surprise, Toni gave her a reassuring look.

Blake introduced the three girls by name. "They were saying . . ."

Caroline gave Girl #3, the leader of the pack, a questioning look.

"J.D. was in my history class," the girl offered. "This is so bad."

"He was in my math class," said Girl #1. "We did a worksheet together. He was nice."

Girls #1 and #2 exchanged a nervous glance and took a step back from Caroline.

"In the bathroom, you said we shouldn't talk to any of you, but yesterday . . ." Girl #3 trailed off.

"Yesterday one of the athletes hit my brother," Girl #2 looked at the ground as she spoke. "They called him a f—. Well, you know what they called him. The guy and his friends thought it was funny. My brother stayed home from school today. His eye's swollen shut."

"Is your brother gay?" Carlos asked.

The girl didn't answer.

"It's easy for people to pick on someone and get carried away," said Girl #3. "Then really bad things happen."

"Anyway," Girl #2 looked at Caroline, "we'll go now if you want."

Caroline took a deep breath. "I'm sorry that happened to your brother. You don't have to go, as long as it's okay with Toni and Blake."

"It's okay with us," Toni said and Blake nodded.

The next morning, the steps were clear. Mrs. Richardson summoned Billy to her office and gave him a box filled with the notes and stuffed animals. The previous evening, she had pressed the flowers and put them in a small, leather-bound book. She told him that grief was normal and encouraged him to schedule an appointment with the school psychologist.

"I wasn't sure what to do with the cookies," she indicated the plate on her desk.

"It's a private joke," Billy smiled sadly, carefully balancing the paper plate in the box on top of a teddy bear.

Later that day, Vincent received a summons. Mrs Richardson asked his permission to hang his painting in the school's main entrance.

"Wow . . . that's . . . I mean yes. Totally yes." Vincent stammered.

"Thank you. It's beautiful."

"Mrs. Richardson, can I ask for a favor?"

"Of course."

"At the end of the year, on the last day of school, can you give the painting to Billy?"

"That's a wonderful gift," Mrs. Richardson's eyes misted. "Would you like to name the painting?"

She waited while Vincent thought for a full minute. He began to speak a few times, then changed his mind. Finally, he met her eyes and nodded.

"Got it?" she asked.

"J.D.'s Sunset."

CHAPTER 46

The next weekend, Caroline spent Saturday at the beach house with her Hollywood High friends and Valerie. The sun was strong, bringing temperatures into the high seventies and warming the ocean. In the surprising winter heat, the beach was unusually active with frisbees, swimmers and surfers.

Gary and Vincent went for a walk, and Caroline stood at the water's edge with Valerie, Kayla, and Irene. Five surfers stood to their right. They watched another adolescent boy swim alone. He moved gracefully through the water, attuned to the currents. The girls exchanged admiring glances. Then they realized the surfers were angling for their attention.

"Look at that jerk!"

"He can barely keep his head above water!"

The boys pointed to the swimmer who navigated the waves like a dolphin.

"What a moron!"

The swimmer, around seventeen, caught a wave and expertly rode it to shore. He rose to his feet and headed back out, diving through the breakers in a perfect arc. His timing was impeccable, his muscles sleek.

"He's a fag!"

"Total fag!"

"Definitely a fag!"

The gentlemen exchanged high fives.

"Let's go," Valerie whispered and turned to walk away. Caroline and Irene took one step to follow her, but Kayla held her ground.

"What if he is?"

Kayla spoke so softly that the pack exchanged confused glances.

"Huh?"

"What'd you say?"

"I said, what if he is?" This time Kayla's speech was unmistakable.

The surfers stared at her. Then one pointed to the water. "FAG!"

"What if he is?" she repeated.

Kayla wore a yellow bikini, her body slim and strong. She had grown an inch since September, bringing her to five-foot-three. Her feet were sandy as she took a step forward to meet the tide. The breeze caught her black curls, gently lifting her thick hair. She stood stunningly beautiful, her eyes dark gold, her skin medium brown. She shrugged disarmingly and said again, "What if he is?"

The surfers shifted uncomfortably, and one of them muttered, "Well, nothing, I guess."

Kayla held their eyes for a long moment, then turned to her friends. "Let's swim."

For the next hour, they bodysurfed with the swimmer. He was stronger in the water than any of them and when he realized, he coached them so they could keep up. He was an excellent teacher, zeroing in on the most helpful tip for each girl. They left the ocean together, streaming water, warm in the salty sun. They thanked him for the suggestions, and he said he worked every summer as a lifeguard and swim teacher, earning money for college. He invited them to join his friends and they feasted on veggies, hummus, chips, and guacamole.

Caroline and Valerie returned to the beach house and brought back iced tea, cheddar cheese, crackers, and a mountain of peanut butter cookies. Gary and Vincent joined them.

They devoured the food until only one cookie was left.

"Who gets the last cookie?" Irene joked.

The lifeguard picked it up and gave it to Kayla. "I heard what those guys said and what you said."

Kayla took the cookie and broke it into small pieces for them all to share.

Nobody asked anybody if they were gay.

It didn't matter.

CHAPTER 47

February, 1974.

For the past four weeks, Caroline had been wrestling with herself over driving. In January, when she reached fifteen years six months, her parents offered to bring her to the Department of Motor Vehicles for a Learner's Permit. Gary also offered, as did the rest of her crew. The minute her friends had hit that golden age, they arrived at the DMV to begin the process of acquiring their ticket to adulthood. Caroline knew she wasn't ready, but didn't know how to explain. Instead, she quashed the notion with such vehemence that nobody uttered a word. Yes, she wanted to drive, more than she could admit even to herself. But powering a 3,000 pound vehicle was too big a threat, jeopardizing her allegiance to the Holy Order of the Nerds. Instead of driving, she began reading a ton of Shakespeare.

Unfortunately, Shakespeare failed her. As she began Act Two, scene one of *The Tempest*, the next wave crashed, instigated by one simple smile. They sat in their lunchtime circle, toasting Valerie. On Saturday night, she had kept them in hysterics. Six Laurel Clovers had received one week's detention and a full month's probation, punishment for

Conduct Unbecoming a Lady. For the entire football season of Driscoll Preparatory Academy for Boys, during every fourth quarter, these half dozen seniors pranced into their brother school's empty locker room, equipped with every colored condom imaginable. They stripped and waited for their conquering or conquered heroes. Finally, and quite inevitably, someone's father came in to console his son after a spectacular trouncing (seventy to three), and found another sort of consolation in full swing.

As Gary declared his disappointment that Hollywood High girls lacked proper support for his team, Caroline turned to Kayla to joke about beginning training sessions. But Kayla wasn't looking at Caroline. She stared across their circle at Vincent. In a shared moment, they half shrugged, slightly blushing. And then, the smile.

Kayla and Vincent.

What is this sex thing? Is it addictive? Could I overdose? No, Kayla wouldn't do something that wasn't safe . . . and polite. When I find the right guy, then I could . . . whoa, hold on, no I absolutely could not! Too risky, an uncontrolled free fall. I need to think it over, think it through, think it out.

Tricky, figuring out how to shield herself from something so alluring. Especially when, in spite of her best efforts, she grew more confident in her body, the latest incident the previous day in gym class. For the past month, every P.E. class was focused on the National Physical Fitness Test. Push-ups, sit-ups, pull-ups. Hurdles, long jump, hundred-yard dash. The monster mile run.

They counted down, and the previous day was showtime. As Caroline finished her second lap marking one-half mile, she found herself sweating, panting, and vaguely frightened. She had little faith in her endurance and expected to faint, even as she felt the steady rhythm of her pulse. Fascination with the girls kept her on the basketball team, where she comfortably spent the season on the bench. She had yet to enjoy any sport for its own sake.

Her gym class had practiced the mile run more than any other event. Their P.E. teacher jogged with the girls, stride for stride with the slowest student. She calmed them on the testing day, narrowed their focus, and all sixty girls passed every test, including the mile run.

They ran in groups of thirty, with the other half yelling encouragement. To Caroline's amazement, she not only finished in the allotted time, she finished number eleven, and allowed herself a shot of triumph. She threw back her head, stepped to her right onto a thin strip of grass next to the track, and began jumping in place.

This turned out to be an unfortunate choice.

Since the beginning of the school year when Della beat up Nellie in the girls' bathroom, the two girls had declared open warfare. Their hostility was an ongoing issue in their P.E. class, and they rejected every effort from their teacher to negotiate a détente. They had been sent to the Vice Principal's office countless times, returning after each visit to resume battle. Then the class began a unit of volleyball and both Nellie and Della turned out to be outstanding players. At their teacher's suggestion, they tried out for the team, where they excelled and were voted co-captains for the following year. Now, they were great friends. Nellie settled down, but Della was always hunting for a new target. This time, Caroline drew the short straw.

As Caroline jumped in place, Della finished her mile run three steps behind and, by chance, stepped to the right onto the same patch of grass at the same moment … except Caroline jumped and Della kept running, smack into her. Caroline stumbled forward unhurt and caught herself before she fell. Della crashed hard, leaped to her feet and advanced threateningly. Caroline flashed on Nellie, curled on the bathroom floor, and knew that a few months ago, she would have quaked in terror. Instead, her self-defense training was at her fingertips. Outwardly ready for war, Della closed in, swearing in English and Portuguese. Instead of cowering, Caroline evaluated her through Linda and Quincy's eyes.

Della's shoulders caved just enough, her stance weakened slightly, her eyes darting and unstable. Caroline pointed to an imaginary line four feet in front of her and Della glared in confusion.

"Don't cross that line."

As fifty-eight girls stared, as their teacher prepared to intervene, Della stopped at the invisible line, snarled, dropped her fists, and turned away.

A new something rippled through Caroline's gut. Athletic confidence, followed by bodily confidence, followed by — before she could stop it — sexual confidence.

The next day, Caroline took several weeks' allowance and shot her wad on a Latin-English dictionary, a gargantuan text with a bright magenta cover. For a week, she memorized Latin vocabulary, her bodily confidence and sexuality blanketed under a dead language.

But Latin vocabulary couldn't stop Irene from falling headlong in love with a political activist she met at a rally for socialized medicine. Her boyfriend was premed at UCLA, an older man of nineteen, meaning sex was a certainty.

Discovering this new world of sensuality, drugs inevitably followed. Both Irene and Kayla confided that "coming" was awesomely different after a few hits of Hawaiian Gold.

Different from what? Coming where?

No, they weren't dipping into anything stronger and yes, they were using protection. They were happy, glowing, and obviously holding onto their higher evolutionary faculties. Still, sex, drugs, and a driver's license were more than Caroline could handle, so she listened and watched and filed the information in an inner rolodex.

With this turn of events, their weekend gatherings became irregularly attended. On a Saturday with Gary and Caroline, Valerie broached a sticky subject, the Laurel St. Patrick's Day Dance, also known as Sophomore Prom. Attendance was mandatory for someone of her social standing. Would Gary go with her? He agreed, curious to experience a Laurel extravaganza. Valerie thanked him, but she didn't look pleased. As the event loomed closer, she grew increasingly irritable.

The following Saturday, as Gary reclined on Caroline's bed with his long legs dangling off the end, Valerie snapped at him. "Sit up! You're abnormally tall!"

"I'm so glad you put Gary in his place." Caroline couldn't contain her laughter. "Being tall is a massive character flaw, and he owes the world an apology for his obscene height!"

Gary grinned. Valerie didn't.

"What's your problem?" Caroline looked at her friend. "You're acting like you're auditioning for *The Exorcist*."

"Did I get the part?"

"Yes!" Caroline and Gary in perfect unison.

"I'm sorry," Valerie blushed. "It . . . I . . . Gary, I'm afraid you might be really mad at me. It's just that nobody at Laurel knows."

"Knows what?" he asked.

"That I'm . . ." Valerie's voice failed.

Caroline stared. "Say it."

Valerie shook her head.

"You have to be able to say it."

"Gay, okay?" Valerie glared.

"Okay with me," Caroline kept her voice steady.

"Me, too," Gary sat up on the bed and crossed his legs.

"I'm sorry," Valerie said again, biting her lip. "I'm so nervous. I know this is going to sound stupid, but at school everyone wanted to set me up. On and on, every day. I felt like I was going to punch the next girl who offered me a Harvard-bound purebred gentleman. So, I told them I had a boyfriend, to get them to leave me alone."

"That's not so bad," Gary reassured her.

"There's more, and it gets worse," Valerie said flatly. "At Laurel, there's a timetable about boys. You go out twice, you're an item. A month, you're a couple. Six weeks, you're serious. People act like you're getting married."

"Unlike Hollywood High," Gary grinned. "Twice, you're naked. A month, you remember the condoms. Six weeks, regular sex. And what's marriage?"

Valerie laughed.

"How do you know about that? Where do you go on Friday nights?" Caroline blurted, then blushed.

"Nowhere. But every day at practice the football players brag about their conquests."

"So, Valerie and Mr. Fantasy are practically engaged." Caroline tried to cover her embarrassment.

Valerie nodded, her anxious eyes on Gary.

"What's wrong?" he asked.

She didn't answer.

"Valerie, what is it?" Gary impatiently.

Caroline began to laugh. "Okay, I get it."

Valerie buried her head in her hands.

"Would someone let me in on the joke?" Gary snapped.

Valerie still beyond speech, Caroline stepped in. "Gary, here's a hint. She's taking you to her dance."

"Yeah, so wha . . . wait, you mean it's me?"

Valerie had described Gary in detail to her friends. Met through Caroline, studied Latin, a science jock, played football. His letterman jacket drew high marks, although a social register listing would have been preferable. Still, Valerie's pedigree more than balanced out his immigrant roots.

"Are you mad at me?" asked Valerie anxiously.

"While you're at it, make me first string. Quarterback would work."

"You're not mad?"

"Coordinated and graceful. A contender on any playing field and debonair on the dance floor."

"Gary . . ."

"I'm not mad," he smiled. "I'll pretend to be your betrothed."

"It's really okay? I mean, there'll be all sorts of comments." Valerie blushed. "They might even say something about our sex life."

A thud of silence.

"You've told them about sex with Gary?" Caroline demanded. "Told them details?"

Valerie seemed to shrink. "I'm sorry, Gary. They kept asking. You should hear the details they give about themselves. I told them about Celia, said it was you."

"What does Celia think about it?" Caroline asked.

"Nobody knows about her except me. Her friends in New York don't have a clue, and her family would disown her. She wants me to play it up, as straight as I can get."

"It's gotta be tough on both of you, but I understand why you're doing it this way." Gary smiled. "Okay, let's go to your prom. What should I get you? A corsage? A diamond?"

Two weeks later, they arrived. Gary wore a tux borrowed from Uncle James, and Valerie glowed in a floor length formal. Nicole and her boyfriend, Hance Bartell, III, arrived in his red Porsche for their double date. The night was perfect, allowing the girls to go strapless in designer creations. A minority sported steady boyfriends, usually from Driscoll Academy. The majority panned around until eureka! — an available male of suitable age (older, never even a minute younger) and appropriate color (white or whiter). A friend's brother, cousin, next-door neighbor. Anyone with a pulse, a penis, and the correct trappings. Prom dates were often first dates, filling the room with awkward conversation. The prom was held in the auditorium, cleared of folding chairs, decked out with gold and white streamers, humongous green four-leaf clovers taped to the walls for St. Patrick's Day.

Valerie introduced Gary to her classmates. Princess Valerie and her famous boyfriend. The multitudes tracked their every move. They stood with the Platinum Ring, and Gary surveyed the scene. Nicole wore an antique diamond choker. Bronwyn and Trisha hugged their own shoulders, self-conscious in mink stoles. Lelia flaunted a magenta leather minidress, her date in black leather pants, a black leather jacket, and wrap-around mirrored sunglasses.

Valerie wore a tight bodice and hoop skirt under a gown that grazed the tips of her silver Cinderella slippers. The rich violet silk turned her eyes lavender. As Valerie twirled gracefully, Gary concentrated on counting the beats.

"The Four-Leaf Clover Crown will be awarded in a few minutes."

He laughed at her gravity.

A quartet of Clovers was always elected at the Sophomore Prom, the number one princess, along with the three trailing votes.

Resigned and amused, Valerie warned him, "Make no mistake. I'm going to win, and they'll insist on a photo of us kissing."

"It's okay, don't worry."

But Valerie was worried, and Gary didn't know why. He was enjoying himself, after all the stories, meeting the faces to go with the names. He asked Valerie to point out Caroline's crowd — Vicki, Maren, and Tory. Then the lights dimmed, and Mr. Hammer took the stage. As expected, Bronwyn, Nicole, and Trisha filled the runner up slots and Valerie received her floral crown. From the audience, Gary watched closely, not liking what he saw. Valerie's composure was forced, her smile more porcelain than real. She blinked too often, too hard. He mouthed, "It's okay," but he suddenly realized it wasn't okay. She'd finally had it with pretending.

Valerie made it through the congratulatory hugs from Nicole,

Bronwyn, and Trisha, shining with blonde hair, blue eyes, ski slope noses. She acknowledged the crowd and accepted her bouquet of white baby roses laced with gold ribbon.

Then photos. First, the four beauties. Next, the girls with their dates. Finally, the three blondes, followed by Valerie left profile, Valerie right profile, Valerie head on. ("They're going to take everything except a fucking x-ray," murmured Valerie, swaggering with her ability to cuss.)

"Let's do Valerie and Gary, side by side!" The jovial photographer carefully posed their hands.

Then the inevitable, "How about a kiss!"

Self-conscious, Valerie and Gary touched lips.

The camera clicked, but no flash.

"Let's try that again." Once more, a click, no flash.

By now, Valerie and Gary warded off hysteria, putting their heads together, trying to stifle their laughter.

"This is ridiculous!" Valerie whispered.

"Can I smash the camera?" Gary whispered back.

"If this keeps up, I'm going to eat my crown," she murmured.

"Can I have a bite?"

The photographer scowled, increasingly edgy, his camera in a mindless state of rebellion. Meanwhile, the droves of sixteen-year-olds turned restless and rowdy.

"Hey, Valerie, your boyfriend's really cute!"

Gary felt Valerie stiffen.

"You two are the cutest couple!"

Valerie was radiating something Gary couldn't identify. He flashed on their first meeting, months ago at Caroline's house, and he suddenly knew what was coming. He reached for her arm and whispered, "Slow down, Valerie."

Valerie's smile was a post mortem grimace, teeth gritted into a grin.

"Hey Valerie, forget the camera, go ahead and kiss your boyfriend!"

"Hey Valerie—"

"THAT'S ENOUGH!" Valerie shouted.

The room froze.

"It's okay," Gary tried to throw her a lifeline. "Slow down."

Valerie shook him off, sick of secrets and shame. Most powerful, J.D.'s memory, the look in Billy's eyes, their spirits circling. Valerie glowered at the sea of astounded teenagers.

"EVERYONE, MEET GARY, MY GOOD FRIEND! HE'S NOT MY BOYFRIEND!" Deep breath. "I'M G—"

Gary gripped her arm. "Stop and think!" he whispered urgently.

"I want to tell them." Valerie was barely audible.

"That's good. But now's not the time or the place."

"Why not?"

"Too staged. You don't want to turn it into a soap opera." He held her eyes. "It's too important. Tell your friends later."

A long pause, then Valerie grabbed Gary's hand and walked, then trotted, then bolted out the door, leaving the baffled boy-girl couples to fend for themselves.

They lurked in the parking lot until they spotted Nicole and Hance.

"Val, what happened?" Nicole rushed over. "Everyone thinks you broke up with Gary, onstage!"

"No," Valerie shook her head. "That's not what happened. I'm—"

"Wait!" Gary commanded. "In the car. Then we'll talk."

Easier said than done. Four adolescents, one over six feet, stuffing themselves into a Porsche. The two girls scrunched in the backseat and as Hance drove out of the parking lot, Gary turned to Valerie.

"Go for it."

Valerie turned to Nicole and said simply, "Brace yourself. I'm gay."

Silence.

Hance glanced in the rearview mirror at Laurel's crown princess. Next to Valerie, Nicole drained sheet white.

"Nicole, you're my best friend at Laurel, and I want you to be the first one at school to know."

Silence.

"Nothing's different between us. I just don't want to have this big secret."

Silence.

"Nicole, say something."

Silence.

"Nicole . . ."

But Nicole wasn't listening to Valerie. She stared ahead, through Hance, into her father's eyes. Her unconscious boiled over. The business lunches when his phone stopped working. The missed dinners. The long weekends away for meetings and conferences, destinations hazy, questions met with an irritable brush off.

"You can't know that about yourself!" Nicole finally blurted, tears spilling.

"Yes, I can. I've known for years."

"How can you do this?"

"Nicole, what do you mean?"

"Don't you care about the rest of us?"

"I don't understand . . ."

"How could you keep it a secret?"

"I'm sorry I didn't tell you sooner, but . . ."

"How can you tell me this now?"

"Nicole, you're not making sense!" Valerie broke into tears.

"Get out of the car!" Nicole screamed.

"Nicole," Hance said softly, "it's not the end of the world. I have friends who are gay. Our class treasurer. The captain of the water polo team. My next-door neighbor. My cousin. This doesn't change your friendship with Valerie. It's okay."

"It's not okay! Nothing about this is okay!"

"Nicole, please . . ." Valerie reached for her friend.

"Don't touch me!" Nicole shrank back. "Get out!"

"Wait a second—" Hance tried to speak, but Nicole began to scream.

"GET OUT! GET OUT OF THE CAR! GET OUT!"

Over Hance's protests, ignoring Gary's attempts at reason, in spite of Valerie's tears, Nicole shoved them into the night.

Valerie and Gary stared as the Porsche disappeared around a corner.

"It's only two blocks to my house," Valerie finally whispered.

"Take off your heels," Gary said. "You'll break an ankle."

"I'm already broken."

Valerie dropped her head into her hands and began to sob. Gary lifted her in his arms. She cried on his shoulder as he carried her home.

"Hold on tight," he whispered. "I've got you."

CHAPTER 48

"Caroline, wait up!" Elton jogged over. "Why are you here after school?"

"Science lab. You?"

"Sewing project."

"You take sewing?"

"The class was empty after the tattoo skin graft mess. So, The Eltons signed up. The teacher lets us play our music in every class. We made outfits for the next Elton John concert. Mine's orange, green, and silver, lots of glitter."

"Wow, that's . . . well . . . wow."

"That's the exact reaction I'm looking for."

"When's the concert?"

"Tomorrow. That's why I had to finish. I'm going with the other Eltons. We got seats together."

"Good job. Well, see you around." She turned to leave.

"Wait up! I have an extra ticket. Want to go?"

"I . . ." she hesitated. Elton was nice. Although she'd seen countless theatre productions, she'd never been to a rock concert. Still, if she said yes, he might assume it was a date and . . . wait a moment . . . he *was* asking for a date. "No thanks, I don't think so."

"Oh. Okay."

"Thanks for asking."

Elton didn't answer, turned, walked away.

Caroline stared after him. How could any boy possibly notice her next to Lacey? Her pom-poms might be absurd, but she'd look gorgeous in a gunnysack. Why didn't Elton offer the ticket to her? It made no sense.

She shrugged and hurried toward the building's main entrance. She paused for a moment to look at Vincent's painting — the orange sun reflected in the gray ocean, J.D.'s flowing blond hair. Mrs. Richardson had added a simple cardboard plaque: J.D.'s Sunset, by Vincent Takayama. Caroline wondered if J.D. liked it, then caught herself. *Am I losing my mind? He's dead!* She rushed to catch her bus.

The next evening, instead of enjoying a glittery concert with multiple Eltons, Caroline crowded into Gary's small apartment with her five closest friends. Valerie's week had been a nightmare.

"They wouldn't even speak to me," Valerie's tears spilled. "Every Platinum Ringlet walked by like I didn't exist."

"Assholes," Irene clenched her fists.

"By Monday morning, everyone knew. Everywhere I went, they watched me. If I looked at anyone, she looked away. I went into the bathroom, and everyone walked out." Valerie reached for a tissue and looked at Caroline. "Your friends have been great. Vicki, Maren, and Tory. They found me on the lawn on Monday. They asked if they could join me, and we ate lunch together. They've eaten with me every day. Otherwise, I would have been alone."

"Nicole's boyfriend Hance was okay," Gary growled, "but Nicole was well-packaged afterbirth."

"Nicole's afraid of me, and I don't know why."

Caroline tensed. *I should tell her. This isn't about her. It's about Nicole and her father. Valerie would feel better if she knew. But then she'd know something about Nicole that's a huge secret. It would make their relationship even more impossible. And if she ever lost her temper and told Nicole . . .* Caroline clamped her mouth shut.

"She probably thinks you want to jump her," Vincent said.

"Not if she were the last debutante on earth!" Valerie burst into fresh tears. "I was the most popular girl at Laurel! Now it's ruined!"

"You can transfer to Hollywood High with us," Kayla comforted her. "You can list my house as your address."

"It's illegal for Valerie to use a false address. Are you offering to break the law?" Irene raised an eyebrow.

"To save our friend from Clover poisoning? Absolutely yes!" Kayla shot back.

"It would be a noble induction into criminal life, but I think I need to tough it out at Laurel." Valerie dried her tears. "Our headmaster, Mr. Hammer, was really nice. He found me first thing Monday morning and told me I could use his office any time I needed a break. He said you can't argue with statistics, and the numbers say I'm not the only lesbian in my class. He told me not to worry, the girls would get used to it."

Then Valerie's face clouded.

"What is it?" Caroline asked.

"I called Celia on Sunday. I thought she'd understand, but she started screaming that I betrayed her. I tried to explain that I only told people about me. I didn't tell anyone about her. She kept yelling that I broke her trust, and she never wants to speak to me again. I told her that my mom and my brother were behind me. She said that was lucky for me, because she was telling her parents that I was sick and perverted, and she was shocked when she found out. Then she hung up on me."

"Let's introduce Celia to that lacquered bitch Nicole," Gary glowered. "They'd make a perfect couple."

"Valerie, I'm so sorry," Caroline said.

"Celia told me that knowing she was different made her rethink everything. But she's just like her parents. Her ultimate goal in life is to join the ranks of the Upper East Side. She wants to get written up in the society pages, preferably with photos, so she can show her friends and complain that publicity is so vulgar and watch them try to hide their envy."

"It sounds like you and Celia want totally different things in life," Kayla quietly.

"Yeah, starting with the fact that Celia's a steaming elephant turd and Valerie isn't!" Irene snapped.

"Now she's going to tell her parents that I'm a pervert, and they'll hate me, and she'll look so perfect!"

"You don't need that shit!" Irene was incensed. "And there's nothing imperfect about being a lesbian. It's not a character flaw."

"She makes me sick!" Valerie's tears spilled again. "She has her whole life mapped out. Go to college to find a husband whose family came here on the Mayflower. Paris fashion week. Box seats at the opera. First born son. Second born daughter."

Caroline hugged her friend's shoulders. "It won't be a pretty sight when tragedy strikes and her firstborn is a girl."

Valerie blew her nose. "I seem to have chosen poorly for my first lover."

"You and me both."

Every head turned to Kayla. Her first reference to Ray.

Valerie dried her eyes and smiled at Kayla and Vincent. "You did better the second time around. I will, too."

"Way to go, Valerie!" Vincent gave her a high five.

"It must have been hard to go to school," Caroline sympathetically.

"Tuesday was awful, but Maren's my new hero. I was sitting with her,

Vicki, and Tory on the lawn at lunch. Out of nowhere, three girls were standing over us. I guess they figured it was safe to approach in a pack. Remember when my art class sketched portraits of the nude model, and then someone wrecked them with orange paint?" Her friends nodded. "They told me they knew I did it. They said nobody except me would do such a sick thing, and I must have had some kind of apoplectic reaction to the model's naked female body."

"Why in the world would they say that?" Kayla stared.

"Because Valerie's an easy target," Irene answered. "Y'know, she's a lesbian, so she's depraved. She responsible for everything that's messed up in the world. Jackie Robinson died. Watergate. The terrorist attack at the Munich Olympics. Air pollution. It's all Valerie's fault."

"What'd you say to that girl?" Caroline asked.

"I didn't say anything," Valerie grinned. "Maren said it for me. She spouted this phrase nobody could understand. She's really good at languages. Turns out she's been taking private lessons in Yiddish. So the leader of the posse said, 'Huh?' and Maren gave her this hitman stare and said, 'Rough translation: Go Shit on a Wave!'"

"What does that mean?" Vincent laughed.

"Who knows? Who cares? I love Maren!" Irene gloated.

"Wait, there's more," Valerie continued. "That afternoon, they caught the leader of the heterosexual brigade in the ceramics classroom, with a can of spray paint. Orange, of course. It turns out she was expelled from Exeter for . . . um . . . redecorating their chem lab. She also repainted a set in their theater three hours before a production of *The Miracle Worker*. Mr. Hammer asked why she wrecked our sketches and the ceramics, especially after being booted from Exeter, and she said, 'I like orange.'"

"That's really twisted. If someone did that to one of my paintings . . ." Vincent shook his head.

"The biggest surprise was Miss MacIsaac," Valerie said to Caroline, then turned to the others, "Laurel's guidance counselor. She's the most prim and proper lady I've ever met. I always assumed she was orgasmic every night reading Emily Post's etiquette book and—"

"Valerie!" Kayla was utterly scandalized.

"Kayla has come a long way this year," Irene grinned, "but apparently jokes about orgasms remain off limits."

"Deepest apologies," Valerie couldn't stifle her grin. "Anyway, on Wednesday, Miss MacIsaac called me out of gym class, into her office. Just as well, because we were supposed to play catch, and nobody would be my partner and—"

"Thank the Gods and the Goddesses!" Gary cut in. "Everyone knows that homosexuality is a virulent disease, airborne microbes, transmitted through catching a softball."

"At the beginning of the year, I would have believed that," Vincent admitted. "I would have thought saying the word *lesbian* or *gay* or *trans* was wrong, like it was encouraging a bad thing to happen. I feel like an idiot."

"It's okay, Vincent. We're all idiots sometimes," Valerie earnestly.

"I'm not an idiot," Irene stated. "Too bad Vincent is."

"He's not!" Valerie's intensity surprised the group. She turned to Vincent. "After I came out to you all at Caroline's house, you invited me to your house for the next weekend. That was my first invitation from someone who knew I was gay."

Vincent stared. "So, you're not mad that I was an asshole?"

"You asked questions. You listened. You changed. I'm not mad."

Vincent opened his mouth, but no words came out.

"Anyway, about Miss MacIsaac," Valerie picked up the slack. "I always thought she was the most pathologically polite person on the planet. If I had a choice, I would have gone anywhere except her office. But when you get that pink summons with the clover at the top of the page, you drop everything and go. She offered me English tea, served in a gold and white china teacup, our school colors of course, with the clover crest. She sipped like a lady and lifted her pinkie, and I was waiting for her to lecture me that I was ruining my chances to marry an upstanding gentleman and make the Social Register. Then she told me that although most Laurel girls might be surprised, she went to Africa last summer to help set up a school in one of the villages. She met another teacher from Los Angeles. He's twelve years her junior, he's Jewish, and they're totally in love. They moved in together in October, but he wasn't comfortable in her Pacific Palisades mansion. So, they sold it and bought a smaller house in Malibu, on the beach."

"Miss MacIsaac lives with her boyfriend?" Caroline was incredulous. "Do you think she wears her Chanel suits to bed?"

"Caroline!" Kayla sternly. "Chanel suits and orgasms are both off limits!"

Valerie's lips twitched. "Leaving aside her choice in lingerie, Miss MacIsaac told me her boyfriend loves to surf. He bought her a surf-board for her birthday, and they hit the waves every weekend. She said most people prefer their stereotypes, but I was free to talk about her boyfriend and her surfboard and the Shabbat candles they light every Friday evening, and she hoped I'd never hide my self again."

"Miss MacIsaac surfs?" Caroline asked blankly. "She lights Shabbat candles?"

"Oh!" Valerie brightened. "I forgot the best part. I was at my locker, and Lelia shoved a note into my hand. You've got to read this." She rummaged through her purse and pulled out a plain black envelope. Her friends crowded around, and Gary tossed aside his copy of their high school's monthly literary magazine. Inside the envelope was a plain black card with glittery silver writing.

Dear Valerie,

You are rude and inconsiderate, forcing your beloved Clover classmates to trade a fantasy for a human being. Hang in there. Give me a few days and I'll do something to take the heat off you.

Courage,

Lelia

"It was brilliant," Valerie put the note back in her purse. "Friday morning, I was slinking into school, and Maren dragged me to the hallway outside Mr. Hammer's office. There's this gallery of glossies of the Board of Trustees. Lelia changed the photos. They're Magilla Gorilla, Mighty Mouse, Porky Pig, Pebbles Flintstone, and the evil cat from *Cinderella*. The Board was furious, but Mr. Hammer thought it was hilarious, especially his picture which is Tweety Bird. He said he's leaving the pictures up for the rest of the year." Valerie eased back, relaxed for the first time that night. "Last Saturday was everything I dreaded, but I'm going to be okay."

They all hugged her, except Gary, who was reading intently.

"Hey Gary," Valerie waved, "I'm having an epiphany over here. Do you mind?"

Gary held up *The Literary Crimson*. "Any of you seen this?"

The group crowded around to read the poem.

"Another epiphany," Valerie said quietly.

"Wow," Kayla's eyes were wide. "The school's toughest student is apologizing to everyone for everything he's done wrong."

Gary shook his head. "Not for everything. Not to everyone. He's apologizing to Caroline."

I AM

I hurt, I crunch, I thrash,
I break.
I break, I rage, I shout,
I stop.
I stop, I think, I feel,
I breathe.
I breathe, I see, I am
Sorry.

By Duke Hunter

CHAPTER 49

"Are you going to the talent show?" Caroline asked Toni and Blake as they circled the quad before school began.

"Maybe," Toni shrugged. "Those shows have a reputation for winning the annual Waste of Time Award. But I've heard the girl in charge this year is really good."

"Her name's Kayla. She's a friend of mine, and she's great. I'm betting on the best talent show Hollywood High has ever seen."

"Then I'll go." Toni looked at Blake.

"I'll go, too," Blake smiled at their girlfriend, "even though I hate to miss my art class. Sculpture from Scraps. It's the best course I've ever taken. We went on a field trip the first day and collected a ton of materials. Wood, steel, wire, plastic, rocks. Then we went to a few crafts stores, and they gave us boxes of stuff they were throwing away. Slightly damaged buttons, ribbons, wires, chains. I'm working on a piece about J.D."

"Are you building a sculpture of him?" Toni asked.

Blake shook their head. "It's not about him individually. It's more about the way things work, so that someone like J.D. could end up dead for no good reason."

"I started a project," Toni said. "It's not for a class. I'm doing it at home."

"You're doing an art project?" Caroline looked at Toni in surprise.

"I'm writing my own American history textbook. It's going to include everyone who mattered, not just straight white men. I'm going to show how people came here to escape oppression, and then they created a society based on oppression, all over again."

"Can I read your book?" Caroline asked.

"Are you sure you want to?"

"Of course, why wouldn't I?"

"Well . . . I mean . . . you're white and straight. It's going to include some bad stuff that white and straight people did."

"It sounds like you're writing the truth. Yeah, I'm definitely reading it. I might learn something, because I'm white and straight." Caroline smiled.

Blake turned to Toni. "Have you noticed that she smiles when she talks about learning history?"

"Yep."

"You're both douchebags," Caroline stated.

A few hours later, in row fourteen of the auditorium, Gary sat on Caroline's left, Vincent and Irene on her right. The annual spring talent show was always the third Friday in April. Kayla was voted "Master of Ceremonies," a great honor. She would cap off the show with a solo.

Whenever Kayla took the stage, an expectant hush fell over the audience. She'd played the leads in *Hello, Dolly!* and *Grease*, and had brought down the house. A television news station scouted young talent in Los Angeles and aired a feature spotlighting three adolescents. Kayla was number two, on national television. Still, she kept her head and remained Hollywood High's thoughtful, excruciatingly polite, entertainment dynamo.

The Duke led his gang to rows eight and nine. As he sat, he caught Caroline's eye and mouthed, "We need to talk."

She nodded and they both looked away, carefully aloof.

To Caroline's left, three rows back, hulked an angry pack of football players. The athletes were loudly vocal that Hollywood High was "overreacting" to J.D.'s death. The memorial tribute at school lasted a full day and was more than plenty. Enough already. Incarceration, in their considered opinions, was a travesty.

Two police officers posted themselves at the exit doors of the auditorium. They radiated annoyance at having to waste an hour at a high school display of non-talent.

Irene and Vincent had warned their friends about the previous two years' shows, tepid in their top-forty predictability. Kayla promised to buck the trend and scouted campus for weeks.

"A show to remember," she assured them.

"Kayla better keep her word," Vincent growled, irritated to miss Sculpture from Scraps.

"If she lets us down, y'know, I'll kill her," Irene stated flatly.

"You won't kill her," Gary shot back. "You'll unleash Caroline."

Irene leaned past Vincent to punch Caroline's arm. "When did you become a holy terror?"

"Who, me?"

"You told The Duke to go to hell. Nobody's ever done that and lived to tell the tale. I'm so proud." Vincent patted her shoulder. "You've become a menace to society."

"Only to jerks who deserve it." Caroline glanced at The Duke as he tucked some stapled pages into his jacket pocket. Maybe the pages were his *To Kill a Mockingbird* paper about names. In spite of herself, she wondered if Mr. Cohen liked his topic.

The lights dimmed, and a spotlight hit the stage. Kayla entered wearing jeans and a Hollywood High t-shirt, white with a red emblem.

The school's *Achieve the Honorable* motto was too small for the audience to read. She welcomed the crowd and introduced Act One.

The Twins were renowned throughout campus, with matted bronze dreadlocks and hazy brown eyes. Invariably stoned, impossible to converse, they grunted unintelligibly and tossed a variety of small objects, juggling their way through every break at school. They faced the audience, startled to find the seats filled, unlike in their rehearsals.

"Like, wow!" Twin One.

"Tubular!" Twin Two.

Before their improvisational dialogue could continue, Dr. Hook and the Medicine Show blasted "Cover of the Rolling Stone." The twins began to juggle with three tennis balls each. They added a fourth, then a fifth. Still juggling, they turned to face each other, moved six feet apart, their profiles to the audience. With artistic precision, they hurled the ten balls back and forth. The stage lights dimmed, and the audience broke into spontaneous applause. The balls were spray painted glow-in-the-dark neon. The bright colors seemed to bounce on the air.

With no finesse whatsoever, no bow, no parting wave, The Twins abruptly exited stage left. The music faded as they hit the backstage door and emerged into the spring sunshine to light up a celebratory joint. The police officers let it go.

Next, one of Kayla's creations. Four boys, three girls, seven languages. She joined them to form an octet, adding English. She divided "America the Beautiful" into eight equal parts and translated each section into a different language. To a taped instrumental background, united in diversity, eight kids sang a tribute to one nation in English, Korean, Portuguese, Armenian, Japanese, Mandarin, Spanish, and Hindi. They stood in a line, dressed in jeans and Hollywood High t-shirts donated by Mrs. Cuthbertson.

Act Three. The I.D. King, a senior who liked to drink, the school's go-to entrepreneur for fake I.D. cards. At rehearsals, he never wavered.

Sporting his black hat, waving his wand, he dropped a maraschino cherry into an empty highball glass, placed his hat over the display, tapped the hat and the cherry disappeared. This was followed by a few sleight of hand numbers, a fluffy rabbit, and a quick exit.

But this show was live, and The King had loftier plans.

Having gained the stage and dropped his maraschino cherry into the glass, he challenged the audience, "Bet I can get the cherry out using only my tongue!" The glass was eight inches tall. He tossed his wand into the wings and proceeded to eat the glass until he easily lapped up the cherry. He then bowed to horrified applause, lifted a confused rabbit, and marched off.

Kayla hustled Act Four onstage, a barbershop quartet that performed an original, surprisingly clever *a cappella* version of "Monster Mash" by Bobby 'Boris' Pickett and The Crypt Kickers. Next, an athletic tap dance to Aerosmith's "Dream On," followed by a gymnastics routine to John Denver's "Rocky Mountain High."

Lacey, dressed in a flaring poodle skirt and saddle shoes, skipped onstage and danced an exuberant jitterbug with her newest boyfriend to Elton John's "Crocodile Rock." The Eltons, seated together in row twenty, went wild.

As Lacey left the stage blowing kisses, Kayla announced that Jeremy Kline would perform a Taekwondo demonstration.

"That's Jeremy!" Gary clutched Caroline's arm. "That's him! The guy who got beat up!"

Jeremy moved with a lean grace, like a tiger. He tied back his brown hair in traditional Korean style, blue eyes focused, feet bare. He looked so fit, you'd never know he'd been beaten nearly senseless only one semester before. He stood still, feeling the opening of Queen's "Keep Yourself Alive," then sprang into the music. He moved with precision and power, his body trained to never again be anybody's victim. He wore his *gi*, a black belt around his waist, and nobody doubted that he owned the stage.

To Caroline's left and three rows back, sounds of discontent escalated, first as the football stars felt a competitive force in their arena, then as they realized who they watched.

Gary's eyes shifted nervously from Jeremy to his teammates. "This isn't happening again. If they don't back off, I'm going in. I can't sit here and watch."

"I'll go with you," Caroline whispered, clutching the arms of her seat as her palms broke with sweat. Automatically, she began to rehearse self-defense moves in her head. She figured she'd at least have the advantage of surprise. The athletes might expect her to bonk them over the head with an *Oxford English Dictionary*, but never to kick them to the ground.

To conclude his final sequence, Jeremy leaped in the air with a dazzling series of kicks. He landed on all fours, then jumped to his feet and bowed. He breathed hard, through a healthy sheen of boy sweat. He faced the crowd, triumphant.

"That took guts," Irene said.

Then it began.

"Hey, Sweetheart, where's your boyfriend?" a football player called.

"You're strong for a girl!"

"You're cute when you fight!"

Jeremy blushed, then his eyes widened. Six team members were on their feet, moving toward the stage.

"Think you can take all of us?"

"Who does your hair? You're pretty."

"Oh, no!" an exaggerated falsetto. "It's Jeremy, the Taekwondo monster! I'm scared!"

The six now mincing, wrists limp and fluttery.

"That's disgusting!" Gary hissed and Caroline broke into a cold sweat.

The crowd began to jeer and with their response, Jeremy took a step back.

Suddenly alert, the police officers yelled for everyone to sit down. Instead, groups of kids swarmed the cops, making Jeremy impossible for them to reach.

"Let's go!" Gary spoke sharply and Caroline nodded, terrified but committed. The two friends shot to their feet as the team reached the steps leading from the aisle to the stage, ready to gang up on one boy in front of the entire auditorium.

They never made it.

The Duke hurtled down the aisle and took the stage in one gigantic leap. "NOBODY MOVE!" he bellowed.

The football players stopped in their tracks. Jeremy was one thing. The Duke was quite another. One of the athletes tried a small step, an experiment.

"I SAID NOBODY MOVE!"

The boy went rigid.

Caroline and Gary dropped back into their seats.

Jeremy cautiously approached The Duke who spoke, this time low. "Get behind me. I'll protect you."

"It's okay. I know Taekwondo."

"Yeah, but there are six of them."

Jeremy sized up the athletes. "The one in the black t-shirt. He's the alpha asshole. I can knock him out with one kick. The rest will fall apart. Pack mentality."

"Fine," The Duke said evenly. "We'll take them together."

The two boys moved side by side, facing the audience.

"BACK OFF THE COPS!" The Duke ordered at the top of his lungs. "TAKE YOUR SEATS!"

Slight hesitation in the crowd.

"I SAID BACK OFF THE COPS AND SIT DOWN!"

The police officers moved toward the stage.

The Duke turned to Jeremy and nodded. They walked down the

steps into the aisle, up to the boulder of athletes blocking their path. The audience held its breath. Slowly, the boy in the black t-shirt moved aside and the other five followed. The Duke and Jeremy walked the length of the auditorium and out the exit door.

When the students turned back to the stage, Kayla stood alone.

"That," she stated, "is the hardest act I'll ever have to follow." The crowd broke into relieved laughter. "If everyone wants to take a deep breath, I'll sing 'Send in the Clowns.' It's from a Broadway show called *A Little Night Music.*"

Caroline bit her lip, looking back and forth from Kayla to the exit door.

"Go!" Gary whispered. "You need to go to The Duke!"

"Kayla's solo . . . she's been rehearsing for weeks . . . I can't . . ."

"Kayla will understand," Irene tugged Caroline out of her seat.

"Go!" Vincent urgently. "Go now!"

Caroline awkwardly worked her way to the aisle and turned to the stage. Kayla gave her a tiny nod and she ran for the exit.

Outside, The Duke and Jeremy stood in the shadow of the next building. Caroline started to rush over, then stopped. This was between the two boys. She ducked into a doorway as Jeremy turned to The Duke.

"I don't know how to thank you."

"No problem," The Duke answered as a wave of nausea hit. Gang leaders never declared an alliance with an openly gay student. What's more, he sided with the cops. The Duke planted his feet, trying to sustain his equilibrium.

"Are your friends going to give you a hard time?"

The Duke shrugged, outwardly impassive. "If they do, they'll regret it."

"Thanks again." Jeremy put out his hand.

The Duke froze. It wasn't just a hand. It was a homosexual hand. And he was supposed to touch it. Standing up to those jerk-off football players who acted like they owned the planet, taking them down in front of a packed auditorium — that was a rush, better than drugs. But shaking hands with a gay boy . . . what if someone saw them? What if Jeremy tried to pounce on him? What if being gay was contagious?

Jeremy smiled sadly and dropped his hand. "It's okay. You've done enough for one day." He turned to walk away.

"Jeremy."

The Duke reached, hand outstretched. Jeremy strode back, stopped a respectful three feet away and their hands met. A long moment and Jeremy let go first, not wanting to frighten the larger boy. Their eyes held, each honoring the other's courage. Then they separated.

The Duke stared down at his own hand, knowing he'd taken the road not taken, instant ejection from his own gang.

Caroline moved toward him, and their eyes met.

Before either could speak, Jay and Tom catapulted into The Duke, punching the air. They brayed and howled, delighted at besting the jocks, any deeper significance miles outside of their realm.

From the corner of his eye, The Duke saw his other gang members file out of the talent show, glare at him, turn their backs and walk away.

Caroline blinked back tears, took a step forward.

The Duke shook his head slightly. Through a shock wave of sadness, he moved toward the quad where Doraine would be waiting.

Caroline shrank into the shelter of her doorway while the crowd poured from the auditorium. She felt her tears rise and automatically stiffened, regaining composure. She breathed deeply, dampening the voltage. Then she realized what she was doing. She took another breath, reversed the process, and allowed her tears to flow.

CHAPTER 50

Carlos rushed through a heavy rainstorm and arrived at the classroom as the bell rang. He shrugged out of his dripping raincoat, lifted the notebook for roll call, and picked up a pencil. Instead of following his usual routine, Mr. Cohen nodded at Caroline, who turned to Kayla and Gary, who glanced at Elvia and Sharon.

Seeing his students hesitate, Mr. Cohen stepped in, speaking with his signature matter-of-fact calm. "It's been quite a year. Too much gang violence. Too much violence against our gay students. We've had one student murdered on campus. I've also been told that our trans students feel threatened every day. We need to work together to change the culture of violence here at Hollywood High." He waited for that to sink in, then he looked at Caroline. "Would you and your friends like to take it from here?"

Caroline stood.

"Carlos, we all want to thank you for being Mr. Cohen's assistant. A really bad thing happened that brought you into our classroom. We're sorry it happened, but we're glad you're here. Since the assembly, it seems safer now at school. We wanted to get you something."

Caroline nodded at Elvia and Sharon, who walked to the front of the room. Sharon handed Carlos a small package and Elvia spoke.

"It was Caroline, Kayla, and Gary's idea. They needed our help because they don't wear makeup. I'm good with different brands, and Sharon's good with color. Everyone in the class pitched in."

Sharon stepped forward. "We all think you look good in your jeans. We like your white pants, too." She paused awkwardly. "Open the package."

Carlos loosened the ribbon and his jaw dropped. Almost tenderly, he lifted from the box a new tube of lipstick and mascara, top quality brands.

"Did I get your colors right?" Sharon nervously.

Carlos nodded.

"If you want . . ." Sharon rummaged through her purse and offered a small mirror.

Carlos carefully applied his makeup. When he finished, the entire class broke into applause, including Mr. Cohen, who shook Carlos's hand.

"Okay, let's get down to business." Mr. Cohen completed roll call and Carlos handed each student a few typed pages. "Today, we'll read and discuss an excerpt from a book. Each student will read three sentences out loud."

The story involved a relationship between two friends, struggling with a betrayal they both thought was irreparable. They turned out to be wrong. Although each was deeply hurt by the other, they found a way to forgive each other and reconnect.

Caroline barely made it through her three sentences. During the discussion, she held herself icy still, trying to freeze her tears at their source. Ideas ricocheted around the room, but she was caught on a parallel track. Over and over in her head, she heard The Duke's words. *We were never friends.*

When the class ended, Caroline was the last to leave. As she walked past Mr. Cohen, he spoke quietly.

"The way you read — literature transports you. That's good. You'll want to hold onto that. Don't let yourself grow out of it."

Caroline's breath hitched. To her absolute horror, her tears broke the surface. Mr. Cohen led her to Carlos's seat at the front of the classroom. She dropped her head into her hands and tried to stifle her sobs. Students filed in for Mr. Cohen's next class. Some stared as Caroline continued to cry. Her teacher began roll call, allowing Caroline the time she needed to regain her composure. She arrived ten minutes late for her second period class, the only unexcused tardy in her high school career.

For the next few hours, Caroline remained unable to speak, treading silently to her classes, never raising her hand. At lunch, her friends bantered while she remained mute. The rain had stopped, but the ground was still wet, so they stood in a circle as they ate.

Suddenly the quad erupted. A boy threw his raincoat to the ground and continued his career as the campus streaker. Like his first foray back in the fall, he wore a furry gorilla mask. He streaked toward Sunset Boulevard where a car waited. His previous success had ended in a victorious getaway. This time, he ran directly into the arms of the campus cop.

"Good afternoon." The officer took the boy's shoulders, holding his naked body at arm's length. "Toss his raincoat to me!" he ordered another student. "Put this on." He handed the coat to the boy. "Now, take off the mask."

The streaker turned rigid.

"What's the problem? You were glad to show the world everything else. Take off your mask!"

Slowly, the boy obeyed.

"Holy shit!" Irene exclaimed.

"Are you kidding?" Gary's jaw dropped.

"I can't believe . . ." Vincent trailed off.

"It's Kurt!" Kayla stared.

"He ran buck naked into the policeman's arms," Irene grinned. "I almost feel sorry for him."

"I feel sorry for the cop," Caroline said dryly.

Her friends burst out laughing, and Caroline smiled with relief. She'd always remember the gorilla streaker, and her gratitude toward Kurt for unlocking her voice.

CHAPTER 51

The Spring Art Show was up and running. The library's chairs were pushed to the side and the tables were covered with jewelry, sculptures, ceramics. Paintings and drawings had been carefully propped on the empty bookshelves.

Vincent joined his friends at lunch and began wolfing his food. "Eat quickly!" he ordered. "We have to go to the art show. Someone in my Sculpture from Scraps class did an incredible carving with wood and wire and paint and . . . I can't explain it. You have to see it."

They entered the library five minutes later. As Caroline walked in, she realized this was her first time in the building since she stumbled into a knife fight, then into a hedge and into The Duke.

"Over here." Vincent led them to a table and pointed.

The artist had built a ship from wood. They had carved out a half-watermelon shape and lined the edge with a thin slat. Next, they sawed a flat cover, which was the ship's deck. Carefully nailed or glued to the slat were carvings, an anchor, rope, sails, flag. Every inch was painted meticulously.

"Amazing detail," Caroline admired.

"It's beautiful." Kayla nodded.

"The deck is a cover," Vincent said. "You have to lift the cover off the slat to see what's underneath."

Carefully, Irene followed his direction.

The artist had carved the area below deck. Wire stick figures were seated around the perimeter, crowded side by side. A thin chain looped around their legs. In contrast to the ship above, the area below deck held no decoration, only stark figures, chains and darkness. Each figure's arms were dropped by their sides or folded over their chest — except one, whose arms were lifted, stretching up through the darkness.

The five friends stood speechless.

"Who did this?" Gary wondered. "Who's the artist?"

"Someone named Blake," Vincent answered.

Caroline's eyes filled. She blinked hard, fighting for control.

What's wrong with me? Crying after the talent show, then about a story in English class, now over a sculpture? I'm losing my shit! Get a grip!

"Look what Blake named the sculpture." Kayla pointed to the small cardboard plaque: J.D. Reaching for the Light.

Caroline's tears broke free.

CHAPTER 52

Since Kayla's talent show, school was relatively quiet. Graduation neared, and the campus gravitated to a holding pattern — fewer gang fights, assignments carefully turned in on time. Physical attacks targeting the gay and trans students stopped, and verbal harassment weakened. The students were ready for summer vacation and in the fall, Vincent would begin UCLA, majoring in art.

Caroline searched for The Duke every day, but he seemed to have gone underground. She began to bite her nails. What if her temper had blown it? More to the point, why would someone as big and powerful as The Duke care about a hopelessly uncool girl whose favorite sport was reading? Maybe she really was an idiot to think they could be friends.

The night after the talent show, Caroline's dream returned. Blond hair, lollipop, noise, confusion. Eduardo, Doris, Eric, Anna, Christopher. The shattering. Every part of the dream traced back to J.D. and Blue Shirt, except the names. Caroline had the uneasy feeling that those names held the key to put her nightmare to rest, but it made no sense. The only Eric and Christopher she'd ever met were in elementary school, she'd never laid eyes on a Doris, and the Eduardo and Anna she knew were two juniors in her Latin class who barely spoke.

Back at school the next day, tired from her restless sleep, Caroline was relieved when the final bell rang. The day was warm with a gentle breeze and surprisingly little smog. She and Kayla shouldered their backpacks and decided to walk home. Two streets from campus, they turned left and the crowd thinned, nobody in sight for the remainder of the block. They chatted about Kurt, who had been released from police custody after his streaking debacle and was back on campus, strutting shamelessly, always fully dressed, wearing his gorilla mask between classes.

"We need a new streaker," Kayla raised an eyebrow. "Any chance you're interested in filling the position?"

"I'm not qualified. I don't own a gorilla mask."

"No problem. Let's go shopping. I—"

Suddenly a hand snaked from a doorway, grabbed Caroline's arm and spun her around so her backpack was against his chest. His other arm crooked around her breasts, his hand circling her throat.

"You move, you scream, you die," Drake hissed. Then loudly to Kayla, "Get lost!"

Caroline broke into a sweat and began to hyperventilate. For an instant, the two girls locked eyes, then Kayla ran. It took Caroline a moment to process that she disappeared in the wrong direction, back toward school.

Before Caroline could stop herself, she began to whimper. She wanted to plead, "Don't hurt me," but only a primal animal sound escaped.

"Scared, bitch?" Drake rasped. "I'm gonna do you better than The Duke ever did. You're mine now. I live here. I've seen you walk by lots of times."

Caroline flashed on the self-defense demonstration at school. Look to the right, to the left. Her knees buckled. She stumbled backwards into Drake and he turned to slam her against the wall of the entry, to the left of the door. Her backpack took the brunt of the impact, but the violence stunned her.

"You ever had a real man?" He watched her reaction and began to laugh. "Perfect, I'll be your first. I'm gonna make you beg. Maybe you'll like it and beg for more."

Drake's first mistake.

Linda and Quincy had studied transcripts of rape trials and practiced with the self-defense class, immunizing them against the most common threats. As soon as Drake promised to make her beg, he entered a world she was trained to find familiar. Through her panic, Caroline heard Linda's voice, steady and strong.

"Let the words roll down like water off a duck. The words can't hurt you, so let him talk and while he's talking, you get ready to fight."

Caroline and Drake stood face to face, with Drake's right forearm across her chest, pinning her to the wall. Her arms hung limply, his left hand around her throat. Caroline felt his need to exert power, to break her. He smiled not wolfishly, not sadistically, but with an eerie pleasure. She searched his eyes and found murky, chilled emptiness.

Caroline's thinking began to roll, gather momentum, gain velocity, and she lost control, careening into panic. She panted, mentally flailing, when she remembered in a silver flash: Linda never said we couldn't be frightened.

"It's a normal reaction to feel afraid. You can fight through your fear."

In that instant, Caroline began to grow dangerous.

"I'm inviting you into my home. We're going to have a nice long visit." Drake shifted his weight and she realized he needed to let go of her with one hand to fish his keys out of his pocket. He wanted to force her inside for a protracted ordeal.

Drake's second mistake.

"If he wants to take you somewhere else," Linda explained, *"it will be more dangerous. Time to turn ballistic."*

No way was Caroline entering Drake's lair.

"*Wait for your opening,*" Linda said before every fight, during every demonstration. "*Watch for your window. Don't make your move until he gives you the chance.*"

Caroline began to study Drake, anticipating him. He pushed his body against hers and she felt his erection through his gold polyester slacks. She gauged the contours of his build, his weight, gathering information, ready to strike.

"The Duke won't protect you now, honey."

She could smell his sweat.

"You're gonna enjoy some real hospitality."

Drake tightened his left hand around her throat and stuck his right hand in his pocket for his keys.

"*NOW!*"

Caroline heard Linda shout and a surge of energy propelled her into the fight.

"*DROP!*"

Seven teen girls yelled, and Caroline realized she carried the voices of every member of her self-defense class.

She hurtled herself down, dropping to the ground, and Drake fell forward into the wall. Automatically, he took a step back as Caroline rolled over and rooted her hands on the pavement. She took a moment to orient herself from her awkward summersault as she brought her knee to her chin. Aiming almost straight up, she crashed her heel into his crotch.

Drake fell backwards, his mouth open in a soundless scream, his face contorted with amazement and pain. He landed hard on his butt, hands covering his penis. He sat on the sidewalk, knocked several feet back.

Caroline jumped up, teeth bared, and feral.

He raised his eyes, red with malevolence. "I'll kill you, bitch!"

Gathering steam, Caroline slammed into him, and he watched in shock as she ran through him, her knee bashing his head which snapped back and thudded against the concrete.

Caroline fell as expected, rolled, hopped up and saw him lying unconscious. Her first thought was that he'd done exactly what Linda had promised, followed the director's orders like a good actor. Caroline rolled her shoulders, bouncing on the balls of her feet. She'd been taught to yell "*NO*," followed by "*9-1-1*," and run to safety. Instead, she stayed, wrestling down the urge to kick him again. She glared at his body sprawled on the pavement, blood streaming from his nose, trickling from his mouth, his left cheek puffy, one eye starting to swell.

Caroline remembered her instructions, but as she yelled "*NO!*" the post-adrenaline crash hit. She swayed on her feet, heard a rustling, black spots and flickering lights obscuring her vision. Her stomach began to churn, and she felt light headed.

Drake stirred, moaned, tried to sit up.

She heard feet pounding, people shouting. She gripped her head to clear the confusion and felt hands grab her arms. Kayla supported her left, The Duke on her right. Tom and Jay stood over Drake.

"You hurt, Professor?" Even in her compromised state, Caroline heard the fear in The Duke's voice.

"No," she managed to whisper. He gathered her to his chest, and she sagged against him.

"I'm sorry," he murmured into her hair.

"I'm sorry, too."

"I shouldn't have said we weren't friends."

"You mean . . ." the words caught in her throat.

"I was an asshole. I . . ." He felt her struggling for balance and he steadied her. "Are you sure you're not hurt?"

"I'm okay. But . . . do you mean . . . we're . . ."

"Friends," he said huskily.

Caroline began to cry. "Where've you been? I've been looking for you."

"I needed some time. Lots going on. Tell you later." He shook his head in wonder. "Damn, girl. You beat him up."

"I guess I finally climbed out of my head." She clutched him.

"No shit! You took him down and you did it by yourself. I guess . . . you . . . you didn't need me."

"I need you now."

Then he realized the shape she was in.

"Professor, you're safe, but it's not quite over." He held her by the shoulders. "You have to walk away. He has to see you walk away."

"Okay. I . . . wait . . . did Mr. Cohen like your paper about names?"

The Duke, Kayla, Tom, and Jay all stared.

"Drake tried to rape you, you knocked the shit out of him, and you're asking about my paper on *To Kill a Mockingbird*?" The Duke was incredulous.

Caroline's tears welled up. "I don't know why I said that."

"Girl, you're in shock. You need to walk away, leave him on the ground. He needs to watch you go." He took her elbow firmly. "I got an A+ on the paper."

"Mazel tov," she murmured, and her friends exchanged alarmed glances.

Jay slipped off her backpack and carried it. Kayla took her hand as her vision turned gray and fuzzy. She could barely hear The Duke.

"This is going to feel like the longest walk of your life, but you can do it. Put one foot in front of the other."

Her chin began to droop.

"Hold your head high, Professor. Half a block, around the corner and I'll carry you. For now, keep walking."

Caroline obeyed, in a fugue state, moving forward to the rhythm of — she identified the beat through a thick layer of cotton — the names. Eduardo, Doris, Eric, Anna, Christopher. An anagram, she thought, drugged and foggy. Rearranging the letters to form a new word. No. An acronym. The first letter of each name. E-D-E-A-C. No. Try the last letters. O-S-C-A-R. Oscar. Who was Oscar? And then she knew. The Oscars. Academy Awards.

By now, Caroline shook so badly she could barely control her movements.

"I'm gonna kill that motherfucker," The Duke growled.

That cleared some of the cobwebs. She mumbled incoherently.

"Say what, Professor?"

"Don't touch him."

"I'm gonna break every bone in his body!"

"You'll get arrested."

"I don't care!"

"He's not worth it."

"I told you, I don't care!"

Logic going nowhere, Caroline resorted to threats. "Go near him and I'll . . ."

The Duke patted her arm affectionately. "Don't let this go to your head, girl. You can't beat me up."

"I have no intention of trying. But I swear if you lay a finger on Drake, I'll barf all over you!"

The Duke broke into laughter.

"I'm completely serious!" she shouted, but it came out a slurred whisper. "This is no idle threat! I have the urge and the firepower! You lay a hand on him, and I'll cover you with puke!"

"You're in mortal danger." Kayla to The Duke. "I'd back down if I were you."

"Okay girl, don't barf on me, I'm begging you."

Caroline would have smiled, but she was approaching dire straits. The Duke returned to coaching.

"Just walk to the corner. Ten steps, nine . . ."

Caroline made it to four before she collapsed to her hands and knees. As she began to heave, she crawled to the curb and vomited into the gutter. Kayla held her hair while The Duke gently patted her back saying, "It's okay, lots of people throw up after a fight."

Caroline finished, staring at the mess, beyond embarrassment. The Duke and Kayla helped her up.

"Drink this." Tom pulled a flask from his hip pocket. She took a swallow of something perfectly awful. "Mad Dog 20/20," he swaggered.

The taste was a slap in the face. Caroline breathed deeply, felt her contours, intact and sturdy. She turned to Tom. "Thank you for sharing your beverage."

To her complete surprise, they burst out laughing.

"She's back!" The Duke punched the air.

They skipped through campus, across the quad and into Mrs. Richardson's office. "Thank goodness!" Their guidance counselor's eyes filled with tears of relief as Leah and Geoff took their daughter in their arms.

When Kayla raced back to the quad after Drake told her to get lost, she first saw Doraine, who hurried to Mrs. Richardson, who called the police and Caroline's parents. Kayla grabbed The Duke, Jay and Tom at his heels, and they pelted back to find Caroline standing unsteadily over Drake, who lay crumpled on the sidewalk.

Now they all crowded around Mrs. Richardson's desk. Two female police officers stood to the side with the school nurse, who moved next to Caroline.

"Where are you hurting the most?" she asked gently.

"I'm fine," Caroline answered, sandwiched between her parents.

The nurse then pointed to Caroline's ripped jeans, bleeding knees, scraped arms, raw hands, bruised neck, cut right cheek and gently probed a lump on her forehead. She checked Caroline for signs of a concussion but found none. For the first time, Caroline felt pain from tumbling on the concrete. Later, she'd go over the fear, the expected tearing of her clothes, her body, her dignity. She'd cry and shiver and vomit many times before she found a place inside, under emotional lock and key, where it couldn't haunt her.

Leah and Geoff embraced Kayla and Doraine, shook hands with Jay and Tom, and finally turned to The Duke. Geoff spoke first.

"I'm glad to meet you."

"You, too, Sir."

Leah extended her dainty hand. The Duke reached for her, then for Geoff. The three moved together, holding each other. Finally, they broke contact.

Two male police officers arrived and eyed The Duke warily. He glared back and they stepped toward him, reaching for their handcuffs.

"What's going on?" Caroline began, then her eyes widened. "No, wait! You've got it wrong!" She moved next to The Duke. "He didn't hurt me. He came to help me, with Kayla, Jay, and Tom. But it was already over when they got there."

"Drake had already raped you?" one of the female officers asked empathically.

"Of course not!" Caroline was puzzled.

"What do you mean *of course not?*" the other female officer asked.

"I stopped him."

"How?" Mrs. Richardson asked.

Caroline suddenly understood their confusion. "I took a self-defense class. I knocked him out."

Leah and Geoff caught their breath. The other adults exchanged amazed glances.

"When we came back to school, we left Drake bleeding on the ground," Caroline looked from one officer to the next. "We should call an ambulance."

The two male officers stepped back from The Duke and verified Drake's address. They called the officers at the scene, who reported that Drake had disappeared. Maybe it was the impending charge of assault and attempted rape. Maybe it was being beaten up by a girl. Whatever Drake's reasons, Caroline couldn't ask for a better script, and with that thought, she chuckled. A child of the industry to the end. Then pure astonishment washed over her. The Duke looked down.

"What now, girl?"

"When we were walking back to school," she dropped her voice to a whisper, "I kept thinking about this dream . . . well, I was actually thinking about all the men in the industry who . . ." she trailed off.

The Duke's eyes widened and he guided her to the far corner of the room. "You've been assaulted before?" he spoke low.

"No, I never was assaulted until today," Caroline was barely audible. "But it felt like I was constantly fighting to keep people away. People in the industry have been telling me I was fat since I was a kid. Men—"

"You've got to be kidding!" The Duke burst out, then quickly lowered his voice as Caroline's parents glanced over. "The only way for you to lose weight would be to amputate a limb!"

"Most of the girls choose to keep their limbs. They stop eating. I knew a girl who died of anorexia."

The Duke shook his head. "That's messed up. Girl, you . . . wait, what were you going to say about men?"

"Men in the industry are always trying to have sex with me."

"Guys our age? Actors?"

"No," she shook her head. "Adults. Older. Actually, a lot older."

"Were your parents upset when you told them?"

"It happened right in front of them."

"You mean—" he caught himself and dropped his tone. "It was okay with your mom and dad to have a bunch of old men trying to sleep with you?"

Caroline's eyes flickered at her parents, who were talking to Mrs. Richardson.

"They . . ." It was suddenly so clear, she couldn't believe she had missed it. "Whenever a famous man hit on me, they liked it. They were proud."

"That's totally fu—" The Duke stopped in the middle of his sentence. "I'm sorry."

"You're right. It's totally fucked up."

"So that's the real film industry, not the tabloid version." The Duke paused, thinking. "Were you ever in a movie? Did you ever try acting?"

"Once, when I was a kid."

"Did you like it?"

She shook her head. "They dressed me, pinned on a wig, covered my face with makeup. The clothes weren't mine. The hair wasn't mine. My face wasn't mine. The director said to cry, so I cried. Everything felt completely artificial. I hated being on the set. But being cool, being in the club — I liked it too much. If it meant I had to act, then I'd act."

"With all that shit going down, why'd being in the club feel cool to you?"

She thought carefully, no time to be flippant. "I wanted to recapture those perfect two months when I was in elementary school, and everyone thought I was the industry's next in line. It was like living the happily ever after part of the fairy tale. I knew I could never get that back. It was a total accident that I had it in the first place. But I couldn't talk myself out of wanting the fairy tale." She wiped her eyes with her sleeve. "I was a coward."

"A coward. Yeah, right, I'm sure Drake would agree." The Duke almost grinned and she almost grinned back, surprised she still knew how. "Girl, no offense, but you make a lousy coward. And you'd make a worse actor. Acting is too . . ." The Duke searched for the right words. "It's too much . . . do this, do that, sit, stand, jump. You're too in-your-head. You'd be a disaster. Get over it."

Caroline paused, tremulous, aware of a cleansing pain, a wound stretching to heal. "You're right, but I hate that I'm such a hypocrite." She blushed so deeply her skin burned.

"You think you're a hypocrite if your thoughts and feelings don't line up like the military, in precise formation. Girl, you expect your head to be perfect. Brains come in a lot of shapes and sizes, but they don't come in perfect."

"Not even . . ."

"Nope, not even yours." He raised an eyebrow and they began to laugh. The others tried to be discreet as they exchanged alarmed glances. Caroline and The Duke caught it and plunged into hysteria. It was out of place, inappropriate, and as they settled down, Caroline felt almost okay.

Finally composed, she turned to her parents. Leah and Geoff stood together on the other side of the room, arms around each other, watching her closely. "Mom and Dad want people to think they're good parents," she said so quietly that The Duke leaned toward her to hear. "When other people are around, they put on a show, like they're doing now. They're protective and horrified that Drake tried to rape me. But tomorrow they'll be fine if a fifty-year-old producer tries to have sex with me, as long as he's famous."

The Duke sized up Leah and Geoff. "The way they care about you is real. They're not putting on a show. Different situations bring out the best and the worst in them. They're . . . it's like . . . they're messed up, but they love you. It's real."

Caroline looked down. "You're right. I'm an asshole. They've given me a lot. I should just love them."

"Nope, wrong again," he whispered. "You're not an asshole. You're just . . ."

"What?"

"You're just human. And . . ." he trailed off.

"And what?"

"You're stronger than they are."

"I'm . . . I . . . what?" Even as she sputtered, she knew he was right. She also knew she didn't have to run from that part of herself anymore.

She could live with her strengths, with her nerd-in-overdrive flaws, with her parents' weaknesses, with their love. And she could live without the entertainment industry.

With one exception.

"Kayla. She's a performer, and I love her."

"You're a very strange girl, and I love you."

"I love you, too."

Doraine saw them from across the room, calm in her understanding, a rare moment of adolescent wisdom and balance. Mrs. Richardson offered her chair to Doraine, who looked ready to collapse under her front-heavy load. The Duke went to check on her and Caroline followed.

"What are you and your friends doing on Saturday?" Doraine smiled at Caroline.

"Anything you want."

"Church at the corner of Hollywood Boulevard and Silliman Court. Ten in the morning. The Duke and I are getting married."

"I wouldn't miss it for anything."

Leah and Geoff looked composed, talking to the uniformed women about Caroline's self-defense class. Kayla, Jay, and Tom were giving statements to another officer, interrupting each other at every turn. Finally, the paperwork was completed and the officers walked Leah, Geoff, and Caroline to their car.

Driving home, Caroline opened the window and let the breeze flow through her tangled hair. Her mother turned in the front seat and her father glanced in the rear view mirror every few moments, checking that their daughter was safe. They didn't know it yet, but Drake would never return. In a month, Caroline would realize her nightmare was gone as well.

"Mom, Dad, I decided something."

"Go ahead, tell us." Her father drove carefully, stopping at the yellow lights, never exceeding the speed limit.

"I'm not going to another opening. If there's an industry event, I'll have other plans. I'm done with showings at The Academy. If you throw a party at our house, I'll be out with my friends or in my room with the door closed. Except Gretchen and Janet. I like them. If they're at our house, I'm glad to see them."

"Is the industry really that bad?" her father asked.

"Not for you. You're a great cinematographer, and you like being a part of that world. But for me, yeah, it's really that bad."

"Then you're making the right choice," said her mother firmly.

"I understand," her father said, and Caroline realized that even if he didn't fully understand, he understood enough.

To her parents' surprise, their daughter was up and ready for school the next morning.

"You can take the day at home," Leah offered.

"I want to go back. I need to be there."

"Okay," Geoff said. "I'll drive you and . . . hold on. I just remembered. Maybe you'd prefer to take the bus."

She nodded. "Yeah, but thanks anyway."

She couldn't explain why returning to campus felt so necessary. She hurt all over. Her face and neck were bruised. Her arms and hands were scraped. She knew the numb feeling was residual shock, and the out-of-nowhere spikes of anxiety would settle down over time. She didn't know how to define her path to healing, but she knew with absolute certainty that Hollywood High was a crucial part of her recovery.

She hugged her parents, shouldered her backpack, and walked to meet her bus.

CHAPTER 53

Toni and Blake took one look at Caroline and turned still.

"What happened to your face?" Toni in a hushed voice.

As Caroline told them, Kayla and Vincent spotted the three girls from across the quad and rushed over.

"Kayla called me last night," Vincent said. "I can't believe—"

He was interrupted as Irene and Gary joined them. Duke and Doraine followed, along with Jay and Tom. Caroline introduced everyone.

"Blake . . ." Kayla looked thoughtful. "Why do I know your name?"

"The art show," Vincent answered. "Blake did the sculpture I showed you."

"That was amazing," Gary smiled.

"Thanks." Blake smiled back.

To Caroline's surprise, The Duke moved close and studied her face. He took her hands, looked carefully at her scraped palms and forearms. He asked for permission to lift her hair and peered at her neck where Drake had put his hands. He nodded, satisfied.

"What?" she asked.

"Your first fight." No bravado whatsoever. "When people aren't used to fighting, they don't get that even if you win a fight, you get knocked around. If you hit someone, your hand hurts. You're probably worried about the cuts and bruises, especially on your face. It's very clean, not too swollen, not too deep. You'll heal fine."

Miss Orville walked onto campus, scanned the crowd for Caroline, hugged her without speaking.

When they entered Mr. Cohen's classroom, Carlos immediately went to Caroline. "Are you okay?"

"Yeah. Thanks for asking."

"You look . . ."

"I know. I look beat up. Actually, he barely hurt me. The cuts and scrapes and bruises are mostly from the sidewalk when I . . ."

"When she knocked him out!" Kayla proudly finished her friend's sentence.

"Damn, Caroline." Carlos shook his head. "You kicked his butt."

"You're The Professor," Dreads tossed over his shoulder as he walked by. "You're supposed to kick ass in the chess club. Way to go!"

"Who knew?" Carlos grinned.

"Yeah, who knew?" Caroline repeated softly.

Mr. Cohen called Caroline to his desk. "I heard about what happened. Do you need anything?"

"I'm okay, but I appreciate your checking."

"If it gets to be too much, you can hang out in my classroom during your breaks. Your friends can be here with you. It's quiet in here. During high voltage times, quiet can be good."

She thanked him and sat down as Kurt zoomed toward Kayla, hand over his heart, declaring his undying love. He hadn't hassled her since his failed attempt at streaking. Now he was back, full throttle. This time Kayla was ready.

He reached toward the ceiling, beseeching Cupid to bring Kayla to her senses.

"My senses are fine, thanks," she shot back.

Mr. Cohen stepped forward to begin roll call, but stopped as Kurt launched into "Ode to Eyes of Unsurpassed Hazel," which he had composed on the school bus that morning. Kayla looked at Mr. Cohen, who gave her a thumbs up. Kurt, tunnel vision on Kayla, didn't notice.

"Bad poem, Kurt," she interrupted his rhapsody. "It's time to stop."

"I never know when to stop."

"I'm going to show you," she stood facing him. "You're not cute. You're not funny. You're a serious pain. Back off!"

The class turned still, aware that this was Kayla's moment. The only one who missed the obvious was Kurt.

"I wore my favorite shirt for you. It's a t-shirt from the Bob Dylan concert. He's my hero."

"Your favorite shirt is in imminent danger." Kayla reached into her backpack and pulled out two squirt guns. She stuck them in the pockets of her painter's pants, then pulled two more firearms from her purse. She faced Kurt, a bright, plastic weapon in each hand. "You take two steps away from me, or I'll fire!"

"Fire what?" He didn't back up, but he stopped bearing down on her.

"Indelible paint."

"A rainbow of love!" he cried and leaped toward her.

Aiming steadily, she unloaded green and pink smack in his face.

"Cut it out!" he yelled and then choked as she plugged him in the mouth with blue.

She lowered her hand, aiming at Bob Dylan. "Your hero is about to turn into a rainbow of love."

"I am smote!" he cried, lunging for her. Kayla shot a jet at his chest, and he jumped back angrily. "That's my favorite shirt! It's a limited edition! You ruined it!"

"This is my favorite class, and you've been ruining it since the first day of school!" Kayla shouted as she emptied yellow.

Kurt curled around his sopping hero. "They only made fifty of these shirts," he whined. "It can't be replaced."

"Neither can the piece of my year that you wrecked," she stared him down. "I'm out of ammunition, so listen carefully."

"Why should I listen to you?"

"Because the next girl might choose something more harmful than a squirt gun."

"Fine," he glared. "What's the message?"

"When a girl says to stop, it's time to stop."

"Stupidest thing I've ever heard . . ."

Kurt was drowned out as the entire room, including Mr. Cohen, broke into applause.

Students and faculty approached Caroline throughout the day. Lacey and Elton from ceramics, Della and Nellie from P.E., Girls #1, #2, and #3 from the bathroom, the basketball team with Lureen punching the air and Shawna shouting "We always knew you had it in you!"

J.D.'s friends found her during the morning break. "Drake disappeared," Gren told them. "Good riddance."

"Will you guys be okay?" Caroline asked.

"We have other people to work for," Billy answered. "One of my clients wants me to move in with him. So yeah, we'll be okay. What about you? You look . . ."

"Yeah, I look like hell, but I'm okay."

At lunch, Toni and Blake joined their circle, sitting protectively on either side of Caroline. Duke and Doraine made a point of walking by several times. Caroline wondered why they didn't approach, then realized that Doraine could no longer sit comfortably on the ground.

Kayla was regaling the group with her morning triumph and the demise of Kurt's treasured t-shirt when a teacher approached, patted

Caroline's shoulder, and hurried into the administration building.

"Who is she?" Gary asked.

"No idea," Caroline shook her head. "Does the entire school know what happened?"

"Best gossip in my three years here," Vincent answered.

"You're an impossible act to follow," Kayla grinned.

"You did fine this morning with Kurt," Gary looked at Kayla. "He'll have nightmares about squirt guns for years."

"I'm just glad Drake didn't—" Toni's voice hitched.

Blake nodded, tears in their eyes.

"I'm going to be fine," Caroline said softly.

"You're more than fine," Kayla sincerely. "You're The Professor."

"I'm the most nerdy girl on campus and I'm famous for beating up a pimp."

Caroline looked around her circle of friends through a strangely bright lens. Toni and Blake radiated support. Kayla and Vincent sat close to each other, the creative forces in the group. Gary's thoughtfulness balanced Irene's fire. Caroline had spoken to Valerie on the phone the night before and could feel her caring from miles away at Laurel. The Duke smiled and Doraine waved. They were together and strong and vulnerable and ready.

Caroline's healing had begun.

CHAPTER 54

The telephone rang in the Hartnet's family room.

"I'll get it!" Valerie reached for the receiver.

Mrs. Hartnet was in the kitchen making popcorn, and Lincoln was flipping through the channels, searching for the Dodgers baseball game.

"Hello?"

Lincoln looked up to see his sister's complexion drain to ash. "Mom, come quickly!" he called.

Mrs. Hartnet hurried in, glancing from her son to her daughter.

"Yes, Mrs. Compston. She's right here."

Valerie held out the receiver to her mother, who covered it with her hand. "Why are you upset? What did Celia's mother say to you?"

"It's Celia." Valerie's hands were shaking.

"Celia is on the phone, and she wants to talk to me?"

"No, Mrs. Compston is on the phone, and she wants to talk to you. But . . . it's Celia."

"You're kidding!" Lincoln's eyes popped. "Celia? Really?"

Valerie blinked back tears.

"I'm missing something," Mrs. Hartnet watched her children.

"It's Celia," Valerie repeated. "Or it was." She wiped her eyes.

Mrs. Hartnet froze for a moment. "I see." With one hand still covering the receiver, she stroked her daughter's hair. "There's nothing like the first break up." Valerie bucked up against her mother.

"This explains a lot." Lincoln thought through their vacations on the Riviera with Celia's family. "I always felt like Mr. and Mrs. Compston wanted me to ask Celia out, but she never took her eyes off you. I assumed she wasn't interested in me." He grinned. "Correct conclusion, incorrect reason."

"Do her parents know?" Mrs. Hartnet whispered.

"I think they know about me. I'll bet they don't know about Celia."

"I'll handle this."

"Mom . . ." Valerie struggled against panic.

"Trust me," Mrs. Hartnet held her daughter's eyes. Then in the proper phone voice of a trained debutante, "Hello, I apologize for the delay. How are you?"

Valerie hunched on the couch, and Lincoln put an arm around his sister.

"Yes, it's a convenient time to speak" . . . "No, I'm not aware that Valerie has a problem I should know about" . . . "Yes, I am aware that my daughter is a lesbian, but I don't consider it a problem" . . . "No, I am not interested in the name of a doctor to cure her" . . . "Excuse me, I regret having to cut this conversation short, but I have an urgent situation I must attend to" . . . "No, it's nothing about Valerie. It's a popcorn emergency" . . . "Yes, I said popcorn. I also said emergency. Goodbye." She gently hung up the phone and faced her children. "I don't think she's ever heard of popcorn. I guess they don't sell it at Tiffany's."

"Mom, I'm sorr—"

Mrs. Hartnet held up her hand. "Valerie, don't ever apologize for being who you are. Be gay and be proud. That goes for you, too, Lincoln. Be straight and be proud. You're both fine people. I'm proud to be your mother."

Without another word, she hurried into the kitchen to rescue her popcorn.

They settled on the couch to watch baseball. The first pitch to Steve Garvey, a perfect swing, a solid crack and the ball soared for a double.

"Yes!" Lincoln punched the air.

"Good hit!" Valerie scooped a handful of popcorn.

"That woman is a narcissistic hairball!"

Valerie and Lincoln stared at their mother, and the family collapsed in each other's arms.

"I'm thinking of a lifetime of future summers anywhere except the Riviera with the Compstons," Lincoln grinned.

"I've always wanted to visit the mosaics in Ravenna," Mrs. Hartnet said.

They both looked at Valerie.

"I'm good right here."

CHAPTER 55

The following Monday, Caroline waited impatiently in the quad with Toni and Blake. After a few minutes, Irene and her journalism friends carried stacks of newspapers to the outdoor tables, the year's final edition of the *Hollywood Crimson*. Caroline, Toni, and Blake grabbed copies and read with an intense focus. The three friends looked up at the same time.

"You did it," Blake said to Toni.

"I did it," said Toni to Blake.

"Congratulations," said Caroline to Toni.

"You really think it's good?" Toni asked Caroline.

"It's a show-stopper."

Hollywood Crimson Newspaper
June, 1974
Letter to the Editor

Dear Editor,

I'm a student at Hollywood High. Every day I come to school, and I'm afraid. If people realize what's going on with me, I'll be beaten. The last time someone was beaten at our school, he ended up dead. I don't think the people who assaulted him meant to kill him. I also don't think it bothers them that he never got up from the beating. It could have been me, and I live with that fear every day. Someone once asked, if I'm scared here, why don't I switch schools? My answer is that there's nowhere safe for me to go. Why? Because I'm trans.

I want an education. I want to become a history teacher. I'm going to rewrite history books so they make sense, so they're not the most boring books on the planet, so they're not filled with lies. Those are my career goals. But I have other goals, too. I'd like to walk on campus without fear. I'd like to know that when I use the bathroom that's right for me, nobody will threaten me, or grab me, or shove me, or say things that hurt me.

The bathroom is a scary place for trans students. A lot of violence, verbal and physical, takes place in the bathrooms. I try not to use the restrooms during school, but sometimes I need to. Each time, I don't know if I'll be recognized as trans. Take a quick moment and think what that would be like. What if you were afraid of being beaten or killed, every minute of every day, for something as basic as having to pee.

Before we leave the subject of restrooms, would you like to know what I do in there? Let's start with what I DON'T do. I don't grab the opportunity to catch a glimpse of the private parts of other people's bodies. I don't look for an opportunity to be hurtful with my words or violent with my fists. I have no interest in having a sexual encounter in a stall next to a toilet.

Here's what I do. I've made a list so everyone can follow along.

First, I pee.

Second, I wash my hands.

Third, I leave.

Fourth, there is no fourth. That's it.

There's really nothing about me that's scary. I've never been violent. I try to be nice. I'm polite. Even when people say or do awful things to me, I don't retaliate. Yes, part of that is because I'm afraid. But even if I didn't feel frightened, I still wouldn't be out for revenge. That's not who I am.

I'm just a high school student with a female identity, but I got there in a way that a lot of people think is abnormal. So, what should you do if you think being trans is scary or bizarre? Even though I'm writing this anonymously for my own safety, I hope our paths will cross. I hope you'll allow us to talk. It's okay to ask questions, as long as you're open to answers. Please keep in mind that the level of respect in the answer will match the level of respect in the question.

If you doubt that trans is real, please allow someone who is trans to share their experience. You might be surprised to discover that along with your differences, you share some common ground.

Next September, I'll be back here at Hollywood High. I hope I'll love some classes, tolerate others, be interested, be bored, eat lunch, make friends — all without fear. I wish the same for you.

Have a good summer.

Sincerely,

Anonymous

CHAPTER 56

The Duke and Doraine were married. Their wedding pulsed with a joy so pure that Caroline forgot to overthink it and had a great time. After the ceremony, Doraine's cousins hoisted the newlyweds onto their shoulders and carried them two blocks to the small house where The Duke grew up. Then more feasting and drinking and singing and dancing until The Duke and Doraine disappeared into Irene's car and spent their one-day honeymoon at Leah and Geoff's beach house.

With J.D. no longer haunting her dreams, Caroline surprised herself by thinking of him in odd waking moments, bringing him with her, wherever she went. She imagined tutoring him in math and English, helping him prepare for the high school equivalency exam that he'd never take. Her fantasies made her uncomfortable, and she told nobody. She wished she could talk to a friend and sort it out, but she didn't know what to say. *For months I had a recurring nightmare about a boy I never spoke to, who doesn't have a name, who was murdered because he was gay. Now I'm having recurring daydreams about tutoring him.* Nope, she'd keep that to herself. Even more strange, she imagined conversations where she turned to J.D. for help in understanding her obsession with him.

Why do I care so much about you? He'd try to explain, but never offered a clear answer. Sometimes their imaginary conversations turned in a different direction, and they'd tell each other about their lives — his growing up on the streets, gay and parentless — her being a bookworm, which was incomprehensible to her parents and their industry friends. Once, they talked about Vincent's painting, J.D.'s Sunset. She cried, and she could feel J.D. crying with her. Another time, he talked about his community of friends, falling in love with Billy. These conversations were so detailed that they felt like actual memories, both speaking softly, no judgments, honest and true. Whatever form her fantasies took, one fact was crystal clear. If J.D. hadn't been in school, he'd still be alive. He had literally died for an education.

Now, for the first time, The Duke and Doraine joined the Saturday night gathering at Vincent's house. The group crowded into Vincent's bedroom, and he put Frank Zappa's *Over-Nite Sensation* on the stereo. They were laughing at "Montana" and dental floss tycoons when Valerie rang the doorbell. She and Caroline exchanged a triumphant smile. The girls had hung up an hour before, after Valerie reported, word for word, the phone call from Celia's mother.

Caroline watched carefully as The Duke and Doraine met the debutante.

Irene grabbed a gigantic sugar cookie and turned to The Duke, cutting off Caroline's proper introduction.

"So, when are you going to tell us?"

"Tell you what?" Duke and Doraine each bit into a cookie.

"Duh," Irene hit her own head. "What changed your mind about Jeremy."

The Duke looked at Doraine.

"I told you they'd ask, but I thought it would take at least one full minute to get there." Doraine handed her cookie, minus one bite, to her new husband. "Heartburn," she grimaced.

The Duke took the cookie, hesitated to speak, glanced at Valerie.

"It's okay," said Gary. "We told her about the assembly."

"Nice going," Valerie smiled at The Duke.

"*Yeah, nice going,*" *J.D. echoed silently, and Caroline nodded.*

"Does she know Jeremy's gay?" Doraine whispered to Caroline, indicating Valerie.

"She's gay, too," Valerie answered calmly.

The Duke and Doraine gaped. "But you're so feminine!" and "But you're so pretty!" they blurted simultaneously.

"And you're so teen-pregnant," Valerie said, thoroughly composed.

The Duke began to laugh. "Caroline, are you trying to kill us?" Before she could answer, he and Doraine each gave Valerie a high five.

"Y'know," Irene raised an eyebrow at The Duke, "your performance at Kayla's talent show was improvisation at its finest. We thought you were a leaking bag of douche."

"Yeah," Vincent nodded, "it's great to be wrong."

"What changed your mind?" Caroline asked The Duke.

"I met a judge."

"Oh, my gosh!" Kayla breathed. "You had your court date."

"Three weeks ago, a day to remember."

"Nine in the morning," Doraine stepped in. "Courtroom of Judge Angney."

"You were there?" Vincent asked Doraine.

"Of course. I thought I was saying goodbye to my man and sending him to be locked up."

"When's your due date?" Gary offered her Vincent's desk chair.

"Any moment." Doraine carefully sat and stared at her own belly. "I'm trying not to think about my very large baby finding its way out of my very small—"

"Someone needs to change the subject!" Kayla leaped in.

"Caroline, say something! Say anything!" J.D. was half amused and half concerned. "Kayla looks like she might puke!"

"I've never been in a courtroom," Caroline broke the horrified silence.

"Mahogany paneling everywhere," The Duke swallowed a huge bite of cookie. "That gavel could kill a grizzly bear. I was scared shitless and—"

"Me too," Doraine broke in. "The Duke's mom was gripping my hand and I was trying not to miscarry and I looked at his useless lawyer . . ."

"Mr. Balfour," The Duke finished Doraine's cookie. "Total waste of space. He—"

"So, what happened?" Irene cut in.

"His Royal Honor Judge Angney walked in. The bailiff called 'All Rise,' and my heart was beating so hard I was sure everyone could hear. My lawyer hauled me up and the judge said, 'Mr. Duke Hunter. We meet again. It's been a while. I was hoping I wouldn't see you back here.' And I thought, I'm totally screwed, because His Highness sent me to Juvie when I was eleven."

"Where?" Valerie was confused.

"Juvenile Hall," Doraine explained. "I could see The Duke panicking, and I thought great, just great, I'm gonna be a single mom."

Valerie's mouth hung open.

"Hey, Valerie, don't go into shock yet." The Duke gently punched her shoulder. "We're just getting started."

They all laughed, including Valerie.

"So, we were shitting bricks," The Duke continued, "and the judge asked, 'Is there anything you'd like to say?' I was under Mr. Balfour's strict orders to keep my trap shut. But when he started to talk, Judge Angney held up a hand and said, 'I'd like to hear from Mr. Hunter.'" The Duke paused, picturing the judge. "He's wearing formal black robes. His desk and chair are huge, like he's a king, on this raised platform above the rest of us. He has these turquoise eyes, crazy bushy eyebrows, bald as a pig. That's when I realized he was looking at me like he really cared."

"What'd you say?" Kayla asked softly.

"That I was sorry."

"Go on," Doraine took his hand.

The Duke nodded at his wife. "So His Lordship asked, 'Sorry for what?' He was weighing every word, so I kept it simple. I said, 'I've been angry all my life. I hurt people I love. I shouldn't have stolen the Coke. I'm sorry.'"

"His mom was whispering this endless string of prayers," Doraine added, "and I was thinking, please, please . . .'"

"Then the judge asked, 'Why'd you take the soda?' I didn't know what to say. I was standing there like a moron and Brainless Balfour whispered, 'Don't tell him,' so I knew I had to tell him."

"You told him the truth?" Kayla was incredulous.

"Yep. Doraine was sitting in the front row, and she's hard to hide."

J.D. laughed softly, and Caroline grinned.

Doraine slugged The Duke's arm. He tenderly placed his hand on her belly for a moment before he continued.

"So, I said to the judge that I found out my girlfriend was pregnant, and I lost my head. No excuses, but that's why."

"That was my cue to swoon for sympathy," Doraine grinned, "but I didn't have time. His Honor nodded at me and asked, 'That's the lady?'"

"I said, 'Yes, Sir. Her name's Doraine.' Then Judge Angney asked the question I was hoping he wouldn't ask — 'Will you marry her?'"

"We talked it over for hours," Doraine brushed her long hair out of her eyes, "but we didn't know how the judge would take it."

The Duke nodded. "I was standing there like an idiot again. I think Judge Angney realized that I didn't know what to do because he said, 'I'm not going to lecture you on morality. I'm interested in how you'll handle this situation.' Then Mr. Balfour, my guiding light, whispered, 'Say yes, you'll marry her,' so I knew that was the wrong thing to do."

"Can you, y'know, cut to the chase?" Irene drummed her fingers.

"I . . . well . . . I told the truth." The Duke shifted.

Doraine squeezed his hand. "I think they can deal with it."

The Duke looked around the room slowly, and finally at Caroline. "Something I've never told you. My dad's in prison for murder. Has been since I was a baby. Has no contact with my mom or me."

Caroline held his eyes and gave a small nod.

The Duke smiled. "That's what Judge Angney did when I told him. Nodded, like he really cared. So, I told him that I didn't want to let it happen again, that Doraine and I decided if I had to do time, I wouldn't marry her. When I got out, I'd always send child support, always be in contact. I'd be as much of a father as she'd let me. But she'd be free to find a good man." The Duke stared at the floor.

"Hey," Caroline gently kicked The Duke's shoe. "It's okay."

The Duke cleared his throat. "I know it's a lot to hear. I mean, this changes things. I get it. If you don't want . . ."

"Friends," Caroline said firmly. "Don't forget, we're friends."

The Duke was unable to speak for a moment. Then he turned to Valerie. "How about you? Are you in shock?"

"A bit," she answered honestly. "But since I'm now the Horrific Homosexual Hartnet, and half our relatives aren't speaking to us, and the other half can't figure out how generations of gentle breeding could go so embarrassingly wrong . . ." she shrugged. "You seem okay to me."

"*I like your friends,*" J.D. whispered.

"What did the judge say?" Irene demanded impatiently.

"I wish you could have seen it," Doraine's lips twitched. "Mr. Balfour looked like a blown hemorrhoid. Then the judge said to The Duke, 'Suppose you don't go to jail?'"

"There was this electric silence in the courtroom." The Duke took over the story. "I stared at Judge Angney and said, 'I didn't think that was a possibility, but Doraine and I have a marriage license. We took the blood tests. We did the paperwork, just in case. If I don't go to jail, we'll get married.' The judge looked like he was thinking everything over. Then he asked, 'How will you support your young family?' I told him about a job in a law office where the managing partner is a friend of Mrs. Richardson's. I told him I'd go to community college at night, maybe transfer to UCLA in a few years.'"

"His turquoise eyes bulged out of his bald head," Doraine laughed. "Our man Judge Angney boomed, 'College! That's a new development!'"

"Then he asked, 'How do you think you can best serve your community?'" The Duke shook his head. "I didn't know what he was talking about. I said the first thing that popped into my head, that I'd like to tutor kids in math. Suddenly he turned formal, and he announced, 'I sentence you to ten hours of community service.' The gavel banged and I jumped about a foot, and he said, 'Hey Duke, Doraine might have already found a good man. Think that's possible?' And he walked out."

"I've never felt so relieved in my life and—" Doraine turned rigid.

"*And there she goes . . .*" J.D. said.

"*What's going on?*" Caroline asked silently. When J.D. didn't answer, she turned to Doraine.

"Are you okay?"

"Doraine . . ." The Duke began.

"My water broke."

CHAPTER 57

Caroline perched on the edge of her chair, gnawing a thumbnail. Mr. Cohen smiled reassuringly as he called for order. Caroline's final requirement for Sophomore Honors English was due today, the last day of school before summer vacation.

Instead of an exam, Mr. Cohen had offered two options for the end-of-year project. They could recite a poem or song from memory, or they could write an original poem or essay and read it to the class. His only parameters were "no bigotry" and "no glorifying violence." Caroline was surprised to learn that she was the only student who chose Option #2.

"I want to recite my favorite poem," Kayla told her friends as they ate lunch.

"Most people chose the first option because writing takes a lot more time." Gary looked at Caroline. "What are you going to write about?"

"Ninth grade. The reason I transferred schools."

"When we first met . . ." — Irene thought back to their conversation in the fall — ". . . you told us about those three girls who smoked pot on campus and were expelled. Then they were brought back because one of the families was a huge donor. I thought you left Laurel because you were tired of the snobbery and the hypocrisy."

"That's all true, but it's not why I left."

"Then why?" Vincent asked.

Caroline turned silent.

"Does anyone know the real reason?" Kayla watched her friend closely.

"Valerie knows everything. She was at Laurel. She saw it happen."

"She never said anything," Kayla was puzzled.

"Before she met you, I made her promise not to tell. Now I feel like I need to tell you and everyone else, too."

Gary realized that this was big, whatever *this* was. "Do you want to tell us now? Would that make it easier to tell everyone else later?"

Caroline shook her head.

"We love you, no matter what happened," Kayla said gently.

"Seems like writing a paper is a lot of work when you could say it." Irene narrowed her eyes. "There's something else going on."

"Yeah, there's something else," Caroline admitted.

"What is it?" Kayla quietly. "Why are you really writing this essay?"

"Yeah," echoed J.D. *"Why are you really writing this essay?"*

"Because . . . actually, I'm not sure what the *Because* is. I mean, I know why I left Laurel, but I don't know why I need to tell everyone. I thought I'd never tell, then something changed." She shrugged. "I'll let you know when I figure it out."

For the final two weeks of school, Mr. Cohen scheduled three students each day. Presto kicked off day one with The Beach Boys' "Catch A Wave." When he finished, he surprised the class with an interpretation. "I get up at four in the morning every day to surf before school. This is my favorite song. But people love The Beach Boys even if they don't surf, so I think surfing is a metaphor. Get a dream. Work hard. Follow your dream wherever it takes you. Sometimes you'll ride it, and sometimes you'll wipe out. Either way, if you stick with your dream, you'll get a seat on top of the world."

Every night, Caroline shut the door to her bedroom and wrote.

Sometimes she scribbled sentences already written in her head. Sometimes the ideas flowed from an unknown source. *"Because,"* she whispered as her words shaped themselves into a cohesive structure. "I have to find the *Because.*"

"You don't have to find the Because," *J.D. smiled gently. "The Because has already found you."*

"What do you mean?" she asked, but he didn't answer.

On day three, Kayla recited Walt Whitman's "I Hear America Singing," and Gary followed with his favorite song, The Beatles' "The Long and Winding Road." Kurt, faintly blotchy from his showdown with Kayla, recited a wooden "Tambourine Man," a tribute to his hero Bob Dylan.

When the final bell rang that afternoon, Caroline and her friends walked to The Duke's house. Doraine had given birth to a healthy baby girl, seven pounds four ounces. When they arrived, The Duke's mother opened the door. "They're all sleeping," she whispered.

"Can you please give this to The Duke and Doraine?" Caroline handed Mrs. Hunter an enormous diaper bag overflowing with bottles, onesies, hats, baby blankets, bibs, a bright magenta stuffed bear, a teething ring, and a rattle. The Duke's mother hugged her.

Day four in Honors English would be talked about for the entire summer. First, Dreads composed a merging of Emily Dickinson's "Because I Could Not Stop for Death" and Sylvia Plath's "Lady Lazarus."

Mr. Cohen had him run through it twice. "Dreads took two familiar works and combined them into his own original medley. It's smart, creative, cutting edge."

The class applauded. When Dreads smiled to acknowledge the compliment, his eyes never left Elvia.

Then Elvia's turn.

"Can I change poets?" she asked, and Mr. Cohen nodded. "I was going to recite a part of Allen Ginsberg's 'Howl.' It's a cool poem, and everyone should read it. Anyway, this is Robert Frost's 'The Road Not Taken.'" The poem rang out clear and pure.

"Thank you, Elvia," Mr. Cohen said when she finished.

"I'm changing that, too," Elvia said, and the class groaned. "Actually, I'm stopping with the changes. You can call me by my real name. Andrea Krause." She glared at the classroom, daring anyone to challenge her.

The students broke into cheers.

That night, as Caroline prepared to work on her essay, the words stopped. "*Because*," she whispered. "Find the *Because*." She waited, pen poised, but nothing came. "What is it?" she asked herself. "Why am I writing this essay?" She felt something stir and she held herself still, letting the thought clarify itself. Then the idea took hold. The *Because* wasn't an *it*; the *Because* was a *who*.

"*Took you long enough!*" J.D. grinned.

Her words poured onto the paper.

Caroline was last on the agenda, sharing her limelight with Sharon and Mort. Even as she felt compelled to tell her story, she had been dreading this moment. She knew it was time to let go of her secret, but *knowing* and *feeling* were different, and her fear heightened as the day approached. She tried to wake up nauseous, with a sore throat or even better, laryngitis. Maybe she dislocated her jaw in her sleep. Instead, she jerked awake sweaty, anxious and worst of all, healthy.

When Caroline arrived at school, she handed Toni, Blake, Irene, and Vincent each a sealed envelope. "This is the essay I wrote for my English class. I'll be reading it aloud. Kayla and Gary will hear it, but I want you all to know what it says." Irene began to rip the envelope. "Wait!" Caroline said sharply and Irene stopped. "Don't read it now. You can read it when the bell rings. I want you all to know at the same time."

"Know what?" Toni asked.

"Why I left Laurel."

The bell blared, and Caroline's palms broke with sweat.

Following Mr. Cohen's roll call, Sharon recited A.A. Milne's "Now We Are Six," holding a humongous stuffed Winnie the Pooh, capturing the poignancy of a teenage girl's nostalgia for childhood. When Caroline lifted her hands to clap, she left two perfect prints of sweat on her jeans.

"Next," Mr. Cohen announced, "Mort will bring us E.E. Cummings."

The first three lines were seamless. But on line four of "anyone lived in a pretty how town," Mort's voice began to crack, and crack, and crack. As the class's hysteria threatened to spin out, as Mort prepared to die of terminal humiliation, Mr. Cohen stood up.

First, he told the class that when he was in tenth grade, his voice cracked every time he talked to his secret crush. For an extremely long month, he became a class joke with students imitating him, often to his face. Next, Mr. Cohen described his embarrassment at the beach, being the last boy in his grade to grow chest hair, and his intense jealousy of his older brother's physique. Years later, his brother would confess that he was equally embarrassed because at age fourteen, he sported a fully developed hairy chest and extra large shoulders on his five-foot-five frame. In time, he'd grow to be six feet, but nobody knew back then, when he lived his life as a human baboon. Now the class was laughing at Mr. Cohen, not at Mort. But their teacher wasn't finished. He offered ten points extra credit if every student told a story about themselves. To earn the prize, he required one hundred percent participation.

Caroline related her cloak and dagger storing used menstrual pads in her lunch bags at Windy Canyon Elementary Education. When she finished, Mr. Cohen nodded with empathy, and she realized he had known from the start that her "fiction" assignment was autobiographical fact.

Andrea, no longer Elvia, admitted that she slept with a faded yellow stuffed bunny, a gift for her second birthday. Dreads, age thirteen, ate nine candy bars on a dare, went to church and hurled all over his priest. Sharon gave a hug to her newly toilet trained toddler cousin at the precise wrong moment and had to complete her Bat Mitzvah in a pink lace dress soaked with pee. Presto, taking his dad's convertible for a spin, waved to some pretty girls and rear ended a police car. Gary, always gigantic for his age, playfully sat on his friend's lap in kindergarten, and the kid was on crutches for a week with a squashed leg.

Kurt's turn arrived and he glowered, "I don't have anything to say. I've never been humiliated in my life!"

Ignoring the gorilla mask under Kurt's desk, Mr. Cohen granted him and Kayla a free pass.

Finally bonded and relaxed, the class listened calmly as Mort returned to Cummings. His voice cracked only twice and at the end, they gave him a huge ovation.

As the applause tapered, through a fog of nerves, Caroline heard Mr. Cohen's voice. "Caroline will wrap up this project with an essay of her own."

Caroline clutched her typed pages. She watched herself walk to Mr. Cohen's desk. She turned to face the class. Mr. Cohen nodded for her to begin, and she froze. *I'm not doing this! No way! I'll take an F on the assignment!*

"You can do this," J.D. said firmly. *"You need to stop hiding, be honest, step into the light."*

"I'm scared," she answered silently.

"That fear means you're doing the right thing."

Holding no other options, she plunged. "My essay is called 'Hollywood Pride.' In ninth grade, everything blew up."

"We can't hear you!" A student in the back row.

Caroline cleared her throat.

"I was the perfect student at Laurel Academy for Girls. I never broke the rules, never scored less than ninety-two percent on an exam, never got in trouble. But I was hiding so many parts of myself, I didn't know who I was anymore.

"I was good at hiding things. I was born into an entertainment industry family. I was raised to be an actor, and my role at Laurel was to be the model student. I played my role well, until I just couldn't do it anymore.

"What pushed me over the edge was an annual Laurel Academy tradition, the May Day Festival, and I wrecked it."

Caroline hadn't meant to be funny and was completely surprised when the class broke into friendly laughter.

"A girl from each grade was voted to be a May Princess, with the senior class winner getting crowned as the May Queen. The girls walked down a garden path in floor length dresses that cost a fortune. I learned later that they had brought in an aging ex-May-Queen to teach them how to walk properly, more like sashaying. I also learned that on the morning of the event, the May Court met at the Beverly Hills Hotel for breakfast in the bridal suite, which luckily was minus a real bride. Blinis with caviar, eggs Benedict, croissants, muffins, berries, tea, coffee, fresh squeezed orange juice. A stylist from a Beverly Hills salon teamed up with a florist to weave white baby's breath and gold streamers into their hair, to highlight Laurel's gold and white school colors.

"The processional was backed by a taped string quartet. The audience was smiling, and it seemed like everyone thought the May Day tradition was totally normal. I thought it was revolting, and I assumed I was the only one. But I was wrong.

"There's a girl in my grade at Laurel. I'll call her Genevieve. If I was my grade's good girl, then Genevieve was our bad girl. Her biggest triumph was removing her edible underwear like a striptease artist and eating it onstage."

The class burst out laughing, including Mr. Cohen.

"But there's a lot more to Genevieve than her pranks. I was surprised to find out that she takes Russian and Mandarin at UCLA, along with Spanish at Laurel. She's been taking AP Calculus in tenth grade and she's #1 in our class. Anyway, she came up to me as the May Day processional began and whispered that I looked as disgusted as she felt. She took me into the building and picked the lock to the art room in about two seconds. We each took a bucket of paint to the roof. Mine was lime green and hers was grainy purple. She told me she knows the roof well because she goes there to ditch class when she gets too bored. She showed me where to stand, so we were directly above the processional, but nobody could see us. Then we poured paint all over the queen and her princesses."

"YES!" Andrea/Elvia shouted and punched the air. The class laughed again. Caroline smiled nervously.

"You'd think Genevieve and I had launched a guerrilla warfare ambush. The girls and their parents were screaming, ducking for cover, running for their lives. The princesses and their queen were crying about their ruined dresses, except one. The princess from my grade, Valerie, stood her ground. She's one of my best friends and months later, she told me that her peach taffeta dress looked like a spoiled eighteenth-century marshmallow, and she thanked me for ruining it."

Another wave of laughter, but this time Caroline was unable to muster even a small smile.

"Before anyone noticed that Genevieve and I were missing, we joined the panic below. Genevieve talked to several girls to make sure she was seen, then she left for a family reunion in Oregon. I stayed."

"Is this for real?" Dreads called from the second row. "You're not exaggerating to make a point?"

"It's for real." Caroline steeled herself to read the next paragraph.

"After about ten minutes, some of the girls started doing burlesque imitations of the panic, mimicking the distraught May Court. A lot of people thought it was funny, and our headmaster was furious. He's famous for pitching fits and this time he outdid himself. He was ranting and raving and railing that he was going to expel the person who ruined the processional. When nobody confessed, he threatened to expel every girl who thought it was funny. He started picking them out, herding them to the side, and yelling that they'd never set foot on campus again. They stopped laughing and started crying, and some of their moms were crying, too. A bunch of the parents were yelling at our headmaster, and others were begging him to reconsider. He kept screaming. It was total pandemonium, and I was the only one who could make it stop.

"So, I said I did it. I had to repeat it several times for everyone to hear. The entire place turned silent. Everyone was staring at me like I was a three-headed gargoyle. Maybe they were right.

"I was expelled."

Caroline closed her eyes for a long moment. When she opened them, she saw Kayla's mouth hanging open. Gary looked stunned. The classroom was absolutely still. Caroline took a quaking breath.

"When Genevieve got back from Oregon, she called me. We talked for days. She offered to confess, but when I asked if she liked Laurel, she told me there's no better place to get shock reactions. Also, she loves the arrangement to take extra classes at UCLA. I said she shouldn't tell. Laurel was right for her, but it was wrong for me. I felt like the walls were closing in, and I needed to get out. I didn't think my parents would let me transfer, but they agreed before they found out I was expelled. That's how I ended up at Hollywood High."

Caroline's voice shook slightly.

"Everything at Hollywood High has been new to me, even my desk in this classroom. There's a carving of a fist, middle finger raised. At Laurel, there would have been an investigation, and the person who defiled the desk would have been suspended, maybe expelled. The desk would have been immediately replaced, shiny and clean. Hollywood High isn't shiny and clean, but it's honest, and here's the truth: It's a good carving, and I think the person who did it is an artist. I'm not saying it's okay to carve up the desks. I'm saying there are all kinds of people here, with all kinds of talents, shown in all kinds of ways. Hollywood High is a much bigger world than Laurel Academy. It's raw, and it's real, and there's a place for everyone, even a nerd like me."

The class laughed again and for the first time in several days, Caroline felt the tension in her shoulders begin to ease.

"I grew up in an academic family. My parents went to Harvard and Radcliffe. My family's intellectual icon lives in an ivory tower, on an Ivy League campus. Now my intellectual icon is different, and it changed because of the people I've met here, especially the gay and trans students. When I was at Laurel, I didn't know any girls who were lesbians and out of the closet. If there were any trans students, they were hiding it. I didn't understand why, but now I do. One of my friends at Hollywood High is a trans girl who is scared she'll be beaten if other students realize. Still, she shows up at school every day to get an education, knowing she might be hurt, even killed. The courage of the gay and trans students blows my mind. They're my new intellectual icons."

Caroline locked eyes for a fleeting moment with Carlos, then stepped into her final paragraph.

"I'm not who you think I am, and I'm not who I thought I was. Most of the girls at Laurel wouldn't understand why I like going to school here. They wouldn't understand that Hollywood High has its own kind of pride. It's not the same pride as Laurel Academy, with its wealthy campus and college admissions track record. On this campus, it's pride in who we are as people. It's Hollywood pride."

Caroline finished reading and looked up. Sharon's hands were clasped, her braids untouched. Mort's pencil lay on his desk. Dreads and Presto stared. Kayla, Gary, and Carlos had tears in their eyes.

"You did it," J.D. *said softly. "Congratulations."*

A long beat and, to Caroline's astonishment, Elvia/Andrea jumped to her feet, clapping fiercely. The rest of the students followed, the only standing ovation of Caroline's life. The rush transported her and she saw lights, cameras, and stardom. The feeling was tremendous and the moment was fine.

It was also enough.

People surrounded Caroline, Sharon, and Mort to offer congratulations. From across the room, Kayla smiled. The love Caroline felt for her was powerful, moving, comfortable, like her love for Irene, Vincent, and Valerie.

Then she met Gary's eyes. Her gut twisted, but it felt oddly good. For a moment, she was puzzled, balancing on an unfamiliar ledge. Then she stepped over the line. How long had Gary been waiting for her to catch up to herself?

The small crowd around Caroline thinned, and Kayla hugged her. "I love you," she whispered.

"I love you, too," Caroline whispered back.

"Good job," and "Cool essay," Sharon and Mort said as they walked past.

Suddenly Sharon shoved something at Mort, shouldered her enormous Pooh, and hurried to the far side of the room where a group stood with Mr. Cohen. Mort stared at the box of shiny new pencils in his hand.

"Okay," he shrugged angrily, "I get it. She thinks I'm a moron."

"She thinks everyone's a moron," Kayla grinned. "Don't take it personally."

Andrea raised an eyebrow, "Maybe she thinks everyone's a moron, except you."

"Huh?" Mort was confused.

"Hey, man, catch a wave," Presto punched his arm. "Her braids are cute."

"Me? You mean me? Sharon likes me?" Mort bounded across the room to join her.

Caroline turned and found Gary standing next to her. They both began to speak, then hesitated as Dreads tapped Andrea's shoulder.

"Hey, Elvia, I mean Andrea."

"Hey what?"

"I want to make a deal."

"What kind of a deal?"

"If I promise not to eat any candy bars, will you go out with me?"

Dreads, Caroline, and Gary held their breath.

"Yeah, sure. But if you even look at a piece of chocolate, I'll . . . never mind. Sure. Yeah, sure."

"Way to go, Dreads and Andrea," Gary murmured, then he met Caroline's eyes. "Your essay is really great and—"

"What are you doing after school today?" she blurted.

"Oh, um, I'm going to dinner and a movie with you."

"Thanks," she smiled. "What about right after school?"

"What do you want?"

"I want you to take me to the DMV to get my permit. I want to learn to drive."

Gary nodded. "Yeah, that makes sense."

"What makes sense?"

Slowly Gary smiled. "Everything."

Kayla walked over from a conversation with Presto about summer surfing competitions. She took Caroline's shoulders. "A May Court mutiny. You're a woman of ill repute. I'm so proud!"

The bell blared. During the last week of school, the schedule was different, with a ten minute break between classes to let students regroup between finals and end of term projects. Mr. Cohen stood at the door to shake each student's hand as they left for summer vacation. He held Caroline's hand an extra second and said quietly, "Gutsy essay. Well done. Keep writing."

Caroline, Gary, and Kayla walked outside as the quad's speakers crackled and Jim Croce's "I Got a Name" reverberated through campus. As soon as they reached the quad, Caroline slowed her pace. She breathed the music, the noise, the heat, the cracked asphalt. She thought of her first anxious moments on campus and fast-forwarded through tenth grade — every sound, every sense, every notion.

"I'll always remember this year at Hollywood High," she said. "Maybe I'll write a novel about it."

"Who will be the main character?" Kayla asked.

"My new hero."

Kayla and Gary stopped walking. Both of their eyes misted.

Gary nodded. "He's my hero, too."

"He's my *Because*," Caroline said quietly. "I'll never forget him. I'm going to make him live forever."

"*I gotta go now,*" *J.D.'s voice faded as he spoke.* "*Thanks.*"

"*For what?*"

"*For caring.*"

"*Always.*" She breathed deeply. With the layered emotions surrounding J.D., *always* was the right way to say *goodbye*.

Caroline, Kayla, and Gary stood close together as Vincent and Irene joined them.

"I always knew I liked you!" Irene held up Caroline's essay. "Now I know why!"

"Do The Duke and Doraine know what you wrote?" Gary asked.

"I put a copy in their mailbox this morning on my way to school, but I think they have their hands full. I don't expect them to read it for a while and—" she stopped and stared at The Duke, who stood in front of her.

"Doraine's with the baby. I read your essay. I came here to find you."

Caroline's eyes dropped. "Now you know the truth. I'm sorry."

"Sorry for what?"

"For not being who you thought I was. For disappointing everyone."

"Girl," The Duke shook his head and chuckled, "you've got a lot to learn."

"Nobody's disappointed in you," Kayla earnestly.

"We like you better," Irene punched her shoulder. "Y'know, the I'm-so-perfect act gets really annoying!"

The Duke glanced at his watch and looked at Caroline. "I wanted to tell you good job on the essay, and congratulations on blowing up Laurel's May Court, and I gotta run. If the baby wakes up and I'm not home, Doraine will never forgive me."

"What's her name?" Caroline asked.

"Chelby." The Duke beamed. He pulled a photo out of his pocket and his friends crowded around.

"She's beautiful," Caroline breathed. "Wow. You and Doraine created her. Just wow."

"Yeah, just wow." The Duke held the photo tenderly.

"Can I visit you in the summer?" Caroline couldn't tear her eyes from the photo. "I want to meet Chelby, if it's okay with you and Doraine."

"Any time you want!" He hugged Caroline's shoulders and jogged toward his mother's house as Toni and Blake hurried over.

"Best essay ever!" Blake tucked the envelope into their backpack. "Lime green and grainy purple are my new favorite colors!"

As the group laughed, Toni moved to Caroline and opened her arms. The two girls hugged.

"When you're not hanging out with Chelby, what are you going to do for the next few months?" Irene smiled at her ex-Clover friend. "I can't imagine your summer without a nerdy project."

"She's going to write a novel," Kayla announced.

"I love novels!" Blake was pleased. "Are you including your new intellectual icons? The gay and trans kids?"

Caroline nodded.

"Maybe your novel can make things better," Gary smiled.

"With a book?" Irene raised an eyebrow. "You're going to cure homophobia and transphobia with a book?"

Caroline shrugged.

"People should read about how it is now, but it won't stay this bad," Vincent spoke with complete confidence. "It's 1974. In ten years, it'll be different."

"I hope so," Kayla said, "but I wonder if it's like racism. People are always looking for a convenient target."

"I'm with Vincent. People can't be bigots forever." Irene grinned. "If they keep it up, I'll make them read Caroline's book."

"What's your book about?" Toni asked.

The group turned to Caroline. She pictured Vincent's painting, a fiery orange sky, a boy on the brink of manhood.

"J.D. I'm going to write about J.D."

BOOK GROUP DISCUSSION QUESTIONS

Dear Reader,

Thank you for choosing *Hollywood Pride*. I'm aware of how many novels are waiting to be read and I'm grateful you picked this one. I've included book group discussion questions, designed to bring forward different perspectives.

All the best,

Amy

1. This novel has lesbian, gay, trans, nonbinary, cisgender, and straight characters. Have you ever wanted to understand these words, but you didn't feel safe asking?

2. A theme of the novel is defying stereotypes. Some of the stereotypes are racial, sexual, and gender based. Some are about other kinds of

assumptions. For instance, what does it say about a person if they're a sex worker, the leader of a gang, a cheerleader, extremely academic? Have you ever felt stereotyped?

3. A subplot in the book is based on Caroline's growing up in the film industry. Have you ever been in an environment that was a mismatch for your authentic self? How did you navigate the situation?

4. From the first chapter, Caroline builds a friendship group that is racially, sexually, and economically diverse. Is that sort of diversity familiar to you? Did any of the diversity described in the novel make you uncomfortable? Did any of the diversity change your view of a particular group of people?

5. Several characters are hiding secrets — Caroline, The Duke, Valerie, Toni, Ray. As you learned about their secrets, did your feelings about the characters change?

6. Bigotry against the LGBTQ+ community can show itself in many forms. It can be subtle, obvious, damaging, deadly. Different characters demonstrate many forms of homophobia and transphobia. Some of those characters model paths to support and acceptance. Did a particular character's path feel meaningful to you?

7.   In the final chapter, Caroline realizes that J.D. is her "because." What does she mean?

8. Do you have a favorite character in the novel? What do you like about them/her/him?

9. Why is it important for Caroline to return to school the day after Drake assaults her? How do the reactions of people at Hollywood High help her begin to heal?

10. *Hollywood Pride* takes place in the 1973-1974 academic year, and some of the language has changed between then and now. The author chose to capitalize the racial heritage Black, which would have been written as "black" at that time. Back then, the author hadn't heard the acronym LGBTQ+; however, the author chose to incorporate "LGBTQ" in the text. The author used the term "sex workers" (now) rather than "prostitutes" (then). Since the novel deals with many issues of stereotypes, racism and bigotry targeting the LGBTQ+ community, the author had to make several choices regarding whether to use the vocabulary of then or now. Do you agree with the author's choices? Would you have made different choices?

AUTHOR'S NOTE

When I was a student at Hollywood High School, a boy disappeared. I heard a rumor that he had been beaten to death because he was gay. I knew him by sight, but not by name. We shared no classes, had no friends in common. In the sea of 3,000 students, I noticed him because he had the most magnificent blond hair I'd ever seen. He was six feet tall and extremely thin, dressed in white laced up pants, platform shoes, a gauzy shirt.

One day he was gone.

I began to ask about him, but nobody knew anything. Most chilling, nobody knew his name.

Decades later, I told a journalist friend that I was writing a novel about that rumor. She suggested that I visit the archives, do some research, find out if the murder actually took place. I hesitated and to my surprise, I heard myself telling her that I wasn't writing about the real person. As the words came out of my mouth, I realized I had carried this boy deep within me since I was fifteen years old. I was writing about a fantasy figure who had taken on mythical proportions. During that conversation, my novel's silent hero was born.

My country is at a crossroads. As I watched the culture of rage and hatred spread its influence through the Land of the Free, I built characters and situations to highlight today's issues. The divisive values portrayed in *Hollywood Pride* have become our day-to-day reality. In the Divided States of America, all people are not created equal. In the United States of America, our strength is grounded in our diversity and our potential is boundless.

Hollywood Pride is my voice for a stronger today and a better tomorrow.

ACKNOWLEDGMENTS

Deepest thanks to my team, the people who read drafts at different stages — Brandi Askin, Jonine Bernstein, Bernie Burk, Kim Hettena, Margaret Jacobs, Millard Kaufman, Marilyn Krieger, Daphne de Marneffe, Mary McKinney, Kelli Murray, Hope Selinger.

Thanks to Michelle Treffer, a gifted personal trainer. Between planks and lunges, she and I talked about many of the topics I addressed in *Hollywood Pride*. She shared her knowledge with her signature generosity and respect, always motivating me to learn more.

Special thanks to three friends who were students at Hollywood High with me. Helaina Laks Kravitz brought each piece of the manuscript into a brighter light. Linda Chang and Scott Mann, separately and together, spoke to me at length about evolving our high school experience into *Hollywood Pride*. Linda also edited the novel, catching my many and varied errors, offering her perspective with the love of a lifelong friend.

ABOUT THE AUTHOR

Amy Kaufman Burk grew up in the Hollywood Hills surrounded by creativity. Her father wrote screenplays, and her home was filled with artists, dancers, directors, actors, photographers, authors, and thousands of books. Amy graduated from Hollywood High School, then studied psychology at Yale College, graduating *cum laude* with distinction in her major. She earned a master's degree in Health and Medical Sciences from UC Berkeley and a Doctorate in Mental Health from UC San Francisco. After practicing psychotherapy for over twenty years, she began writing. Amy met her husband in college, and they have three grown children.

Hollywood Pride is based on Amy's experience in tenth grade, when she transferred from a college prep academy to the local public high school. At her new school, she found over forty languages spoken among the students, no single racial heritage a majority, and an economic spectrum ranging from kids living on the streets to the wealthy homes in the Hollywood Hills. Being a part of Hollywood High's diverse community shaped Amy's outlook on all aspects of her life going forward.

www.ingramcontent.com/pod-product-compliance
Lightning Source LLC
Chambersburg PA
CBHW070457010826
48976CB00022B/1741